CARRY A
CRUSADING SPIRIT

A CLUBMOBILE GIRLS NOVEL

BUGLE CALL BOOKS
www.buglecallbooks.com

ELERI GRACE

CARRY A CRUSADING SPIRIT

A CLUBMOBILE GIRLS NOVEL

First paperback edition published 2020

Cover designed by Rafael Andres, Cover Kitchen
Map designed by Rafael Andres, Cover Kitchen

ISBN 978-0-9600445-2-8 (pbk.)

Published by Bugle Call Books
www.buglecallbooks.com

Praise for *Courage to be Counted*, the first book in the Clubmobile Girls series

"This is a story that grabbed me from page one, Vivian is such a strong and caring heroine and Jack well what a hero but times are hard for them there is danger everywhere, the tension at base while Vivian is waiting to see if Jack makes it back, and then the worry while Vivian is travelling close to enemy lines through Europe, makes this a story not to be missed."
Helen Sibbritt
Deanna's World Book Reviews

" . . . how beautiful and accurate the era was described. From the first pages, I was transported to that time and it felt truthful and realistic. And that date in NY was so romantic and atmospheric! I just wanted to watch a bunch of old movies from the era (I did actually...), wear red lipstick and swing to jazz melodies."
Victoria
Coffee with Jane Book Blog

"*Courage to Be Counted* balances the realities and horrors of WWII war and mid-20th century stereotypes about a "woman's role" with very engaging and credible examples of strong women finding ways to serve their country, define their own paths, explore the world, and make love to handsome heroes. . . . And for young women readers - this is a story of your great-grandmothers who blazed trails and paved the way for your leadership and creativity to shine now!"
A.G., Amazon Reviewer

"In a sea of WW2 books, this one stands out. Jack and Vivian are compelling characters, real in their flaws and strengths. They manage to be true to their time frame context and also modern. While the romance is the center of moving the plot forward, I think this book is so well researched and has such rich background information that anyone interested in this time period (everyone?) will find it compulsively readable. You will find yourself thinking about these events and characters long after you put the book down."
A. N., Amazon Reviewer

"Eleri Grace's deep knowledge of World War II history comes through on every page. She has unearthed an unending fount of

inspiration in the Red Cross girls who served multiple locations across the globe sometimes behind combat lines. I also learned a lot about the valiant Eighth Air Force."
Amazon Reviewer

"Eleri Grace tells a story about the chance meetings among courageous individuals serving in wartime that lead to friendships, loves, sacrifices, losses and sometimes happy endings despite overwhelming odds."
D.W., Amazon Reviewer

"There's such a thrill in reading a historical novel in which you know very quickly that you are in safe hands, both in terms of the historical accuracy of the period and in terms of the love story. IN COURAGE TO BE COUNTED, Eleri Grace has clearly done a huge amount of research into the amazing women who served with the Red Cross clubmobiles during WW2, and also into the American B-17 bomber crews who flew from English bases, but at no point do we feel like we are being hit over the head with an encyclopedia. The love story between Vivian and Jack is paramount - even during their periods of separation - and the accuracy of the details and descriptions of time and place never get in the way. Quite the opposite, the short life-expectancy of any Allied flyer during World War Two and the very real threat to the lives of the Red Cross girls working near the front lines after D-Day, are so well described, the love story becomes even more poignant."
C. L., Amazon Reviewer

"This was such an authentic, well written novel. The author's sense of time and place, especially through her use of dialogue, was impeccable and made me feel like I had been dropped into the 40s. I was drawn into the story by the history of the amazing Red Cross Girls, but was soon completely swept up in Vivian and Jack's story set against the backdrop of a war filled with horrors and uncertainties. Definitely a page-turner!"
S. V., Amazon Reviewer

To the courageous men and women who served our country during WWII.

To my parents, Hulon and Cheryl Turner, for believing in and supporting my writing dreams.

And finally, as always, to Elizabeth and Harry, who are my everything.

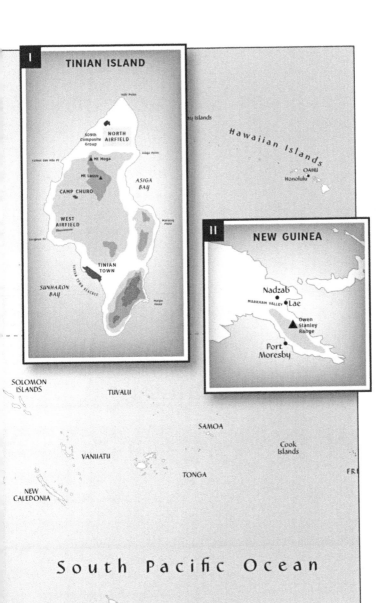

I TINIAN ISLAND

Ushi Point

509th
Composite
Group

NORTH
AIRFIELD

Faibus San Hilo Pt

▲ Mt Maga

Asiga Point

Mt Lasso ▲

ASIGA
BAY

CAMP CHURO

WEST
AIRFIELD

Makalog
Point

Gurguon Pt

TINIAN
TOWN

TINIAN TOWN BEACHES

SUNHARON
BAY

Marpo
Head

II NEW GUINEA

Nadzab

MARKHAM VALLEY ●Lae

▲ Owen
Stanley
Range

Port
Moresby

ay Islands

Hawaiian Islands

○ OAHU

Honolulu ●

SOLOMON
ISLANDS

TUVALU

SAMOA

Cook
Islands

VANUATU

TONGA

FR

NEW
CALEDONIA

South Pacific Ocean

"Human beings forget so fast, if the generation that fights today is to lay the foundations on which a peaceful world can be built, all of us who have seen the war at close range must remember what we see and carry a crusading spirit into all of our work."

Eleanor Roosevelt, "My Day" column, 30 August 1943

CHAPTER ONE

January 6, 1943
U.S.S. West Point
South Pacific Ocean

"Aft starboard, aft starboard, aft starboard," Hadley Claverie chanted as she descended yet another flight of narrow, steep steps to the next deck.

The first deck, home of the chaplain's office, and aft starboard. That's what the crewman had told her. But where had she started? Hadley gripped the cold steel stair railing. *No, ladder. A staircase on a ship was called a ladder.*

Male voices reverberated through the open doorway. Hardly surprising with eight thousand troops aboard.

If this wasn't the right deck, Hadley would backtrack. She stepped over the coaming and through the door. Starboard was on her right, but only if she were facing the front of the ship. Which way was forward?

The rooms on her right were silent, so they were likely storerooms. She turned left.

Swashhhh, plink, plink, plink. Hissssss. Swashhh, plink, plink, plink.

Hadley frowned. Probably sailors hosing the deck.

Crewmen were always cleaning something. Perhaps the officers believed it helped keep sailors out of trouble. Hadley had discovered first-hand that the crew also amused themselves by directing their water hoses toward unsuspecting passengers. Two nights after they had set sail from San Francisco, Hadley and her Red Cross Girl cabin-mates had abandoned the stuffy confines of their cabin for the top deck. Hours later, the drenched women, wringing out sodden bedrolls, conceded that open-air sleeping came with drawbacks.

Hadley continued through the passageway. She caught a whiff of Ivory soap a split-second before she slammed into *him*.

Him being a very tall, very wet, *very* naked man.

"Woy!" Hadley clapped a hand over her eyes. *The showers.* She had blundered into the showers. Male laughter rang out, and a flush heated her neck and face.

"Looking for somethin,' doll?"

"Wanna come join us?"

"I'll share my water point with you, honey."

A tingle of dizziness shot across her forehead. *Move. Get out of here.* Their catcalls would only become bawdier the longer she stood frozen in shock. Keeping her hand over her eyes, Hadley spun to retrace her route back to the ladder.

"Aw, don't leave yet, baby." Louder laughter rang through the steamy compartment.

"Cut it out, fellas!" A strong voice cut through the others.

She raced forward blindly and skidded on the slick surface. Her feet whooshed out from under her, and she landed on her backside on the hard deck with a *thud*.

Red-hot pain pulsed through her hipbone. She gritted her teeth and squirmed against the water seeping through her skirt and underwear. Why were her legs up in the air? Another stab of pain jolted through her hip. *Owww.*

Hadley pried her palm from the wet deck and tugged her skirt down. A half-second later, a pair of strong hands settled around her waist, lifted her up, and set her on her feet. The Ivory soap smell enveloped her again. Ivory soap, mixed with the distinctive mossy-cedar scent of Aqua Velva aftershave.

"Can you walk?" The man's resonant voice put her in mind of a creamy café au lait. He was the one who had told the other men in the showers to shut up.

Leery of slipping again, Hadley took a tentative step forward. Yet before she could take another one, the man gripped her arm with his warm hand and towed her forward.

Lordy, is he still naked? She chanced a sideways glance and was relieved to see he had wrapped a towel around his waist. Water droplets clung to his tanned, muscular chest and lean torso. Hadley swallowed and averted her eyes.

When they reached the narrow door leading back to the ladder, Hadley dropped his hand and stepped over the coaming.

"Thanks," she muttered, setting her foot onto the lowest rung of the ladder.

Laugh lines on either side of his mouth creased with his smile. "Hang on. Where are you headed? I'm guessing you weren't looking for the officers' showers."

Heat flared in Hadley's cheeks again. Nautical terminology might as well be Greek to her. She hadn't gotten seasick, but she was a landlubber. She remained as lost aboard the troop ship as she had when they had first embarked three days ago. As it was, most of the ship was off-limits to her and the other Red Cross Girls. They could roam through *officer country*, but couldn't venture onto the lower decks where the thousands of enlisted men slept and ate in shifts.

Glistening water droplets clung to the hair dusted across the man's well-defined chest. Hadley licked her lips and looked up into his eyes. *What?* "Oh, er, I'm looking for the chaplain. I was told I could find him on the first deck . . . Starboard aft."

"You're in need of the chaplain already?" He deepened his smile.

She stepped off the ladder and pulled a small notepad and pen from her jacket pocket. "I thought he could provide a verse of scripture for the ship's newsletter. I'm the new editor."

"The editor?" He raised an eyebrow.

"Contributing editor," she corrected. The naval officer who wrote and edited the weekly shipboard newsletter had declined her offer to take over the job, even after Hadley had shown him a scrapbook of clippings from high school and college newspapers and the *Times-Picayune*. Though worried she might be crossing that fine line between persistence and pestering, she had returned again with her Underwood typewriter. Today was her first day on the job.

The man pointed up. "He's one deck up. Bulls-eye 1-75-7-Q."

"Ok." She scribbled 1757Q on her pad and capped the pen.

He jabbed a finger at the number and shook his head. "Don't run them together like that. *One* stands for first deck. *Seventy-five* is the frame number. *Seven* is the compartment number. Between starboard beam and starboard quarter."

Hadley stared at him.

He ran a hand through his damp hair. "Hold tight right here. I'll take you."

Before she could tell him she only needed more conventional directions, he strode back toward the showers, rolling his shoulders so that muscles rippled across his upper back.

Hadley inhaled and blew out a breath as he disappeared from view. To know the ship so well, he must be a naval officer. Meaning he wouldn't disembark in Australia, New Zealand, India, or wherever they were headed. Their ultimate destination remained a mystery.

The Pacific Theater. Hadley rubbed the back of her neck. Of all the luck, she was bound for the Pacific rather than England. England, where communication lines were plentiful and easy to access. England, where women journalists were making a name for themselves. England, where she might persuade war correspondents to help her obtain credentials or file stories on her behalf.

Hadley suspected her sense of being disconnected from civilization wouldn't improve after they docked, whether in Sydney or Bombay. She hadn't seen any bylines from female war correspondents reporting from anywhere in the Pacific *or* the Far East.

The man stepped back into view. His hair was considerably fairer now that it was dry. He wore a khaki non-dress officer's uniform, without his service cap, which wasn't required at sea.

"Lieutenant Masterson at your service, Miss . . .?"

"Claverie. Hadley Claverie."

"Clea-Verhee." He drawled the syllables. "French?"

"I'm from New Orleans." Hadley lifted her chin and smiled. Steamy and sophisticated, stimulating and somnolent, free-wheeling and fettered, New Orleans was home.

Masterson tilted his head to one side. "Never been. Jazz music. Parades. Big on parades there, right?"

"Yes. Today is Twelfth Night." A pang of nostalgia zipped through her. "That's the start of Carnival."

"That's parade time?"

"Yes, but the parades and balls will all be cancelled again, like last year." Hadley worried the beads on her bracelet. It didn't matter that she was in the middle of the Pacific Ocean. There would be no floats, marching bands, or riotously festive street celebrations again this year.

He shrugged. "Maybe next year."

"You don't believe the war will end that soon, do you?" She widened her eyes.

"Nope. But you might be home within a year."

"My overseas assignment is for at least two years." Hadley ran her finger over the Red Cross pin fastened to her lapel. Hadley had been unable to secure credentials from the *Times-Picayune* or another Louisiana newspaper, so she had jumped at the chance to get closer to the action overseas with the Red Cross. She could figure out how to file stories from her post.

Masterson made an indistinct noise. Did he think she couldn't hack it? That women had no business near combat zones?

"We signed on for the duration, same as you men. Even if I serve overseas for two years, the Red Cross won't necessarily post me back to New Orleans. That's the way it works for you fellows too, isn't it? You get enough points to rotate back stateside, but the military can station you anywhere."

"Gotta get the points." Masterson shot her a tight smile. "Without dying first."

Hadley's stomach twisted into a tight ball. Her best friend Camille's brother Philip had died on Guadalcanal in August. So many senseless losses. She swallowed. "I —"

He shook his head. "Nah, I know what you meant. Didn't need to remind you we aren't on a pleasure cruise."

"We all want to do our part." Hadley met his eyes. "Men *and* women."

"Do your part for duty, honor, country," he said, quoting a popular patriotic poster and mimicking the dramatic delivery of a newsreel announcer.

Hadley smiled.

Masterson gestured toward the ladder. "Let's go find the chaplain."

"All right." She climbed the steep ladder, stepped off, and glanced over her shoulder. Well, well, well. Hadley had seen that look before. She tucked a strand of hair behind her ear and waited for him.

He paused at the top and moistened his lips before swinging up beside her. He put a gentle hand on her arm and motioned for her to turn left. "That way."

"Okay." Tingles radiated from where his hand rested on her

arm. "How would I know which way to turn?"

"I'm gonna show you." He pointed to a yellow plate affixed to the door on their right. The designation 1-12-3-C was stamped across the plate. "That's a *bullseye*. You'll see those on doors, hatches, and bulkheads. Now, see that the first number is a *one*?"

She nodded.

"*One* means you're on the main deck. If it said *zero two*, you'd be two levels above the main deck. If it said *three*, you'd be two levels below. Now, the next number is *twelve*. That tells you the frame number. Frames are numbered from zero at the forward or bow of the ship and get higher as you move toward the aft or stern. Got it?"

"So is twelve closer to forward or aft?"

"You don't need to know that." Masterson guided her forward and pointed out the next bullseye. "See how this number is higher? That means we're moving aft."

"Okay." Hadley pulled out her notebook and made a note. "What's the next number?"

"Ah, that's the compartment number." He took another step. "That's where it gets complicated. The number *three* means you're starboard from the ship's centerline. The centerline is *zero*. Moving out from center, you'll have even numbered compartments on the port side, with odd numbers on starboard. The numbers grow larger as you move away from the centerline."

"Even is port, odd is starboard. Numbers get bigger out from center," Hadley scribbled.

"Yes, that's it. Now the last letter tells you the purpose of the compartment. *F* stands for *fuel*. *C*, as we have here, is ship *control*."

"All right." Hadley stopped, tapped her pen against her notepad, and winked. "What's the code for showers?"

He laughed. "*L* stands for living space - meaning showers as well as heads, washrooms, berths, and the mess."

"Avoid *L* compartments." Hadley wrote, underlining it several times.

His eyes crinkled at the corners. "You might not want to completely avoid those, or you'll be plenty hungry before we reach port."

"Oh, I know how to get to chow. They don't serve gumbo like we have back home, but the food is better than what they fed us during training in Washington." Hadley wrinkled her nose at the memory.

"Hmph. Navy's got the best chow in the military, so you'd better enjoy it. Wherever you land up, it won't be this good," Masterson said.

He clearly knew his way around a ship. Hadley edged closer and checked his uniform insignia. No dark blue shoulder boards with gold stripes for the navy. Perhaps she still didn't have a good handle on the various insignia. She pointed to the wings pinned above his right shirt pocket. "You're a naval aviator?"

"No." He flattened his mouth into a thin line and quickened his step.

Hadley hurried to keep up. "The wings indicate you're a flying officer, right?"

"I'm army. A USAAF pilot." He offered no further details.

"Oh, you're a fighter pilot?"

"No. My ship is a B-25 bomber."

"Your *ship*?" Bombers and fighters were planes, Hadley was certain of that much.

"Airmen refer to their planes as *ships*. It's short for airship." He lengthened his stride.

Why his sudden change in attitude? And why would a bomber pilot be on a troop transport? Someone had told her the army transported fighter planes to combat theaters via ship, but bomber crews flew their planes to their assigned bases. Hadley half-jogged to catch up with him. "I thought bomber crews flew their planes."

"They do. Gunners and ground crews go by ship."

Now she was really confused. He wore wings and officer insignia. He understood navy lingo on a deeper level than might be expected of an Army Air Forces man. None of it made any sense. "But I thought —"

"Here we are." Masterson pointed toward a bulls-eye stamped 1-75-7-Q. He pushed the door open and gestured for her to proceed inside.

The chaplain looked up. "Good morning. How can I help?"

Masterson cleared his throat. "Miss Claverie needs your assistance for the ship's newsletter."

"Ah, you must be in search of a daily scripture." The chaplain thumbed through sheets of paper stacked on his desk.

"I leave you in good hands," Masterson murmured.

Hadley turned to thank him, but he had already disappeared.

***

Skip Masterson swiped at the sweat beading on his temple. His heart thumped. He hurtled up the ladder, taking the steps two at a time. The weather deck would clear his head.

He stepped toward the side of the ship and tightened his hands around the cold taffrail. He had drawn no more than two lungsful of cool morning air into his tight chest when someone called his name. Thirteen months had passed since Skip had last heard that snarly voice, but he knew before he turned who he would find standing behind him.

"Just the man I need." Commander John Buckley flicked his cool gray eyes over the wings pinned above Skip's right breast pocket.

"Sir?" Hyper aware of the sweat popping up along his hairline despite the brisk breeze ruffling his hair, Skip clenched his fists.

Buckley met his eyes. "I hear one of the lovely Red Cross Girls stumbled into the officer showers. Seems you took an interest in serving as her guide."

"She was looking for the chaplain on the wrong deck." Skip straightened his shoulders. "Got her squared away."

"Captain Donelson says she fancies herself a reporter. She sweet-talked him into letting her help with the newsletter."

"Hmm." Skip injected nonchalance into his tone and ignored the flutters of foreboding stirring in his gut. Buckley was not one to shoot the breeze.

"She'll need an assistant. Someone to act as a guide and obtain information for her from areas she can't access."

Skip made no reply. His clenched fingers had gone numb.

Commander Buckley's eyes sparked with self-satisfaction. "You, Lieutenant Masterson, are the perfect man for the job. You're familiar with ships and the navy's *customs and regulations*." He snapped out the last phrase with extra emphasis.

Flush crept up the back of Skip's neck. "Sir, I'm charged with keeping tabs on my enlisted men, ground crews, and cargo."

"So I heard. Normally, Lieutenant Masterson, flying officers *fly* rather than traveling by troop transport."

Skip tightened his jaw. He wasn't giving Buckley any details.

Buckley cocked his brow. "You won't say why you're here? Based on your history, I can make a good guess. Some things never change."

Skip pressed his lips together and resisted the urge to take the bait. Buckley would make good use of any details Skip divulged in an angry outburst. Being shipboard again was torture enough. He took a deep breath. "As I've said, sir, I already have an assignment."

"One that takes little of your time, Lieutenant. I've noted you spend most of your day up here on the weather deck."

Yes, he did. He slept here too, avoiding the choking confines of the ship's vast interior. He had drawn one of the top bunks in his crowded berth. On the first night at sea, with his face only inches from the overhead, panic had enveloped him like a thick fog, driving him up here. As he had stood shaking in the cool night air, he had vowed to only go belowdecks for chow and a shower.

Buckley curved his lips. "I will inform her that she can expect your assistance, effective immediately, and that you'll meet her in the mess in one hour."

Dammit. Hadley Claverie was attractive, with her inky black hair, dark eyes, and trim figure. But she asked too many questions. After only ten minutes, she had managed to drill him with an uncomfortable array of them. No, he needed to evade this errand boy job. Not only because it would require him to spend more time belowdecks, but also because she was so damned attractive. *That* was the last thing he needed.

Skip cleared his throat. "Sir, I'll be happy to have one of my fellows —"

"No." Buckley shook his head. "None of your men are officers, so they can't access the ship beyond the lowest decks."

"I'm not navy," Skip shot back. "Men with the most leeway and knowledge of this ship are its own crewmen."

"As you well know, our crewmen are busy, Lieutenant Masterson. They aren't sunbathing on the weather deck."

"And if I have to neglect my shipboard orders to play Man Friday for this woman?" Skip squeezed his fists. Sunbathing, his ass. *Surviving* was more like it.

"You have time for both jobs if I say you do, Lieutenant Masterson."

"Sir, as you noticed," Skip said, "I haven't spent much time belowdeck. I don't know the ship well enough to navigate it for Miss Claverie."

"You'll find this ship no different than others in your experience, Lieutenant. It's like riding a bicycle." Buckley smirked. "Oh, and *Captain* Claverie will expect you in the officer's mess at ten hundred."

Captain? The woman outranked him? Swell. Just swell. He bobbed a tight nod at Buckley. "Yes, sir."

Buckley strode past him and disappeared around the corner.

Skip unclenched his fists. He glanced at his watch, still frozen at 08:06. His chest tightened as though secured with a bowline knot.

For Skip, the journey to Brisbane now held hazards and stresses far beyond any danger from Japanese submarines.

CHAPTER TWO

Hadley stopped turning the mimeograph machine's rotary crank and inspected the top copy of the newsletter. It was legible but not for long. She had already dispatched Lieutenant Masterson to find more ink. She hopped onto the counter beside the machine, sipped from her bottle of lukewarm Coke, and drummed her foot against the cupboard. Where was he?

Probably taking his sweet time just to annoy her. Whatever had triggered his transformation from kindly rescuer to surly legman remained a mystery. His lean frame thrummed with resentment at being forced to act as her shipboard gofer.

Hadley slid off the counter and rubbed her aching arm. An electric mimeograph like the one at the *Times-Picayune* would be much more efficient for printing thousands of copies of tomorrow's newsletter. The manufacturer now produced bombsights instead of mimeographs, so Hadley was stuck using this old model.

Perhaps she could churn out a few more copies before the ink faded completely. She closed her hand around the iron crank and made a half-hearted turn of the drum before noticing a rip along the right side of the stencil. The problem wasn't only a dwindling ink supply. The torn stencil was now useless. She was a fast typist, but hell's bells, it was nearly midnight.

Swearing a blue streak, Hadley rooted through the supplies in search of a new stencil. She found one, loaded it into the typewriter, and retrieved a copy of the newsletter from the paper tray to use as a master. Moving back to the desk, Hadley spotted Masterson framed in the doorway. He was empty-handed and appeared more amused than contrite.

"Where's the ink?" Hadley yanked the rolling desk chair from under the desk and sat.

"Purser was asleep. The storeroom's locked." He sidled into the cramped compartment and picked up the discarded stencil. "Looks like you don't need the ink now, anyway."

"A ripped stencil doesn't mean the ink isn't also running low. Can't someone else unlock the storeroom?" Would he give a male officer such a flimsy excuse?

Hadley placed the damp copy next to the typewriter, plopped paperweights onto each corner, then perched her glasses on the end of her nose. Fingers poised over the keys, she looked up to find him watching her. "Again, Lieutenant, I need more ink so I can finish this before dawn. I need to *fais do-do* soon."

"What?"

"Ink, *Lieutenant*." She added a dollop of emphasis on his rank.

He frowned. "No, the last part. Something about *dough*?"

"Oh. *Fais do-do* means sleep. It's an expression from back home in Louisiana." She looked up in time to catch him rolling his eyes and narrowed her own. "What?"

He shrugged. "The whole Southern belle routine."

"Southern belle?" Hadley pulled off her glasses, set them down, and crossed her arms. Was he envisioning her as a modern incarnation of Scarlett O'Hara?

He raked a hand through his hair. "Probably used to servants who'll do your bidding day and night. That's why you've sent me running all over the damned ship."

No. She had attempted to do the legwork herself. Surely he hadn't forgotten her unfortunate foray into the officers' showers. Besides, even if she understood the nautical terminology well enough to navigate the ship, she lacked access to more than half the decks. The restrictions infuriated the ship's female passengers. The Red Cross had deployed thousands of women overseas to provide soldiers, especially enlisted men, with entertainment and recreation opportunities. Without access, how could the Red Cross Girls improve the morale of men who ate and slept in shifts in the overcrowded lower decks?

Hadley stood and faced Masterson. She had kicked off her pumps and now, standing before him in her stocking feet, he loomed over her. "You know full well I've been ordered to stay off the GI decks, which means I can't move about the same way you can."

"Not sure you could find your way to those decks even if they let you." His laugh lines deepened, making Hadley again wonder at their incongruity with his bad-tempered personality.

She straightened her spine. Was he dragging out that tired refrain about women not having a good sense of direction? She was a reporter, dammit. Inquisitive. Intuitive. And by golly, intrepid. "Couldn't be all that difficult. Keep going down until there are no more ladders." She paused and added, "Oh, and listen for the sound of the showers."

"That didn't deter you before." He tilted his head and lifted his eyebrows.

Touché. Her intuition had failed her. She shifted her weight and cast him a devil-may-care smile. "I bet those men were more unnerved than I was."

This time Masterson didn't stifle the smile that transformed his entire face. His broad, infectious grin held more than a hint of a hell-raising past. If only he wore it more often.

He stepped closer, and Hadley caught a whiff of his earthy aftershave. Her pulse skittered.

"*Unnerved* isn't the word those fellas were using," he said.

Her ears burned. The suggestive remarks the men had shouted before Masterson had swooped in were surely nothing compared to the crude jokes they had probably shared later. Hadley had caught their sideways looks and smothered laughter in the officers' mess.

She raised her chin. Some of the moxie that had helped her land a position as the only female reporter at the *Times-Picayune*'s political beat bubbled to the surface. "They should watch what they say. I might have some descriptive words of my own to share."

"I'll just bet you do." Skip laughed. His eyes were a soft, pale green, similar in hue to the small jade elephant her Uncle Victor had brought her from China.

Finally, another glimpse of Skip's more sociable side, complete with that dishy grin. A delicious tingle flitted through her gut.

"Well, anyway. I'm sure the navy doesn't want a repeat of that incident," Hadley said. "I expect that's why Commander Buckley asked you to help me."

"No." His smile vanished as quickly as it had appeared. A flush crept up his neck, and he narrowed his eyes. "That's not why."

He turned and strode toward the door, and Hadley scurried over to block his path. "Oh? If they thought you'd be a friendly liaison between the military and the Red Cross, they misjudged your capacity to be charming."

"No one said I had to be nice to you, doll. Now why don't you move out of my way, Miss Scarlett, so I can wake the purser and get your damned ink."

Hadley pursed her lips. What had caused his abrupt switch from flirty to fractious? Why *had* he been assigned a duty he didn't want?

He waved his hand. "Thought you were anxious to hit the hay, Scarlett."

Sleep was a more immediate need than learning what was

driving his erratic mood swings. Hadley stepped out of his way, but the ship lurched before she planted her feet, pitching her forward against Skip's chest. The desk chair slid on its casters and slammed into one of the cabinets. Skip circled his arms around her and hung on tight.

The ship listed sharply in the other direction. Hadley's stomach roiled. The chair skidded across the deck and banged into another cabinet. Skip tightened his hold on her. She pressed her fingers against his waist and lay her cheek above his heart.

"Just zig-zagging," he murmured.

They had all felt the jarring lists and heels designed to avoid enemy submarines in the ship's path in their berths at night. At times, the movements rolled them against the bulkhead or even sent them toppling from their bunks.

Hadley tilted her head and peered up at him. A small shaving cut marred the underside of his clenched jaw. His Adam's Apple bobbed.

Skip pulled back and turned her around until her back pressed against the bulkhead. Then he leaned close, as if he were about to kiss her. Hadley's heart somersaulted. She parted her lips.

"Watch out. You don't weigh enough to keep that chair from sliding. I'll get someone to bolt it down tomorrow." The barest hint of concern overlay his sharp tone.

Hadley swallowed and nodded.

He released his hold on her. "Going to get the ink now."

"Ink?" She blinked up at him. The scent of his masculinity still hung in the air, that heady mix of mossy cedar, a whiff of mint, and Skip.

Hadley paused to assess the roll of the ship. Then, staying within reach of the bulkhead, she crossed the room, stopping only to retrieve the chair and roll it back to the desk.

Her glasses still sat against the side of the typewriter. Happy they hadn't fallen to the floor and broken, she put them on and braced her foot against the desk. Perhaps it would keep her from careening across the room during the next zig-zag.

The paperweights had done their job. Her master copy sat right where she had left it. Typing a new master was easy. She could finish it and load it onto the mimeograph drum before Skip came back with the ink.

Assuming he returned. Hadley sensed that he had experienced more than a simple startle reflex during the zig-zag. His hammering heart and dilated pupils suggested he suffered from deep anxiety. Why would a man so familiar with ships panic during a simple evasive move? And why was he so uncomfortable belowdecks?

This wasn't the first time Hadley had wondered what mysteries lurked in Skip Masterson's past. Or how she might discover them.

CHAPTER THREE

January 17, 1943

U.S.S. West Point

North Pacific Ocean, near the Equator

Hadley's face slammed into the smelly slop. She pressed her lips together but couldn't prevent the foul odors of vomit, food refuse, and sewage water from filling her nostrils.

You signed up for this. It'll make a great story, you said.

Naval tradition dictated that passengers and crew must produce a shellback card or be branded a tadpole — and tadpoles must be initiated as shellbacks before the ship crossed the Equator, war or no war. The officers in charge of this traditional ritual had warned the women that while it was all in good fun, it would have unpleasant elements. Hadley had decided experiencing the bizarre tradition first-hand would make for a stronger story than if she observed it from the sidelines. But damn! This wasn't any fun at all.

Whoever had sat on the canvas above Hadley finally got up. Relieved, she scrambled onto her hands and knees. With her face out of the muck, she and the others crept forward. Was that light ahead? Whatever came next couldn't be as bad or as smelly as this.

All the gagging, retching, and swearing coming from behind her and in front of her must have muffled the sound of what awaited at the end of the tunnel. Hadley only had a moment's warning before the blast of ice-cold saltwater hit her full in the face.

High-pressure hoses blasted her and the others from all sides as they climbed out of the refuse-filled canvas tunnel. She stood and brushed garbage off her swimsuit, shivering despite the warm sun beaming down overhead.

"Line up, tadpoles! Hurry now. Move along, move along." Brandishing a wooden club, a sailor motioned for them to move forward.

Other Red Cross Girls and nurses were aboard the troop ship, yet Hadley stood in line with men on either side, both officers and GIs. Rank carried no weight in this ceremony. Even President Roosevelt had been initiated as a shellback on a crossing a few years ago.

"Surprised you gals are doing this," the man on her right commented.

"Least you're not wearing those fancy uniforms we've seen y'all in since we set sail," said the fellow on her other side. He flicked an appreciative gaze over Hadley's two-piece bathing suit, lingering on her exposed midriff. She had loaned her modest skirted one-piece to one of the nurses. Determined not to give him the slightest bit of encouragement, she averted her eyes and kept her mouth shut.

"Can't imagine why they didn't hand you a pretty costume and give you a pass."

"A pretty costume? We aren't going overseas to play dress-up." Hadley confirmed her fingers were muck-free and then pushed her sopping hair off her face.

"You a nurse?"

She shook her head. "No, Red Cross."

"Red Cross Girls are nurses, aren't they?" asked the soldier to her left.

"No, the army and navy each have their own nurse corps. We're recreation workers."

"And a *recreation* worker does what, exactly?" he asked with a smirk.

Hadley rolled her eyes. "Not *that* sort of recreation, mister. We set up clubs where you can play ping-pong or throw darts, get a hamburger, talk to American girls."

She would have gone on, but a large man dressed in pirate attire stepped in front of them, wielding a club and shouting for them to move forward. Shellbacks who weren't part of King Neptune's court wore pirate-themed costumes and shepherded the tadpoles through the rituals.

Hadley estimated that only ten percent of the ship's passengers and crew had produced a shellback card, which made sense. How many Americans outside the military would ever have had had the means or opportunity to cross the Equator?

They continued toward the Court of Neptune, stopping first in front of the Royal Photographer.

"Look at the birdie, sweetheart," he sang out.

Hadley closed her eyes just in time to avoid a stream of purple dye. Some folks got a normal photo, but at unpredictable intervals a nozzle near the camera lens shot a stream of purple dye into an unfortunate tadpole's face. She wiped at her face and stumbled forward with her eyes shut.

"Hey!" She poked the man in front of her in the ribs without opening her eyes. "Did I get it out of my eyes?"

"You look like a raccoon that lost a fight, doll, but I figure you can open 'em now."

"Thanks." She blinked and eased them open. Her eyes didn't

sting, but her hand now had a purple stain on it. She wafted it in the
air to dry. Dye stains wouldn't come out of her swimsuit.

"Look, the Tadpole Queen is a fella. You'd think they would
have picked a woman since there's so many of you gals on board,"
the first soldier said.

"That's why there's a Tadpole *King*," Hadley said. The tadpole
pageant the night before had been a riotous, drunken affair. Each
military unit entered one of its number to compete for the title of
Tadpole Queen in a farcical combination of beauty contest and talent
show. Any woman on board was eligible to compete for the
corresponding title of Tadpole King.

Bizzy, the Red Cross Girl from Cleveland who had been
crowned king, sat at the far right of the royal court, observing the
initiation rites with a bemused smile. Bizzy's Tarzan costume from
last night's pageant had been impossible to top. She had used gauze
and medical tape to cover her breasts. Clad only in modest swimsuit
bottoms overlaid with a trademark triangle of green felt fabric and a
fur stole draped around her neck, Bizzy had received a standing
ovation and been crowned with little debate.

Tadpoles lined up in groups before the court. Hadley flicked her
gaze to Skip Masterson, who stood off to one side in the pirate-
themed attire of a shellback with a lazy grin on his face. He tilted his
head and squinted, as though assessing how best to photograph the
scene.

Most of the shellbacks had painted a skull-and-crossbones on a
plain white T-shirt and tied bandanas over their heads. Some carried
cardboard swords and wore face-paint mustaches and scars. But Skip
had gone to more effort. In addition to sporting an elaborately
knotted black head scarf, he had laced twine through the top buttons
of his white shirt and topped it off with a black vest and a red sash
tied around his waist. He might have stepped off the set of an Errol
Flynn movie.

"Are these more tadpoles who have violated the sanctity of my
domain without my permission?" King Neptune boomed.

Hadley tore her gaze away from Skip.

King Neptune sat in the center of the court, his bare muscular chest glistening in the bright sunlight. He wore purple Arabian-style pants and a gold cardboard crown and sported a long, green wig and matching beard. Seashells covered his pants legs, and he held a large cardboard trident in his left hand. On his right sat Queen Amphitrite, clad in seafoam-green linen robes, a gold crown, and several seashell necklaces. On King Neptune's left sat a man wearing a makeshift cloth diaper. His large belly was covered in slimy goop. The Tadpole King and Queen sat next to him.

"On your knees, tadpoles!" King Neptune shouted.

They crawled toward him on their hands and knees, kneeling in small groups before the Royal Court to hear the Royal Prosecutor read the charges against them.

King Neptune declared all tadpoles guilty and sentenced each group separately. The sentences were comical. He ordered one cluster to pair off and dance a jitterbug, while another had to sing the national anthem backwards. Another group was ordered to stage a love scene with Queen Amphitrite.

"Anything that requires kissing one of those fellows is on you, doll," the soldier next to her murmured when they reached the throne. Hadley stifled a giggle.

After each group completed King Neptune's sentence, they were led away by shellbacks.

King Neptune banged his trident. "On your feet for your sentencing, if you please, slimy tadpoles."

As she stood, Hadley nearly lost her footing on the slippery deck and grabbed the elbow of the man next to her.

King Neptune made a show of unfurling a roll of parchment. "Tadpoles, you are hereby found guilty of the following offenses: Transgression into my domain without permission and insubordination to the trusty shellbacks of this vessel. You are hereby sentenced to play a game of Ring-Around-the-Rosie and sing and act out *Pop, Goes the Weasel* for the delight of the Royal Baby. All of you, that is, except for Captain Claverie. Captain, step aside for separate sentencing, if you please."

Hadley fumed while the others in her group played the childish games. King Neptune was one of the men from the shower incident. She had rebuffed his advances one evening in the lounge. She pressed her fingernails into her palms and waited. After her fellow tadpoles finally finished their games, King Neptune beckoned her forward.

"Captain Claverie, you are guilty of the offenses mentioned earlier. But, in addition, you are also hereby found guilty of malicious delegation of unpleasant and tedious tasks, wasteful use of office supplies, and —" He broke off and paused. "A pleasure-seeking intrusion into the sacrosanct domain of male officers."

His last charge sparked a flurry wolf whistles, cheers, and a few bawdy catcalls. When the hubbub died down, King Neptune held up his trident.

"Captain Claverie," he said, "you are hereby sentenced to sit on the Royal Baby's lap, blow raspberries on his belly, and sing him a lullaby."

Grit your teeth and smile, girl. If he sees he's gotten under your skin, he'll keep it up.

Hadley plastered a grin on her face and approached the Royal Baby. His belly was slathered with a gelatinous goop that looked like a mixture of Vaseline and egg whites and protruded so far, he had no lap. She perched on one of his knees and did her best to ignore the jibes from all around as she pressed her lips to his slick stomach. She gagged and recoiled, but someone, perhaps the baby, pushed her face into the gloppy mess.

Definitely Vaseline and eggs, mixed with castor oil.

Her gag reflex, combined with the slippery concoction, made it difficult for her to produce the requested sounds even though she blew hard. Determined to do it, she kept going until she finally produced a succession of raspberries. He laughed, and his belly vibrated against her lips. She took that as a sign to stop.

She surreptitiously wiped her hand across her mouth and waved, smiling, at the throng of cheering men surrounding them. Skip stood nearby with a deep frown creasing his forehead.

Hadley ignored him and turned back to the baby. She kissed his face several times for dramatic effect and launched into a lullaby Fanelia had often sung to her and her sisters when they were little.

She had sung only a few lines when someone shouted, "English, please!"

Hadley held up one finger, finished crooning in French, and then said, "Now in English."

The men roared with laughter when she reached the part threatening that if the baby didn't go to sleep, a crab would eat him. After taking a bow, Hadley got up and slipped and slid across the deck to her group of tadpoles, who waited for her.

The Royal Doctor swabbed their throats with something that made the men curse, spit, and beg for water. Hadley recognized the substance immediately. Tabasco sauce. The Royal Dentist wielded a squirt gun filled with beer spiked with mustard, black pepper, and more Tabasco. He declared that each tadpole must rinse with this foul blend.

Next came the Royal Barber, who gave some of the men the Southern Cross, a close-cut military buzz in the shape of a cross. As disgusting as her hair was at the moment, Hadley didn't want him or his shears anywhere near it.

The barber's helper stirred the sloppy contents of the bucket beside his chair. By the looks of it, they had mixed lard with eggs and God knew what else.

Determined to exude nonchalance, Hadley plopped into the barber's chair.

A great story. This will be a great story for the folks back home.

"Well, well, well, looks like we have a lady in need of a shampoo and cut." He ran his fingers through the sodden mess that was her pride and joy. Her hair had an inky, blue-black hue courtesy of her French forbears and held its curl and shape, even on searing days drenched with humidity back home in New Orleans.

Hadley fought back the temptation to ask — or plead if need be — for just a shampoo. The disgusting mess would come out eventually, even washing it in saltwater aboard ship.

She closed her eyes and mouth and sat motionless as the Royal Barber massaged handfuls of slimy goop from his bucket into her scalp. The excess ran in rivulets down her face.

"Hmm. A little trim, perhaps?" he asked.

No, no, no!

A pair of strong, firm hands hauled her out of the chair, set her on her feet, and prodded her forward. "Move, tadpole!"

Skip. She would thank him later.

He pushed her hard enough in the center of her back to propel her past a gauntlet of laughing shellbacks wielding paddles. A few of them took what she assumed was a perfunctory swat at her rear as she stumbled through. A chair perched over a swimming tank lay ahead.

Shellbacks shoved the man in front of her into the chair and tipped him backward into the tank. "Swim, tadpole!"

At least she would clean off with a swim. Maybe this was the end of the ritual?

With the barber's gloopy concoction sliding down her face, Hadley barely realized she had been crammed into the chair before a shellback tipped her backward. Her throat too dry to scream, she barely had time to suck in a panicked breath before wind-milling her arms and plunging into the water. She swallowed a mouthful of saltwater and came up sputtering and choking. Then she went down again. Was one of the shellbacks dunking her? She might drown, dammit. Hadley gulped in air as he hauled her up and then pushed her under again.

The water around her rocked with the force of someone diving into the water. Seconds later, a pair of strong hands pulled her upright.

"Enough," a familiar voice said. "I've got this one from here."

Hadley blinked and peered through the curtain of hair hanging over her face at Skip, who bobbed in front of her, holding her wrists to keep her upright. Somehow, his pirate headscarf still remained in place.

"Hope you can swim, tadpole." His words would have been a taunt without their warm tone and his accompanying grin.

The man who had been dunked before her had already been sent back to Hadley's side of the tank several times. Each time he crossed the pool, the shellbacks shouted, "Who are you?" and he answered, "I'm a tadpole, a lowly tadpole," the line she and the others had been forced to recite all day. But that wasn't the response the shellbacks wanted, so they made him swim back again and start over.

"What's he doing wrong? Who is he *now,* Hadley? Think," Skip said, his voice a husky whisper in her ear. In a louder voice, he said, "You swim across too, tadpole. See if you can get it right the first time."

Hadley set off using an easy crawl stroke, her mouth closed tight against the disgusting garbage floating in the tank. She treaded water at the other end and looked up at the waiting shellback, who shouted, "Who are you?"

Ah, this *was* the end. A thrill of recognition buzzed inside her.

"I'm a shellback," she shouted in response.

He grinned and gestured for her to climb the rope ladder dangling over the side. She did so, then glanced back at Skip, who still treaded water on the other side. A trace of a smile played over his mouth before he turned toward the other ladder and climbed out.

The fellas in her group waved her forward. Someone put a beer in her hand. She smiled when presented with a card decorated with pictures of King Neptune, mermaids, and a variety of colorful fish. The shellback card declared that Captain Hadley Claverie was free to roam at will over the Seven Seas, as long as she carried this card.

She would bet money that all the shellbacks were navy men, most of them career navy and in the service long before Pearl

Harbor. How did Skip Masterson, who wore the wings of a USAAF flying officer, have a shellback card?

Hadley's curiosity was always fine-tuned for a good story, and she resolved to learn the answer — not only to that question but also to the other mysteries surrounding him.

CHAPTER FOUR

January 20, 1943

Brisbane, Australia

Skip pointed toward the convoy of parked army trucks. "The first four are for passengers. Hop in the last one. We'll be on our way after they load our cargo."

"Okay." Dewey pushed up his shirt sleeves. Cloying heat hung in the air. "Seen the rest of our crew?"

"Dunno why they'd be here. Army's trucking us north to somewhere called *Townsville*. We'll fly to our base in New Guinea from there." Skip stepped a few paces off the road to allow a line of trucks towing half-assembled P-38 fighter planes to trundle past.

Dewey shook his head. "Huh. Could've sworn I saw Rafe."

Rafe Lopez, their crew's radio operator, was the only enlisted man to join the skeleton crew who had flown their B-25 bomber from California to Australia. The group commander had taken Skip's seat after Skip had been ordered off the roster.

Skip tightened his jaw. Traveling by ship was a steep price to pay for a momentary lapse in judgment. For nothing more than a moment of exhilarated vindication, he had landed himself in his own personal version of hell. He had since resolved to follow the straight and narrow.

"All I know is, we're headed north," he said. They would join the rest of their squadron in Townsville, where he would reclaim the left seat of his ship and the authority and respect that went along with it.

"Loads of P-38s coming off that carrier," Dewey observed.

Skip looked up. The tower crane's jib swung over the river, hoisting yet another fighter plane from the U.S.S. *Barnes,* which was anchored near the U.S.S. *West Point*. He bobbed his head in agreement. "We'll be happy to have 'em soon enough."

Listening in on a few shipboard bull sessions, Skip had gleaned that the European Theater was receiving the lion's share of resources at the moment. He gritted his teeth. *Europe first. What a crock. The Japanese attacked us, not the Germans*.

"Charlie already in?" He swiped at the sweat beading on his temples.

"Yep," Dewey chuckled. "He was the first one off the damned ship. Says if the Japanese don't get him, he may stay here cuz he's not gettin' on another boat."

Skip grinned. Plagued by severe seasickness, their tail gunner had lost at least ten pounds during their weeks at sea. Seasickness hadn't factored into Skip's haste in debarking, but he was also happy to leave the U.S.S. *West Point* behind.

He cut his eyes toward the steady stream of soldiers pouring down the gangway. Fifth Air Force, 503rd Parachute Infantry, plus large numbers of Navy Seabees — and of course, the women. A bevy of nurses and Red Cross Girls, laden with musette bags, had gathered along the wharf. Skip scanned the crowd for Hadley.

Yes, there she was, clutching her typewriter case. Her shiny indigo curls spilled from her cap, and her slender eyebrows arched over her dark, inquisitive eyes. Her ever-present notebook stuck out of her jacket pocket. Her nails were painted in what Skip took was her signature style — vibrant fire-engine red nail polish, with perfect white half-moons on their bases and tips. Were her toes painted to match?

He swallowed when she met his eyes, bobbed his head, and swiped his damp palms down his pants legs. Last thing he needed right now was a woman. Especially *that* woman, with her boundless curiosity. Good thing he would never see her again. He was headed to New Guinea, while the Red Cross Girls were sure to be stationed in large Australian cities, well away from danger. He had survived his tour of duty as her shipboard errand boy, and the sooner he shook free of her and everything associated with the ship, the better.

"Well, well, well, dat boat finally got you here."

Skip tore his gaze away from Hadley and pivoted on his heel. A summer-weight flight suit did little to disguise Leo Kozlowski's burly frame. Skip's navigator stood only a few yards away, flanked by their other crewmates.

"See you got a nice suntan on your long voyage, Skipper. You're as dark as Rafe here." His copilot, Mike Flannery, clapped a hand onto the shoulder of their wiry radio operator. Ah, so Dewey *had* spotted Rafe.

Rafe stepped forward, pushed up one of his shirt-sleeves, and shoved his forearm beside Skip's to compare the hues of their skin. "Almost, Skipper. Spend a few more weeks in the tropics, and we'll pass for brothers."

"Looks like you've been camped in a poolside chair all month. Wasn't such hard duty after all, was it?" Mike grinned and punched Skip's arm.

Rafe waved toward the milling women. "These gals serve you drinks while you sunbathed? Maybe you knew what you were doin' when you landed yourself on ship duty."

Hyper-aware of Hadley's proximity, Skip made of pretense of laughing.

"Think they'll send you by ship to Townsville? Or take you off the leash, let you stretch your wings again?" Mike gestured at the wings pinned over Skip's right breast pocket.

He swallowed. Traveling by water might be preferable to the vast distances in Australia, with them sweltering inside an army truck to Townsville.

"Nope." Skip compressed his lips and pointed out the waiting convoy. "That's my ride to Townsville."

"You're going by *truck*? Whew, bet you wish you hadn't buzzed that navy ship. Man, I'll never forget those swabbies ducking and running for cover." Mike guffawed.

Skip glimpsed Hadley edging closer. His pulse jerked in his neck. Last thing he wanted was her scrutiny and endless well of questions, although she was sharp and had doubtless overheard enough to piece together his story. Skip fought the urge to invite her to join them, to relate an appropriately embellished version of the buzzing incident that had landed him on the troop ship, to flirt with her.

"Save the hedge-hopping for those enemy convoys next time, eh?" Leo said.

Dewey pointed out a forklift laden with wooden crates that was depositing its contents beside a truck in the convoy. "Looks like the last bit of our cargo, Skipper."

Skip nodded at Dewey. "Go on and hop in. Tell the driver to wait for me. Gonna go double-check everything's off the ship."

"Shame you can't stay and see the sights with us." Mike clapped a hand on Skip's shoulder. "Even cooling our heels here for another day, we'll probably still beat you to Townsville."

"Why are you sticking around?" Skip asked. "You could fly out today."

"Cause they got our ships in the repair hangar over at Eagle

Farm for combat modifications." Leo held out a pack of cigarettes.

Skip waved off the offer of a smoke. "Combat modifications?"

"Fella named Pappy Gunn's been changing our B-25s from bombers to strafers. Installing eight machine guns in the nose. Pilots will fire 'em from the cockpit." The glint in Mike's eyes suggested he looked forward to combining flying with gunning.

"In the nose? What about Leo?" Skip frowned. Leo, in his dual role of navigator and bombardier, operated from a battle station in the Plexiglass nose of their B-25 Mitchell.

Leo blew out a smoke ring. "I'll still navigate and man the top turret gun. Just not from the nose." He winked. "You boys in the cockpit will control the bomb release and all those snazzy guns in da front."

"Strafers, you say?"

"Yep." Mike mimed a swooping plane with his hand. "Going in at treetop level."

So their months of boring, repetitious training in bombing from altitude had been a waste of time. Boredom had led to Skip's lapse in judgment.

"Gotta go make sure none of our cargo is still over there." Skip jerked his thumb back toward the wooden crates and metal containers still stacked along the wharf. "See you later."

"We'll be waiting for you in Townsville." Mike curved his lips in a wide grin.

Skip rolled his eyes and strode toward the cargo staging area.

"Enjoy your ride, Skipper," Leo called after him.

A crewman stood at the entrance to the gangway leading into the cargo hold. Skip cupped his hand over his mouth and yelled, "All the cargo out?"

The sailor peered into the hold, turned back, and nodded.

Skip snaked through the lines of stacked cargo, examining the unit identification stamps on each pile. All remaining boxes belonged to the Seabees.

He paused beside the main gangway. Hadley and the other

women still stood on the wharf awaiting their rides. He slid his hand into his pocket and closed his fingers around his light meter. It could be a good photograph — American women disembarking into the Pacific Theater, their normal lives upended to play a direct role in the war. Skip tilted his head, judging how he might frame a shot of Hadley, how he might capture the expectancy in her expression.

She tucked a strand of hair behind her ear, giving him another peek at her pretty nails. He swallowed. Wouldn't hurt to stop and say a quick goodbye and wish her luck.

"You headed to Townsville, Lieutenant?" a man behind him asked.

Skip turned and met the eyes of a USAAF major with a cloth pouch slung across his chest. The dark brown eyes of some sort of animal peered out of the pouch.

Skip pulled his gaze from the mysterious creature and snapped a salute. "Yes, sir."

"Lieutenant, I need you to make a delivery to Townsville for me. I leave on a flight in less than an hour, and my buddy has been delayed there."

"Of course, sir." The major wasn't carrying anything. Did he need Skip to take money to his friend? Perhaps payment of a gambling debt or a loan to tide the fella over until payday.

The major pulled the cloth pouch off over his head.

"Sir?" Skip frowned and held up his hand as the major looped the pouch over Skip's head and draped it across his shoulders. The warm weight of the animal, whatever it was, settled against his chest. The creature's heavy tail thumped his waist. *What the hell?*

The animal's narrow face, with bone structure resembling that of a fawn, had large, dark brown eyes that peeked out at him with curiosity. The bit of an ear he could see also put him in mind of a fawn. The creature thumped its tail again. That was no deer. A large rodent? His gut churned.

The major smiled. "She's a wallaby."

"A wallaby?" Skip repeated.

"Kind of like a small kangaroo. Same family, anyway."

"Oh?" Skip raised his eyebrows. Kangaroos grew to be quite large, didn't they?

"She belongs to my buddy. Long story as to how she ended up with me, but she ought to go back to him in Townsville." The major pulled a slip of paper from his pocket and passed it to Skip. "That's her owner. Captain Rick Oglethorpe with the 22nd Bomb Group."

A jeep pulled up alongside the wharf and blared its horn.

"There you are, George. Hop in!" the driver called. "We gotta get to the flight line."

"Thanks, Lieutenant." The major waved at Skip and set off at a jog, pausing only to call over his shoulder, "Her name's Lucinda. Named after the town where Rick found her."

Skip stared at the wallaby. *Lucinda.* What the hell was he going to do with a wallaby while riding for days in a truck? Questions tumbled one over the other in his head.

"Wait!" he yelled. "What does she eat?"

Too late. The jeep had roared out of sight.

"What do you eat, Lucy?" She blinked up at him.

Skip bit his lip. She was cute, but he didn't know the first thing about wallabies or any other animal. He sighed and set off toward the line of waiting trucks. He and a truck full of Americans were about to learn first-hand about wallabies.

"She eats grass, leaves, twigs, that sort of thing," Hadley said as she fell into step beside him. Groups of Red Cross Girls and nurses headed toward a line of jeeps teemed around them.

Skip halted and stared at her. "Do they have wallabies in New Orleans?"

"No." Hadley tilted her head and met his eyes with one slender brow lifted. Her lips twitched. "There was a book about Australian animals in the ship's library. Apparently you should have read it too."

"Did the book say if they're meant to be pets?" Skip glanced warily at Lucinda. What if she was prone to biting? He hadn't grown up with pets, but a neighbor's cat had once given him a reason to keep a respectful distance from felines.

Hadley leaned in close to peek inside the pouch, and Skip inhaled the pleasant spicy citrus scent of her perfume.

"She looks perfectly friendly," Hadley said. "Hello, Lucinda."

Lucinda thumped her tail. Hadley raised her hand and put it, palm up, near the wallaby's nose before Skip could stop her.

His pulse jumped, and he jerked sideways. "What if she bites?"

"Oh for pity's sake, Skip. Look, she's adorable. Aren't you, cher?" Hadley slid her hand inside the pouch. The wallaby's nostrils quivered as Hadley stroked the top of Lucinda's head and behind her ears with her glossy red and white polished fingertip.

Lucinda shot out a paw and grasped Hadley's wrist.

She giggled as the wallaby nuzzled her hand. "Awww, she's so sweet."

"Yeah?" Skip blew out a breath. "Well, maybe you should take her with you."

"I would, but I'm not going to Townsville." Hadley tickled the fur beneath Lucinda's muzzle. "Not that I've heard anyway."

"Hadley, come on! We're the last ones." A tall, skinny Red Cross Girl with wild blonde curls waved from the curb.

"Coming, Bizzy!" Hadley scratched the wallaby's ears one last time. "Bye, sweet Lucy." She giggled and mock-whispered. "Skip is a little bit afraid of you, cher, so be gentle with him."

Skip opened his mouth to protest, but Hadley rose onto her toes and pressed her soft lips to his cheek, catching him off-guard. His heart thrummed in his chest.

"Oh, and bye to you too, Skip!" She waved and set off at a light jog to meet her friend.

"Bye. Bye, Hadley," he whispered after her. He looked down at the wallaby. "All right, Lucy, I guess we're off to Townsville."

He tentatively stuck his finger into the pouch and stroked her soft fur. Her nose quivered, and she sniffed his wrist. "You liked Hadley, so you might be all right."

＊

February 27, 1943, 4:00 a.m.

Archerfield Aerodrome, near Brisbane, Australia

Hadley dropped slices of bread into several neat rows on the counter. Bizzy followed behind her with a jar of peanut butter, while JoJo added grape jelly.

"With these, we'll have one hundred and twenty sandwiches. I'll go check on the coffee." Hadley pushed a strand of hair from her face. The sun wouldn't rise for another hour yet, but the humidity was already high.

She stepped into a small adjacent space crowded with coffee urns, a doughnut machine, wire racks, and other supplies. Stella turned, holding tongs clutching a piping hot doughnut.

"First batch is cooling in the racks," she said. "Almost done with this round."

"Do I need to make coffee?" Hadley asked.

"No. I turned off the heat before I started this batch of doughnuts. Maybe find some fella to carry those out to the Clubmobile?" Stella pointed at two five-gallon ceramic urns.

Hadley nodded. Finding help wouldn't be a problem. Even at this ungodly hour, men from the signal corps would be loitering nearby, eager to snag a hot doughnut and a cup of coffee in exchange for their assistance.

She opened the door, stepped out into Archerfield's steamy pre-dawn darkness, and paused to allow her eyes to adjust. Cicadas hummed in the trees beyond the hangars and depot repair facilities. Their two Clubmobiles, the *Palm Beach* and the *Coconut Grove*, waited a few hundred yards away. Just as the men named their planes, or *ships* as they referred to them, the Red Cross Girls bestowed creative names on their Clubmobiles.

She jerked on the iron handle to open the *Palm Beach*'s back door and hoisted herself into its cramped compartment. Once inside, she pulled out her flashlight, directed its beam toward the floor, and closed the door. No amount of Lysol could cut the odor of greasy doughnuts and coffee inside the Clubmobile. After making sure the space for the urns and doughnut trays was clean and ready, she clambered out and repeated the process inside the other vehicle.

She then set out for the nearest repair shop. Men worked in shifts day and night to repair or retrofit the planes for the Fifth Air Force.

"Hiya, Red Cross. Got any doughnuts?" Private Anderson, his face spattered with grease, looked up from a bomber's turret assembly.

A grimy sergeant peeked out from under a P-38 wing section. "Sure could use a cup of hot Joe over here."

"You know the drill." Hadley leaned against the door frame. "Extra doughnuts and coffee for the first four fellas who help us load the Clubmobiles."

Men scrambled toward her from all directions.

"Not yet." Hadley placed her hand on the first eager helper's shoulders and steered him toward the sink. "Wash your hands first if you're gonna carry food."

The men chatted with her nonstop on their way to the outbuilding the USAAF had allocated to the Red Cross as a staging area.

Hadley stepped inside and pointed to the wire doughnut trays Stella had piled on every available surface and to the coffee urns crowded on the stovetop. "Mack and Wes, you can carry the urns. Andy, you and BJ take the trays. Divide everything between the two Clubmobiles."

Bizzy and JoJo piled sandwiches wrapped in wax paper inside cardboard boxes already brimming with candy bars, packaged almonds, oranges, and bananas. Hadley grabbed more sandwiches and helped to fill the remaining boxes. The GIs carried them outside while the women cleaned the staging area.

Once they finished, Hadley clapped her hands and motioned for everyone to go outside.

"Let's head out," she said. "The sooner we leave, the faster we'll be done."

"What's your hurry?" Bizzy untied her head scarf and fluffed her curls.

"We've all got other things to do." Hadley hoped the implication of laundry, shopping, and other mundane errands would prevent the others from pressing her for details about her plans. The less her friends knew about how she spent her free time, the better. She didn't want the bigwigs at the Red Cross to get a whiff of what she was up to.

"I don't know about the rest of you," Stella tapped her fingers against her mouth to stifle a yawn. "But I'm gonna get some more shut-eye before my shift at Amberley."

Damn. Hadley also needed to be at the Amberley Airfield canteen by ten o'clock. She had to allow an hour to get there via tram, bus, and train. She wouldn't have enough time to join the press corps at General MacArthur's headquarters. His press officer sometimes held a late morning briefing — and at other times MacArthur himself might answer questions from reporters before joining his family for lunch at their residence at the Lennons Hotel.

Hadley jiggled the doorknob to make sure the door was locked. "Anyone willing to trade for a late shift?"

"Ooh, golly, yes." Bizzy climbed in on the driver's side of the *Palm Beach* and started the engine. She leaned out the window. "I've been trying to figure out how to juggle my two dates tonight since I don't finish until eight o'clock."

"Deal." Hadley exchanged grins with JoJo and Stella. They were all amused by Bizzy's whirlwind social life. Did she ever sleep? She often arrived at their flat after midnight, even though their shift started at three-thirty. "If you'll promise to be at Amberley by ten."

"I'll be there." Bizzy held up three fingers. "My scheduled shift starts at three, okay?"

"Perfect. Thanks, Bizzy." Hadley jumped into the passenger side of the *Coconut Grove* next to JoJo and shut the door.

JoJo started the engine, shifted into gear, and released the clutch. The Clubmobile lurched forward with a sharp jerk, and Hadley pitched forward. She slammed her hands against the dash to break her momentum.

"Sorry." JoJo shot her a sheepish smile. "I'll get the hang of it."

"It's all right." Hadley had little room to complain. She hadn't driven much back home in New Orleans. Trolleys and her feet had gotten her around. She chuckled. "We'll both be experts before long. Unless . . ."

"Unless?" JoJo turned toward the radio site.

Hadley looked out the window. "Unless a new crop of Red Cross Girls arrives in time to save us from this lousy shift."

That much was true. Their arrival last month had relieved another crew of Red Cross Girls of this pre-dawn work. She had stopped short of voicing her immediate goal. The fellas at the airfields were fun and appreciative of Clubmobile services. But General MacArthur and the headquarters operations for the US Army Forces in the Far East were in Brisbane, not in these outlying area airfields. The action — and the stories — were in Brisbane.

Terrica House, the first and largest Red Cross service club in Australia, was only a short walk from MacArthur's headquarters, but any of the other Red Cross clubs in Brisbane would suit Hadley fine. She only had to stick it out until the next batch of Red Cross Girls arrived and then, with any luck, she could nab a transfer. Brisbane wasn't London, but it had its advantages.

JoJo parked the Clubmobile in front of the Signal Corps building. "I hope they hurry, those new women. Brisbane isn't much of a city, and nothing like New York." JoJo had grown up in Brooklyn, earned a degree from Barnard, and hadn't spent any significant time outside the Big Apple until now.

Hadley hopped out, walked around to the rear compartment,

and tugged it open. "It's nothing like New Orleans either. No wonder the boys are so bored here."

Violent street brawls had broken out between Australian and American soldiers a few months ago, spurring the authorities to demand longer operating hours for movie theaters and other entertainment venues — except bars. The Red Cross had also expanded its hours and opened additional clubs.

"I'd like to work at one of our beach resorts." JoJo got out a small wooden serving table. "Might as well enjoy some sun and surf on my days off, you know?"

"Not me. I want to go to New Guinea as soon as they let us." Hadley stepped into the crowded compartment's center aisle and handed JoJo a tray of doughnuts. Rumor had it the Red Cross would soon establish service in Port Moresby, home to multiple army airfields and a sizable navy presence. Moving closer to the combat zone would give her access to real stories. Not only the action, what was happening on the ground, but also the truth of how the war was being waged and how the soldiers were faring. That would be even better than scooping General MacArthur in Brisbane.

Hadley moved the coffee urn to the edge of the compartment and squeezed around it so she could jump down. Then she and JoJo each took a handle and carried it to the table.

"You'd rather be in the jungle than on a nice beach?" JoJo stepped back into the compartment and handed Hadley a tray of coffee cups.

Hesitant to reveal her plans to gain accreditation as a war correspondent, Hadley merely shrugged. Once Mr. Dupre, the editor of the *Times-Picayune*, read her stories from the front lines of the Pacific Theater, he would be sure to give her credentials. But until she got to New Guinea, the next best place for Hadley was Brisbane, with its headquarters for the US Army and Air Forces.

***

March 2, 1943

Brisbane, Australia

Hadley had no war correspondent band around her arm, no credentials, no press badge. She pocketed her Red Cross pin and draped a shawl over her shoulders to hide her ARC insignia. By blending in with the mass of reporters entering the lobby of the AMP building, General Headquarters for the Southwest Pacific Area, Hadley intended to finally attend one of MacArthur's press briefings.

She had loitered among the press pool for several weeks and struck up a friendship with Lorraine Shaw, the sole female correspondent covering MacArthur and SWPA headquarters. Lorraine was a native of Australia but had credentials from the *London Daily Mirror*. She had already worked as a foreign correspondent for more than five years, though she wasn't much older than Hadley. She had started on Fleet Street in London before following her husband to a post in Singapore. They had escaped ahead of the Japanese invasion, and Lorraine had reluctantly returned home to Australia.

"Reckon the general will give us any real information today?" Lorraine fiddled with a hairpin. "Press releases haven't been all that right."

"Something big is afoot," Hadley said. "Loads of planes took off from Archerfield this morning." The Red Cross had taken orders for three hundred boxed lunches, double the usual amount, and Hadley and Stella had stayed late to fill last minute requests for over a hundred more. "Some of the pilots hinted they aren't flying a usual mission today."

The heavy bronze doors opened, and milling reporters rushed forward.

"Bloke at Somerville said the same over brekky this morning."

Lorraine had a good contact at the US Army Base 3 headquarters who often passed along tips over breakfast.

The MP stood checking press badges at the door. Hadley's heart hammered, and she shot Lorraine a nervous glance. Worst case, he would refuse her admittance, but he would remember her if she tried it again another day.

"Have your notebook in hand and prattle on about something with me. Don't make eye contact with him," Lorraine murmured in a low rush.

Hadley pulled out her pad and jabbed her finger at her notes, as though passing along critical information and unable to pull out her credentials.

Lorraine gesticulated toward Hadley's notes, asked several nonsensical questions, and flashed her press badge while sailing forward with Hadley hurrying along beside her. They scurried deeper into the scrum of reporters headed toward the briefing room before the MP could stop them. Hadley slid into a chair beside Lorraine, looked behind her to confirm that he wasn't chasing after them, and exhaled in relief. "I think it worked."

"Too many journos after us for him to bother following you. That's why I wanted us to come in toward the middle." Lorraine pulled her notebook and pen from her bag.

Within minutes, an army officer dressed in the standard Southwest Pacific attire of a khaki shirt and khaki pants strode up to the podium.

"Eh, he's only the press officer," Lorraine whispered. "Whatever's going on, we won't learn it from him."

Hadley had spotted this man, and a woman known openly as his mistress, coming and going from the Lennons Hotel. Every correspondent in Brisbane resented Colonel Diller's approach to the press that ranged from nonexistent access to General MacArthur and his principal military officers to his ruthless blue censor pencil. No story could ever deviate from the official communiqués that painted MacArthur, his strategy, and his results in a glowing, inaccurate light.

Sure enough, Colonel Diller began by reciting the day's communiqué. Hadley exchanged a frustrated glance with Lorraine. The colonel stated that reconnaissance planes had spotted a Japanese convoy moving toward the northern coast of New Guinea under cover of a weather front and that Allied air forces were preparing to attack, weather permitting. That explained the extraordinary number of planes taking off from Archerfield this morning.

Diller looked up from the communiqué. "The general will permit a few correspondents to fly to Port Moresby to cover this operation. Departure from Archerfield at fifteen hundred."

Several correspondents shot to their feet, and a loud babble of names and news outlets rang through the crowded room.

Diller put up his hand to quiet the clamor. "If you're interested, come to the podium at the conclusion of this briefing."

He would choose the journalists most apt to attribute all success to MacArthur without deviating from the SWPA Headquarters line.

The press officer studied the seated press members, finally settling his gaze on Lorraine and then lingering on Hadley, no doubt wondering which paper or wire service had a new female correspondent. He lifted his chin. "*Men* only, of course."

Of course. Hadley gritted her teeth. Lorraine's fingers clenched and unclenched around her pencil. Under MacArthur's regime, Lorraine's years of experience counted for nothing. He couldn't revoke her credentials, but he could make damned sure she had no opportunity for a scoop.

Hadley faced many obstacles beyond her gender. Mr. Dupre might remedy her lack of credentials if she could send him a few stories. She had written three last week but hadn't worked out a way to deliver them. Mailing them wasn't an option, because the censor would strip them down to nothing and report her to MacArthur's press staff. She had no access to an overseas telephone line or teletype. If she were in England, she might be able to get a piece or two through the censor without losing substance, but censorship was far stricter here.

Lorraine had offered to send Hadley's work to the *Daily Mirror* under her credentials and follow it with a telegram asking her editor to transmit the pieces to Dupre at the *Times-Picayune*, attributed to H. G. Claverie. Hadley didn't see the point in going to this trouble for the articles she had written so far. She needed a unique angle. Not a big scoop, just something to entice Dupre into securing credentials for her.

Short of an assignment near combat action in New Guinea, Hadley would best meet her goals if she worked at the main Brisbane club, which was close to SWPA headquarters, the Lennons Hotel, and Lorraine and her contacts.

Most of the men in the room surged up to Diller's podium at the end of the briefing.

Lorraine shook her head and beckoned for Hadley to follow her. "Let's go," she said. "Won't change anything to get crook over it."

"Crook?"

"Pissy." Lorraine shot her a tight smile. "Angry."

Hadley sighed. No, arguing with MacArthur's press officer would only serve to reinforce his antiquated view that women were too emotional to cover anything beyond the society pages. Hadley eyed the MP at the door as they left the building, but he didn't ask for any identification for people exiting.

She followed Lorraine outside into the damp air. The sidewalk was wet, and what had been sprinkles earlier had turned into a downpour.

Her friend gestured toward a small cafe. "Time to join me for a cuppa?"

Hadley opened her umbrella and shook her head. "I'd love to, but I want to swing by Terrica House before I go out to Amberley for my shift."

She waved Lorraine off and continued down Queen Street for the short walk to the largest Red Cross Services Club in Brisbane.

Hadley opened the outside door to the field director's office.

Miss Browne looked up from her ledger book and smiled. "Oh, Hadley, I hoped I would see you today. I have good news."

Finally. An assignment here. Hadley's heartbeat accelerated. Perhaps Miss Browne would ask Hadley to organize their larger entertainment shows or coordinate the recruitment and vetting of young Australian women who attended their bi-weekly dances. Supervising the restaurant staff and operations would also be fine. Whatever Miss Browne had in mind, Hadley would dive in with enthusiasm.

Miss Browne's terrier, Pogo, lifted his head, thumped his tail against the floor in greeting, and then laid his head back onto his paws.

Miss Browne riffled through a stack of papers on her desk. "You expressed a desire to coordinate more entertainment options."

"Oh, yes." Hadley had finally settled on a strategy for winning her desired assignment. Her shifts at the airfields didn't involve organizing entertainment, so she had dropped her desire into several conversations with the director. Apparently her hints had worked. She smiled at Miss Browne. "I've got so many ideas for how to expand the Sunday night show and perhaps add an afternoon event."

"They'll need more than Sunday events. Probably a rotating daily schedule."

They? Miss Browne must be talking about Riverview, the other Brisbane club.

Miss Browne passed Hadley a slip of paper. "Your lifeguard certification will also come in handy."

That did not sound like Brisbane.

Hadley glanced down at the paper. "Sans Souci?"

"It's lovely. Absolutely lovely." Miss Browne smiled. "I toured it last week. We have several rest homes for officers alongside the beach at Surfers' Paradise. You'll have many options for offering recreation and entertainment to the men there. Horseback riding, boat rides, beach barbecues, biking, sailing, swimming lessons. Oh, and best of all, tennis." Mary Browne was a former national tennis champion.

Hadley cringed. This was JoJo's dream job, not hers. She cleared her throat. "I'd feel awful taking this job, when JoJo wants it. What if she does this, while I wait for something else?"

"Oh, JoJo is going with you. You, JoJo, Stella, and Bizzy are all going to Sans Souci. They desperately need more staff. Once you get the club organized and running, it'll be a dream job. Absolutely tops. Away from all the hustle and bustle of Brisbane."

Hadley pasted a smile on her face. "We can still visit on a day off though, right?"

"You won't want to leave once you're there." Miss Browne waved a hand. "Southport is about fifty miles south, but in this country, fifty miles might as well be five hundred. But no matter. You're headed to paradise, Hadley."

Paradise? An assignment near a sunny tropical beach *would* be paradise for most people, but not for a reporter desperate to cover the war.

CHAPTER FIVE

March 2, 1943

Durand Airfield (17 Mile Drome), Port Moresby, New Guinea

"Scuttlebutt has it we'll go up." Leo ducked inside the tent.

Skip looked up from his book. Mess chatter tonight had suggested a large-scale mission was in the works. A mission worthy of the weeks they'd spent practicing strafing runs on the Moresby wreck in the harbor. Pilots perfected the technique of strafing the deck from stem to stern, then pulling up sharply over the masthead, while copilots mastered General Kenney's new skip-bombing tactics.

He peered through the open tent flaps and gestured toward the brilliant fiery red and orange clouds towering over the sun, which would soon slip out of sight beyond the distant Owen Stanley mountains. "We've seen that before."

Tonight's sunset, staggering even by tropical standards, signaled clear weather for tomorrow — and clear weather translated into an upcoming mission.

Skip dog-eared his page, closed *For Whom the Bell Tolls*, and set the book on the small bedside table he shared with Mike. He had first read the novel when it had come out several years ago. Good thing it was worth a re-read. Unless he got leave soon, he would run out of books. He had already swapped what he had with every other reader on base. If the Red Cross set up a club, it might include a library, but none of the men expected the Red Cross to show up in this godforsaken jungle hellhole anytime soon. A male field director visited them every few weeks, but so far he had only brought candy, razors, toothbrushes, soap, and cigarettes.

Skip picked up each boot in turn, flipped them over, and gave them a good shake to dislodge any creepy-crawlies, especially scorpions, before tugging them on. Twilight segued into pitch-black nightfall within seconds at their jungle base. Time to retrieve Lucy.

When Skip had reached Townsville last month with the wallaby, he had learned that her owner's squadron had been sent to Port Moresby. Skip's squadron was preparing to relocate to Durand Field outside Port Moresby, so he had told Oglethorpe's buddies that he would deliver Lucy to New Guinea.

He had worried the flight would stress her, but Lucy had been a trooper. Granted, she had burrowed herself deep into the canvas pouch Skip had hung on the back of his pilot seat and didn't reemerge until they were back on the ground. The next day, Skip had borrowed a jeep and set off for Jackson Field. Officers there had informed him that Oglethorpe's plane had been shot down in a mission over Lae. No survivors. Skip hadn't asked if any of the fellas in Oglethorpe's group wanted Lucy. She was his now.

He ducked out of the tent and strode down the hillside to her fenced enclosure. He had traded two bottles of Scotch for the Marston mat materials from a crew of Seabees. The black market for enough dunnage wood to create a solid fence would have set him back far more than the booze had. Everyone wanted wood to create raised platform flooring inside their tents.

After scrounging for several good-size limbs, Skip and his crewmates had staked them at intervals to form an enclosure, a tough job in this thin, rocky soil. After that, they nailed Marston matting to the stakes. The material was normally used to surface runways, so he figured it should keep out crocodiles and other predators. Their ground crew also pitched in by building Lucy a small lean-to so she could escape the daily downpours.

Normally, she would be running the perimeter of the fence while he walked up, eager to use her last chance for exercise for the day. But she had a visitor. Skip picked up her collar and leash, unhooked the fence's rope latch, and stepped inside the makeshift enclosure.

Pat Flannery, pilot of *Southie in the South Seas* and Skip's wing-man, waved in greeting from where he sat on his haunches, feeding Lucy bits of chopped apple from his hand.

She nibbled the last piece and hopped toward Skip.

"Thought she might like a treat today." Pat rose and walked toward Skip. "Got an apple from the mess."

"She's always happy to have more food." Skip laughed. Lucy's paws pressed against his right pants pocket. She knew he had something for her from the mess.

He laughed and pushed her paws away. "Hey, little miss greedy, you just ate an apple Pat gave you. Be grateful. I haven't been able to nab any apples for you in awhile."

Lucy gave up on him and bounded toward the perimeter fence.

"Mac hid the apples." Pat's freckled face split into a wide grin. "Guess he wanted his mess boys to have first dibs. Not like they're rationed, so I don't know why he's hoarding them."

Nothing Skip had eaten in the mess since disembarking at Brisbane had been tasty enough to warrant hoarding. "Guess I'll remind him Lucy needs fruit now and then."

"Don't reckon she'd find apples in the wild here, do you?" Pat winked.

Skip laughed. "Naw, probably not." He swept his arm around the enclosure. "Just not sure this bit of grass has everything she needs."

"You gonna take her back home with you, after the war?"

Home? Last time he had visited his parents, he had only stayed long enough to eat Thanksgiving dinner and engage in at least three separate arguments with his father. Did his folks even still live there? He addressed his letters to Mama and Molly at the family's long-standing FPO address. None of the dozen houses Skip had lived in during his childhood held any association of *home* for him.

More immediate was the question of survival.

He shrugged. "I'll think about it when I've got the points. Hardly worth considering yet."

Eyes trained on the ground, Pat scuffed the toe of his boot toe in the dirt. "Reckon I could be home by the start of football season."

"Oh, yeah?" Skip clenched his hands into fists until his fingernails dug into his palms. Making such concrete plans for the future, let alone giving them voice, was bad luck. He forced a measure of nonchalance into his tone. "Early polls have Notre Dame winning the championship next year."

"Bushwa," Pat scoffed. "BC's gonna take it. They got so close last fall."

Pat and Mike, Skip's copilot, had grown up together in the same south Boston neighborhood. Both had gone to Boston College, then enlisted together after Pearl. They were rabid about all Boston sports teams, especially those of their alma mater.

"My money's on Navy." Skip relaxed his fists and tightened the knot in Lucy's leash.

Pat barked a laugh. "The swabbies? Have some service pride, Masterson."

Lack of service pride wasn't the issue. Skip had so far avoided divulging any details about his own college days, going so far as to hide his class ring from the Naval Academy — an item he had once seen as a symbol of accomplishment and a source of pride — inside his kit. Of all his fellow officers, Pat might best understand Skip's unconventional path to the USAAF and refrain from judging his choices, his mistakes, his hubris. Pat had his own demons.

"Been thinking about what you said the other night." Pat extracted a rubber ball from his pocket and tossed it toward Lucy. She bounded after it, although she didn't understand the concept of playing fetch enough to bring it back. "You know, about how we only get one life and I should do what I want, not what my Pops wants or what Mike wants."

I said that? Skip scratched his jaw. Old Skip, sure. Old Skip had enthusiastically embraced that outlook. Not now. Not after Pearl.

The war had changed everything.

Pat cleared his throat. "Wrote to a few vet schools to ask about enrolling after I get home."

"You said anything to Mike yet?"

"Nah." Pat shook his head. "Soon as I'm gettin' close on the points, I'll talk to him and write Pops. No reason why Mike shouldn't take over the bar on his own or find another partner."

The war had disrupted everything from Pat's father's retirement to Mike's plans to marry Pat's younger sister Fiona — and Pat's combat service had certainly altered his perspective about taking over the family bar in partnership with Mike. He had confided his dream of becoming a veterinarian to Skip, said he could no longer ignore how short and fragile life could be.

Right. One life. They each had one life, a life that might have to substitute for another that had been needlessly lost. Skip's gut twisted in familiar spasms. He stuck his hand into his pocket and closed his fingers around the light meter he carried with him at all times.

The light meter was a cherished gift from his older brother Chet. It represented an acknowledgment of Skip's individuality and stood as an invitation for Skip to follow his heart. The war, however, had upended his plans and forced him to bury his dream. After serving his country, he would take up where Chet left off. Well, not exactly. Skip had no intention of rejoining the navy, but he would become an engineer, settle down, and raise a family.

He looked up. Variegated streaks of orange over the distant mountain peaks topped the dark purple sky. Full darkness would be upon them in minutes.

Skip extracted a few bits of chopped carrot from his pocket, whistled, and squatted with the treat atop his upturned palm. That did the trick. Lucy bounded over and nibbled on the carrots while Skip fastened her collar around her neck.

"Time to sleep soon, Lucy." He stood, led the wallaby through the gate, and turned to make sure Pat latched it behind him.

Skip took no more than a few strides up the sloping footpath toward their tents when Lucy's paws hit the backs of his knees. Skip's lips quivered, and he suppressed the urge to laugh but continued on. More insistent swats of her paws followed. He exchanged a grin with Pat and took a few more steps. Poke, swat, poke.

Skip laughed, swung around, and scooped the wallaby up in his arms.

Pat waved off Skip's offer for him to join them in their tent for a poker game. "Might join you fellas later. Gonna go try to get some sleep."

Lucy leapt out of Skip's arms as soon as he stepped through the open canvas tent flaps and hopped from one cot to another, happy to greet her people. Skip secured the end of her rope leash around a post. The night was far too warm from them to close the tent flaps, but the rope was long enough for Lucy to move about the tent without wandering outside.

"Hiya, Lucy Lou." Rafe pulled a few chopped bits of carrot from his pocket and sprinkled them onto his cot.

Skip unlatched his trunk and took out his knives. He picked up a leather strop and sat on the edge of his cot to sharpen them. "Try to keep her over there while I strop my knives."

Lucy would pick up anything lying about inside the tent, but the biggest danger was her tail. She knocked things over on a regular basis. Their field lantern now hung from a center post.

Skip unsheathed his hunting knife, angled the blade against the leather, and drew it backward across the strop. Then he flipped the blade over and stropped the other side. After twelve passes, he held it up to the light. Sharp enough. He slid the glistening knife back into its sheath and repeated the process with a second knife and a folding machete.

Mike looked up from a letter. "Aren't you worried you're overdoing it with those knives?"

"You'll be damned glad I've got sharp knives if we go down in the jungle." Skip dipped a rag into a tin of boot crème, ran it up and down the strop, and hung it on a peg. "When was the last time you fellas even looked inside your kits?"

"I figure you and Mike will make sure we go down in the water instead of the jungle, and a sharp knife won't count for shit against those sharks we see from the air," Leo said.

Skip couldn't argue either point. Their survival odds would be considerably higher if they ditched into a mass of swarming sharks rather than crash-landing in the jungle. Assuming a crash into dense vegetation didn't kill them outright, their odds of navigating out of the jungle without succumbing to its myriad dangers were almost zero.

Yet something drove him to double-check the contents of his jungle survival kit each night. He retrieved his pack and spread it out on his cot, then pulled out each item, confirming his water purification tablets and matches were intact and dry, the packets of bouillon powder weren't ripped, and there were plenty of bandages.

"Anything changed in your kit since *last night*, Skipper?" Rafe rolled a rubber ball toward Lucy, and she hopped after it. "From the mission we didn't fly today?"

"You clowns haven't checked yours since we got here. If your purification tablets are ruined, I guess I'm the only one who'll survive, eh?" Skip replaced each item inside his pack, rolled it up, and closed the fastenings.

Leo pulled off his uniform shirt, shook it out, and hung it on a peg on the makeshift shelving unit. "We're betting you won't leave your buddies behind to die."

Skip didn't speak, but his heart tightened. He hadn't intended for any of his buddies to die. If he hadn't let his temper get away from him, if the attack on Pearl had happened one day earlier while he was still on board — well, he couldn't have prevented it. He knew that. He might have died too. But he might have survived, might have been able to save some of them, might have saved his brother. Instead they had all died, and he was left with an outsized helping of guilt, grief, and anger. Anger he now channeled into combat missions.

Anger might drive Skip, but he now worked overtime to keep his worst impulses in check.

Be prepared. Follow all the rules. Play it safe. No more hell-raising. No more bucking authority. No more emotional ties.

"At least clean and load your damned side-arms, all right? And don't forget to put tracers in the magazine." Skip ejected the magazine from his Colt .45 and checked its contents. Tracer ammo could signal their location to would-be rescuers.

He then field-stripped the pistol, cleaned and oiled each part, reassembled it, and pushed the magazine back into the grip until it clicked. Humidity and rain did more than ruin their boots and clothing. The dampness would also rust their weapons.

Skip returned the pistol to his shoulder holster and looped it over a peg. He always took the weapon with him to the trenches when Japanese bombers came overhead. He didn't fire it at the enormous jungle rats that roamed the trenches and campsite, but he would take no chances with a crocodile. Their hastily-constructed air bases had disturbed the reptile's natural habitat, and the beasts had become, according to both locals and Aussies, particularly aggressive and dangerous.

Mike capped his pen, folded his letter, and slipped it into an envelope. "What's the dope on the briefing time?"

"Thirty minutes after the final raid ends, right as you're dropping off to sleep. Isn't that always the way?" Leo stretched his arms, then picked up a deck of cards.

Skip sighed. Japanese bombers raided the airfields clustered around Port Moresby every night. They rarely hit anything, but whenever the siren sounded, the men ran to the slit trenches nearest their tent. The trenches were slick with foul-smelling mud and swarmed with mosquitos. Many men declared that a direct bomb blast would be preferable to slumping for hours inside a fetid trench fighting off giant rats, biting insects, and snakes.

Leo ambled over to the small card table in the center of the tent, pulled out a rickety folding chair, and sat. He shuffled the deck. "Who's in?"

"What else are we gonna do until those bombers send us to the damn trenches?" Mike pulled out another chair and plopped into it.

Rafe tossed his letter onto his bedside table and moved to take a seat. "Too early for bed. No bar, no club, no women. Wish we were based in Australia."

"The Red Cross clubs in Brisbane were tops." Leo dealt the cards. "Milkshakes and burgers, dances with pretty Aussie girls, ping-pong tables, pinball machines, the works."

Skip rolled his eyes. He had left Brisbane within hours of debarking the ship and had bounced along horrible roads for fifteen hours with a restless wallaby in tow. Was Hadley working at one of those Brisbane clubs? Maybe she was in Sydney or Melbourne or working in one of the beachside rest homes. He quirked his mouth. Wherever she was, she was probably running the show.

"Heard they're bringing Red Cross gals over here soon," Rafe said.

Leo laughed. "Here? No, they won't be starting a club in this jungle anytime soon."

Conditions were far too primitive and dangerous for women

here. Skip grinned as he considered what Hadley would have to say on that score. Old Skip would have found Hadley Claverie to be very compelling and very, very attractive. All that crusading passion and feisty independence would have made her irresistible. But new Skip had sworn off all emotional entanglements. No point in thinking about her or any other woman. Leo was right. No jungle club here anytime soon.

He rose to join the poker game, and his boot crunched something on the ground. He bent to retrieve it. A lid from a tin of Kiwi boot crème.

Uh-oh. He must not have closed the tin after he wiped down his strop, and Lucy had found it. He scanned the tent until he found her.

"Aw, Lucy," Skip groaned.

The wallaby was covered from head to toe with dark brown boot crème. Worse still, she had dabbed her crème-coated paws all over the clean uniform shirts the men had hung on pegs to dry.

His crewmates burst into such raucous laughter, they were soon joined by a half dozen men from nearby tents.

***

March 3, 1943, 4:45 a.m.

Durand Airfield (17 Mile Drome), Port Moresby, New Guinea

Perhaps the chatter and calls of birds from the surrounding jungle woke Skip. Perched on the fine edge that separated its nighttime menace from the approaching dawn, the jungle yawned, stretched, and eased into the day. The tent remained enveloped in smothering, dense blackness. Thanks to the close confines of his mosquito bar, his sense of entrapment multiplied and his heart pounded.

Leo's snores, the harsh stench of mildew, and Lucy rustling inside her pouch next to him signaled where he was. Skip's mind darted with dread to what today held. It wasn't his first combat mission, not by a long stretch. He had flown six others before orders came to stand down and practice the new strafing and skip-bombing tactics. Tactics they would employ in combat for the first time today.

God knows they had practiced enough. Skip wasn't worried about the mechanics. But, spraying up to eight hundred rounds per minute onto the deck of the Moresby *wreck* was one thing. It was a stationary target. No ack-ack guns firing at them, no helmsman maneuvering the vessel out of their path, and no enemy soldiers to shoot or shoot back.

His crew and squadron would dive closer to the enemy than ever before, putting them in more danger but also giving them more control. He would fly the ship *and* direct the firepower of the forward-facing guns. It was a chance to even the score. Better yet, he would be part of a force that stood to earn the respect of General Kenney, maybe even General MacArthur.

Revealed through the gap in the tent flap, the thick, oppressive darkness tapered into a soft, pale gray before becoming suffused with the soft lavenders and vivid pinks of the impending sunrise. Skip eased out from under the netting, shook out his boots, and stepped into them, then looped the shoulder holster with his .45 over his head. Crocs and snakes were most active at night, but they had also been spotted early in the morning.

Lucy peeked out of her pouch and stretched her paw toward him.

"Not yet," he whispered. "You stay put." He worried that nocturnal predators might still lurk at this hour. Whenever he flew early morning missions, he left Nate, his ground crew chief, in charge of moving Lucy to her enclosure. The ground crew fellas often ribbed him about turning her into the Australian delicacy of roo tail soup in his absence, but they coddled her as much as Skip and his crew did.

Skip double-checked that the wallaby's rope leash was securely lashed to the post before ducking outside through the open flap. Humidity hung thick in the air.

He closed his mouth and swatted at a cloud of swarming gnats before setting off for the nearest latrine, situated over a mile away in a pointless attempt to minimize odor. The sickly-sweet stench of dank decay seeped from the dense jungle that pressed close to the campsite, the mess and ops buildings, and the revetments for their ships.

He climbed a small hill and paused to scan his surroundings. Shrill calls and warbles from brightly colored birds rang out. He stomped his feet to scare off a few rats. No point wasting ammo on them. Even if the foul scavengers were the largest the Americans had ever seen, they skittered away in the light of day.

After using the latrine, Skip hiked up the slope of another hill and sat on a log to watch the sunrise. Damn, this light was perfect. His once-beloved Graflex camera was buried at the bottom of his trunk, but he knew how he would frame his shots. He had several new canisters of Kodachrome film packed alongside the ones he had used the morning of the attack, the morning when everything had changed in the whistle of a bomb hurtling into the fleet at anchor.

He hadn't had time to ship those rolls to the lab for processing. At least, that's what he had told himself during his months of USAAF training. Now he was in the New Guinea jungle, he couldn't see the point until after the war. After the war. He would get that film developed *after the war*.

The peace of breaking dawn would end at any moment. Skip lifted his hand to shade his eyes and peered downhill at the cluster of Ops tents. Their front flaps were tied back, but any time now, the Ops staff would come out and roust the combat crews from their tents. Skip was surprised they hadn't done so already.

Two officers exited the Squadron Ops tent and beckoned for a man from the Intelligence tent to join them. The three men then strode toward the hillside tents. Skip stood. He would save them the trouble and wake his crew.

***

March 3, 1943, 8:45 a.m.

Crossing Owen Stanley mountain range

Heading: Cape Ward Hunt, southeast of Lae, New Guinea

A flight from Port Moresby on New Guinea's southeast coast to the day's assembly point at Cape Ward Hunt on the northeast coast was a straight-line shot. A flight path that nonetheless required them to traverse the rugged, cloud-shrouded Owen Stanley mountains that rose to over thirteen thousand feet and could throw up treacherous storms and weather with no warning.

Weather was reportedly clear over today's target, a large Japanese convoy intended to supply its forces at Lae. But the propensity for unpredictable, violent weather dictated that they remain alert and cautious.

Skip wiped sweat from his brow and flipped the selector switch from command function, which allowed him to communicate with other pilots in the group, to intercom for inter-plane conversations. "Pilot to navigator: Course all right?"

"Adjust one degree right, hold altitude," Leo responded.

"Copilot to crew: Oxygen check." Mike made check-marks in his logbook as each crew member responded in turn. Once they cleared the mountains, they would descend below eight thousand feet and remove their oxygen masks.

Skip tucked his ship, christened *Bourbon Street Belle*, closer into the element. Dewey, their flight engineer, had grown up in southern Louisiana. He had raised his eyebrows when he had first read the name emblazoned on the plane, but if he had connected the name to the attractive Red Cross Girl from the docks in Brisbane, he had made no comment. Honestly, the name had taken Skip by surprise too, and he had given it to the group artist before he changed his mind.

Southie in the South Seas was on his left, *Pinball Princess* on his right, and *Devil's Delight* behind him.

When they crossed the final peaks of the Owen Stanleys, Skip let down to 7,500 feet, and Mike told the crew they could remove their oxygen masks. Tracking a northeasterly course parallel to the Mambare River, the formation decreased altitude, crossed the lowland hills close to the coast, and flew to their assembly point.

Good God. They had been briefed on the composition of the strike force, but Skip's chest swelled with pride and a surge of adrenaline at the sight of the growing armada of Allied aircraft. His skin prickled with energy.

"Even the fighter boys joined us today," Mike noted. "Good."

"Got drop-tanks, remember?" Leo reminded him.

They had been told in briefing that the fighters had been equipped with extra fuel tanks to boost their range for today's mission. They would release their empty drop-tanks at the start of battle, leaving them with a full tank of fuel and a lighter load.

The P-38 fighters circled above the B-17s, and the non-strafer B-25s that would bomb from medium altitude flew below them. Aussie A-20 bombers assembled beneath them, followed by the Royal Australian Air Force Beaufighters. Skip and the other strafer B-25s flew into formation alongside the A20s and the Beaufighters.

Command function went silent.

Skip maneuvered *Bourbon Street Belle* to follow the lead squadron as the formation hugged the coast and flew toward a point south of Lae before flying over the Huon Gulf and circling to the Viatriz Strait.

And there below them, spread over the sparkling blue water like ducks on a pond, sailed a large Japanese convoy of destroyers, cruisers, transports, and cargo ships. Thanks to today's rare clear skies, what airmen called CAVU - ceiling and visibility unlimited — they had a perfect visual sighting of their target. Ships as far as the eye could see. Skip's heart thrummed hard. *Ships.*

"Prepare for action," he barked into the intercom. He jammed his helmet on over his headset and adjusted his flak vest. He hoped it would take the brunt of any flak that might penetrate from below.

The B-17s dropped bombs on the convoy from eight thousand feet and achieved their primary objective. They couldn't bomb with enough precision from higher altitudes to sink ships, but they could force them out of their tightly packed convoy. Japanese ships dispersed even farther when the A-20s and B-25s bombed from medium altitude, adding their payload to the mayhem. Now the Allies had them right where they wanted them.

Almost time. Skip tightened his grip on the yoke. Sweat sheened his forehead.

The Beaufighters had to do their job first. Fifth Air Force brass hoped the Japanese anti-aircraft gunners would focus their fire on the bombers at medium altitude and fail to notice the low-level strafers moving in. If they could achieve that, the Japanese gunners would be unable to recalibrate their fire until they were either mowed down or forced to abandon their guns to seek cover.

As the Beaufighters approached the convoy, they dodged the P-38 drop-tanks falling into the sea. Each P-38 fighter was now lean and trim, with optimal maneuverability to protect the Allied bombers and strafers. The lethal RAAF Beaufighters, armed with four front-facing cannons and six machine guns, raced ahead in a high-speed, single-file formation just above the waves and peeled off for the attack, raking the Japanese vessels from stem to stern with blazing, concentrated firepower.

Skip's group descended several miles from the convoy and dropped down to skim the surface of the water. Spray from the waves hit the belly of their planes.

Smoking, smoldering vessels stretched over the deep blue water for miles. Skip shook his head to clear the visual from his past. This wasn't Pearl Harbor. He sharpened his focus as though he had a single destroyer centered in the rangefinder of his Graflex camera.

Mike closed the cowl flaps, set the mixture to full and rich, and pushed the throttle forward to 38 inches of manifold pressure.

"I'm making a run on that lead cruiser," Major Larner snapped in Skip's ear on the squadron frequency. "Everyone pick your target."

Larner's plane dove toward the cruiser with his wingman close behind.

"Which one we gonna nab, Skipper?" Skip's wingman Pat asked.

His first thought was of those other ships, the ones destroyed on that fateful Sunday morning, but the ships at hand were in the Bismarck Sea.

Enemy ships, not my buddies. Not Chet.

His fellas were counting on him to have a steady hand and the iron will to do the job. *Breathe and focus.*

"Follow me." Skip accelerated and climbed to five hundred feet, dodging and weaving among the mass of Allied aircraft pelting into battle. A destroyer bobbed in his rangefinder.

Two thousand yards out, he dove steeply to port at high speed. *Bourbon Street Belle's* straining engines thrummed and the high-pitched screech of air whistled through the cockpit. He would attack on the bow, while Pat took his ship across their target on the beam.

Jinking his ship closer, Skip hit the fire button on the yoke, sending several bursts of fire from the powerful nose guns toward the target. A thousand yards. Blood thundered in his ears. He pressed on the rudders to yaw the nose from side-to-side while keeping his thumb depressed on the fire button. The ship's airframe vibrated with a rattling, concussive crescendo of staccato bursts as he unleashed *Bourbon Street Belle's* full firepower of eight hundred rounds per minute over the destroyer's deck.

Carnage. Skip's stomach roiled. Even at this supercharged speed, he couldn't miss the blood bath their planes were unleashing on the enemy.

Enemy. The fucking enemy. The Japanese were the enemy, and this was his job. A job that had nonetheless just gotten a helluva lot more personal being this close to *the deck* of the damned ship rather than dropping bombs from seven thousand feet above it.

Images flashed through Skip's mind. Towering masses of black smoke, blazing infernos, listing and sinking ships, enemy planes exacting destruction at will, desperate wounded men swimming through burning oil slicks. A scene not unlike the one unfolding below him now. A sharp thrill of vengeance warred with a healthy dose of fear and desire for self-preservation. His heart pounded in tempo with the bullets spraying from his guns.

Mike opened the bomb bay doors. If all went to plan, one or both of their 500-pound bombs would skip from the water into the hull of the destroyer at midship. The objective was for the remaining bombs to score direct hits on the deck and take out the ship's bridge and superstructure. At this low level, it would be damned near impossible for them to miss.

Skip leveled off at twenty feet but continued flying at high speed as Mike triggered the successive release of the bombs. *Bourbon Street Belle* jerked up sharply with the release of a thousand pounds from her load.

The bombs had a five-second delay fuse. Skip pulled back on the control column, hurtled *Bourbon Street Belle* over the ship's mast at breakneck speed, and dove back down to water-level in a tight left-hand turn to escape the explosion.

"Blasted her in half, Skipper!" Whoops from his gunners burst from the intercom. "She's blazing and sinking."

Skip allowed himself to glance back and take in the clouds of thick black smoke billowing from the conflagration. Torn between pride and self-loathing, he scanned their surroundings, searching for an exit path. *Get out, get out, get out.*

"Let's take another one! That one!" Mike screamed into the intercom, gesturing out the cockpit window at a cargo ship in their path.

Skip's mouth went dry. The idea of wreaking such savagery on another target filled him with disgust and relish in equal measure.

That half-beat of hesitation bought him a reprieve. *Annie Get*

Your Guns tore across their path in a steep dive to bomb the ship broadside. Skip maneuvered around the massive plume of smoke pouring from the damaged ship. Sweat dripped down his neck.

"The cruiser at two o'clock is limping," Leo said. "Let's finish her off."

"You see her, Skipper?" Dewey called out. "Right there."

"One more run, and she's a goner," Charlie chimed in.

They already had a hit, damn it. Why should they risk their lives to chalk up another score? His cautionary pause again spared him from having to make a decision. Large flumes of water shot skyward in front of the windshield. The B-17s were bombing again, and their aim was notoriously poor from their high altitude.

"Forts are bombing again," Skip shouted, accelerating and climbing fast as he scanned for a viable exit path. "We gotta get out of their way."

"Let's take out another one on our way out." A note of judgment filtered through Leo's voice. "Everyone else attacked another target."

Skip gritted his teeth and pressed the call button. "Our *orders* are to move out so the heavies can have another go from altitude. This is a coordinated assault."

Sure, old Skip would have thrown the rulebook out the window, but his fellas ought to be damned glad he was following it now. Did they want to chance getting hit by friendly fire?

"Fucking cowards!" Charlie's voice pulsed with raw rage. "You see what they're doing?"

"Those *bastards!*" Dewey screamed.

What the hell? Skip's heart hammered. He couldn't see anything.

Mike leaned out his side window, looked back at Skip, and shook his head.

Skip toggled the cockpit radio to the command frequency. Through the babble of profanity-laced exclamations from the other pilots, he pieced it together. Several crewmen had bailed out of a stricken B-17, and Japanese fighter pilots strafed them as they floated down in their parachutes. Dishonorable. Cowardly. Indecent.

Skip continued to jink at high speed toward the coast.

"Gunner to cockpit: Let down lower, and we can shoot up that fucking lifeboat."

"Yeah, I've got plenty of ammo left for those bastards," Charlie bellowed.

Several dozen enemy soldiers clung to a small rubber dinghy that threatened to topple its passengers into the sea. Others fought against the current to reach it.

Burning soldiers swimming through water laced with oil and fuel, clinging to floating debris and rafts, amidst the enemy's bombs and gunfire. Horrific images seared in his memory from that December morning competed with today's carnage in his mind.

This was no time for a lecture in the rules of war or morality.

Mike edged his hand toward the controls. In response, Skip pushed the throttles up and pulled back on the yoke to gain altitude.

His men went silent.

"Sharks'll get 'em," Skip said flatly.

No one could dispute his prediction. Rivulets of blood tainted the clear blue water below, tempting the plethora of sharks visible from the air.

Minutes later, he sucked in a steadying breath and pulled *Bourbon Street Belle* into the gathering formation of Allied planes.

No question the modified B-25 planes could do exactly what the Fifth Air Force designed them to do. None of them needed official reports to confirm what they had seen with their own eyes. With these modified low-level strafers, the Allies could sink ships, damage aircraft on the ground, and kill enemy soldiers.

All at point-blank range.

CHAPTER SIX

May 10, 1943

American Red Cross Officers' Rest Home, Hotel Sans Souci

Southport, Queensland, Australia

Hadley tacked two more signup sheets to the bulletin board. One for a hot dog and marshmallow roast on the beach tomorrow night, and the other for a boat ride on the river the following day.

She strode back to the reception desk and thumbed through a volunteer list for the navy dance on Saturday night. Plenty of local young women had already signed up to attend. Hopefully the kitchen staff would find the ingredients to prepare either chicken salad or pimento cheese sandwiches. They had no Kraft cheese, but Bizzy's aunt had sent several jars of canned peppers. They would serve sandwiches, cookies, cordials, and a fizzy punch the naval officers would probably spike from their flasks.

JoJo had sweet-talked several naval officers into supplying them with a large number of frankfurters for tomorrow night's beach cook-out.

"Navy's got the best chow in the U.S. military." Every time Hadley had eaten in an army mess, Skip Masterson's words rang in her ears, and she couldn't help but wonder where the enigmatic lieutenant had ended up. Was he still in Townsville? Or was he . . .

No. She closed her mind against the inevitable question.

Hadley glanced at the clock. Could she put off doing her laundry for another day? If she skipped that chore, she would have some free time before her afternoon shift at the beachfront snack bar. Time better spent snooping to learn if the rumors she had heard about General MacArthur's plans to bring his young son to this beach were on the level.

Even if she wasn't able to speak with the general, she could write a human-interest piece. A first-hand observation of him building sandcastles and splashing in the surf with his child would humanize him.

Hadley had already mailed several short pieces to Mr. Dupre. Nothing newsworthy, just stories about her interactions with American soldiers *down under*. Stories the censor couldn't rip apart. Dupre had scribbled *Thanks - keep 'em coming* on the clippings from the society pages he sent back to her. *MacArthur's Day at the Beach* might merit a better slot.

Where was Bizzy? Hadley looked around. Her friend was due to take over the information desk. She had been asleep when Hadley left their room hours ago, thanks no doubt to another late-night date.

"Hey, doll, where are the tennis racquets?" Two Marines, dressed in shorts and short-sleeved shirts, wandered into the reception area and walked over to her.

She directed them to the recreation supply storage closet. "Don't forget to sign them out on the clipboard and return them when you're done."

"Sorry, sorry." Bizzy raced in, swiping her bushy curls out of her eyes. "Lana asked me to help her show several officers to their rooms. About three dozen airmen on combat leave from New Guinea."

"Good grief. Did we have enough rooms?"

"Barely." Bizzy pulled a handkerchief from her pocket and dabbed at the perspiration glistening on her temple. "Would have felt bad for the fellow bunking with a wallaby, except he seemed familiar with it."

"A wallaby?" Hadley, who had one foot out the door, paused and turned back. "Really?"

"Yes, it's a pet. On a leash and everything." Bizzy laughed. "I didn't see its owner, but Lana says he was persuasive and charming and that he assured her he'll take the wallaby outdoors to do her business. He swears she'll be no trouble."

Many men had adopted pets, ranging from the usual assortment of dogs and cats to snakes, lizards, cockatoos, parrots, koalas, and yes, the occasional wallaby and even kangaroos. But they normally left their pets back at their base.

"It's cute." Bizzy winked. "Wonder if its owner is too?"

Hadley laughed and waved. Bizzy would probably have a date with the wallaby's owner in no time. Her active social life hadn't slowed one bit since they had left Brisbane. If anything, she had found more dates here. Large numbers of American and Australian servicemen spent their leave here on Australia's Gold Coast with its mild temperatures, sunny days, and lovely beaches.

The amenities made the location popular with the men, but its isolation was not a selling point for Hadley, who remained antsy to move on. If she couldn't be posted to New Guinea, she wanted to go back to Brisbane. Miss Browne was due to arrive for an inspection of their facilities any day now, and Hadley had a plan. A plan that was sure to get her what she wanted.

***

Hadley located a rag hanging on the back railing and used it to scrub sand from her legs. She then stepped out of her shoes, clapped them together, and wiped down the soles.

She had served hamburgers, banana splits, and Cokes all afternoon at the beachside snack bar. No MacArthur today. She had only gotten more of the same, stories that didn't even merit the censor's scissors. In her next packet to Dupre, Hadley wanted to include something — anything — with more pizzazz, more punch, more power.

She opened the door and crossed the hallway separating the kitchen from the laundry room. A strong odor of bleach enveloped her.

"And who'll clean up after it if it isn't trained like he says?" a woman snapped from the laundry room. "It's been living in a tent in the jungle. How would he know if it pisses indoors?"

Hadley stepped into the room where Rhoda and Daphne, two Australian cleaning ladies, stood folding towels. Neither looked happy.

"Bizzy said one of the men brought a pet wallaby with him," Hadley said. "Is that —"

"Yes." Rhoda rolled her eyes. "It belongs in the wild, not in a fancy resort hotel."

"So where is it?" Hadley refrained from mentioning that this so-called *fancy resort hotel* had no hot water heater. Even their navy buddies hadn't been able to provide them with a solution. She looked from one woman to the other. "The wallaby, I mean."

"Wandering around on a bloody leash, last I saw." Daphne shook her head.

Hadley waved at the women and continued down the hallway, circling her stiff shoulders. If only she could have a hot shower. She was tired of settling for sponge baths.

The one plus of a fast sponge bath was having time to put a

finishing touch on a half-completed story about soldiers and their pets. An AP photographer had arrived here on leave. She might persuade him to take a photo of the wallaby and send it and the story over the wireless. That would be better than any of the other fluff pieces she had ready to send.

Lana, a Red Cross Girl from Asheville, breezed through the front door with an armload of fresh flowers.

"Oh, Hadley, am I glad to see you." Lana pointed toward a box of books sitting by the stairwell. "Another shipment of books came in today. Will you take them to the library? I know you love arranging them."

That was overstating things. Hadley's schedule was too jam-packed for non-essential tasks. Lana, who had run the place on her own until Hadley and her friends had arrived in March, tended toward bossy — or *biggity* as the folks back home would say. She forced a smile. "I'll do it as soon as I freshen up. I've been in the snack bar all afternoon."

"Fine, but can you at least move the box to get it out of the way?" Lana frowned. "Miss Browne will be here any minute."

Miss Browne? All thoughts of wallabies and exotic pets vanished from Hadley's mind. She had read the woman's report to Australian club directors last month that noted the Red Cross hoped to soon open a new club in Brisbane with nightly jazz music entertainment. Who better to arrange for jazz musicians than a New Orleans girl? She swallowed past the unexpected lump in her throat. No point in getting bogged down with homesickness and memories. Persuading Miss Browne to transfer her back to Brisbane had to be her focus.

"Will Miss Browne be here for dinner?" she asked.

Lana nodded. "Yes, her assistant called to ask if she had arrived. With so many airmen arriving today, we're running behind."

Hadley stooped to lift the carton of books. "I'll drop these in the library, get cleaned up, and come help."

Lana called out her thanks and hurried into the kitchen with the flowers.

The library was in a room that had originally been a small parlor. They had placed two bookcases against the wall and left the chairs and divan in place so the men would have a quiet space to relax and read.

Hadley was only steps from the library when a familiar voice carried into the hallway.

"Hmm, *The Lost Horizon*," the man said. "The pilot dies in this one, so you wouldn't like it. Besides, we sure as hell aren't in Shangri-La. Are we, Lucy?"

Skip Masterson. He must have kept that wallaby after all. She choked back laughter at the memory of him at the harbor, floundering and half-afraid of Lucy. Now he was discussing book plots with her?

"Agatha Christie writes a tight mystery," he said. "You'd love this one. Trouble is, I already know how it ends."

Hadley peeked around the corner. As Daphne had said, Skip had Lucy on a leash. The wallaby hopped in circles around him while he browsed their books. She frowned. She couldn't go in now, not when she was sweaty and disheveled. She would take the box of books to her room and bring them down later.

"How about *Gone with the Wind*? The heroine is a selfish, ruthless schemer, but she blazes her path on her own terms. Reminds me of —"

Hadley snagged her heel on the carpet and pitched forward. Books flew out of the box, and she stumbled into the door jam. Pain streaked up her arm. "Ow!"

Skip whipped around as the empty box hit the floor. The corners of his eyes crinkled, and he curved his lips. He held a worn copy of *Gone with the Wind* in his hand.

"Well, speaking of Miss Scarlett," he said with a laugh.

She clutched her arm and blushed. Had he been about to tell Lucy that Scarlett reminded him of Hadley? No, he had made that earlier comparison in anger and meant it to be an insult. He would never believe Hadley shared any of Scarlett's positive qualities. Especially now, when she had a large pickle juice stain on the pocket of her plain white blouse and streaks of chocolate sauce down the length of her pale blue skirt. She had never felt less like a Southern belle.

"So you're one of the airmen who arrived from New Guinea this morning?" she asked to fill the tense silence that enveloped them. *What a vapid observation.* Her cheeks heated. She looked away and stooped to retrieve the scattered books.

Skip put *Gone with the Wind* back on the shelf, then knelt beside her with the leash in his right hand so he could stack books with his left. "Yep. We flew into Townsville yesterday and took a C-47 here this morning. Lucy's happy to be back on solid ground."

"You kept her?" Hadley's amusement at the memory of his initial discomfort with the wallaby overrode her fluster. She looked sideways at him and grinned.

He averted his eyes. His Adam's Apple bobbed. "Let's just say we've grown on one another."

She nodded. Without probing further, she knew Lucy's original owner had died. She pointed toward a book in hopes of shifting their conversation to a cheerier topic.

"Maybe Lucy would enjoy this one?"

"*The Jungle Book*?" Skip turned the stack sideways so he could read the titles. "Shere Khan might frighten her. What about Kipling's poetry? Do you have *Gunga Din*?"

Hadley blinked. A well-read man. Surprising and yet, Skip *had* often had a book in hand the few times she had seen him on the top deck of the ship.

"I haven't seen any poetry here." Hadley lifted another stack of books and turned the spines toward him. "Have you read any of these?"

"Yeah." He held his palms up in a guilty-as-charged gesture. "Was hoping to find some newer books."

"Hmmm, you're a tough customer." Hadley tapped her finger

against the spines. "I can look in Ludoma's library for you tomorrow."

"Ludoma?"

"It's another rest home, also for officers." Hadley pointed to her right. "It's a couple of miles from here."

"And you can borrow books from their library?"

"Sure. You can come with me. We can ride bikes over there." *Oh, Lordy.* She had forgotten she was talking to Skip. Aloof, mercurial Skip. A heated flush warmed her neck. He wouldn't want to spend time with her, not even to get something new to read.

Hadley reached for another book just as he closed his hand around its spine. A kick of adrenaline buzzed through her veins at his touch and the waft of his woodsy aftershave.

"I'd like that," he said, his voice as smooth as honey and without the bite of irritation it had held aboard ship. Maybe his animosity hadn't been personal after all, and he had merely resented being obliged to act as her errand boy.

She smiled and tilted her head. "I'm glad to see Lucy again, but wouldn't it have been less trouble to leave her back at your base?"

"Nah. Fellas and I built her a fenced area, but she sleeps inside at night. I'd worry they'd forget to bring her in. Or they wouldn't keep her leash tied up good, and she'd get lost. We've spotted crocodiles nearby." Skip looked at his hands. "Besides, she's attached to me."

No matter how insufferable, how inauthentic, how inscrutable Skip had been aboard ship, his revelation of a tender soft spot for his pet sent Hadley's heart flipping in her chest.

Lucy hopped closer at the sound of her name. Hadley smiled and held out her hand as she would with a dog. Lucy's nostrils quivered, and she tickled Hadley's hand with several feather-light licks of her tongue.

Hadley giggled. "Aw, cher, you remember me, don't you?"

"If you hold her leash, I'll be happy to put these books on the shelves for you." Skip passed her the lead.

She closed her palm around its leather handle and rubbed Lucy's ears with her free hand. Lucy lifted her head, and Hadley scratched under her chin. "Thank you."

"She loves that." Skip nodded approvingly and scooped up a stack of books.

Oh my. Hadley inhaled. The rear view of Skip Masterson's broad back and trim hips was nice too. He picked up a book, paused, and then tapped its spine against his palm. He traced a finger along the books on the top shelf.

"Are they organized by author or subject?"

"Neither." She cleared her throat to find her voice. "I've been meaning to organize them, but can never find the time. Just stack them on top of the bookcases for now."

"Okay." After making several trips across the room to scoop up stacks of books, Skip grabbed the last tottering pile and stepped toward the bookcases. "That should do it."

"Thanks, Skip." Hadley giggled as Lucy swiped her paw at Hadley's hair and tore out her hair clip. It fell into her lap. She smiled, pushed the leash under her thigh, and retrieved the clip.

"And our library for the men is right here," Lana said, her voice carrying down the hall.

Oh damn. Hadley shoved the clip back into her hair. She hadn't yet changed clothes so she could help the others make the dinner tables look especially nice for Mary Browne.

Deep barks tore from the throat of Miss Browne's pet terrier in the hallway. Lucy jumped several feet into the air, and her back claws gouged Hadley's legs as she came down. The wallaby turned and hopped from one chair to the other at breakneck speed, then leapt onto the divan and used it as a springboard to vault onto the bookcases. The books Skip had just stacked atop them cascaded to the floor. Lucy's long, thick tail hit a porcelain vase, which fell and shattered on the floor. Water pooled around the shattered shards of porcelain and the flowers.

Hopping rapidly back and forth across the top of the bookcases,

Lucy squeaked and chirped and thumped her tail against the wall.

"All right, Luce." Skip lunged for her leash. "Settle down, settle down."

Hadley threw a glance at the people gathered at the door. Miss Browne had scooped up Pogo, who continued to yelp but didn't seem inclined to break free. Lana thinned her lips as her gaze roved over the mess the wallaby had made.

"Hello, Miss Browne." Hadley scrambled to her feet. A surge of dizziness rippled through her. She swallowed and smoothed out her stained skirt. "Lana mentioned you would be here tonight. I hope you had a pleasant drive."

"Hello, Hadley. I had a lovely trip, thank you." She smiled. "This scene would delight any film director. *Screwball comedy* — isn't that the term?"

Playing part in that comedy would *not* get Hadley transferred back to Brisbane. Or maybe Miss Browne would decide to send Hadley as far from civilization as possible. She might make it to the front lines in New Guinea after all.

Skip cleared his throat.

Hadley turned and eyed Lucy, whom he had coaxed down from the bookcase. The wallaby slammed her paws against his legs, apparently demanding he pick her up.

"My apologies." Skip gave Miss Browne a rueful smile. "Some fellas at my base have pet dogs, and she's usually fine with them. Your little guy startled her, that's all. I'll help Miss Claverie put things right in here."

Oh, no, no, no. Hadley cringed. The men, especially the enlisted ones, might pitch in and help around Red Cross clubs, but that was not official policy. The Red Cross promoted an idealized image of enthusiastic and efficient service to the armed forces. Accepting Skip's offer of help would *not* further Hadley's ambitions.

"Oh, no, Lieutenant, I wouldn't dream of it," Hadley blurted before he could say anything else. She plastered on her best Southern belle smile. The kind of smile that averted trouble, won favors, and melted hearts. "We'll be serving lemon cordials and hors d'oeuvres in the front parlor shortly. You should go join the other guests. I'll clean this up."

Skip ignored her and leaned down to grab a handful of books with his free hand. He deposited them back on top of the bookcase. Lucy, who apparently sensed that her nemesis was no longer a threat, hopped over to pick up one of the flowers from the broken vase with her paws and munched on the leaves.

Hadley hurried forward. "No, stop. I'll have this cleaned up in no time. You should leave it to me and go get ready for dinner."

"I'll put these away while you get a broom and a dustpan." He picked up another pile of books and gave her a go-weak-in-the-knees grin. "Lucy's taking care of the flowers."

"Heard there was a wallaby here," a man said. *Click, click.*

Hadley turned. Oh, swell. The AP photographer chose to capture *this* moment? She side-stepped out of his frame.

"Looks like she might have also had some water along with the flowers," Bizzy piped up, visibly fighting laughter as she peeked into the room over Miss Browne's shoulder.

Hadley glanced back at Lucy as an unmistakable yellow stain spread across the rug beneath her.

Click, click, click.

Hadley tightened her jaw and looked from Lucy to Skip, who gritted his teeth in a sheepish smile and rubbed the back of his neck.

"I recommend asking if the kitchen has baking soda and vinegar to clean that stain." Miss Browne smiled and gave Hadley a cheery wave.

CHAPTER SEVEN

Hadley signaled for a left turn onto the barely-there footpath that led through the coastal grasses and scrub brush to Mermaid Beach.

"This way," she called over her shoulder. "Follow me."

"Wait," Skip shouted. He braked to adjust the pile of books balanced in his bicycle basket. Ludoma's library had received a shipment of new ASEs, books distributed to the armed forces, and Hadley had talked the director into letting him have eight books, even though the normal checkout limit was three.

She had been surprised when Skip had appeared in the lobby this afternoon with a picnic basket and no Lucy. A flush had colored his cheeks when he explained that his roommate was nursing a hangover and planned to stay in the rest of the day. Had Skip arranged a babysitter for Lucy so he could accompany her on this carefree outing? Did he consider this a date?

She had counted on taking him on a short bike tour to Ludoma to visit their library, returning in time to spend the afternoon at Surfer's Paradise beach so she could keep an eye out for General MacArthur. But she hadn't had the heart to cut the outing with Skip short. Not when he had gone to the trouble of getting the kitchen to prepare a picnic for them.

They got off their bicycles and set their kickstands on the solidly packed path near the sandy beach. Skip pulled out a rain poncho and tucked it around the books in the basket.

"Just in case," he said.

Hadley picked up the blanket and gave him the picnic basket. "It doesn't rain often here."

"Habit." He shrugged. "In New Guinea, weather ranges from rainy to downpour to torrential to monsoon. Never a day without rain."

Hadley spread the blanket under a palm tree. "Hope I get a chance to get out my rain slicker soon."

"You mean go to New Guinea?"

"Yes." She nodded. "I'm on the list, but they're fully staffed for now. I'm keeping my fingers crossed."

"Why would you want to give up sun and surf for a soggy, mosquito-infested jungle?" Skip gestured toward the picture-perfect beach where gentle waves rolled in, depositing layer upon layer of white foam across the stretch of smooth, glistening sand.

"You forget — I'm *from* a soggy, mosquito-infested swamp." Hadley kicked off her shoes and placed them on opposite corners of the blanket to anchor it.

Skip laughed. "Trust me, nowhere in America gets weather that foul. Besides, it's not only the rain and mud that ought to keep you gals here."

"I know it's more primitive, but I don't mind a little discomfort." Hadley took a deep breath. "We came to build morale — and not just at leave destinations."

"Life in New Guinea comes with more than a little discomfort." He frowned. "Enemy bombers send us into trenches every night.

Trenches filled with mud and rank water up to here." He slashed a line just below his knees. "And we share the space with snakes, rats the size of dogs, and every biting insect on that godforsaken island. Tons of fellas are in the hospital with all sorts of weird infections."

"There's a Red Cross club in Port Moresby." Hadley lowered herself onto the blanket, tucked her legs to one side, and smoothed her skirt.

Skip knelt and drummed his fingers on the top of the picnic basket. "Well, the club in Moresby is one thing. The enemy's targeting our airfields, not that little half-assed village."

"One of my friends is posted there." Hadley had fumed for days after receiving a letter from Dora, one of her shipboard cabin-mates. "She says they take jeeps out to the airfields to meet the missions and serve cookies and lemonade."

"Humph. Well, my base is seventeen miles from Moresby, so I doubt we'll get service." Skip opened the basket, pulled out two bottles of Australian beer, and arched his eyebrow in question.

At Hadley's nod, he opened one of the bottles and passed it to her. The beer was warm and more bitter than she liked, but it was a welcome change.

He plopped down next to her and took a swig from his bottle. "Why are you so determined to go to New Guinea?"

"That's where things are happening, where I can get material for stories to send to my editor back home." She lifted her chin. "Australia's no longer under threat of invasion, so there's no real war news here."

"If you really want to be a journalist, why aren't you doing that instead of working for the Red Cross?" He frowned.

Hadley blew out an exasperated sigh. "Not for lack of trying. I worked for years as a reporter for the *Times-Picayune*, even covered the political beat. And believe me, covering politics in Louisiana, especially New Orleans, isn't for the faint of heart. But my editor flat-out refused to get me War Department credentials, said it was too dangerous. Too dangerous for a *woman*."

"So you decided to join the Red Cross so you could go overseas?"

"Exactly." She bobbed her head. "But I banked on being sent to Europe. Plenty of women are reporting from London. Margaret Bourke-White even flew a combat mission. *Life* published her photos last month, did you see?"

"No." Skip shook his head and pulled the picnic basket closer. "So is that what you'll do after the war? Go back to reporting?"

"Yes . . . and no. It depends." Hadley paused, struggling to decide how to best explain the competing impulses that might shape her professional future. The lure of earning enough standing to expose injustices back home, balanced against the temptation to reach higher and maybe try her luck in New York or Washington.

He opened the basket and rummaged inside. "Depends on what? When you tie the knot?"

"Honestly!" She inclined her head and lifted a brow. "Are you ever all wet."

Hadley was torn between irritation and amusement. What a typical man, assuming a woman would only work while chasing after a husband and would quit her job the minute she had a ring on her finger. That must be what he envisioned for himself — marriage to a woman who would keep a tidy house and bear and raise his children.

"Not every woman is after a husband," she chided.

"Aw, give a fella a break." Skip clutched his heart and cast her a sheepish smile. "You're too beautiful to stay single."

"What piffle." Hadley stretched her legs forward and nudged her foot playfully against his. He nudged her back, his eyes sparking with amusement and perhaps a flash of desire. No point in indulging *that*. Not when he had made it clear what sort of woman he was after.

Skip held up two packets of potato chips. "Will you forgive me in exchange for these?"

"And how!" Hadley took a bag and turned it over to read the label. "Smith's Potato Crisps. This is an Australian brand, isn't it?"

"They all go to the military." Skip winked. "That's why you

can't find them."

Hadley extracted the small blue packet of salt from the bag, sprinkled it over her chips, and gave the bag a good shake. She bit into a chip. "Ummm."

Skip set out a pair of wrapped sandwiches.

She pointed to them. "What kind did Millie give you?"

"Ham and cheddar, with tomato relish. She called it *chutney*." He passed one to her.

Hadley stared at it. "Tomato relish? With sliced cheddar? You must have been incredibly charming to get sandwiches this fancy."

The bread also appeared to be fresh. The kitchen usually sent PB&J or egg salad sandwiches when they organized picnic outings for their guests.

"I might have used a few candy bars for her children as an incentive." His laugh lines deepened with his grin.

Hadley picked up a small glass jar and strained to open the lid. "Are these pickles?"

Skip took the jar from her, opened it, and handed it back. "Yeah. Courtesy of my sister. I brought them along in my kit, hoping to find a good occasion to break them out."

"Ummm." Hadley savored the first delectable bite with its sour crunch. "These are *perfect*. Did she put them up herself?"

He shrugged and averted his eyes.

"Where —"

"I also grabbed a few of these in the Townsville PX." He pulled out two candy bars packaged in white wrapping.

She gaped at him. "Milky Way bars? This picnic is tops, Skip."

"Figured you might like something besides Aussie biscuits."

A rosy flush lingered at his temples. He had cut off her question asking where he was from and deflected her attention with the candy bars. Why wouldn't he discuss his background or family? Nothing in his accent pegged a particular region. The man held so much mystery — and so much magnetism, if she were being honest.

No. That was stupid. His unpredictable mood shifts rattled her.

He clearly envisioned his homemaker wife, and no matter how attractive or charming he might be or how adorable she found his wallaby, it made no sense to make an emotional connection with a serviceman. Too much uncertainty, too much torment, too much risk.

They quickly polished off the food. Skip opened another bottle of beer for each of them and then turned the conversation back to Hadley's plans. "What about transferring to Brisbane? MacArthur's there, so stands to reason the press can get more information."

"I was there for two months." Hadley sipped her beer. "I'd go back, but even there, they filter the news. The press gets a daily communiqué from MacArthur's press officer, but it's all white-washed puffery."

He snorted. "You can bet it puts MacArthur in the best light possible."

"Yes, and that's not truthful coverage." Hadley leaned closer to him. "The American people deserve the truth. So do soldiers in the fight."

"Hmph." He swigged his beer. "I dunno. What is the *truth*?"

"It starts with the facts, doesn't it? So people can make good choices."

"Whose version of the facts?" Skip leaned back on his elbows. "They aren't necessarily black or white, especially in war."

"Plenty of things are factual." Hadley scrunched her nose. "If the papers report the Allies destroyed fifty Japanese ships, the number's either right or wrong. If the public finds out they actually only destroyed five — and not fifty — it will change their perception."

"That assumes we can say for sure how many ships we destroyed." He widened his eyes and tilted his head to one side.

"Why can't you do that?" She frowned and raked a hand through her hair. Strategic questions might have nuances. But numbers? Numbers were simple.

"Take the battle of Bismarck Sea." Skip set down his beer and bit his bottom lip. "I was there, and I couldn't tell you how many ships were in that convoy. I was too busy sweating like hell and focusing on our plan of attack. And I damn sure didn't count 'em before we got the hell outta there."

Skip had been in *that* battle? She clenched her beer. Why was she surprised? The Fifth Air Force had put up everything they had that morning. Maybe she wasn't surprised so much as concerned. And *that* was concerning. She couldn't afford to become emotionally entangled with any man, least of all one serving in a hot combat zone.

She pursed her lips. "Okay, maybe that isn't the best example. But we can do better than spewing out the sugarcoated nonsense MacArthur's press officer puts out as news."

"How would you get around the censors? MacArthur runs a tight ship."

Hadley had wondered the same thing. If she did get a good scoop, how would she get it out? Lorraine could file it for her, with a separate note asking the *Daily Mail* to forward the piece to Dupre — *if* they would honor her request. But Lorraine was in Brisbane, not New Guinea. And if Hadley were in New Guinea, all communications would run through the military censors, who would never approve a piece written by a journalist without credentials, especially a woman.

She tapped her lip. "I haven't worked that out yet. I've sent several stories back to my editor in New Orleans by regular mail. Folksy columns featuring chats with the boys about Australia. The censor didn't touch them, because they didn't contain any real news."

"Did you include names, hometowns, that sort of thing?"

"Oh, sure." Hadley nodded. "But nothing about their military assignments. Just *Yanks Down Under* pieces about how they cope with confusing Aussie money, what they think about warm beer, what they miss most. Nothing exciting."

"Probably plenty exciting to the folks back home, especially to the family and friends of the fellas you named, right?" Skip cast her a relaxed smile.

She rolled her eyes. That wasn't news. "Maybe so, but real news gives readers the bigger picture, the truth about what's happening in the world. How and why we're waging the war."

Hadley longed to send dispatches with more substance. Dispatches containing the truth, the unvarnished truth about what was really happening, were now more important than ever. Skip was right that fluffy "woman's angle" features served a purpose. But she had bigger goals, ambitions she could further more effectively under the exigencies of war. Making a name for herself now could give her a solid start after the war, whether in New Orleans or New York.

Skip wadded up his empty potato chip packet and tossed it into the basket. "You could be the woman's version of Ernie Pyle, Hadley. People like him and his columns."

"He's with the troops in North Africa." Hadley read the popular journalist's column every week in *Stars and Stripes*. "Not stuck in a leave resort town."

"Doesn't matter *where* he is. It's his perspective that resonates with folks. You could capture how the war affects us all by talking to soldiers on leave. Nurses, doctors, Seabees, engineers. They all take leave here, right?"

"Sure, but that's not . . ." Hadley let her words trail away. Individual portraits seemed too narrow and unimportant right now. Each individual contributed to the war effort, but what would readers gain from reading stories focused on one individual?

A faint smile played over Skip's mouth. "Didn't you read Pyle's columns back when you were a girl? When he traveled the country, writing about the common man — and gals too?"

Hadley bit her lip. Ernie Pyle had built a name for himself *before* the war. Because he was now the most admired war correspondent in America, he could afford to focus on the little guy and leave the big picture to others. Most importantly, he was a *man* — not a woman struggling to make inroads in a man's world. Even if all Hadley ever wrote were features aimed at women on the home front, they would carry more substance from the battlegrounds in New Guinea rather than the vacation beaches of Australia.

"The real war is in New Guinea," she finally said.

Skip drew his eyebrows together and set down his bottle. "That it is."

"Red Cross Girl Hadley isn't supposed to ask questions." She rolled the beads of her bracelet. "Or remind you of what you've been through, what you're headed back to do."

"But reporter Hadley wants to ask." Skip rubbed his jawline and picked up his beer, then set it down again. He had rolled up his sleeves, exposing his lean, tanned forearms.

She laid a gentle hand on his arm. The caramel brown hair was soft beneath her fingertips and touching him sent a crackling charge cascading across her shoulders. She swallowed. "Only what you're comfortable sharing."

"What do you want to know?"

"Anything. Everything."

"I figured." Skip laughed. "You've got an insatiable curiosity, and it's enough to drive a man crazy. But right now . . . right now, doll, you're making me crazy in a different way."

He scooted closer to her and took her hand.

Hadley's stomach flipped in time to the waves breaking against the shore. He interlocked his strong fingers with hers and circled his thumb over the surface of her polished thumbnail.

"Might be hard to keep your nails this pretty in New Guinea."

"We Red Cross Girls are the enterprising sort. You might be surprised." Her low, rich voice was redolent like a sultry saxophone blues number.

Skip met her eyes. His lush lips quirked up with the wolfish confidence of a consummate hell-raiser, a man with a wild side and a grin that melted hearts, stole hearts, broke hearts.

He tipped his mouth closer to hers and chuckled. "You always surprise me, Miss Scarlett."

Before she could catch her breath and protest that she detested the Southern belle cliché, he cupped her face, leaned in, and closed his lips over hers.

Skip knew how to kiss. My land, the man knew how to kiss. How to kiss, how to intoxicate, how to send her.

She shouldn't be surprised. Skip exuded raw sensuality, even in his most infuriating, baffling moments.

He released her hand and pulled her deeper into his embrace. Hadley's heartbeat roared in her ears. She threaded her fingers into his hair and opened her mouth under his, devouring the tang of salt in his whiskers from the sea-spray and the malty taste of beer on his breath.

Skip's lips were everywhere — crushing her mouth, trailing across her jawline, nibbling her earlobe. He pulled her onto his lap and trailed his hand up her leg, caressing her tender skin, before sliding it beneath her skirt to stroke her thigh. *Oh, lordy. What are we doing?*

Hadley's frantic breath came fast. Skip Masterson was all kinds of wrong for her, but just now? Just now he felt exactly right. *This* was the driving force behind jazz and its sensual rhythms, the energy powering the ardent, feverishly soulful lyrics of the best jazz and blues musicians in those backatown nightclubs. Now she understood.

He groaned against her mouth, renewing his kisses with breathless, ferocious intensity and unleashing desire within her until it rained down like a pelting tropical rainstorm.

She dismissed the first few drops, believing them the product of her imagination. She had rainstorms on her mind. Just sprinkles from the humidity. But as the drops grew larger and pounded down, Hadley and Skip pulled apart and looked up at the sky.

"Guess it's a day for the unexpected." Skip's husky laugh sent a tingle through her. He pulled her into a tight embrace to shield her from the onslaught and unbuttoned his shirt.

Hadley met his eyes. Did he mean to carry on canoodling in the rain?

He tugged off his shirt, draped it over her shoulders, and guided her arms into the sleeves before settling his gaze on the front of her soaked white blouse.

"Mmmm, mmmm, mmm," he murmured as he pulled the shirt closed and did up the buttons. "Good thing I'm a gentleman."

Her eyes traveled from his broad shoulders to his tanned, well-defined chest that was speckled with water droplets, over his rippling abdominal muscles and lower still to the line of tawny hair that began at his navel and disappeared into his pants. Hadley gulped and fought the urge to tell him to ditch his gentlemanly impulses. Whatever reasons he had for hiding his true nature, Skip was far more Rhett Butler than Ashley Wilkes. She was sure of it.

"You didn't need to do that." She tucked damp tendrils of hair behind her ears.

"Oh yes, I did." He wrapped his arms around her, pulled her close, and lowered his face until his mouth hovered above hers. "I'd toss out every bit of restraint if I had to keep looking at you in that wet blouse."

He kissed her again. A kiss that was inexplicably hot, even with the cool breeze from the rain squall. Hadley kept forgetting that it *was* nearly winter here. She wrapped her arms around Skip's neck and pulled him closer. Warmth rolled over her.

"We'd better go. Be dark soon," he whispered.

Hadley looked over his shoulder. An edge of darkness hovered in the sky. He was right. It was much later than she had realized, and riding bicycles down the narrow coastal road in the blackout wouldn't be safe.

Skip released her with reluctance, stood, and helped her to her feet. He shook out the blanket and carried it and the picnic basket back to the bicycles. He pulled a handkerchief from his pocket and dried off their seats.

She unbuttoned his shirt. "You can have this back. I'll wrap the blanket around my shoulders."

"No." He shook his head and placed his hand over hers. "It won't stay fastened, and we'll end up chasing it down the road.

Besides, I've got a better use for it."

"You do?"

"Yep." Skip winked and tucked the blanket around the poncho-wrapped books. "Gotta protect these books."

***

"What happened to you?" Stella waved her hand over Hadley from head to toe.

She must look a fright. Rain followed them the entire way from Mermaid Beach, alternating between a steady smatter and short, battering bursts. Thanks to wearing Skip's shirt, her blouse was only damp, though wrinkled and disheveled.

Hadley had given his shirt back to him when they returned the bicycles to the storage shed. After he took her in his arms, pressed himself against her, and kissed her with the same scorching fervor they'd shared on the beach.

"We, er . . . got caught in a rainstorm." She looked away from Stella and ran her fingers through her damp hair.

Her friend tapped her watch and widened her eyes. "You left with Lieutenant Dreamboat hours ago."

"He had Millie pack us a picnic. We stopped at one of the beaches and ate sandwiches and drank a beer." *And kissed each other senseless.*

Stella smirked. "Did the rain smear your lipstick too?"

Hadley's cheeks burned. She grabbed a tissue from the reception desk and wiped her mouth. Wait. She turned the tissue over and examined it. No lipstick stains.

Stella smiled. "That's what I thought."

"Think whatever you like." Hadley tossed the tissue into the wastebasket under the desk and swatted playfully at Stella's arm. "I don't care."

"Bizzy says Lieutenant Dreamboat was your assistant on the ship coming over. Helped you with stories for the ship's newsletter."

"Um-hmm." Hadley averted her gaze and straightened a pile of Gold Coast tourist maps on the front desk.

"She also said he looked as gone on you then as he does now."

Gone on her? No. What had happened on Mermaid Beach was . . . well it had only happened because they had been alone in a beautiful, relaxed setting and let their guard down. That was all. Nothing more.

Still avoiding eye contact, Hadley rubbed her hands over her arms. "It's cool in here. Think I'll go change and check with the others to see if they need help."

"Hadley, it doesn't hurt to have a little fun." Stella's voice lost its teasing note. "You don't have to adopt Bizzy's whirlwind social life. But your fella seems like a nice guy who enjoys your company. Nothing wrong with spending time with him."

For now. There was nothing wrong with it for now. That was the part Stella hadn't voiced. Hadley could have fun with Skip for now, but he would soon return to New Guinea. Back into combat. Back into danger.

She moved toward the door. "Want me to bring you a sweater?"

Stella shook her head. "I'm fine. You're probably chilled from being out in the rain."

Hadley nodded and left. She had one foot on the staircase when someone in the dining room called her name. She backtracked and peeked around the corner. The room was empty except for Bizzy, who was setting out fresh linens for tomorrow's breakfast.

Bizzy beckoned her in. "Where have you *been*?"

"I went to Ludoma with one of the guests." Hadley stepped inside and took a napkin from the pile, folded it, and set it at one of the place settings. "We stopped at Mermaid Beach and had a picnic — after I finished my last shift."

"I know you had the afternoon and evening off today, but oh, Hadley. Of all the times for you to be away. Did you see him at all before he left?"

Him? Her stomach tautened. "See who?"

Bizzy knitted her eyebrows together, stepped closer, and whispered, "General MacArthur."

Hadley's heart contracted to the size of a button. *No. No, no, no.* MacArthur had been *here*? After spending weeks on the lookout for him, she had missed her chance?

She swept her hand over the table. Surely Bizzy didn't mean he'd had dinner in this room. "Here?"

Bizzy placed a gentle hand on Hadley's arm. "I had Daphne ring Ludoma, but they said you'd already left. When you still weren't back a half-hour later, I sent the two boys who help Millie out to look for you. They didn't find you on the road or on any of the beaches between here and there."

The boys had turned back at Ludoma. If only Skip hadn't persuaded her to go all the way to Mermaid Beach — and she hadn't let him initiate that first kiss and then let him carry on. If she hadn't responded in kind, hadn't relished his every touch, hadn't reveled in their passionate interlude.

"How long was he here?" Hadley pressed her fingers to her throbbing temples. "When did he leave?"

"He had his son Arthur with him. They spent the afternoon at the beach, used the showers, and then the general joined Miss Browne and Lana for cordials and hors d'oeuvres in the front parlor. They came in for the final dinner seating."

"And they've left?" She swallowed.

"Yes. I'm sorry, Hadley." Bizzy bit her lip. "I know you've been trying to meet him for months. I tried everything I could think of to find you."

Hadley nodded jerkily. "I know you did."

A burning flush popped up on her cheeks, and Hadley clenched her hands into fists by her sides. Bizzy probably assumed Hadley was angry, and she was. But not at Bizzy. Not even at Skip. She should have fibbed and told him her schedule had changed, that she needed to fill in for someone else — and given him directions to Ludoma so he could go alone.

She had no one to blame for missing MacArthur but herself. He'd had plans to come to this beach, and it made sense that Miss Browne had timed her trip to coincide with his visit. Her presence should have been a clue. How had Hadley missed it?

If she had spent more time with Miss Browne last evening, the director might have mentioned the general's visit. Instead, Hadley had allowed Skip to sit next to her at dinner. Sure, she had gotten plenty of details about Lucy, enough to finish off her piece about servicemen and their exotic pets. Yet she should have been buttering up Miss Browne for a transfer to New Guinea or Brisbane, not flirting with him. Hotcha he might be, but he was completely unsuitable for her. Missing a huge opportunity for a MacArthur scoop to neck with him on a beach was all the proof she needed.

She swallowed. "Thanks for trying, Bizz. It's not your fault I missed him."

"Don't worry about helping me." Bizzy took the napkin from Hadley's hand. "Go relax. You're off this evening."

"Yeah, I can take a nice bath in four inches of ice water. No thanks." Hadley shook her head. "We should host a few parties for the Seabees. All these dances we've held for the navy fellas, and we still don't have a hot water heater."

"Not a bad idea." Bizzy wrapped her arm around Hadley's shoulders and kissed her cheek. "I hope that dreamy pilot at least showed you a fun time."

"Which dreamy pilot?" Hadley's shoulder muscles tightened.

Bizzy nudged her elbow into Hadley's ribs. "The dishy one who's had his eye on you since you met. Who else?"

"Masterson?" Hadley snorted. "He detests my company."

"He detested you having authority over him on the ship, that's all. You can't see it, but he's a smitten kitten, completely gone on you." Bizzy squeezed Hadley's shoulders.

Hadley shrugged out of her friend's embrace. "Oh, piffle. He is *not*."

You always surprise me, Miss Scarlett. Hadley scowled. Had that been a compliment? No. Skip wanted his wife to be a traditional homemaker, not a career girl. He especially wouldn't want to marry a journalist. Their helter-skelter lives stood in sharp contrast to his dreams.

Hadley took a few steps toward the door before turning around. "Besides, nothing would be worth me missing my chance to meet General MacArthur."

"You'll get another opportunity." Bizzy waved her hand.

She snorted. "Not if I'm stuck here."

"You may be in luck. Miss Browne told Lana she plans to make some staffing changes. You should catch her before she leaves in the morning." Bizzy folded another napkin.

Hadley paused in the doorway. "Do you know if she's already gone up to her room?"

"She followed Lana to the staff office after MacArthur left. She might still be there."

"Oh good." Hadley turned away and hurried down the hall. The office door was open, but Lana was probably alone, working on their expense ledgers or preparing a shopping list for the kitchen staff. The hair on Hadley's neck prickled when her name emanated from the room.

She edged closer and stopped to listen.

Miss Browne's modulated voice filtered out into the hallway. "Yes, I believe Hadley will do well there. Apart from her nails, she's not a glamour puss who would resent living in primitive conditions. And she's not the type to go all khaki wacky over the soldiers."

Oh thank God. They're transferring me to New Guinea. She had missed MacArthur, but writing about him near the front lines would be so much better than writing a woman's piece about him stopping at a Red Cross club to dine with some soldiers on leave.

"She's a self-starter, all right. But —" Lana broke off. "Well…"

"You have concerns about her work?" Miss Browne prompted.

Hadley frowned. She worked twice as hard as Lana.

"No, she pulls her weight. It's . . . well, her focus isn't always on her work. She was a reporter before the war, and she's been writing stories here in her off hours. I guess she's mailed them back home."

"Well, as long as she isn't short shrifting her work, I have no problem with her writing in her free time," Miss Browne said in a brisk tone. "She won't have as much of that at her next assignment anyway."

"From what you describe, that's probably true," Lana said.

"Right, so that settles our staffing changes. You'll move back to Brisbane with me at the end of the month. JoJo will step into your role here, and Stella and Bizzy will continue as they have been for the moment. And we'll send Hadley to Cannes."

Cans? Or is it Cannes? Hadley wrinkled her nose. Where was that in relation to Port Moresby? From what Skip had said, Port Moresby was the base of operations for the Fifth Air Force. Maybe infantry units were stationed at Cannes.

A jitter of adrenaline flashed through Hadley. A post there might be even better than she had dreamed. No wonder Miss Browne had mentioned primitive conditions. If she was sending Hadley to provide recreation for forward ground forces, she would definitely be roughing it. With tents, K-rations, and first-hand access to the real war. After she told Mr. Dupre where she was, he would finally get her credentials.

"I'll speak with Hadley tomorrow morning before I leave. Given the chaos in Cannes, it's probably best if she packs and boards a train as soon as possible," Miss Browne said.

A train? Hadley went cold. Trains didn't go to New Guinea. Maybe Miss Browne meant for her to take a train to Townsville and board a flight from there. That must be it.

"Is it in Queensland?" Lana asked.

Miss Browne chuckled. "Oh my, yes. She won't even need to disembark and board another train. What an inefficient railroad system Australia has. Different gauges in each state."

Townsville was in Queensland, as were the leave destinations at

Mackay and Rockhampton. Further north, Cairns and Darwin had clubs. No one wanted to be assigned there — the most isolated places in Australia.

Miss Browne sighed. "I hope she won't be too disappointed. Cannes is a far cry from Brisbane, or even here."

Disappointed? Hadley must not have communicated her wish to experience jungle life in New Guinea as well as she had imagined. No matter. Her enthusiasm for her new assignment would be hard to miss. She would start packing now.

Hadley turned to leave, but paused when Lana's voice again carried out into the hallway.

"How odd that the Aussies pronounce it Cannes when the name is clearly spelled C-a-i-r-n-s, like those cute little terriers."

Cairns? I'm being banished to a remote northeast coast backwater? Hadley's heart slammed into her knees. Being there might put her physically closer to New Guinea, but she would be more isolated than ever — and even further from the actual war.

Dammit, dammit, dammit.

CHAPTER EIGHT

August 5, 1943

Mission against Japanese barges near Madang, Papua New Guinea

Where the hell were the Lightnings? P-38 fighters based out of Port Moresby were supposed to escort their mission to strafe and bomb Japanese supply barges near Madang.

At the Battle of Bismarck Sea, the Allies had knocked out the ability of the Japanese navy to resupply their base at Lae, so the Japanese now relied on a fleet of small barges to bring in men and supplies. Camouflaged and motionless during the day, the maneuverable barges operated from dusk to dawn. The B-25s must strike before they went into hiding for the day.

"All right, fellas," Skip spoke into the intercom when he at last spotted the P-38s. "Owen Stanleys, here we come."

Wispy, silver-white clouds floated around the purple mountain peaks, melding seamlessly with the hazy, predawn gray. Striations of melon orange and pale pink threaded across the distant horizon. Skip closed one eye, rubbed his thumb over the light meter in his pocket, and allowed himself to consider how he would frame a shot of the stunning vista.

Full daylight would soon arrive. The barges would go into hiding, and Allied planes would be at greater risk from the Japanese fighter planes, known as *Zeros*.

Leo announced they had cleared the highest peak along their plotted route. Clouds shrouded not only the jagged peaks but also the steep slopes of New Guinea's mountains, their hostile clusters indiscriminately segueing from one range to another. Cumulonimbus clouds had already gathered into vertical masses, signaling savage weather to come. Skip clenched the throttle. With any luck, they would be back over the inhospitable interior ranges before the weather changed.

The formation descended to a lower altitude over the Bulolo valley. Low enough to see the occasional thatched roofs of small villages dotted among the verdant hills. Streams and ponds bisected the idyllic landscape. The place was bucolic, even oddly pastoral, from the air. Air crews admired its rugged beauty from the safety of their ships, thousands of feet above. But going down in this primeval land, even into the deceptively peaceful valley below them, would be a death sentence. The jungle was forbidding and impenetrable, with dangerous rivers and impassable mountain terrain that would separate them from any hope of rescue.

Mike broke the silence. "We've got leave next month. Who's gonna join me in Sydney this time?"

"I dunno. Getting there will cut into our time. Think we can get them to cut orders directly to Sydney instead of Brisbane?" Rafe asked.

"Ain't no one gettin' leave to Sydney except the navy." Dewey's thick Cajun accent rang out in Skip's ear. "You know that."

"Chuck and his fellas bided their time for an afternoon around one of those Brisbane airfields and codged a ride," Leo said. "Shouldn't be too hard to work out."

"There you go," Mike said. "We won't have to spend days on a train. Pat and his crew are game. He keeps yammering on about the zoo there. Has a soft spot for animals."

Skip squirmed. Didn't sound like Pat had told Mike about his plans to pursue a veterinary career after the war rather than helping Mike run the family business.

"You in, Skipper?"

"I don't know. Have to see how Lucy does with the flights."

How she did with her *first* flight, that is. Men en route to leave Down Under made a refueling stop, and Skip had a short detour in mind. Although Cairns was principally a naval base, it had a small airstrip for emergency landings. He planned to convince their pilot to make an unplanned stop there.

Hadley might not still be in Cairns, but he wanted to check. The day after their beach picnic, he had resolved to sign up for whatever activity she led at Sans Souci during the rest of his leave. A boat tour, horseback riding on the beach, golf — whatever she did, he would sign up for it. If she worked the reception desk, he would plant himself in a chair in the foyer. Or if she manned the beachside snack bar, he would read a book during her shift. Hell, he'd hang laundry on a line if necessary, just to spend time with her.

He hadn't counted on finding her standing in the entryway with a packed trunk and a musette bag when he'd gone downstairs for breakfast the next morning. Her porcelain skin had been tinged with a faint pink flush, and she had given him only clipped responses in answer to his questions.

Skip had even suggested that he would gather his things and Lucy and catch the train to Cairns with her. The USAAF didn't care where he spent his leave, as long as he returned to Brisbane in ten days for his return flight.

Later at the breakfast table, Skip finally pieced together the rest of the story. With his heart shrinking in his chest, he realized why Hadley had cut him off, why she had been so coolly dismissive. MacArthur and his son had dined at Sans Souci while Skip had wooed her on the beach. She hadn't just missed a chance to watch MacArthur from afar or have a short conversation with him; she had missed spending an entire evening with him, missed an opportunity to convince the general of the value of female war correspondents. That would have been far more important than gleaning material for a story to persuade her editor in New Orleans to obtain War Department credentials for her. No wonder she had given Skip the boot.

She might be no happier with him now than she had been three months ago, but seeing her would be worth a shot. But before he connived his way into stopping at Cairns, he needed to lead his men through today's mission. Survival was today's priority. He had to survive and stay in the good graces of his squadron commander, Major Cheli.

The familiar whiff of disappointment he sensed from Cheli echoed a pattern from his childhood. Skip had never measured up, not to his parents, not to teachers, not to superior officers. Surely the reproach he sensed from Cheli was only in his head. The major had no reason to suspect that each mission tormented Skip. He had followed the order of battle every time. To a goddamn tee.

Many other pilots used the cover of battle to skirt the line or outright flout briefed orders. One of their pilots had attacked a formation of Japanese bombers while returning from a mission over the Owen Stanleys. Skip sensed that Cheli — not to mention his crew — wanted more of *that*. More boldness, more spirit, more heart.

The swashbuckling approach looked all well and good after-the-fact, if the pilot and crew came out the other side in one piece. Why couldn't they see that he was doing his damnedest to be sure they all survived?

"Navigator to cockpit: Approach to Isumrud Strait coming up."

"Roger," Mike responded.

Skip pushed the yoke forward to descend, keeping Pat and his ship, *Southie in the South Seas,* on his right wing.

They swept over the water, flying only a few hundred feet above the swells of the Bismarck Sea, careful to keep out of range of any Japanese coastal radar or anti-aircraft defenses. If they had even the smallest warning, the Japanese would radio their supply barges — and they would vanish.

With the land mass of Kar Kar island barely visible through the misty dawn, the 38th navigated through the Isumrud Strait before turning a few degrees southeast.

"Pilot to crew: Keep alert for Zeros."

Enemy fighter patrols were common. Zeros could materialize with no warning, despite the infinite expanse of sea that held yet another danger.

"Christ. Look at 'em." Awe and a trill of terror sounded in Charlie's voice.

No one needed to ask what Charlie was referring to. They could all see the large school of sharks with silvery undulating bodies zipping through the clear water below. A shudder rippled down Skip's spine.

"Navigator to cockpit: Rounding Bil Bil island in approximately five minutes."

They pointed their ships toward New Guinea's wild, ragged coastline. Barely skimming the crest of the breakers crashing against the shore below, the 38th split up, with each two-ship element hunting its own prey before rendezvousing with the others over Mount Yule.

Several pairs turned inland to scout small inlets and streams, while others scoured coastal waters. Skip and Pat flew parallel to the coast.

Minutes later, they spotted what they had hoped to find. A large barge steamed toward the mouth of the Gogol river, its smokestack belching black smoke. Skip judged it to be fifty feet long and yep, there were the commensurate guns. This was a target the enemy would defend with vigor.

The barge initiated characteristic evasive maneuvers. Barges couldn't outrun the B-25s, but they knew how to draw the strafers into range of their deadly gunfire.

Skip flipped the selector switch to command function to radio his wingman.

"Watch out, Pat," he said. "Sucker's got a second gun nest on the deck, aft of the deckhouse."

Pat didn't acknowledge Skip's warning. He must be giving battle orders to his crew. Skip made a mental note to remind Norm, Pat's copilot, to monitor the command function at this juncture of every mission.

"Copilot to engineer: Shoot a flare toward *Southie*. Wanna get their attention, be sure they heard Skipper's warning."

Skip shook his head at Mike. "Pilot to engineer: Save that flare. Won't be visible and no way Flannery can miss that extra set of guns."

Mike's cheeks flushed.

Skip wouldn't normally countermand his copilot. But dammit they might need those flares. If they were shot down, signal flares could save their lives.

He lined up at five hundred feet and jammed his helmet on over his headset. He would attack the barge at 90% power, leaving reserves to evade the ack-ack. Pat would make the first pass, sweeping his ship across the barge from bow to stern to silence or slow its guns.

Southie careened toward the barge, tracers blazing from her guns. Skip frowned and gritted his teeth. Pat should be compensating for that second gun-nest. If he took the usual path across the deck, when he bounded over the second mast, his ship would be dead to rights in the sights of the guns mounted aft.

"Flannery, you see that second gun nest?" Skip called, perspiration beading on his upper lip.

No response. *Southie* held her course.

Could Skip take his ship down fast enough to take out the aft guns ahead of Pat's sweep? Order of battle had him taking *Bourbon Street Belle* across the beam behind *Southie in the South Seas*, not directly in *front* of Pat's firing guns. Sweat slicked the sides of his face, while adrenaline sent waves of blood thundering through his ears.

Engines roaring in an escalating wailing crescendo, Skip clutched the yoke and aimed *Bourbon Street Belle*'s nose perpendicular to *Southie in the South Seas*. No time to ask Leo to calculate. Only his gut could judge whether he had enough speed to blaze across and take out the aft guns without risking a hit from Pat's own guns.

Old Skip wouldn't have hesitated. He would have burned the engines to dust in a death-defying dive, would have viewed it as a worthy challenge of his piloting skills, would have whooped in exhilaration when he knocked out those aft guns right under Pat's nose. The entire maneuver and outcome flashed across his mind's eye in a split second.

Skip's ribs tightened into a burning knot of pressure. He couldn't suck in any air. No time to jam his oxygen mask back on.

He had full power. He only needed to hold his course, and yet something held him in check. And then he had lost that edge, the slimmest moment when he still might have dared to strike aft. Pat was a scant hundred yards from the bow.

Towering masses of black smoke burst in front of the windshield. An acrid burning smell coated his throat. *Christ, is that barge carrying a fuel tank?*

Coughing and blinded by smoke, Skip held his course by instinct. Billowing layers of smoke peeled toward the edges of the windshield before he took his ship across the beam amidship. He depressed the fire button and held it steady to unleash a maelstrom of firepower. A cloud of sawdust and wood fragments flew through the air as his guns tore into the wooden barge.

Into the barge and its occupants. His heart thundered. Would he ever become numb to the human carnage so evident at masthead level?

Skip flipped through the images seared into his mental catalogue until he settled on those of his shell-shocked and gravely wounded comrades at Pearl Harbor, swimming through burning water, clinging to debris, fighting for their lives. The Japanese had done that. They had started this whole damned war.

Not the men he was mowing down. Like Skip and his crew, they were only following orders. Dammit, he should request a transfer to a squadron flying B-25s at altitude. Or give up the left seat. As far as Skip could tell, Mike suffered no qualms of conscience about waging warfare at tree-top level.

Skip gulped in air. He had to focus on completing the mission. Surviving and keeping his men alive had to be his immediate priority. He could wrestle with his conscience later.

He gritted his teeth and turned *Bourbon Street Belle* in a tight arc so he could swoop back over the barge, this time running lengthwise from bow to stern. Tracers arced in a steady stream around the ship while his pulse beat a staccato tattoo in time with the enemy ack-ack guns aimed at his ship.

Pat's strafing run should have either knocked out the guns or sent the gunners leaping overboard. The pungent smoke had signaled a hit on a fuel drum, so how was the enemy still able to continue shooting? Where the hell was Pat and his ship? He should be making another run.

"The fuck is Pat?" he growled into the intercom. He saw *Southie* a split second before Mike swore, and a wave of ice-cold water splashed over Skip from head to toe.

Goddammit.

Southie in the South Seas was the source of the conflagration. With her right engine and wing engulfed in reddish-orange flames, she trailed copious amounts of black smoke and pitched violently into an uncontrollable death spiral toward the sea. And in a flash the only trace of *Southie* and her men remaining in the blue waters of the

Bismarck Sea was a white fizzle of steam.

Skip's stomach plunged in a cold dive, might have fallen into the fathomless sea right along with Pat and his crew.

He should have made certain Pat had seen the second set of guns. Shouldn't have cut off Mike's order for a flare. Should have taken the gamble and taken out that second gun-nest. A rope-like vise tightened around Skip's chest, securing his heart with a boom hitch knot.

Boom-Ack. Ping, ping, ping.

An unmistakable shrill grinding whine issued from *Bourbon Street Belle*, and she listed to the right. That could only mean one thing. Flak had hit the right engine.

Mike feathered the prop and switched all fuel to the left engine, while Skip frantically trimmed the controls. The cockpit frame rattled with the choppy bark of Dewey's turret guns and were soon joined by the vibrations from the high-volume tracers fired from Leo and Rafe. Charlie's guns in the rear remained silent. Slight uncommanded movement in the rudder pedals signaled that her tail section might be damaged, but he didn't have time to ask Charlie for a report.

He had squandered valuable time watching *Southie in the South Seas* sink below the surface. He had allowed grief to overshadow vigilance, the very thing he had warned his crew against from the beginning. A man couldn't afford to wallow or send up a prayer. The enemy would exploit Allied softness every single time.

They were hit, but not down.

Those bastards had killed six good men. A wave of anger sharpened Skip's focus. He aimed his guns dead center into the second gun nest as if framing it in the viewfinder of his Graflex camera. Wind whistled through the cockpit and seared his face. Blood thundered in his ears.

He yanked on the throttles with such force, his teeth jarred. He dove straight into the swells of dust and smoke, raining his fusillade of destruction along the barge from bow to stern. The enemy's gunners would sure as shit abandon their guns now.

He banked in a sharp turn off the stern and pulled back on the yoke to gain whatever altitude she could manage with one engine. He and Pat would normally continue further down the coast to scout more targets. But without her wingman and badly battle-damaged, *Bourbon Street Belle*'s best hope was to head home.

Skip slowed her speed and flew parallel to the coast so they could assess the damage to the ship before proceeding.

"Cockpit to crew: Status report, one at a time." Mike's voice splintered like concentric circles of cat-ice. He wiped a handkerchief over his face and averted his eyes.

Skip couldn't swallow past the knot in his throat.

Leo and Dewey responded to Mike's call, followed by Rafe.

"Radio to cockpit: Charlie's hit. He's bleeding so damned fast, I can't stop it." A high note of panic crept into Rafe's voice.

"Dewey, take Rafe the medical kit and see if you can help. Report back." Skip's chopped words came out in a rasp, his throat still too dry to swallow.

Flying home would be slower on a single engine, and they would be vulnerable if an enemy fighter spotted them. Staying over water risked that very encounter, because the Japanese fighters patrolled the skies to protect their barges. Skip decided to move inland and find the shortest route over the mountains.

The intercom crackled. "Dewey here. Charlie's in a bad way, Skipper. Rafe already gave him morphine, and we're trying to staunch the blood. But Christ —"

"Where's he hit? Have you used a tourniquet?" Leo's nasal tone cut into Dewey's nervous prattle.

Skip glanced over his shoulder as his burly navigator crawled over the bomb bay and into the belly of the ship to assist Dewey and Rafe.

Towering clouds with inky bases and gray, turbulent tops loomed to their right. The colossal clouds were so laden with moisture Skip couldn't imagine how they hung in the sky. They stretched east and west as far as he could see, standing sentry before the mountain ranges they must cross. The perilous coastal mountains rose steeply no more than a couple of miles from shore. On their other side, a long valley separated them from the higher interior ranges.

He fought with the ailerons and rudders to keep the plane steady. She was slow and strained to gain altitude.

"We need more, sweetheart," Skip muttered. "Come on."

When his ship reached the minimum altitude needed to clear the Finisterre range, Skip exhaled. He would try to gain another thousand feet, but this should be enough.

He made successive attempts to enter the thunderhead at an oblique angle, testing the turbulent air before edging them out each time, leery of throwing his ship into that hellish churning vortex with only one engine.

"Pilot to crew: Status report on Charlie?"

"Dewey here. Leo's working on him now, got the bleeding mostly stopped. Leo thinks he's in shock. Leo says . . ." Dewey's voice caught. "Leo says hurry. Hurry if you can, sir."

Skip's chest tightened.

"Since when am I *sir*?" He coughed to clear the gruffness from his voice. "Tell Leo I'm gonna get Charlie home."

His caution may have contributed to Pat's death and the loss of *Southie*'s crew, but Skip had no intention of losing his chain-smoking Okie tail gunner.

Skip eased up on the throttles and hurtled toward the Finisterres. From the moment *Bourbon Street Belle* entered the clouds, turbulent currents popped her right and left and violent downdrafts caused her to lose altitude. Skip clutched the yoke, his knuckles white, as torrential sheets of rain pounded against the bomber's thin skin.

He glanced sideways at Mike. Tear tracks glistened on his copilot's cheeks below his goggles. He clenched his jaw tight as he struggled to help Skip with the ailerons.

A terrifying cloud cave closed around them, obscuring both the sky above and the mountaintops below. Mike pointed toward the artificial horizon indicator, which indicated her nose was pointed upward fifteen degrees even though the altimeter showed a dizzying rate of descent. *Fuck, fuck, fuck.*

They had to regain enough altitude to avoid ramming into the side of a mountain.

Skip leaned forward and squinted out the windshield. A narrow opening out of their current hellscape had materialized about a mile ahead at three o'clock. He rammed the throttles forward to gain as much speed and altitude as the lone engine could muster, urging his ship to hurry, desperate to reach the aperture before those quicksilver clouds denied them clear passage.

Bourbon Street Belle shot through the opening, and they emerged into blue skies and clear weather. Skip leveled off, switched his oxygen regulator to pure, and gulped in air.

Unstable winds remained an issue, but they were high enough to clear the shrouded peaks with confidence. His biggest worries now were fuel and the exceptional strain he was putting on their one remaining engine to maintain this altitude.

This was the narrowest point across the Finisterres. Trouble was, Leo was with Charlie. Skip and Mike would either have to calculate the heading or make their best guess when to descend into the Ramu Valley. Once they did, Skip could fly fast and low and reduce the strain on the engine.

Mike scribbled calculations onto a notepad with shaking hands. He glanced up from the pad, peered out the side window, and shook his head. "Hell if I know where we are."

"Me either." Skip's stomach roiled. Descending too soon could be fatal. If they overshot the Ramu Valley, they could easily wind up over Mount Wilhelm, New Guinea's highest peak, and Skip doubted the power of their single engine would allow them to climb high enough to clear it. They didn't have enough fuel or time for error.

"Leo," Skip called into the intercom. "We need you to give us an accurate heading."

After a short pause, the intercom sputtered, and Dewey said, "Leo's —"

"Goddammit," Skip cut in, "We'll all die if we don't descend in time to cut across the valley. Calculate our position and give me a heading. That's an order."

Pain shot from his clenched jaw to his forehead. He sensed Leo's approach and glanced back just as his navigator squatted on the ledge behind his seat. He squinted at the instruments and jotted down a few readings, then went to his station.

"You can descend," Leo said, "But adjust three degrees south."

Skip made the adjustment to their course and the clouds thinned, allowing him to see the river below. He took his ship to 90% power and pointed her nose downward for a sharp rate of descent. *Hurry, hurry, hurry.*

Had his order for Leo to navigate sealed Charlie's fate?

He urged *Bourbon Street Belle* onward at full power, flying a scant fifty feet above the raging muddy waters of the Ramu River, still swollen from recent monsoons.

He flicked his gaze from the gas gauge to the cylinder head temperature gauge. The metal arrow on the temperature gauge ticked past the red line.

Mike swiped a hand down his pants leg. Skip wasn't indifferent to their predicament. Racing to save Charlie's life could end in tragedy for them all. He should nurse their remaining engine, not overtax it. Yet instinct urged him to take advantage of the respite from Mother Nature because even a clear pass over the Owen Stanleys would cost them valuable time.

Skip clutched the throttles. Did they have enough fuel to keep up this pace? Mountains and high ridges pressed close on their right, and he had to fight the ailerons to keep the ship flying straight while he followed the winding river. He had to keep the wing low on the left, where they had power, to avoid rolling the ship.

"Navigator to cockpit: The Watut River will branch off to the south in five miles."

The Watut River's channel was essentially a narrow gorge that cut through towering canyons rising over three thousand feet on each side. If threading their damaged bird over the Markham with a ridge pressing close on one side had been challenging, braving the perilous dangers over the Watut River Valley would be even worse. Every time clouds blocked the sun, gloom settled over the gorge and masked the dangerous cliff faces.

Once they finally emerged over the high plains nestled at the base of the Owen Stanleys, Skip released the breath he had been holding and eased up on the throttles to increase airspeed. What should have been evident earlier manifested itself plainly in the instruments: Crossing the Owen Stanleys with only one functioning engine would be improbable, if not impossible.

Skip's gut twisted. *Should we have ditched in the ocean?*

No. They would never have survived long in shark-infested waters with Charlie bleeding so profusely. And even if they had managed to swim to shore, they would have been in enemy territory and would have been captured in short order.

So if he had done the right thing in taking them over the coastal ranges, they remained faced with the reality that bailing out over the Owen Stanleys wouldn't improve their chances for survival.

"Skipper!" Leo shouted in excitement, tapping Skip on the shoulder. He thrust a map between the cockpit seats and jabbed his finger at the high plains interspersed near the base of the Owen Stanleys. "Tsilli Tsilli."

"What about it?" Mike leaned closer.

Leo tapped the map. "We've got fighters based there. They've got an airstrip. Just occupied it last week."

Skip winced and circled his cramped shoulders. They could land there and save themselves, but what about Charlie? A new outpost might not have a doctor, let alone a field hospital. Yet pressing on with *Bourbon Street Belle* in such bad shape would be foolhardy. Saving everyone else had to take precedence. If there was no hospital, maybe one of the fighter planes could transport Charlie to one.

"Pilot to radio: Contact the control tower at Tsili Tsili. Let 'em know we're coming in and need medical assistance if they've got it."

Leo passed on an adjusted heading.

Rafe's voice rang out. "Radio to pilot: We're cleared to land. No hospital on base, but a C-47 with medics is standing by. They're readying it to take off as soon as they've got Charlie."

Thank God. Now Skip only had to land the ship safely. Not a foregone conclusion with one engine out and the other one running too fast and too hot. He advanced the throttles to over ninety percent power, ignoring the creep of the gauge indicators above the red line. The runway came into sight, and Skip nosed her down at a sharp rate of descent.

"Use thirty degrees on the flaps to slow us faster," Skip said to Mike. "And open the cowl flaps to cool the engines."

They came down fast but controlled. He maneuvered *Bourbon Street Belle* off the runway, onto a perimeter road, and then into the closest empty hardstand. The fuel gauge showed less than ten percent remaining. They couldn't have cleared the Owen Stanleys. He inhaled deeply and drummed his fingers on the yoke.

The rear hatch opened, and Dewey and Leo's voices mixed with those of the medics who had pulled an ambulance next to the hardstand.

"Type O," Leo called out. "I already checked his tag."

Skip and Mike exited through the front hatch and joined the others, who were clustered around Charlie and the medics. His heart jittered at the sight of Charlie's ghostly pallor and his still form. The medics had started a transfusion, but were they too late? Now he understood the panic of his men, why Leo had urged him to hurry.

Skip grabbed one end of the stretcher and helped to load his crewmate into the ambulance. The C-47 was lined up at the other end of the runway, engines running and ready to take-off once they had Charlie on board.

"Where will you take him?" Leo asked.

A medic hopped into the ambulance. "Moresby," he yelled before slamming the door.

Good. Skip blew out a breath. Port Moresby had a stationary hospital, not a field hospital like those at outlying airfield bases. They could save his life in Moresby.

The ambulance roared along the perimeter road toward the waiting C-47.

Skip stood in a cluster with his men. They shaded their eyes and squinted as the medics lifted Charlie's stretcher through the hatch and closed it behind them. Minutes later, the C-47 barreled down the runway, gathering speed. She lifted into the sky and clawed furiously for altitude before disappearing from view over the hazy purple mountaintops of the Owen Stanleys.

He swallowed. Either he or Rafe needed to radio their base to report their whereabouts, then Skip had to determine if the ground crews here could repair the damaged ship. But his first order of business was to tackle the thornier issue of how things stood with his men.

With Mike.

Skip cleared his throat and gestured for his men to circle closer. Mike stood stiffly off to one side with narrowed eyes.

"Rafe, find their ops tent and contact our base. Let 'em know we landed safely, that Charlie was airlifted to Moresby —"

"And that *Southie*'s crew was killed in action," Mike snapped, a harsh note overlaying his pronounced Boston accent. "*Needlessly* killed in action."

Skip bit his lip. *Don't engage. His grief is too raw.*

"Dewey, go find the ground crews, see if any of 'em have worked on B-25s," Skip said. "Then supervise whatever they do. If no one is competent to repair our damage, let me know. In that case, we'll need to radio Durand and get 'em to send us mechanics and parts."

He inclined his head toward Leo. "Figure out if they've got

room in any of their tents to house us. We may be stuck here overnight or longer, while they patch up our girl."

Skip waved the three of them toward an idling jeep.

"Send it back to get us," he told Leo.

Mouth too dry to swallow, Skip considered hoisting himself into the cockpit to retrieve his canteen. No, he should speak to Mike first, while they had privacy. He edged closer but still allowed his grieving crewmate a measure of personal space.

He scuffed his boot on the dusty ground and struggled to find the right words. "He wouldn't have seen the flare. Not from that direction, not in daylight."

"Should've tried." Mike tightened his jaw. "It wasn't our last goddamned flare."

"No, it wasn't. But, look here, if we'd needed to ditch in the water or the jungle, we'd need every one of 'em." Skip rubbed his hand over his chest. Ditching had seemed their only option more than once today.

"I wouldn't have. Looking out for the other fella means something to me."

Heat rose in Skip's cheeks. "Looking out for all of *you* means a damned sight more to me than what happens in other men's ships."

"We knew Pat hadn't responded. We knew —"

"Right. And that's on him and on Norm, not us. One of them should have monitored the command frequency. We all know that, Mike."

A mottled flush rose up Mike's neck and across his cheeks. "We're supposed to look out for each other up there —"

"Exactly." Skip closed the distance between them. "That moment of inattention, when we were shocked about Pat and his fellas, that's when we got hit. And then I had to think about Charlie, about *us* makin' it back alive. It's my job to put all of *you* first."

A jeep sputtered down the perimeter road toward them.

Mike thinned his lips into a sharp line and stepped toward Skip. "Before that though — before we attacked. You could've saved Pat then."

Skip hadn't given voice to any of that, hadn't said one word to indicate he thought it was possible he might dive fast enough to streak in front of Pat's guns and take out the second gun-nest. His parched throat burned.

He frowned and shook his head as the jeep pulled up alongside them.

Mike put his hand on the vehicle's back railing and turned to look at Skip. "You had it. You coulda made it. You lost yeh nerve."

CHAPTER NINE

September 10, 1943

Yorkeys Knob Rest Home

Cairns, Queensland, Australia

Hadley dabbed at her face and neck with a handkerchief and pushed sweaty tendrils of hair off her face. The daily fourteen-mile drive from the Red Cross officer's hotel at Yorkeys Knob into the town of Cairns for groceries became more monotonous and uncomfortable as the weather grew warmer.

The forested mountains of the Great Dividing Range loomed over fields of leafy green sugarcane on the inland side of the road, while the Coral Sea lay a short distance beyond the fields on the coastal side.

Rounding a bend in the road, Hadley spotted clouds of billowing black smoke. Burning the cane fields sloughed off the leafy tops and destroyed weedy undergrowth, allowing the locals to harvest the crop more efficiently. She reluctantly rolled up her window and stopped so she could lean across the truck cab to roll up the other one. Heat and smothering stuffiness instantly overwhelmed the small cab. Hadley accelerated, anxious to move past the burning fields.

As she approached the narrow footbridge spanning the Barron River, she noticed movement below it near the riverbank. Men in canoes.

She frowned and shook her head. With heavy smoke from burning sugarcane filling the area and rough rapids up ahead on the river, this was hardly an ideal spot for a relaxing canoe expedition. Her curiosity got the better of her not long past the bridge, and she turned the truck around. Once she got back to the bridge, she pulled off the road, cut the engine, and hopped out.

She started toward the river, only to double back for her binoculars. She trained them toward the east, where she had spotted the canoes, but saw nothing but churning brown water.

Hadley hiked closer, peered through the binoculars, and adjusted both lenses. Still nothing. On the verge of giving up and returning to the truck, she shifted her stance and spotted some unexpected movement among the trees.

The men had left the river and now strode through the trees atop the riverbank, carrying their canoes overhead in pairs. They were young and fit. The type of men one might expect to be in military service, not traipsing about the countryside for fun. Perhaps they were American or Australian soldiers enjoying the outdoors during leave with borrowed canoes from the nearest Red Cross club.

Except they weren't headed for Cairns. Nor did they seem to be on a pleasure jaunt. Hadley adjusted the lenses again and struggled to keep the men in sight. They stayed inside the tree-line, yet she sensed purpose and a certain measure of stealth in their movements.

Hadley crossed the road, ducked behind a copse of trees, and trained her binoculars across the river. When she had them in sight again, she zoomed in closer. American and Australian infantry and air units and the U.S. Navy had a large presence in the area, but Hadley wasn't aware of any bases this far outside town.

Why were the men out here in the back of the beyond? Military intelligence? Secret operatives? She had heard about a *house on the hill* that was allegedly being used for clandestine purposes. No one had divulged its whereabouts, only made offhand remarks about an isolated location in the bush. To the Australians, that could mean anywhere outside the Cairns city limits.

The men quickened their pace, and she broke into a jog, taking care to stay out of sight behind the trees. When she judged that she had gotten ahead of them, she stopped to catch her breath and refocus her binoculars on the men. Then she tore her gaze away from them to assess her position. She had moved a good distance from the road.

Keenly aware that her skirt and blouse, and especially her flimsy shoes, were unsuitable attire for tromping around in the bush, she weighed her curiosity against her common sense. She ought to turn back. Retracing the route she had taken should minimize her chances of encountering dangerous animals. And after all, the men might only lead her to an isolated conventional military installation.

Hadley swatted at a swarm of mosquitos. She had forgotten to use the insect repellent the Australian cooks had provided, a mix of lemon eucalyptus oil, vanilla extract, and distilled water. She pulled a handkerchief from her skirt pocket and swiped sweat from the back of her neck. Yes, she would turn back. Never mind predatory and poisonous reptiles, the insects would soon do her in.

She took one last look at the men and was startled to see them heading toward a large house she hadn't noticed before. A house with wrap-around verandas on both levels that sat on a small rise surrounded by dense brush and trees. She caught her breath and zoomed in as far as the binoculars would allow, then panned to examine the house and grounds.

This must be the elusive *house on the hill* of local lore that presumably served as some sort of covert training grounds. Hadley bit her lip and focused on the surrounding countryside. No visible road led to the house. Perhaps it was accessible only from the river.

She lowered the binoculars. After she finished shopping in Cairns, she would explore the byways north of the river that traversed in this direction. Then she would —

A hand clapped over her mouth.

She gasped.

Her captor knocked the binoculars from her grasp and wrapped his other arm around her waist, immobilizing her arms and pinning her against his hard body.

Her heart jumped into her throat and thudded erratically. She attempted to kick him and tear free of his grip, but he stepped on her feet and tightened his hold. A mix of sweat, masculine musk, and eucalyptus oil clung to his skin.

Adrenaline coursed through Hadley faster than river rapids. She was unable to move and tried to bite him. Firm pressure from his hand prevented her defensive move.

"Thought we didn't spot you having a gander, Sheila?" he murmured in her ear. His accent would have pegged him as Aussie even without the slang term for a woman. "We took note of your every move. From when you crossed the bridge, parked your truck, went back for the binoculars, and followed us."

Her heart thudded. Her sleuthing skills, honed on the political beat in New Orleans, had been a source of pride, but they obviously weren't as effective in the Australian countryside as they were at home. Her instincts had proven to be correct — it was clear these men were engaged in covert operations or training — but that was small comfort to her now.

Whether from the physical pressure of the man's hold or her reaction to the adrenaline and panic flooding her system, her field of vision narrowed to a pinprick of light with black edges. Nausea rose in her throat.

"I could kill you." The prick of cold metal against her throat told her his words carried no idle threat. "Could've killed you before you even finished whatever thought was running through your pretty head."

Could. Did that mean he wouldn't? Ripples of lightheadedness flashed through her head. She needed air.

"But I won't," he whispered. He removed his hand from her mouth and pushed her against a tree trunk with her arms pinned at her sides. He nodded at her Red Cross pin. "Red Cross. American or Australian?"

"American," Hadley choked out. She screwed up her face and tried to halt the bile rising up her throat. "American Red Cross."

"Fancy yourself a detective, do you?"

"No." She gulped in air and shook her head.

A lock of dark hair fell across his forehead. He quirked his lips and leaned close. "Right. Ordinary curiosity prompted you to look at us with binoculars you just happened to have with you and then trek into the bush, heedless of native wildlife."

"No. I was birdwatching." Hadley thrust out her chin. "That's why I had the binoculars."

"Birdwatching, eh?" He raised his eyebrow. "What sort of birds are you looking for?"

She sucked in a breath. A generic type of bird like *robins* wouldn't cut it. She had to do better than that. Did Australia have egrets or sand plovers, the kinds of birds that might live near rivers back home? Enid's husband had mentioned a New Guinea bird that migrated to the Cairns area each summer to breed and nest. What had he called them?

"Metallic starlings," she blurted out. "They've migrated here to breed."

"Metallic starlings." He gave a curt nod. "Fair dinkum, Sheila. What else?"

"Cockatoos." Hadley's palms were slick with sweat. She curled her fingers and pictured the flying foxes that gorged themselves on ripening mangos and sweet-scented melaleucas near the hotel. She could have focused on them, but they were large tropical bats, not birds. The boys brought in white parrot-like cockatoos as pets.

He narrowed his eyes. "No cockies in this vicinity. You find them in rainforests."

"I didn't say I saw any," she snapped. "I'm an American, so how am I supposed to know where I might see cockatoos?"

"Well, Sheila, how am I supposed to know whether you're a spy or only a stickybeak?"

"A *spy?*" Laughter burbled despite her nerves. "I'm no spy. Besides, we're allies, remember?"

"Being a Yank doesn't make you a mate and doesn't mean you aren't spying. Back to the birds — maybe you were looking for cassowaries."

Cassowaries. She frowned. He must be trying to trick her. Cassowaries were large, dangerous, ostrich-like birds. Mr. Pittman, the field director for the Cairns area, had warned Hadley about them when she had first arrived at Yorkeys. She shook her head. "They're dangerous. I've heard they can be found around here but prefer to live in rainforests."

"All right, you know a bit about Australian birds. But apparently you don't have good sense about other animals in the bush." The man straightened his shoulders and leaned closer. "You were so focused on keeping us in sight, you got far too close to a crocodile."

A sharp stab of cold fear pierced Hadley's gut. *A crocodile?* As a Louisiana girl, she appreciated the dangers of coming too close to those large predators.

"I stayed away from the river." Sweat beaded on her upper lip. Crocodiles, she had been told, didn't venture far from water.

"Right." He swiveled her around and pointed. "But you tramped right next to that billabong."

"Billabong?"

"You Yanks call it a pond."

"That?" Hadley pointed toward a patch of standing water and marshy vegetation she had skirted around earlier. He was right. She hadn't paid it much mind beyond trying to keep her feet dry. "I'll pay better attention on my way back."

"You're assuming I'll let you go."

"I told you, I was only birdwatching." A spasm shot down Hadley's spine. She wanted to rub her muscles, but he had too firm a grip on her upper arms. "I won't stray this far off the road from now on."

"Let's dispense with the pretense of birdwatching, shall we?" His warm breath bathed her cheek. "When I bailed you up, you had your binoculars trained on that house on the hill."

"I —"

"Don't lie to me," he said, his eyes going flinty and cold. He released one of her arms and waved at the structure on the opposite side of the river. "Forget about that house. Don't try to find it. Don't ask questions about it. Don't yabber about it at the Red Cross club. And — don't *write* about it."

"Fine." How could he have any idea she was a journalist? She would say whatever it took to escape his clutches. "So can I be on my way now? I've got errands in town."

He tilted his head and appraised her. Hadley's stomach fluttered. Her neck flushed with heat. At last he nodded, released his hold on her, and shoved the binoculars into her hand. "I'll escort you back to the road."

Hadley didn't protest. With his guidance, she wouldn't have to worry about running into dangerous wildlife. She fell in step behind him, gripping the binoculars. She ought to take one last look at the house before it disappeared from view.

"No binoculars, Sheila," he said without slowing his pace or glancing at her over his shoulder. Did he have eyes in the back of his head?

She exhaled, dropped the binoculars, and lowered her hands.

They sidestepped around the marshy waters of the billabong, and her guide paused to point out the crocodile she had missed earlier. A shudder slithered across her shoulders. Her fear and the tightness in her chest didn't ease until she glimpsed her truck up ahead. The man had made no threats along the way, but a note of menace still hung about him. She would be more than relieved to part ways with him.

When they finally reached the truck, he raised his eyebrows and tapped his fingers against the notepad in her skirt pocket. "Let me repeat. Do not *write* about the house."

"I won't." Hadley put her hand on the door handle.

He closed his large hand over hers. *"Birdwatcher Mauled by Crocodile* is a tragic headline, righto?"

Ignoring this threat, she wrenched the handle to open the door, clambered into the truck, and slammed the door.

Safe at last. Hadley drew in a calming breath and turned to give him a cheery wave — but he was already gone. She peered out the passenger side glass, then looked at the rearview mirror. He was nowhere in sight. He had melted into the bush.

Unable to swallow past the knot of anxiety lodged in her throat, Hadley grabbed her canteen off the passenger seat and took a deep drink. Her hands trembled as she recapped the container and started the truck. Before she drove away, she leaned her forehead against the steering wheel and rubbed the back of her neck.

We took note of every move you made. His words haunted her. From somewhere nearby, the man probably watched her now. Would he follow her into Cairns and back to Yorkeys Knob?

He would if he were serious about her staying mum. No. She scowled. She was being melodramatic. He couldn't tail her into town on foot, and she hadn't seen any vehicles near the house. But he knew she was with the American Red Cross, and the Cairns area only had eight female ARC staff assistants. He would have no difficulty locating her.

Hadley didn't know *how* he would find out if she wrote about the mysterious house for her New Orleans paper, but she had no doubt that he would. Why did the place demand such secrecy? And what risks was she willing to take to find out?

***

Hadley hit the brakes and peered at the road ahead through the dust-coated windshield. About a half mile away, a crew of army engineers operated a scraper and a grader.

"My land, who lit a fire under the army to get this done?" she murmured. Fixing the four-mile stretch of road leading to the officers' rest home hotel at Yorkeys Knob hadn't been a military priority up to now.

Hadley eased the truck to the side of the road, lowered the window, and leaned out. "Hi, fellas, can I squeeze past you?"

One of the men walked over, peered into the bed of the truck, and laughed. "Chickens?"

Hadley shrugged. "We serve ten dozen eggs a day."

He patted the truck door, then yelled and gestured for the heavy equipment operators to move to the side of the road so she could get by.

Hadley waved as she chugged past them. She parked around the back of the hotel so she could unload the food near the kitchen door and take the chickens to the coop.

Hefting a two-gallon steel canister of ice cream in each hand, she paused midway up the path and turned to stare at the alley where two new refrigerators had stood for three months. They had disappeared. Her mouth fell open. Was the army fixing the road and installing the refrigerators on the same day? Someone important must be visiting soon.

She continued up the path and banged her foot against the kitchen door to get someone's attention. Moments later, Enid, one of the Australian cooks, swung the door open and held out her hands to take the canisters.

Hadley handed them to her. "Thanks, I've got more. Where's Juan?" The young Filipino boy should be helping in the kitchen at this time of day.

Enid rolled her eyes. "He's *assisting* the detail installing the fridges."

Hadley shook her head and returned to the truck. She hauled in several wooden crates filled with bottles of milk from the army commissary, boxes of vegetables from the Chinese grocer, stacks of steaks from the butcher, and cartons of bread from the bakery. Then she returned to move the two wire crates full of squawking chickens. She couldn't lift them by herself, and Enid and Madge were busy putting away the groceries.

She crouched to peer into the crates and scrunched her nose. No way around it, she would have to transfer the chickens one by one. Hadley released a weary breath, opened the closest crate's wire latch, and snatched out the first chicken within reach by its feet. It squawked as she closed the crate. Taking them into the chicken yard one by one, mucking out the yard, and returning the crates to the musty storage shed took her over an hour.

She swatted at a cloud of midges and wiped a sweaty hand down her skirt. If only she could take a shower. The generator pumped sun-warmed water from a tank over to the lone shower on the back patio. Yet despite the wooden frame around three sides of the cubicle and the crude curtain across the front, she worried about privacy — especially at this time of day. Too many male guests roamed about the property.

Speaking of men, an army truck pulled up alongside the hotel just as she returned, and several Air Forces men climbed out carrying kit bags. She turned away and blew out an exasperated breath. She needed a sponge bath and a change of clothes before she could greet new guests. Hoping they wouldn't notice her, she scurried toward the back door.

"Hadley," one of the men called out in a familiar voice.

She started and turned around. Skip Masterson had a knack for turning up at the wrong moment. She was disheveled and grimy from her foray into the bush and then manhandling two dozen chickens, not to mention that she was still shaken from her encounter with the Aussie spy, or commando, or whatever he was.

So of course, Skip stood in the yard immaculately-dressed and as handsome as ever with Lucy's rope leash in his hand, while the wallaby hopped around him in excitement.

Hadley wanted nothing more than to flee into the hotel so she could bathe and change before interacting with him. Instead, she pulled out a handkerchief and wiped her face and neck before pocketing the dirty cloth and walking toward him.

Keeping her gaze averted, she stooped to greet Lucy. "Hello, cher. You're still a sweet little thing, aren't you? But we'd better keep you off the rugs."

Hadley gathered her courage, patted Lucy, and then stood to reluctantly make eye contact with Skip. His lips turned up crookedly on one side, and a zing fluttered across her chest. Hard as she tried, she hadn't been able to get him out of her head. She had forgotten how utterly dishy his lopsided grin could be. Under the right circumstances, she could be gone on Skip Masterson in a flash. And that was why she needed to keep her distance. No more smooching.

She smiled. "We don't get many flyboys here on leave. Cairns is a naval depot, so most of our guests are navy officers."

"Brisbane was our destination, but our pilot was forced to make an unplanned stop here due to engine malfunction." Skip's eyes crinkled at the corners. Laugh lines outlined his smile.

His companions looked far less amused. Had Skip suspected he might find her here? Tingles goosed down her spine. She rubbed the back of her neck and turned to the stocky fella with close-cropped dark hair. She had met him before but couldn't remember his name.

"Welcome to Yorkeys Knob," Hadley said. "I believe I've met you on the Gold Coast at Sans Souci. I'm Hadley Claverie."

"Lieutenant Leo Kozlowski." He bobbed his head in acknowledgment. "Good memory, Miss Hadley. We did meet at Sans Souci. Real nice place, that was."

He knitted his brows and swept his gaze over the Yorkeys Knob hotel and club. Hadley understood his skepticism. Sans Souci *was* much nicer. This place had served as a brothel before the Red Cross had taken it over, and it remained a bit ramshackle, with few amenities.

Even so, the northern beaches were spectacular and much quieter than those near the larger cities to the south. Green Island and the Great Barrier Reef were only a short boat ride out from Yorkeys Knob's harbor.

"Will you fellas need rooms?" Hadley asked. Clara had mentioned that they had special guests arriving tomorrow, but Hadley could find rooms for Skip and the others tonight if necessary. She met Skip's eyes. "Or will your plane be repaired today?"

"A couple of rooms would be swell."

"We won't need rooms."

Skip's request clashed with the declaration from a man she didn't know. She flicked her gaze from Skip to the stranger, whose clothes hung on his slight frame in a way that suggested he had recently lost a good bit of weight. She had seen his vacant stare on other men many times before and pegged him as a fella in desperate need of a break from the war. Skip and Leo looked worn, if not as thin and shell-shocked as their crewmate.

"Hadley, this is my copilot, Mike Flannery," Skip offered in a rush. "He's hoping we can fly on to Brisbane this afternoon, but repairs to the plane may take longer. Our other crewmates stayed in Cairns and will call us when we're cleared to leave."

"All right." She gestured toward the hotel. "Let's find you boys a room or two where you can stow your kits. After you've freshened up, I'll suggest some activities to pass the time while you wait for the repairs to be done."

"That's swell, thanks. We're due some fun, aren't we, fellas?" Skip glanced at Mike, who looked away.

They'd flown some rough missions, from the sound of it. Hadley's gut twisted. Yet another reason to keep her distance from Lieutenant Masterson. She led them around the hotel to the front door. She brushed dirt from her skirt and blouse while she and Clara conferred about rooms, then Hadley motioned for the men to follow her upstairs.

"Shoulda left our kits with the others at the club in Cairns," Mike groused in a stiff undertone as they climbed the stairs. "Don't know why we had to trek all the way up here. They could call any time to tell us the plane's ready."

He had a good point. She glanced at Skip. Why *had* they come all the way to Yorkeys Knob — almost an hour from Cairns — if they didn't plan to stay overnight?

Hadley turned back and caught Leo nudging Mike and gesturing in her direction. A pink flush bloomed across Skip's cheeks.

Her stomach flipped. So he *had* thought he might find her in Cairns.

CHAPTER TEN

"Every time she finishes a game, another fella swoops in," Skip muttered to Lucy. Hadley had spent the last hour playing one game of ping-pong after another, while he watched with mounting frustration.

He was further aggravated by the naval officer who kept replaying a scratchy *Java Jive* record. Didn't they have any others? The song's repetitive refrain and silly rhymes were driving him crazy. Happy to be off the leash, Lucy bounded out of his lap and hopped around the perimeter of the club.

Despite the hotel's spartan appearance, it did have a phone, and Skip had confirmed that repairs to the plane might take several days. Turns out the excuse he had invented to persuade the pilot to land at Cairns had actually been a stroke of luck. The maintenance crew had discovered a serious issue with the plane that needed attention, and since Cairns only had an emergency air strip, they had little hope of codging a ride to Brisbane on another flight. They would have to stay in Cairns over the weekend.

Hadley's conversation with the naval captain was finally winding down. Clutching *A Tree Grows in Brooklyn* to his chest, Skip rose and hurried toward the ping-pong table. Hadley waved goodnight to the officer and his friends as they left the club.

"I didn't see any of those fellas at dinner tonight," Skip said.

She lowered her arm. "They aren't overnight guests. They're from the naval base a few miles up the coast. Naval officers sometimes pass their evenings here."

Skip scooped up the paddle abandoned by the naval captain and drummed it against the book. "You play a good game."

"I get loads of practice. We don't have many entertainment options here." Hadley fiddled with the other paddle, drawing Skip's attention to her slim hands.

She still wore the same pretty red nail polish she had on the ship. His pulse whirred as a cascade of sensations flooded his senses — rubbing his thumb over those nails, the feel of her slender fingers twining in his hair, and the way she had skimmed them down the back of his neck. He couldn't help but imagine her raking those same nails over his chest, digging them into his back, or grasping him in the heat of passion. Heat rolled through him in fiery waves. He looked away and swallowed.

Don't want to jump the gun and scare her off. He rubbed the back of his neck. Hadley was a unique woman who wouldn't be seduced by flamboyance, flattery, or flirtation. Up to now, Skip hadn't needed to call on anything more than superficial charm and an instinctive magnetism most women found alluring. None of that would work with Hadley Claverie. Sparks of his former esprit flared.

"I'm surprised we can't swim. We saw signs posted at the beach."

"Too many sharks." Hadley sighed. "We've been trying to get a net installed for months."

"You also don't have many books." Skip frowned and pointed

at the small bookcase in the corner. "Is there a better library at one of the other clubs?"

"You mean the one in Cairns that's almost an hour away?" Hadley arched her pencil-thin brows. "Or the one that's three hours south? Or the one in Port Moresby?"

"Sounds like I'll have to make do with what you have," Skip said. Hadley's isolation at Yorkeys Knob was clearly a sticking point. He tried another tack. "Fella at the beach said a boat will take folks out to an island near the Great Barrier Reef. Could we do that tomorrow?"

"He was talking about Green Island." She held out her hand to take the ping-pong paddle from him and then placed both paddles into a bag attached to the table. "Sure. All you need to do is show up at the harbor by eight o'clock. Be on time, because it leaves promptly at eight."

She grabbed a tray and began collecting discarded coffee mugs.

"Wait." Skip followed her. "By *we*, I meant the two of us. You and me."

"Well . . ." She paused with her fingers wrapped around the handle of a white ceramic mug, her red fingernail polish vibrant against it. "I don't normally work on Saturdays."

Skip had asked the staff about her availability earlier and already knew she had Saturdays off. He studied her face and waited.

"But, someone important — we don't know who yet — is arriving tomorrow." Hadley placed the mug on the tray and moved to another table.

She hadn't said no. Skip hurried after her. He touched her upper arm and pointed at her tray. "May I take that for you?"

His experience working with Hadley aboard the U.S.S. *West Point* had taught him that she bristled at the slightest hint that women couldn't handle certain tasks. Driven by fierce independence and a relentless need to prove her worth, Hadley was no vapid dream puss.

She held his gaze for a few beats, perhaps sizing up his motivation. She finally nodded and held out the tray. "Thanks. The hotel staff is already overworked readying the place for the bigwig coming tomorrow."

"Must be someone important." Skip set the book onto the table and accepted the tray of mugs. "Say, do you think the other guests will get to meet him?"

He couldn't help but wonder if the bigwig might be General MacArthur. Then he remembered the disastrous end to his last date with Hadley.

"Who says it's a man?" Hadley asked with a hint of suppressed laughter and none of the sharpness that would signal true annoyance.

He cast her a sheepish smile. "Fair point. Maybe it's the woman with the dog that scared Lucy. What was her name?"

"Mary Browne. She's the Director of the American Red Cross in Australia. A visit from her wouldn't prompt the work the army has done around the property today."

"They've made improvements?" Skip gaped at her. The hotel wasn't merely spartan from an aesthetic perspective; it was only one step shy of primitive. The building had no running water beyond a tap in the kitchen and a single outdoor shower — and worst of all, the men were forced to use outdoor privies no better than the ones back at base.

Hadley settled her mouth into a relaxed smile and tilted her head. "Believe me, yes. Until yesterday, we ladies used the same privies as you fellas. Fighting off rats, spiders, and snakes."

She shuddered.

So the indoor restroom is new. He lifted his eyebrows.

Hadley stacked two more cups and saucers onto the tray. "Did you see the army detail smoothing out our road when you came in? Clara asked for that long before I got here. And two new refrigerators sat in the yard for months until the men finally installed them today. Now if someone would only fix our fish trap, our menus wouldn't be so heavy on beef."

"As long as it's not that disgusting Aussie bully beef, we'll be happy. Could also live without the gelatin fruit salad." He winked.

She swiped cookie crumbs off the table into her palm and dumped them into one of the dirty mugs. "Sorry to say, the *Aeroplane Jelly*, as the Aussies call it, is a daily staple. Enid and Madge would revolt if we removed it from the menu."

"The spaghetti and meatballs tonight sure hit the spot." He grinned. "Did your staff make the ice cream we had for dessert?"

"No, we get it from the army commissary. I had just come back from making the groceries when you arrived."

"*Making* groceries?" He lifted his brows.

Hadley clapped a hand to her forehead. "Sorry. That's how we say it in New Orleans. No one here knows what I mean. *Shopping* for groceries."

"You drive forty minutes each way for the food?" He shifted the tray so she could add more cups.

She nodded. "Every day."

"All that driving probably doesn't leave you much time to write stories, unless you find something newsworthy in Cairns." The small coastal town had struck Skip as a sleepy backwater. He and his crew had stopped by the Cairns Red Cross club for enlisted men to find rooms for Dewey, Rafe, and Charlie — and to find out if Hadley was there.

She dropped a coffee cup onto the tray with a clatter and knocked over several other cups. He pressed the tray against his chest to keep the two mugs teetering on the edge from shattering on the floor.

"Sorry, sorry," Hadley muttered. Her hands trembled and her pupils dilated as she righted the fallen mugs. She looked away.

Skip set down the tray and placed his hand over hers. "Didn't mean to upset you."

"No, no, it's fine," she said. Her hands trembled, and she wouldn't meet his eyes. "We've all been stretched a little thin, that's all."

"Hmph." Skip scowled. From what he had observed, Hadley hadn't had any free time at all today. Overwork and no time to focus on her writing was taking its toll. "Can't they bring in more women to help?"

"Yorkeys Knob isn't as popular a leave destination as the Gold Coast or Sydney, so we're less of a priority." She shrugged.

The motion and her tone's affected nonchalance weren't enough to override Skip's instincts. He rubbed a finger over his lips. Hadley was overworked and stressed from lack of time to pursue journalism. But that didn't account for her odd startle response. Something else had to be bothering her.

"You still ought to ask them to send another gal or two up here. You'd feel better if you had more time for yourself — and time to chase a few stories. You're bound to find something worth writing about, even if you aren't in New Guinea."

"Here?" Her snort of laughter did nothing to allay his concern. Her genuine laugh started deep in her diaphragm and built into infectious peals. "We're in the Outback, Skip."

"Technically not."

She rolled her eyes and pulled her hand from beneath his. Calculated to convey composure, her expression might fool someone less observant.

She tapped her toes on the rough cement floor, tented her fingers over her mouth, and scanned the room. Then she waved her hand toward the small desk in the far corner that had a few mugs scattered atop it and walked toward it. "Bring the tray over here, will you?"

"Sure." Skip picked up the tray and followed her. "You said earlier that this place gets more navy fellas than army or air forces."

"That's right." She stacked several saucers and placed them onto the tray. "Ships dock in Cairns to resupply."

"Just our ships?"

"And some from the Royal Australian Navy, I suppose. Australian servicemen are eligible to visit our Red Cross clubs, but they don't come here very often." She gathered a deck of playing cards, tapped the stack against the desk, and slipped them back into their box.

He frowned. "Are there any permanent bases around here?"

"Why would there be a base here?" she asked in a tone permeated with briskness. "All the action is in New Guinea or the Solomon Islands."

"Could be training camps," Skip mused. "Isolated locations are good for training."

Hadley's strangled cough couldn't disguise her sharp intake of breath. No mistaking her expression and stance as anything other than flustered. No, not flustered. Nervous. Nervous — and maybe even frightened.

Skip set the tray onto the desk and gripped her upper arms. "Tell me. *Is* something going on in Cairns, Hadley?"

"How would I know?" A shimmer of sweat beaded on her upper lip.

He laughed and pushed a strand of hair out of her face. "How do you know anything? You're a reporter — and a damned good one. I saw that on the ship. You don't give up."

The pink flush tinging her cheeks probably had nothing to do with him, but damn, she was beautiful. His heart ping-ponged in his chest. She bit her lower lip. "How far . . . how far do you think a reporter should go for a story?"

"Reporters in general, or this particular reporter?" He kept his eyes intent on hers and trailed his index finger through her glossy dark hair.

She swallowed but didn't answer. How did she keep her porcelain skin so perfect in this tropical climate? Irritated that his thoughts had wandered, he frowned. What had he said to prompt such a strong reaction from her? He flicked back through their conversation. He had mentioned training, training in remote locations. Maybe not ordinary training.

"Well, I'm talking about you, of course." He tugged her closer. "You shouldn't take risks. No story is worth that. Especially for a story you can't even get out."

"But, what if —" Hadley broke off and wrinkled her nose.

He met her eyes. "What if what?"

"What if I want to know the truth? Just for me," she whispered. "Even if I can't scoop it."

"Would investigating it put you in danger?" Skip tightened his hold on her.

She blinked, her eyes closing and reopening like a camera shutter.

Dammit. He drew his brows together. "Hadley, listen to me. I can hazard a good guess what you might be trying to uncover. We've got men who operate in the shadows, behind enemy lines. Aussies have 'em too. Commandos. Saboteurs."

He didn't miss her quick half-nod before she retreated behind her inscrutable facade. He was on the right track. Whatever she had found, it wasn't likely in Cairns. It might be near here though, hidden amidst the unending sugar cane fields.

"You found something." Skip leaned closer. "Does anyone else know?"

Hadley moistened her lips and bobbed her head.

His first instinct was to harangue her, but he didn't want to upset her or crush her persistence and crusading spirit. So instead he hitched a deep breath and studied her expression. She would never admit it, but he sensed her trepidation. Had someone warned her off? If so, he had to reinforce that message without goading her into doing something stupid.

"Look," he finally said, twisting his lips. "The usual norms don't apply in war. Threats can be more easily backed up with action. No second chances in war."

"I know that, Skip. I'll —"

"Did someone threaten you?" he interrupted.

She cast him a nervous smile. "It was probably a joke."

"No, it wasn't," Skip said flatly. "Men engaged in clandestine activities don't joke or make idle threats."

"Don't worry." Some of her normal insouciance returned. She

tilted her head and plastered a faux-cheery smile on her face. "I'll watch my step."

She wriggled out of his hold and winked at him. "But if you hear I died in a crocodile attack, remind the authorities that I'm from Louisiana and have an above-average respect for large reptiles."

"Hadley," he growled.

"I'm only joking, Skip. I'm not stupid." She turned away, opened a narrow cupboard, and extracted a broom and a dustpan.

No, she wasn't stupid. But her tenacity and obsession with ferreting out the truth could still land her in danger. He had to impress on her how risky poking into a covert operation might be. Those men didn't operate under traditional rules of engagement.

He held out his hand for the dustpan, and she gave it to him. "Look, all I'm saying is forget about that story. Focus on something else instead."

"Journalists don't suppress the truth."

"Wartime censors do." He stooped and held the dustpan in place for her. "They won't allow you to include even a fraction of what the regular military is up to, much less special forces. You'd never be able to publish anything about them."

"We've already established I'm not planning to publish it." Snappy sparks smothered her soft Southern cadence.

He met her eyes. "Right. So there's no point in pursuing a story that will never see the light of day."

"Again, it's not about the story." Hadley tilted a chair so she could sweep underneath the table, then set the chair back down with a thump. "It's —"

"Your curiosity," he finished for her. "I know. But just this once, set it aside."

"I can watch out for myself." Hadley jutted her chin.

You're lousing things up again, Masterson. Infuriating her wouldn't persuade her to be cautious . . . or encourage her to go on a date with him.

Skip held up his hands in surrender. "I know you can take care of yourself. How about this? I'll drop the over-protectiveness if you'll agree to go to Green Island with me tomorrow."

"Well, if we're negotiating," Hadley said, putting her hand on her hip. "How about you help me finish cleaning in here while I think about it?"

"Deal." He exhaled. "What else do you have to do?"

"Put away the games, wipe down the tables, that sort of thing." She swiped the checker pieces into the proper game box and folded the board.

Skip shuffled a deck of cards and pushed them into a box. "Good thing the club isn't all that large."

"It's got most of what the fellas like, just a scaled-down version. It makes for a tight squeeze during our Wednesday night dances, but we make it work."

"Do folks dance around that?" He nodded at the ping-pong table.

She laughed. "No. We move it and the furniture outside to make more room."

Skip looked around and finally settled his gaze on the small platform stage at the far side of the room. He had assumed it was for skits or singers.

Hadley followed his gaze. "The twelve-piece soldier band we hire barely fits. They nearly blast us out of here, but everyone seems to have a good time."

"Fellas and I might still be here for the next one. Wednesdays, did you say?" He might pass the rest of his leave here and enjoy several Wednesday night dances. He could be sure that Hadley abandoned her notion of investigating the covert operation. Even better, he'd get to hold her close on the dance floor while he breathed in her exotic citrus perfume, stole kisses, and persuaded her to leave the loud club to canoodle on the beach under the brilliant tropical moon. His pulse rate accelerated.

Hadley pulled a dust cloth from her skirt pocket and wiped down the tables. "Your buddy Mike seems anxious to move on to

Brisbane. Can't imagine how unhappy he might be if you fellas stay here past this weekend."

Buddy. His buddy. His buddy, whom he had let down. Skip's throat constricted. He winced and clenched his fists against the pain of the familiar lump rising within it.

She arranged a pile of magazines into a cascading stack. "He must have a girl in Brisbane. Maybe someone he met earlier?"

"No."

She glanced up at the harsh bite in his tone, her head cocked and her eyes narrowed.

Dammit. He didn't want to have to explain about Pat. She would think he was callous — or worse, a coward. God knows he had replayed the maneuver in his head dozens of times since the attack on the barge. Mike had been right. No question, Skip had choked when it counted. He tightened his fingers around the Monopoly box.

Hadley pursed her lips. "Can't blame him if he finds Brisbane and the Gold Coast beaches more fun than this backwater. Were you fellas planning to stay there, or go on to Sydney? Everyone who's been there says it's marvelous. We had sailors in here last week who raved about the zoo there."

Pat had wanted to go to Sydney, had been especially keen on spending time at that zoo. Skip's throat burned. He stepped away from Hadley.

She knit her sculpted brows together and held out her hands for the game. "Skip?"

"I —" He broke off and gave her the box. Self-preservationist reserve warred with his restive impulse to unburden himself about Pat, about his comrades . . . about Chet.

His ping-ponging emotions skittered from one extreme to the other, until he seized on a half-assed excuse he knew was no good before it left his mouth. "I'm just a little flak-happy."

"No, I don't think that's it." Hadley stepped closer with the game box clutched to her chest and her eyes round with concern.

"Something else is wrong."

His neck seized with tension. He wanted nothing more than to confide in her but couldn't bear her thinking of him as a self-serving coward. "I — I can't talk about it."

"It's something to do with Mike, isn't it?" Hadley set the game atop the others and took Skip's hand. "He seems . . . in a bad way."

"Mike?" Skip pressed the fingers of his free hand against the back of his neck and pasted what he hoped passed as a nonchalant smile on his face. "Nah, he'll be just fine after this leave."

Truth was, Mike had struggled to function both in and out of the cockpit since Pat's death. Leo had insisted that Skip handling most of the flying duties was too dangerous and urged Skip to tell the squadron leader or the group doctor about Mike. But Leo only knew half the story. He and the others assumed that Mike was only experiencing prolonged grief over Pat's death. They didn't know about the rift born from Mike's reproach, nor that it had widened into a gulf of guilt. Covering for Mike and keeping his record clean was the least Skip could do.

"Look, it's getting late." Skip grabbed Lucy's leash and attached it to her collar. "I know you want to close the place, and I should take Lucy out to do her business."

He stood and backed toward the door with Lucy hopping along beside him. The worry swamping Hadley's eyes nearly undid him, but he kept going.

"Skip —"

"I'll see you tomorrow, Hadley." He opened the door and strode outside before he could change his mind. He would see her tomorrow — and then what? He had just given her a good reason to probe his secrets. His stomach clenched. He should tell her about Pat, about the *Arizona*, about his brother. About how he spelled nothing but trouble for those he loved.

No. It was better this way. If he allowed her to get too close, she might suffer some great catastrophe.

He shouldn't have dragged Mike and Leo all the way up here.

What on earth had he been thinking? Skip would never be able to satisfy Hadley's innate curiosity. He wasn't willing to reveal anything about himself, his past, or his problems.

A din of trilling and squawking from the mango trees surrounding the club would have startled him if Hadley hadn't already pointed out the colony of flying foxes hanging in them. As it was, he tightened his hold on Lucy's leash and led her past them. He didn't like bats, and these looked large enough to swoop down and carry off a wallaby.

"We'll leave tomorrow, Lucy."

That was the only answer. He had to escape.

***

Hadley fastened her two bronze ARC insignia pins to either side of her jacket collar, after measuring the requisite one-inch distance from the shoulder seam with her finger as they had learned to do while training in Washington — and hadn't done since.

Yet they required spit and polish today.

She stooped to check herself in the mirror to make sure the tips of her regulation white blouse's collar were completely tucked under, then straightened the Red Cross pin fastened at her throat. Her fingers trembled as she picked up her lipstick.

Simmer down. Last thing you need is smeared lipstick. She puckered her lips in the mirror and tilted her head from side to side to check them before smoothing her hair. Should they wear their caps? Mrs. Roosevelt would probably be in her full formal uniform, since she was traveling as a representative of the Red Cross.

Tingles goosed down Hadley's spine. She would soon greet the first lady. She couldn't believe she hadn't guessed the identity of their important guest before. The Australian newspapers had reported every move of Eleanor Roosevelt's official tour across the South Pacific, albeit a day or two later for security reasons.

Hadley jumped when Clara opened the door to their cramped

room off the upstairs porch she was sharing with Hadley for the night. Mrs. Roosevelt had been given the large veranda rooms Hadley and Clara normally occupied.

"Don't forget your cap," Clara said. "She'll be here any minute."

"I know, I know." Hadley opened her trunk, hoping her cap hadn't slipped to the bottom and been crushed. *Oh, thank goodness.* She found it in the velveteen tray where she kept her handkerchiefs, slips, and gloves. "Gloves too?"

"Not yet." Clara bit her lip and shook her head. "But definitely for dinner."

Hadley checked that her cap was straight, then smiled at Clara. "Ready?"

After learning late last night that Eleanor Roosevelt would be their guest for dinner tonight and would stay the night, Hadley and Clara had worked at a frantic pace. Hadley hadn't had even a moment to puzzle over Skip's abrupt departure from the club. Even if she had accepted the date with him to Green Island and their conversation hadn't veered from flirtatious to confusing, she would have had to cancel.

Clara had supervised work at the hotel, while Hadley did their marketing in Cairns. She had been the only person allowed to leave Yorkeys Knob today, because the club was official army property for the weekend and had been put under military guard. This meant Skip and his crewmates had also been confined here.

"Thank goodness we only have the fella with the wallaby and his two friends staying here right now. Mrs. Roosevelt is bringing an entourage of army and navy officers, so we'll need every other room we have," Clara said.

Hadley agreed and walked downstairs with Clara to prepare for their guests.

Skip, Mike, and Leo rose from the trio of chairs in the small front parlor when the women walked in. All three were attired in their formal *pinks and greens*.

"Hope it's all right that we're here," Skip said in his mellifluous voice, without even a hint of awkwardness. "We thought it would be rude for us to miss greeting the first lady, since we're also your guests this weekend."

"Of course. We're so sorry to have inconvenienced you, due to military security." Clara clapped her hands. "We know from the press clippings how much Mrs. Roosevelt enjoys meeting servicemen, so I'm sure she'll be delighted to see you."

Tires crunched on the gravel outside.

"Here we go." Hadley opened the door and beckoned for the others to follow her outside.

By the time they spilled out onto the porch, several generals and admirals had already climbed out of the lead car. One of the men opened the rear door of the second car and extended his hand to Mrs. Roosevelt.

She was much taller than she appeared in newsreel footage. *And . . . oh dear.* Hadley and Clara had worn their tropical uniforms, while Mrs. Roosevelt wore her formal winter blue. The first lady smiled at them as if she hadn't noticed, strode forward, and extended her hand.

Hadley wiped her sweat-slicked palms down her skirt and desperately wished she and Clara had opted to wear their gloves.

"I'm Hadley Claverie. We hope you'll enjoy your time at Yorkeys Knob, Mrs. Roosevelt."

Not that Hadley could call on personal experience — women in New Orleans didn't usually shake hands with one another or with men — but Mrs. Roosevelt's handshake was like a warm beignet dipped in café au lait. She immediately put Hadley at ease. Perhaps it was an innate attribute or a skill she had developed during her years in the public eye. Hadley unfurled her shoulders, and the tension from the previous twenty-four hours melted away.

"Oh, it's been splendid already. A company of engineers demonstrated barge landing exercises off your beach." Her blue eyes conveyed connection and conviviality as she held Hadley's gaze. She then shook hands with Clara before moving down the line to Skip.

"First Lieutenant Skip Masterson of the Fifth Air Force, ma'am. And these are my crewmates, Michael Flannery and Leo Kozlowski."

"I'm so happy to make your acquaintance, gentlemen." Mrs. Roosevelt shook their hands. "You're here on leave?"

"Yes, ma'am. We were forced to land here yesterday and repairs to the plane will take another day."

"Fifth Air Force," she said. "Are you based in New Guinea or northern Australia?"

"We operate out of Durand Airfield near Port Moresby," Skip said.

"That's in New Guinea," Leo added.

Nothing in Mrs. Roosevelt's expression signaled it, but Hadley suspected that the woman could pinpoint Port Moresby on a map more readily than most of the officers in her entourage.

The first lady nodded. "I had hoped to visit our troops in New Guinea, but I'm told that isn't possible. I look forward to hearing about conditions there from you gentlemen over dinner."

"Speaking of dinner, I assume you might enjoy time to rest and freshen up beforehand," Hadley said, leading the way to the front door. "We'll give you a short tour of the downstairs, then show you to your rooms. Our staff will bring in everyone's luggage."

The hotel's spartan furnishings and lack of amenities didn't seem to faze Mrs. Roosevelt. She commented on the striking ocean view visible from the narrow sitting room that ran the length of the hotel and nodded her approval when Hadley led her onto the back porch, where they had removed the partition that usually separated her sleeping quarters from Clara's to make more space. Thank God she didn't have to show Mrs. Roosevelt the outdoor privies, with their assortment of unwelcome wildlife. She opened the door to the brand-new bathroom.

"I'm afraid we only have one outdoor shower, but everything else you might need is right here." Hadley gestured toward the veranda. "Don't mind the lack of a screen. We find the night breeze refreshing. There's a mosquito bar for your bed, although the mosquitos aren't too awful this time of year."

"The engineers told us they detonated a chemical *bug bomb* last night in hopes of driving most of them away." Mrs. Roosevelt peered at the profusion of tropical flowers blooming in the garden off the porch visible through the decorative latticework.

Hadley nodded. "Yes, they've been setting off those bug bombs once or twice a week lately. I hope the military shares the device with the public after the war. Folks back home in New Orleans would sure welcome it."

"You're from New Orleans?"

"Yes, ma'am." Hadley rolled her thumb around a bead on her bracelet. "Apart from spending my college years at Millsaps in Jackson, I've lived there my whole life."

"I stopped in New Orleans on a tour a few years ago. The iron work in the French Quarter is stunning. I would have enjoyed staying longer so I could've seen more of your beautiful city." Mrs. Roosevelt removed her cap and set it on the dresser.

In 1937, while Hadley had been a sophomore at Millsaps College, the first lady had embarked on a lecture tour through the South. "I attended your lecture while I was at Millsaps. You spoke about the duties of citizenship and how the Depression had fostered national unity. You wore a lovely corsage of yellow jonquils."

"Why yes, I remember." Mrs. Roosevelt nodded. "I was in Jackson for a few hours. I only had time to rest, give my lecture, and dine with the governor. Our train left late that same evening for our next stop."

"You also gave a press conference at the Robert E. Lee Hotel."

"Yes." Mrs. Roosevelt tilted her head. "Yes, I remember now."

"I was a journalism student at the time, but I didn't have credentials."

"Are you a journalist now?" the first lady asked. "Or I should say, was that your job before you joined the Red Cross?"

Here was her chance. Could the first lady put in a word for her with the War Department? Well, even if she couldn't personally take that step, she could ask her husband, and he could get Hadley credentials.

Hadley lifted her chin and met Mrs. Roosevelt's eyes. "I am a journalist. I asked for credentials as a foreign correspondent when the war started, but my editor said it was too dangerous. He obtained them for a male reporter instead. So, I decided to go overseas via another channel and write and submit dispatches when and where I could."

"I admire your initiative and tenaciousness. Has your editor published what you've sent?"

"Yes." Hadley paused. "But —"

"Let me guess — he put them on the society pages?" The first lady lifted her brows.

Hadley couldn't contain her snort. "Yes, I've written a few pieces that would have landed on the front page if Ernie Pyle's byline had been attached to them. Mr. Dupre always reframes my pieces as human interest stories and relegates them to the fluffy social section."

"I'm sure you've heard that I host a press conference limited to female journalists at the White House each week when I'm in Washington."

"Oh my, yes." Hadley nodded. Of course she had heard about the unprecedented access the first lady accorded to women journalists. The opportunity had been enticing enough that Hadley had considered moving to either Washington or New York to pursue her career. Only her commitment to exposing injustice at home and her remaining connection with her old nanny, Fanelia, had kept her in New Orleans. The war had changed everything, however, and might yet further upend her trajectory. Hadley smiled. "I would love to be a part of it. Who knows . . . perhaps after the war?"

Would Eleanor Roosevelt still be in the White House then? Her husband would have to win re-election for an unprecedented fourth term next year, and no one knew how long the war might drag on. Yet many people wanted President Roosevelt's steady hand to see the nation through to the end of hostilities.

"How about this?" Mrs. Roosevelt smiled. "Give me half an hour, then come back with your notepad. I'll give you an exclusive interview. I daresay the Red Cross, under whose auspices I travel, would hate to lose you. But the interview might persuade your editor to obtain war correspondent credentials for you."

"Really?" Adrenaline surged through Hadley. She had hated being assigned here, had bitterly resented her isolation. Yet now she had a remarkable opportunity. At any other Red Cross club in Australia, the first lady would have been surrounded by people clamoring for her attention. And if Hadley had been sent to New Guinea, she wouldn't have met the woman at all. She fought to maintain her professional composure. Mrs. Roosevelt probably wouldn't appreciate a spontaneous, bone-crushing hug. "Thank you so much. My editor will be thrilled."

Hadley waved and shut the door behind her. Then she leaned against the wall under the staircase and exhaled. First things first. Before she retrieved her notepad and pencils or composed questions for her interview, she must find Clara and explain why she would be busy at this crucial time. Hadley was in charge, but she didn't need a resentful staff member, especially when Mr. Pittman, her supervisor, would arrive for dinner at any moment.

Clara would settle the officers into their rooms, while Enid and Madge got everything in the kitchen under control. Hadley drummed her fingers against the wall. All that remained was to set up the hors d'oeuvres and cocktails in the front parlor. They would serve drinks tonight, because with Mrs. Roosevelt in residence, Yorkeys was under the control of the army rather than the Red Cross. Clara could focus on that, if they could rely on Juan and Felipe to deliver the luggage to the correct rooms.

She climbed the stairs and hurried toward the men's guest rooms with her mind buzzing between potential interview questions and explanations for Clara. She rounded a corner and slammed headlong into Skip, who had just exited his room.

"Whoa, why the rush?" Skip grasped her upper arm to steady her. "Has the kitchen run out of Aeroplane Jelly?" He hummed the first few bars of the radio jingle.

"Very funny." Hadley fought to suppress her smile. He could be so damned charming. If it wasn't for his inexplicable moodiness, she would be a smitten kitten.

"So if the kitchen is happily creating enough Jell-O molds to impress our distinguished guests, what's got you in a dither?"

"I'm not in a dither," Hadley huffed. "I need to be sure the luggage deliveries are going well, so Clara can prepare for cocktail hour. Mrs. Roosevelt offered me an interview, but —"

"I'll deliver the luggage myself," Skip cut in. His eyes, no longer crinkled with amusement, bored into hers. "You have to do that interview. Does Clara have a list of the room assignments?"

"Yes." Hadley nodded. "But they only gave us ranks, with no names. Connecting the luggage with the right people might be a little tricky."

"I know all of them, so it won't be any trouble." Skip waved his arm to flag down Clara, who was exiting a room two doors down.

"Most of them are navy," Hadley said with a frown. "How do you know them?"

"Don't worry about it. I'll explain later." The hint of curtness in his voice needled Hadley, but his offer to help quashed her aggravation.

Clara was all too happy to pass the chore of moving luggage to Skip.

They headed downstairs. Clara hurried to the parlor, while Skip went outside to examine the suitcases and trunks piled near the front door.

Hadley strode upstairs into the room she would share with Clara tonight. She had fifteen minutes to brainstorm insightful questions for her exclusive interview with the first lady.

***

Hadley restlessly tapped her toes under the table and pushed peas around on her plate. She was torn between joining the swirling conversation and mentally composing her interview into a feature article. Her pulse hammered.

When the servers, navy sailors lent to the hotel for tonight's dinner, had first walked in bearing elaborate fruit salad Jell-O molds, she had inadvertently locked eyes with Skip across the table and had to press her fingers to her mouth to squelch a burbling titter of laughter.

The main course included the usual steak fillets, with mashed potatoes, peas, and baked pumpkin. Hadley's adrenaline levels still ran high from her interview with Mrs. Roosevelt, and she couldn't focus.

Clara couldn't have known, but seating Hadley across from Skip was proving to be a big distraction. She had never seen him dressed in his formal air corps uniform before. The cut of his jacket emphasized his broad shoulders and trim waist, and the color made his eyes look all the more green. As Fanelia might have said, the man cut a fine figure.

Mrs. Roosevelt sat two seats away on Hadley's right, and she kept her ears open for any new tidbits she might incorporate into her piece. She and Mrs. Roosevelt had discussed a wide range of topics, from Red Cross work overseas to troop morale in the Pacific. Her article would impress Mr. Dupre. Hadley was sure of it.

"Tell us, boys, how's the war in New Guinea?" General Buscombe cut open a dinner roll and spread butter on it. "Hear tell General Kenney has the enemy all but vanquished."

"I wouldn't say vanquished, sir." Skip cleared his throat. "But we're on the offensive."

"Well," General Buscombe said, "what do you need to get the job done?"

"More of everything, sir. More men, more supplies, more

planes. Most especially more planes." Skip's tone remained respectful, and he seemed at ease voicing his thoughts to a superior officer.

Hadley smiled at Skip and picked up the bowl of mashed potatoes. "More potatoes, Lieutenant?"

"No, thanks. But I will have more Jell-O fruit salad, if there's any left." He winked at her.

She choked back a laugh. Butterflies fluttered through her stomach. If only he were always this relaxed and charming.

"All I'm saying is, it won't hurt to get to the bottom of it," Admiral Timmons said in a low voice to General Nelson. "You know how it is."

"Ah, now, don't tell me you've fallen for all that talk." General Lowell's jesting tone and grin didn't completely disguise his disdain.

Pearl Harbor was in the news again back home, with some members of Congress demanding that the original congressional investigation be reopened.

"The president doesn't object to fact-finding," Mrs. Roosevelt commented. "But the timing strikes him as being politically-motivated. With the nation waging a two-front war, should we allocate precious resources to reexamining the work of the Roberts Commission?"

"Exactly," General Lowell murmured. "The commission acted with fitting urgency."

"Perhaps too fast. That's what concerns folks." Admiral Timmons leaned forward. "They put out the report a mere seven weeks after the attack, while emotions were still running high. In their haste, they may have missed some critical information."

Navy officers tended to believe they had received a disproportionate share of the blame for the Pearl Harbor attack.

General Lowell snorted. "You're using diplomatic phrasing to allege a cover-up. Convening a joint commission of military leaders from each branch after the war might be useful, but starting another congressional investigation during an election year? No thanks."

"I'm not suggesting the commission effected a cover-up, but the whole process smacks of convenience. Placing the blame on Admiral Kimmel, a principled commander with an impeccable record —"

"And General Short," General Nelson cut in. "Both branches received their fair share of blame."

"*Both* sides?" Admiral Timmons snorted. "I wouldn't go that far."

"Seems to me the destruction of the fleet makes the attack more personal for the navy." General Lowell cleared his throat. "Perhaps they're taking on more guilt and blame than the report assigned."

"The report was put out too fast, that's all we're saying. It may prove to be accurate, but re-examining the evidence in a more deliberate way can't hurt." Admiral Timmons speared a piece of steak with his fork.

Oh dear. Hadley bit her lip. If the conversation continued in this vein, they might soon arrive at the more controversial allegations circulating under the surface of American conversations about the war. Namely that President Roosevelt had been so determined for America to enter the war on the side of the Allies that he had ignored warnings about — or worse, had engineered — the attack on Pearl Harbor.

As Hadley's mind raced through the ways she might redirect their conversation onto safer ground, her gaze settled on Skip, who sat ramrod straight — and not in a way that suggested adherence to military decorum. No, he reminded her of a deer preparing to flee a predator.

Admiral Timmons jabbed his fork at Skip. "Your father agrees with me, doesn't he?"

"We haven't discussed it, sir." Skip gripped the stem of his water goblet.

Mrs. Roosevelt peered at him across the table. "Of course. *Masterson.* I couldn't place the name earlier. You're Admiral Masterson's son."

Admiral. So that's why Skip knew his way around a ship so well, why he spoke the navy slang with such ease, why he had a shellback card. As the son of a naval officer, he must have lived overseas during some part of his childhood. His independent nature must have led him to choose the army when the war broke out, thus avoiding charges of favoritism or comparisons with his successful father.

Skip nodded. "Yes, ma'am."

"The newspapers back home suggest your father is lobbying behind the scenes for Congress to reopen the investigation." Admiral Timmons raised his eyebrows.

Skip took a long, slow sip of water, his fingers white around the goblet stem. "The papers may know better than I do, sir."

"Come on, Masterson." Admiral Timmons set down his highball glass with a sharp clatter. "You must know your father well enough to guess his position."

"I truly can't say, sir." Taut cords stood out in Skip's neck. "I haven't spoken with him in over two years."

Hadley drew her brows together. Skip always deflected conversation away from his family and his past. Was his moodiness attributable to this family rift?

Skip set down his goblet and rubbed a circle over the face of his watch. Hadley intuited more than discomfort motivated his uncharacteristic fidgetiness. An unexpected protective impulse overrode Hadley's usual curiosity. She needed to steer the conversation in another direction.

Before she could open her mouth, Admiral White said, "How did Admiral Masterson's boy end up in the army?"

"The army was willing to put me in the air, sir." Skip compressed his lips into a thin line. Sweat glistened on his temples.

Admiral Timmons sipped his wine. "Naval aviators are in high demand. Your father might have —"

"I wouldn't have asked him to intervene," Skip interrupted. His cheeks flushed, and he cut his eyes toward the door. "Or allowed him to do so."

"We have lemon meringue pie for dessert," Hadley blurted out. "If everyone is done —"

"You must be the maverick in the family," Admiral White continued, as if Hadley hadn't spoken. "Your brother was a navy man."

Registering the admiral's use of the past tense, Hadley's pulse jumped in her neck. So Skip's brother had died, presumably in the war. She normally would press for more details, using the investigatory skills she had honed for years to put the puzzle of Skip Masterson together at last. Yet, everything in his unnaturally stiff posture, in his nervous fiddling with his watch, and especially in his wary expression, signaled vulnerability. If Mrs. Roosevelt hadn't been present, he probably would have already bolted.

Unsettled by this unfamiliar urge to squelch the conversation, Hadley fidgeted with her napkin. Maybe she should stand and repeat her announcement about dessert.

"I was a midshipman with your brother at the academy, Lieutenant," Captain Jensen said to Skip. "He was an outstanding leader and tops at everything. I was sorry to hear about his death."

Skip made an abrupt, jerky nod.

"That's right." Admiral Timmons leaned back in his chair. "He was serving on the *Arizona*, wasn't he?"

The *Arizona*. So he *had* died at Pearl Harbor. Perhaps the loss of his son was one factor spurring Admiral Masterson to press for a renewed investigation. Had any journalists made that connection? She certainly wouldn't write about it. Skip's family deserved privacy and respect.

"My husband knows your father well, dating back to when Franklin served as Assistant Secretary of the Navy." Natural warmth permeated Mrs. Roosevelt's voice. Her experience at putting people at ease was evident. "He called Admiral Masterson to express our sympathies."

"Thank you," Skip said softly. He twirled his water goblet, his eyes fixed on its stem.

Grief for his brother might account for Skip's capricious manner. Hadley's heart fluttered. God knew, she could empathize with the pain of mourning a loved one.

The door from the kitchen banged open, and navy servers carried in Enid's lemon meringue pies. A tart lemon scent, along with a hint of vanilla, wafted into the room.

"The pies smell delicious. But if you'll excuse me, I believe I'll pass on dessert." Skip pushed back his chair, stood, and inclined his head toward Mrs. Roosevelt. "It was an honor to dine with you, ma'am. I hope you enjoy the remainder of your tour."

Though he kept his voice even, his stiff spine signaled tension. Hadley gripped the edge of her chair and fought against the irrational urge to follow him and offer comfort.

For crying out loud, you're having dinner with the first lady of the United States. Missing even a minute of available time with Mrs. Roosevelt would be nuts. She could find Skip later, after he had collected himself. Intruding now would only backfire. She needed to give him space. Besides, Enid's lemon pies *were* delicious.

"Masterson went through the academy too, didn't he?" Admiral White gestured toward the door after Skip left.

"Yep, he was a few years behind me and his brother Chet. Enrolled while we were still there and garnered quite a reputation as a trouble-maker." Captain Jensen shrugged. "Possible he was expelled. He wasn't wearing the ring."

Hadley stared down at her pie. So she hadn't been too far off the mark in pegging Skip as a hell-raiser.

"If he couldn't toe the line, I'd wager that's why he couldn't get into our aviation program." Admiral Timmons cast a self-satisfied smile at General Lowell. "No matter who his father is, we have the highest standards for the men we train."

"Has he mentioned graduating from the Naval Academy?" Captain Jensen asked Mike and Leo.

They exchanged glances and then shook their heads.

"Skip never talks about his family or his past," Leo added.

"Skip. Right, I couldn't remember his first name, but that's what Chet called him. They were as different as night and day, but the best of friends. Chet doted on his little brother."

Best of friends. An older brother who doted on him. Hadley's heart constricted. She abruptly came to her feet. "Excuse me. I'll go see what's holding up the coffee."

Hadley poked her head into the kitchen. "Madge, be sure to send those fellows in with the coffee soon."

"Sure." Madge swiped a strand of hair off her forehead and pointed toward a tray holding a sugar bowl and creamer set. "Will you take that in, while I transfer the coffee to the servers?"

"Sorry, but I need to go to the loo." Hadley smiled in apology, walked down the hallway, and approached the back door. Skip might have gone up to his room, but she decided that he probably would have opted to seek more privacy by retreating someplace outdoors.

She grabbed one of the flashlights they kept by the door, stepped outside, and shut the door behind her. She paused to allow her eyes to adjust to the darkness, then clicked on her flashlight and aimed it toward the ground. Snakes and large tropical rats were active at night.

Squeaky chirps from the flying foxes feasting on ripening mangoes mixed with the rhythmic crash of waves on the beach as Hadley crossed the lawn. She soon found the MP who had suffered the misfortune of being assigned near the privies.

"Did a man come out here a few minutes ago?" Hadley asked.

He gestured toward the beach. "Yeah. Said he was gonna go down toward the water."

Hadley thanked him, gave the privies a wide berth, and followed the path. Alert for any slithering movements, she carefully picked her way through the vegetation beyond the high tide line.

Once she cleared the scrubby grassland, she removed her shoes, curled her toes in the cool sand, and turned in a slow half circle to scan the beach. She finally spotted Skip sitting on a coconut log about fifty yards away. Shoulders slumped forward and arms resting on his knees, his silhouette conveyed evident anguish.

A sharp sting of pain stabbed through her. She drew in a shaky breath and hurried toward him.

"Skip," she said quietly as she approached the log.

He shifted his clasped hands but didn't turn his head.

Even so, Hadley believed he had heard her. She shifted the flashlight to the hand holding her shoes and gently touched his shoulder. Leery of initiating conversation too soon, she squeezed his shoulder and lowered herself onto the log beside him. She turned off the flashlight and set it and her shoes beside her. Then she straightened and pressed her shoulder against the solid warmth of his arm. Her heart contracted.

Swelling waves undulated against the shore, roaring with momentum before subsiding with a low burble. The ocean was impenetrably dark, with only the surf's white foam faintly visible. A cool breeze ruffled her hair. She tucked a few wayward strands behind her ear and impulsively reached for Skip's hand, clasping it tightly with her own. His fingers were firm and warm, and she circled her thumb over them.

If she had learned anything during her eight months overseas, it was how to comfort a grieving man. But she had never held hands with any of the others, nor had she internalized their suffering. An ache built in her gut, and her heart seized at the intensity of emotion emanating from him as they sat in silence, listening to the crash of the surf.

After awhile, he loosened his grip on her hand, his spine lost its strained stiffness, and he looked less like a trapped animal poised to flee.

"Didn't mean for you to follow me out here and miss spending time with Mrs. Roosevelt." Gratitude perfused his statement, despite his gruff tone.

Hadley squeezed his hand. "I had a whole hour with her, thanks to you. I've got plenty of material to write a fabulous interview."

"Good." He nudged his shoulder against the Red Cross service patch on her uniform sleeve. "Maybe now your editor will get you the armband you've wanted to wear all along."

"Hmm, maybe."

"Can't do much better than interviewing the first lady."

"A woman interviewing another woman, even if she is the first lady, may still not merit the front page. Especially in the South." Hadley drew circles in the sand with her toes. "Oh, he might send me a congratulatory letter. But I'd be foolish to expect credentials."

"That's bushwa."

"Thanks." She flashed him a rueful smile. He wanted a traditional wife and home-life, but her heart still fluttered at his support of her career dreams. "I might try my luck somewhere else. After the war."

"Can't you submit your interview to another paper?" He turned and met her eyes for the first time since he had fled the dining room. "One that might give it the due it deserves?"

"I could . . . if I'm ready to commit to leaving New Orleans." She bit her lip. Reporters credentialed to the AP or the UPI got wider coverage than journalists linked to a specific news outlet. Hadley didn't have credentials for any paper or service. Only courtesy and her desire to grease the wheels for a return to her post-war position dictated that she send her material to the *Times-Picayune*. Skip's point was worth considering. If she changed her mind about returning to New Orleans, perhaps she could act as a stringer or a roving journalist.

Skip studied her. "What's holding you there? Your family? Or a fella who might return after the war?"

His last question pulsed with odd energy despite his casual delivery. He wasn't asking out of idle curiosity.

"I'm holding hands with you." Hadley emphasized the point by squeezing his fingers again. "And we did a good bit more than hold hands at Surfer's Paradise. Or have you forgotten?"

"I have most definitely not forgotten, Miss Scarlett." His lips tugged up on one side, and he locked his gaze with hers. "In fact, I very much hope to repeat that experience."

Her breath caught in her throat as he scooted closer and gently traced his finger along her jawline. Everything about him — the glint of his dark stubble in the moonlight, the warmth and intensity of his pale eyes, the hint of scotch from his Rob Roy cocktail on his breath — intoxicated her. If she leaned in, he would kiss her, and Hadley desperately wanted his devouring, scorching kisses again. Truth was, she wanted a hell of a lot more than kissing.

Skip's vulnerability, in addition to the lurking sentries, checked her impulses. He must have also remembered their unseen companions, because he dropped his hand and pulled back.

"You didn't answer," he murmured. "A fella back home or no?"

"No," she whispered. *No, just you. You're the one who sends me.* She might only be a wartime fling. He wanted a traditional home — and now she knew why. With his father being a naval officer, Skip and his family had probably moved many times during his childhood. He wanted a settled life after the war, and she could hardly blame him.

He met her eyes. "So what's keeping you in New Orleans?"

"Fanelia," she said, the name slipping out before she could stop it.

He inclined his head. "Is she one of your sisters?"

"No." Hadley heaved a deep sigh. "This is going to play right into your *Miss Scarlett* nonsense. She was my nanny. My —"

She broke off. She'd been about to say that Fanelia was her best friend, but that wasn't accurate somehow. Fanelia was mother-teacher-confidante-and-mentor all rolled into one. Or rather, she had been. Hadley looked at Skip and then down at the beaded bracelet on her left wrist. Fanelia had given it to her on her tenth birthday.

"She was everything to me for many years."

"Was?"

"We, um . . . fell out of touch." Hadley wasn't prepared to share the entire story, to confide all that had transpired. Too much pain, too much regret, too much cowardice.

Her reticence to unburden herself sparked another surge of empathy inside her for Skip. She understood his desire to hide his vulnerabilities and grieve in solitude. His pain was raw and recent and had resulted in the moodiness that had confounded her until now. But she had suppressed her emotions for so long, she didn't know how to voice them.

Little by little, the bird makes its nest, as Fanelia would have said. With time, everything is possible.

"What about you?" Anxious to avoid any more probing questions Hadley turned the conversation another direction. "You've never said where you grew up, but you must have moved around a lot if your father was a naval officer."

"Yep." He cleared his throat. "We were never in one place all that long."

"Having to start over so often must have been hard. Especially in high school."

"Actually, those years were stable for me, since my parents shipped me off to Western Military Academy, a boarding school north of St. Louis. Guess they thought the place might give me a healthier respect for following rules."

"And did it?"

"What do you think?" His eyes twinkled.

She laughed. "Didn't take, huh?"

"Nope." Skip's mouth curved with that same sultry grin that always melted her heart.

She grinned. "Did you continue flouting authority in college?"

"Proudly. But unfortunately, the Naval Academy has a place for troublemakers — the *bottom of the class*."

"Someone has to be last." She shrugged.

He nodded. "We all got the same diploma, best I can tell."

"If you graduated from the Naval Academy . . ." Hadley let her words trail away. Didn't men who attended military academies have a service commitment?

The relaxed amusement vanished from his eyes. "Yes, I served in the navy. For a while."

Hadley tightened her hold on his hand and squelched the questions his divulgence raised. His tense countenance told her to steer their conversation in yet another direction. She swallowed. "After you left the dining room, Captain Jensen mentioned that he graduated the same year as your brother. Mike or Leo might ask you about it."

Skip made a non-committal noise.

"Your sister who sent the pickles — does she live in Washington with your parents?"

"How do you know my folks live in Washington?" He narrowed his eyes.

"Your father is hard to miss. He's received a good bit of news coverage." That was something of an understatement. The national papers often featured news about Admiral Masterson's campaign to launch a new investigation into the attack on Pearl Harbor.

Skip jerked his hand free and stood. "Yeah, and he doesn't need more. Neither does my sister."

"Oh, Skip, I would never write about your family." Hadley scrambled to her feet. "Of course not. I only wondered — if your sister is still at home, she must be a comfort to your parents, with you in the service."

"You think my brother's death is behind my father's clamor for a new inquiry."

Hadley reached for him, but he side-stepped her. She had only wanted to reassure him that she had no intention of investigating his father's motivations or using his family's tragedy as an angle for a story. Yet before she could say anything else, he grabbed her flashlight, clicked it on, and pressed it into her hand.

"You won't get a scoop from me." He turned and vanished into the night.

CHAPTER ELEVEN

October 22, 1943

Kila Kila Drome

Port Moresby, New Guinea

Hadley pushed her hair out of her face and gripped one of the handles on the big galvanized steel can, while Bizzy grabbed the one on the other side. "One . . . Two. . . Three . . . Now!"

With straining muscles, they shifted the can sloshing with eight gallons of lemon cordial onto the waiting rolling cart.

"Where are those boys?" Bizzy mopped her face with a handkerchief.

The local boys hadn't yet arrived, but Hadley and Bizzy needed counter space to mix more cans of cordial before the morning sun overheated the water.

"I'm sure they'll be along any minute." Hadley peered out the hut's open window at the sliver of pale pink light along the horizon that hinted at sunrise. "It's not daybreak yet."

"Hope JoJo and Stella turn up soon too." Bizzy measured more sugar and poured it into a waiting pot. "The fellas will be pouring in here any second."

JoJo and Stella had stayed behind in Port Moresby to use the doughnut machine at the *Shangri-La* club. The women usually served traditional Red Cross fare of coffee and doughnuts to the men leaving on early morning missions here at Kila Kila, the field closest to Port Moresby. Then each afternoon, they took their Clubmobiles out to the surrounding airfields to meet the returning crews with ice-cold lemon cordials and cookies. Hadley had avoided serving the men at Durand. Seeing Skip Masterson always ended with hurt feelings for one or both of them.

Tires crackled on the crushed-coral road leading to the *Coconut Grove* canteen. Hadley opened the door and stepped back to permit Stella and JoJo, each carrying wire trays laden with doughnuts, to come in. "Are there more out there?"

"Loads. Last night's shift left us a note — today is an all-out effort." JoJo pulled a set of tongs from a drawer and transferred doughnuts to the waiting platters as two young local boys stole quietly through the door.

"Good morning. *Plis kisim wara insait tins.*" Hadley smiled at the boys and gestured toward the remaining empty jugs. She had only been in New Guinea for a short time, but she had already picked up enough Pidgin words and phrases for rudimentary communication.

The boys smiled, revealing teeth stained red with betel nut, and each picked up a jug and hurried outside to fill it with water. How could those scrawny boys carry ten-gallon canisters sloshing with water?

Hadley stepped outside and walked around to the open rear door of the Clubmobile. She hopped inside and shifted the full trays into stacks at the edge of the compartment.

"Hey, doll," a man called out. "Mind if I grab a couple of those?"

Hadley turned, her reflexive rebuff dying on her lips.

Captain Phil Blanchard, a fighter pilot, had become Hadley's good friend after she had arrived in New Guinea. Tall, dark, handsome, and sporting an infectious grin, Captain Blanchard hailed from her home state of Louisiana. He had worked as a photojournalist for the *Houston Chronicle* before the war and had opted to enlist rather than seek correspondent credentials. Phil understood Hadley's desire to pursue every lead that came her way. Moreover, he retained his investigative bent and passed along tips and observations whenever he could.

"You have any scoop to barter for a couple of sinkers?" Hadley ignored his proffered hand and hopped down from the compartment.

Phil dropped his hand and pulled a pack of Lucky Strikes out of his shirt pocket. He leaned against the *Pacific Prowler's* back door, shook out a cigarette, and lit up. "How about a chance for a first-hand scoop?"

"Direct your smoke away from the doughnuts, will you?" She frowned at his cigarette. "And what do you mean by *first-hand?*"

"Said you wanted to see more of New Guinea, right?" He blew a silver smoke ring away from the Clubmobile and tipped the ashes onto the ground.

Another expedition to a native village? Sail to one of the islands near the harbor for a picnic? Or hike to a swimming hole? In the three weeks since she had arrived in Port Moresby, Hadley had already accompanied soldiers on several such recreational outings. "I'm hoping to get closer to the *action*, yes."

Having finally reached New Guinea, Hadley had been disappointed to discover that life in Port Moresby was even more slower-paced than that in Cairns. The Fifth Air Force had already shifted most of its combat forces to the newly opened airfields at Nadzab and Dobodura on the northern coast. *Moresby* only meant more mud, more mosquitos, more malaria.

Probing the secrets of the *House on the Hill* outside Cairns would have been far more exciting than anything she had seen here. Hadley had never gotten a chance to pursue that lead.

"You're in luck. Going up at first light to do some coastal observations," Phil said. "My F-4's out of commission, so they've assigned me a little Grasshopper. It's got two seats, and if I take along someone else, I can also get photos. My tent-mate had too much jungle juice last night, so he's useless. You game?"

Hadley's pulse quickened. Skip had said that photo reconnaissance pilots were the war's unsung heroes, flying without escort, without wingmen, without weapons. Skip's high praise for those pilots gave Hadley the impression that he might have preferred that line of duty. She supposed men with backgrounds in photography were assigned to the reconnaissance squads. The pilots focused on flying, evading enemy fighters, and dodging anti-aircraft fire, all while searching for the mission's photographic objectives, and if one flew solo in an F-4 — a P-38 fighter with camera equipment in place of armament — he also took photographs using the cockpit control buttons.

Even flying along New Guinea's southern coast, well away from any hot action, would give her an incredible perspective for writing a profile of the daring pilots whose exploits received so little coverage.

"Oh, golly, yes," she said. "But I don't know anything about professional cameras."

"You won't be using the fancy mounted cameras in my F-4. Just my Graflex."

"Well . . ." She glanced at the two local boys as they passed by carrying water-filled canisters and was reminded of a much bigger obstacle. How could she get away when they were so busy? She jerked her thumb toward the canteen. "I'm supposed to work here all morning."

"We'll only be up about an hour." Phil took another drag on his cigarette.

Hadley's heart raced. An opportunity like this might not come around again. Surely she could concoct a reason to leave for an hour or so. She met his eyes. "You're sure there's no trouble with you taking a woman along?"

"Don't need to file a flight plan to take up a Piper Cub," he said, "and no one's apt to notice anyway."

Hadley bit her lip. Red Cross rules prohibited them from taking unauthorized flights. Her field director, Luella Brinkman, would definitely put the kibosh on Phil's plan. But he was only taking up a little Piper Cub that couldn't fly all that fast or far — and definitely couldn't go over the Owen Stanley mountains. She wouldn't be in any danger.

"Okay, I'll go. I'll make an excuse and meet you at the plane."

"It's in the second closest revetment." Phil pointed toward the clusters of planes, some no more than a half mile away. "Walk toward the Stokes hills, and you'll see it."

"Okay." She waved her hand over her olive-drab long-sleeved shirt and pants, paired with her lace-up GI boots. Thank goodness she had put on her long pants this morning rather than the culottes the women favored on hot days. "Is this all right?"

"That'll do fine. We aren't going too high, so you won't need a jacket. Do you have a scarf or something you can use to tie your hair back? Gets windy up there."

"I don't think so." Hadley patted her pockets and shook her head. "If I see one inside, I'll grab it."

He nodded.

She gestured toward the doughnut-laden wire trays. "Give me a hand, will you?"

"Sure thing." Phil stacked the trays in her outstretched hands and closed the Clubmobile's rear door for her. "I can't wait long, so hurry."

"I will." She scurried toward the canteen, where another man opened the door for her, and threaded her way into the crowded space. At least double the usual number of men milled around inside.

Must be a big strike force going out. "Excuse me, coming through with hot sinkers."

Several men stepped forward to take the heavy trays and set them on the counter.

JoJo flipped open the top of each tray. "Any more sinkers in the Clubmobile?"

"No, that's it," Hadley said.

Stella and JoJo each scooped up a platter from the serving table and used tongs to add fresh doughnuts to the near-empty plates.

"I'll help Bizzy with the coffee." Hadley strode over to the coffee pots and caught sight of the serving table decor. The women had knotted brightly colored scarves over twine to create decorative banners that hung from each table. She edged around one, unknotted a scarf, and stuffed it into her pocket. As she straightened, Skip Masterson walked in. Her pulse skipped a beat. He wasn't based at Kila Kila, so why was he here?

She turned away. Maybe he hadn't seen her. She cut around a circle of men dunking doughnuts into their coffee mugs and hurried toward the coffee pots.

"Good morning." Skip stopped her with a hand on her shoulder.

She blew out a soft breath and turned to face him, biting back the "why are you *here*" on the tip of her tongue. "Well hello, Skip. I thought only fighters took off from here."

"My squadron's been assigned a recon role today and our briefing was here, so . . . ." He put out his hands, palms-up, and lifted his shoulders.

She tensed. Last thing she needed was for him to see her getting into a plane.

"Be sure to get some doughnuts before you leave." Hadley pasted a charming smile on her face. "We'll be waiting with cookies and lemon cordials when you get back."

Painting an idyllic picture of post-mission treats was the official Red Cross line Hadley typically avoided. She had served doughnuts to far too many men who didn't make it back.

Skip made a jerky motion with his hand, as though to grab her sleeve and hold her back. A flush crept up his neck. "Hadley, look—"

"I've got to go help the others. Maybe I'll see you later." She patted his arm. "The cookies are oatmeal raisin today."

She turned away and spotted Bizzy standing on her tiptoes to add coffee grounds to the filter in one of the big pots so she could brew another batch. Feigning illness, some tropical malady, would be the most plausible reason for Hadley to cut her canteen shift short.

Hadley tapped Bizzy on the shoulder. "Let me finish this. My stomach's cramping something awful, so I probably shouldn't touch the food."

"Uh oh." Bizzy turned to look at her, and her pale brows contracted. "You do look a bit pale. You should go see the base doctor."

"But —"

"No, no. The fellas will soon be on their way out. We can manage. You go on." Bizzy shooed her toward the door.

Hadley flashed her a wan smile. "Thanks. See you back at our tent later."

Phil had promised they would only be gone about an hour. Hadley would be back and lounging on her cot well before the others returned for their mid-morning rest.

***

Hadley secured the scarf in a tight knot under her chin. "Ready."

"Not quite." Phil pulled a parachute pack from his gear stacked on the ground and helped her fasten and adjust the harness so the pack sat across her chest. Then he explained how to use it in case of an emergency. "See? Easy."

"What are the odds I'll need it?" Hadley ran her finger along the ripcord handle.

"None. But I'd definitely be in hot water if I took you up without one."

The pack wasn't uncomfortable, but it weighed more than she had imagined. Phil put his own pack on and bent to retrieve his rifle. He looped the gun strap over his shoulder. He also wore a sidearm in a shoulder holster and had a sheathed hunting knife on his belt.

Hadley raised her eyebrows. "Will you need all that weaponry today?"

"Standard procedure." He tilted his head and grinned. "Might come in handy if we see any cassowaries."

She crinkled her nose. "They don't fly, do they?"

"Nope," Phil said cheerfully. "So we shouldn't see any on this flight."

Hadley rolled her eyes and waved her hand toward the plane's fabric-covered body. "Those guns might weigh more than the plane."

Phil laughed. "She's sturdier than she looks, trust me." He pointed out a steel step attached to the fuselage beneath the two seats. "That should give you enough boost."

The olive green two-seated L-4 or *Grasshopper* was open on one side, with the door dropped down against the fuselage and the window pulled up against the wing. Hadley grabbed one of the wing struts for balance, wedged her right foot into the stirrup, and swung herself into the rear observation seat. Once she was settled, Hadley adjusted the pack, buckled her lap belt, and glanced back over her shoulder. *So far, so good.*

No other crews were near enough to spot her. She had run most of the way here from the canteen, anxious to put distance between herself and anyone who might report her.

Phil pulled a camera from the front seat and looped the strap over Hadley's neck. Between the parachute and the camera, she had almost no clearance between her chest and the back of his seat.

He pointed out the camera's various functions. "See? Not too complicated."

"Hmmm, I'll do my best." Hadley held up the camera and peered through the rangefinder.

He laughed. "Whatever you get is bound to be an improvement

over what my soused tent-mate would've managed."

"How will I know what you want me to photograph?"

Phil tapped his fingers against the edge of the front seat. "I'll wave my hand." He demonstrated with an overhand circling motion. "And I'll try to point where you should aim. You won't hear me for the wind unless . . ."

He rummaged around in a compartment up front and lifted out a device made of rubber tubing. "Aha. It's primitive, but it might work all right."

"What is it?" She frowned.

Phil handed her two lengths of tubing, each with round metal fittings on their ends. "Tuck these over each ear under your scarf. I can talk into the other end, and if we're lucky, you'll hear at least some of what I'm saying."

"All right." Hadley slid the earpieces over her ear and pulled her scarf tight to hold them in place. She draped the talking end of the tube over Phil's seat. "Where are we going again?"

"Brass wants to build a new airstrip down the coast to give the fighters a shorter path over the Owen Stanleys. We'll take photos of the area. Nothing too exciting," he warned. "But it's a different perspective, so it might give you a fresh angle."

The Allies had no combat troops stationed along the southern coast except for Port Moresby and the occasional Australian outpost. She wouldn't see any ground force activity or enemy camps, but she could include a tagline that read *From the Air Over the Jungles of New Guinea*, which should automatically elevate its interest level.

Phil flipped a switch in the cockpit, then walked to the front of the plane and manually spun the prop a few times. The engine sputtered to life.

After slinging his Thompson gun over his shoulder, Phil hoisted himself into the front seat and shut the door. He released the brake, and the plane lurched forward.

"Shouldn't you close the window?" Hadley yelled over the engine noise.

Phil grabbed the end of the Gosport tube. "Nah, it's warm up there. Plus, you can take clearer photos with the window up. Can you hear me?"

"Yes," she called out.

"That may change once we're airborne, but it's a good sign. Here we go."

He steered the bumping Grasshopper along the rough perimeter road and lined up at the end of the runway.

The crystal-clear water of Joyce Bay, bathed in shimmering pinks and lavenders of the unfolding light of dawn, rippled peacefully on Hadley's left. The green rounded hills of Stokes Range, topped by soft puffy clouds, were visible to her right. Phil pushed the stick forward. The plane picked up speed and bobbed toward the end of the runway.

Hadley's heart stood on tiptoes as they lifted into the air. Her first flight ever had been on the noisy C-47 transport that had flown them from Australia to Port Moresby three weeks ago. Flying in the Grasshopper was more intimate and exhilarating. Warm wind whipped at her face and fluttered her shirt sleeves. With each jounce, lift, or dip in altitude, her stomach flipped.

They climbed steadily higher, flying over the bay, hugging the jagged coastline.

"Testing, testing." Phil's tinny voice through the tube startled Hadley. "Let me know if you can hear me."

The chest parachute and camera restricted her mobility, but she was able to stretch forward far enough to tap her fingers against his shoulder.

"Oh good, it's working. We'll continue to head west. Enjoy the ride."

They weren't very high up and yet the dark green expanses of jungle pressing against the sandy beaches below looked so different from this vantage point. The men had said that the forests near Moresby didn't qualify as jungle, but now she begged to differ.

The luminescent pinks and lavenders of early dawn soon gave

way to vibrant purple backlit by the melon-orange rays of the sun, while white clouds of mist puffed over the dense jungle and larger clouds drifted lazily over the hills. Hadley resisted the urge to take pictures of the wondrous vista — even color film couldn't capture the shifting kaleidoscope of colors and patterns over the water, forests, and mountains before them. Not to mention that Phil wouldn't like her to waste his film on nature photography.

Her resolve to preserve film for the area of interest to the military planners was further tested when she spotted a pod of dolphins swimming in the water below. She tapped Phil's shoulder and pointed down toward the water.

"Beauties, aren't they?" Phil said as he stair-stepped them down in altitude until they flew just above the frolicking dolphins.

Hadley leaned out the open window for a closer look. The dolphins' sleek, silvery bodies shot through the water, rising and falling in tandem with one another and occasionally making spectacular leaps through the churning white foam atop the purple-tinged water.

"See if you can get a picture. Good way for you to test the camera."

Hadley brought the camera to her face, leaned out as far as she could, and positioned the rangefinder away from the wing. That alone, she discovered, wasn't easy to do in the bobbing plane. Catching the dolphins in a jump would be impossible. She framed the graceful creatures in the viewfinder as they made several tandem jumps, trying to discern the pattern of their actions. She finally depressed the shutter to snap a picture but with little confidence that she had captured anything more than the glinting surface of the Coral Sea.

"Just take one or two shots, okay? Photo intelligence guys won't be pleased if I show up with nothing more than photos of dolphins," Phil called out. He pulled back on the stick and ascended back to their previous altitude, then banked the plane closer to the coast.

They passed over inlets, streams, swamps, and raging rivers
while local men plied the waterways in wooden canoes, perhaps
spear-fishing. Seeing the landscape from the air confirmed the
daunting challenges faced by airmen who ditched their planes on
land and attempted to return to their base on foot. Following the
coastline, while reasonable in theory, would involve crossing a body
of water every half-mile or so, many of them wide, muddy and
running high and fast. Now Hadley understood why the men
proclaimed that ditching a plane into the shark-infested waters of the
sea had better survival odds.

Phil nosed the plane down and flew across a white-sand beach
before cresting a range of small hills similar to those surrounding the
coast near Port Moresby.

"Showtime," he called out as he pulled back on the throttle.
"We need pictures of this valley. Get as many different angles as you
can. I'll fly slow."

Hadley leaned out the window, once again angling the camera
away from the wing. Wind whipped her face, while Phil crisscrossed
the flat valley nestled between the coastal hills and what must be the
lower range of the Owen Stanley mountains on the interior side.

"Got plenty of pictures for the intelligence fellas?" he finally
asked.

Hadley leaned forward and made the okay sign near his face.

"You're tops. We'll head back now." He banked toward the
cluster of hills separating the valley from the coast, pitching the nose
high enough to cross them.

After cresting yet another series of rolling hills, Phil flew east.
Bright rays of early morning sunshine half-blinded Hadley before he
changed course by a few degrees.

Between the gaps in the hills, she glimpsed water, sparkling and
vibrant turquoise under the morning sun. They would soon fly over
the coast.

Phil pushed the stick to take them over the final cluster of
coastal bluffs, and something like a flash bulb popped in the air

above them. Had it come out of the glaring sun?

"Fuck!" Phil screamed. "Get down *now*!"

Hadley's heart jumped. With the stick and rear seat controls, her parachute, and the camera, she had no room to maneuver. Ducking behind Phil's seat was the best she could do.

She turned her head and looked up — at a plane with a bright red circle painted under its wing. A *Japanese* plane. Hadley gasped, and her muscles seized. What chance did this tiny Grasshopper have against a Japanese fighter?

"Grab the stick and hold it steady!" Phil had dropped the Gosport tube, but his loud words carried over the roar of the engine. "I'm gonna shoot the bastard."

Hadley straightened and grabbed the rear seat stick. Sure, she had seen him fly the plane, but she had never expected to be put to the test herself.

Buck up. Phil will take control if we're about to crash. She gritted her teeth. If she were a real pilot, she could turn the plane to help him hit the enemy fighter. But as it was, she would be lucky to keep them aloft.

She moved the stick to the left, and the plane rolled violently. Her stomach flipped.

No, no, no. She edged the stick back to the right but over-corrected, and the plane listed that direction. She fought to equalize it and level out.

Phil kicked the door open so he could lean out and aim his rifle at the other plane. Hadley's erratic attempts to level the plane obviously weren't helping.

"Keep her steady," he yelled. "You can do it."

Steady, steady, steady. She gripped the stick and held it tight.

"Hold it right there, I've got him in my sights!"

Boom. Boom.

The enemy plane swooped. Phil had either hit it, or it had mechanical issues. Either way, the pilot couldn't evade them or attack.

Boom. Boom.

A gust of wind carried a whiff of gunpowder into Hadley's nostrils. She hung on to the stick as Phil aimed again. *Please let him hit his mark.*

A swelling roar of engines from behind them sent Hadley's heart lurching into her stomach. Oh God, had the enemy pilot radioed for help? She shot a look over her shoulder.

Three planes soared toward them in a steep dive from altitude. Her stomach swooped in time with their bobs in altitude. She had spent time at various airfields, but she couldn't identify specific planes, especially from a distance.

Phil looked up, shook his gun in the air, and whooped.

They must be ours. Tension in Hadley's shoulders eased.

He slid back to his seat and yelled, "My control!"

She let go of the stick and released the breath she had been holding. Phil banked to the left to take them out of the path of the diving planes.

Since Hadley was no longer struggling to keep the plane steady, she leaned sideways and eyed the Japanese plane. Something was definitely wrong with it — and whatever it was, its situation was about to turn more dire. The diving Allied planes bore down on the crippled enemy plane with their engines whining in a shrill crescendo. Then the lead plane, flying only a few hundred feet above the water, sprayed a hailstorm of machine gun fire into the enemy's cockpit, sending the plane into a tight death spiral.

Hadley squinted at the circling Allied planes and then peered down at the water. No sign of the pilot, but the tail section of the Japanese plane, emblazoned with the vivid red circle, jutted out of the water at an odd angle.

She lifted the camera with trembling hands, centered the red circle or *Rising Sun* in the rangefinder, and depressed the shutter. Moments later, as it sunk below the waves, she snapped one last photo.

"Case you didn't know, those were our B-25s," Phil said,

having picked up the Gosport tube. "Must've gone up for a check-ride. Sure as hell glad they turned up when they did."

Hadley was relieved she couldn't verbally respond. Flying a plane in combat, however briefly, was more excitement than she had bargained on.

"Heading back to base." Phil turned the plane toward the coastline.

If dolphins frolicked in the water below or friendly locals waved at them on their return trip, Hadley didn't notice. Her mind vacillated between scanning the sky for other unwelcome planes and formulating the angle she would use while writing her piece about today's fierce excitement. Now that they were no longer in peril, she allowed herself to exult in the experience. She could now write one hell of a story

Shame she couldn't use her real name. Her family would lose their minds, and more importantly, if someone in the Red Cross read it, they would ship her home. No, she would have to give the impression that the piece had been written by a man with *Anonymous* as the byline. Tricky part would be explaining why *she* had forwarded the piece to Dupre.

Now might be a good time for her to send the story to another outlet. If she mailed it anonymously, that might work. But if the outlet declined to publish it, they wouldn't send her a rejection note, and she wouldn't know she needed to resubmit it to another service. Writing as *Anonymous* also wouldn't allow her to take credit for it. Showing her carbon copy after the war, however, would be one way around that problem.

"Looks like our B-25 friends plan to escort us home," Phil said.

Hadley looked out the open right window. Three planes flew in wing formation close behind them, much more slowly than they would normally fly.

"Been thinking about that Japanese plane," Phil continued. "It or its pilot had probably already been injured. Pilot might've lost so much blood he flew off course."

Not a bad theory. Pilots said that with New Guinea's violent weather tossing a plane around, it was easy to lose all sense of direction. The weather guys at their base would know if storms had come through last night.

The base. Oh no. She eyed the B-25s again. Had their saviors radioed to alert those on base about their encounter with the enemy aircraft?

She had assumed she would be able to slip away from the revetment after they landed and hurry back to her tent without anyone being the wiser. Phil hadn't filed a flight plan, so debriefers wouldn't normally meet with them.

Hadley bit her lip. She would still need to escape as soon as they landed. Once she could make herself heard, she would explain that to Phil and assure him she would catch up with him later to get the dope. She couldn't risk Luella — or worse, Mr. Litton, the field director for the Moresby airfield complex — getting wind that she had been on this flight. Catching a ride with a pilot between Australian cities was one thing. The Red Cross would look the other way for that infraction. But flying in a combat zone was another matter.

Phil made a gradual descent.

"Too much traffic on the runways, and we can't communicate with the tower," he said. "I'll set her down on a grass strip near the revetment. Don't worry, I've done it before."

Coasting above the grass, Phil pushed on the stick and allowed the wheels to touch down. The Grasshopper bounced a few times, jostling them from side-to-side before smoothing out.

"Looks like we've got company," Phil said.

Damn. Hadley looked over his shoulder to where two officers waited in a parked jeep.

Phil shut off the engine, opened the door, and hopped out. He leaned into the rear seat, took the camera from her, and muttered, "Let me do the talking."

"All right," she whispered. For once, Hadley agreed that

staying silent was her best option.

The officers got out of the jeep and strode toward them.

"Morning, Lieutenant."

Phil saluted. "Good morning, sir."

"You must be the one ordered to photograph the Kaimuku area." The captain crushed his cigarette under his heel.

Phil held up the camera. "Yes, sir. Hope this holds photos that will help our planners."

"Got a radio report from a B-25 reporting contact between an L-4 and an enemy fighter."

"That's right." Phil repeated his theory about an injured pilot who lost his course heading.

The other officer puckered his lips. "Not a bad theory. The Japanese mounted a small raid over Wards and Schwimmer fields last night. One of their fighters might have gotten hit and been unable to escape with the others."

"He came in out of the sun, like they do when they're attacking. But he didn't target us. And hell, he didn't even shoot back when I fired at him." Phil shifted the rifle on his shoulder. "That's what makes me think he was injured."

"Tell you what, come over to the debriefing tent and give us the details." He pointed at Hadley. "You're with the Red Cross, are you?"

She nodded. Hard to deny it with the Red Cross service patch on her sleeve and the ARC insignia on her collar.

"My ship with installed cameras was out of action, so they told me to take the Grasshopper up. Flying and shooting photos with my Graflex at the same time is difficult, so I asked Miss Claverie to come along." Phil flashed her a conspiratorial look. "She worked with me back home, and her photography skills are tops. Never dreamed we'd encounter a combatant less than a hundred miles down the coast."

"We'll get the details at the debriefing." The first officer gestured toward the jeep. "You can sit in the front, ma'am."

Hadley's stomach turned back-flips, and she gulped. On the short ride to the briefing tent, she went over various scenarios in her head. Her best bet would be to find Luella and put her own spin on the story, doing her best to frame the whole thing as a misunderstanding. She could say she thought Phil was only offering to take her up for a quick joyride. She had still used poor judgment but on a lesser scale than knowingly going along on an observation mission.

Captain Marshall parked the jeep and cut the engine. "All right, here we are."

Her stomach still in knots, Hadley hopped out. Captain Marshall hurried around the jeep and held the tent flap open for her. Normally smoky, noisy, and smelling strongly of whiskey shots during debriefing, the tent was now quiet, dank, and empty. Mission crews weren't due back for hours.

The first officer introduced himself as Captain Sterling, then pointed toward the first empty table. He pulled out a chair for Hadley before grabbing a notebook and pen and sitting beside the second officer, whom he introduced as Captain Marshall.

"Now, while we're waiting on . . ." Sterling broke off and tapped his pen on the table, then turned. "Ah, good, they're here."

A group of ten men wearing tropical flyer uniforms — simple khaki pants and shirts paired with parachute packs and Mae-West life vests — trudged into the tent.

Damn. Skip, Mike, and Leo were among them.

"Come in and join us, gentlemen." Captain Marshall pointed out two adjacent tables.

Skip chose a seat in Hadley's line of sight and pressed his mouth into a thin line. She bit her lip and focused on Captain Sterling, who asked Phil to give his version of events.

Phil led off with the assigned purpose of his mission. Then he repeated the lie about Hadley's photography experience, and Skip lifted his eyebrows. Tight lines around his mouth conveyed his disapproval. He probably assumed that Hadley had fed Phil that line to persuade him to take her along.

Skip's frown deepened when Phil related how he had yelled for Hadley to take the stick to keep the plane level so he could fire at the enemy.

"And that's when these fellas came blazing toward us in a steep dive," Phil said.

Captain Marshall gestured toward the B-25 crewmen. "Who spotted the Grasshopper? Or did the Zero catch your eye?"

Skip cleared his throat. "We had just flown to Yule island on a quick photo recon mission. That's why we didn't have a full crew. We were heading back when I spotted the Zero. As lead ship, I radioed the others that we would it strafe it as a target of opportunity." He paused. "Didn't see the L-4 until we were approximately three hundred feet away, on course to strafe the Zero. Lieutenant Blanchard then attempted to move out of our way, and I made a two-degree correction to avoid them."

A wave of dizziness flashed through Hadley. He made it sound as though his B-25 could have clipped one of their wings, collided with them, or even strafed them. She had presumed the B-25s had spotted their plane and swooped down to rescue them.

Phil went pale. He must have also mistaken the original intent of the B-25 crews.

Captain Sterling tapped his pen against his notepad. "None of you saw the Grasshopper?"

Several men spoke at once, until Captain Sterling waved for silence. The upshot seemed to be that the other crews had all assumed Skip saw the Grasshopper.

Hadley's hands trembled. She clasped them together in her lap to hide it.

Captain Marshall pointed at Leo and Mike. "Neither of you realized his course might imperil the Grasshopper?"

"Our radio was on the fritz," Leo said, "and I was trying to fix it."

"And you?" Captain Sterling frowned at Mike.

Skip glanced at his copilot. "Mike warned me, but I didn't hear him. Was too focused on the Zero. If anyone is to blame, it's me."

One look at the far-away expression in Mike's eyes confirmed what Hadley had decided back in Cairns. This man had no business flying. Skip was covering for him for some reason.

"As you know, Lieutenant, I have to inform your CO. Being aware of your surroundings, especially when attacking a target, is critical for the safety of your crew, your ship, and your comrades."

"Yes, sir." Neither Skip's voice nor his expression revealed anything other than contrition and respect.

After what seemed like hours of endless follow-up questions, Captain Sterling wagged his finger at Hadley. "No more unauthorized flights. Not even in a Grasshopper. Understood?"

"Yes, sir. I'll speak with Ms. Brinkman." Hadley hoped to forestall him and the other officers from reporting the incident to her supervisor.

He stood. "All right. And as for you, Lieutenant Blanchard — find yourself a photographer within the ranks of the military next time, are we clear?"

Phil stood and saluted. "Yes, sir."

Anxious to escape any more prying questions and the waves of emotion rolling off Skip, Hadley got up, nodded at the officers, and followed Phil out of the tent. He steered her some distance away, stopped and put his hand on her arm.

"God, Hadley, I'm so sorry," he said with wide eyes.

Tremors ran down her spine. "You couldn't have foreseen any of that."

"Not the specifics, no." He shook his head. "But that's not the point. I shouldn't have taken you up. Period."

"That's an understatement, Lieutenant." A sharp edge of fury rifled through Skip's voice.

Hadley pressed her shaking hands to her flushed cheeks. She should have trusted her gut and declined Phil's offer. She hadn't fully considered the possibility of danger during their foray, but she had known she was betraying the trust of her supervisor, lying to her fellow Red Cross Girls, and risking her job. And now Skip also had a black mark on *his* record.

A lump rose in her throat. She blinked back tears. Yet despite the jumble of shame, guilt, and shock roiling through her, she only wanted one thing: the comfort and safety of Skip's arms. She lurched toward him, but he put up his hand to forestall her and stepped closer to Phil.

"You know as well as I do that even the most routine flight in this theater can be dangerous. You could've gotten caught in a storm in that kite or experienced mechanical issues. Hell, you could've crashed on take-off."

"You're right. Taking Hadley up was a huge mistake." Phil nodded, apparently under the mistaken impression that respectful conciliation would defuse Skip's anger. "Didn't focus on the risks, and I shoulda known better. All I could think was that it would give her a chance for a good story."

"A story? You took her up on a dangerous flight for a *story*?"

The hairs on the back of Hadley's neck stood on end. Just because Skip couldn't see the point of covering the war from a different perspective didn't mean it had no value.

"Oh, hey now, you heard me in there." Phil ran a hand through his hair. "I was going on a simple photographic mission, much like your own. It shouldn't have been dangerous."

"Shouldn't have been?" Skip's face turned red. "Look, pal —"

"Stop it, Skip." Hadley stepped between them. "Going up with Phil was my idea, so don't blame him. I know you're angry, but leave him out of it."

"Last time I saw you," Skip growled, his eyes holding hers, "I warned you about taking stupid risks for a story. How could you be so foolhardy? And pretending to have photographic expertise?"

"No." Hadley raised both hands. "I didn't —"

"I made up that story," Phil cut in. "Thought they might go easier on her if I made it sound like I had a good reason for taking her up with me."

Skip ignored him. "I thought we agreed you wouldn't pursue any stories that could put you in danger. Why on earth would you ask a pilot to take you along on a mission?"

"Actually, I —"

"She didn't ask," Phil snapped. "I offered. We've been talking shop since she got here. I was a reporter in Houston before the war. I knew she was keen for a good scoop, so —"

"So you thought endangering her life would be a good way to advance her career?"

"Stop it, Skip." Hadley up her hand. "We don't need another lecture."

"I would never have put her in danger, I promise." Phil squeezed Hadley's shoulder.

Skip zeroed in on Phil's hand. His expression hardened. "I see. Well, guess I'm leaving you in good hands then." He turned and stalked off toward the revetments.

Hadley opened her mouth to call after him. He was all wet, had misinterpreted Phil's friendly gesture. But then again, him thinking there was a love affair between her and Phil might be easier to bear than knowing she had lost his respect. He wouldn't want a relationship with her now, that was for sure. Not even a wartime fling. He believed she was reckless and self-centered — that she had finally lived up to his *Miss Scarlett* nickname for her.

No point in trying to apologize. No point in trying to put things right. No point in trying to hold back her tears.

***

Later that evening, Hadley hung her wet poncho on a hook inside her tent and unlaced her boots. She slipped them under her cot, stripped off her wet socks, and set them out to dry. Then she sank onto her cot with relief. Every muscle in her body ached. She wasn't being shipped home, but Mrs. Brinkman obviously believed keeping

Hadley busy every moment of the day would serve as a reprimand and prevent her from being tempted to break any more rules.

The endless succession of chores had also prevented her from dwelling on her argument with Skip. She had disappointed him again. And despite the attraction sparking between them, they clearly weren't good for each other.

She would take care to avoid serving at his airfield. Rumor had it that many of the crews would soon be transferred to the northern coast anyway, so she and Skip would probably never see each other again.

From now on, she would trust her instincts. Hadn't her initial reaction been to avoid emotional entanglements with soldiers? That's what the Red Cross wanted — and that was one Red Cross directive Hadley would embrace from here on out.

After all, she had a new story to write. It may have come at a high price, but she intended to put her experience in the Grasshopper to good use. Dupre should have received her interview with Mrs. Roosevelt by now. She would send him this piece too, but ask that he use only her initials in the byline. That was the perfect solution. No one would ever guess the author was a woman.

Exhaustion aside, she ought to pull out a notebook and record her impressions while they were fresh in her mind. God knew, her work tomorrow would probably be a repeat of today's endless tasks.

The tent's wood plank flooring was smooth and cool under her bare feet as she rose and crossed to the front of the tent. She halted and frowned at the umbrella stand, where their musette bags typically hung on pegs. Where were they? Surely no one would have stolen them. Was this some soldier's idea of a prank?

Hadley turned in a slow half-circle and surveyed the tent. Ah, there they were. Clipped to a small clothesline that ran across the back wall. How odd.

She took a few steps toward the bags, then caught sight of the mail piled on the center table that housed her typewriter when they weren't using it for card games or as a nail salon.

A letter from her sister Cecilia and one from fellow Red Cross Girl Vivian Lambert, who had been Hadley's roommate during their training in Washington, lay on top of the stack. Vivian had landed in England, the lucky duck. Hadley set those letters aside to read later and slit open the third envelope, a note from Mr. Dupre:

"*. . . enclosing clipping from your feature on soldiers and exotic pets in Australia — very well received, many thanks. In your last note, you asked me to let you know when I will publish your interview with Eleanor Roosevelt. Ha, ha, very funny. Did you also interview General MacArthur? Keep up the good work.*

P.S. If you did actually interview the first lady during her tour of the South Pacific, please forward the article to me again pronto, as we did not receive it and would be most anxious to publish it of course. That, my dear, is front-page news."

Hadley stomach dropped. Dupre hadn't received her interview? Of all things for the army mail couriers to lose. Mail was always at risk. Planes crashed, ships sank.

She would type a new original from her carbon copy. She set down the letter and crossed to the musette bags. The moment she touched hers, however, she understood why they were hanging on the line. Soaking wet, all of them.

Heart racing, Hadley unclipped her bag and unbuckled the straps. She kept her carbon copies in a brown clasp envelope in the interior section. She pulled out the sopping envelope, untwirled the wet string to open the back clasp, and then carefully spread it open to peer inside.

The carbon copy was sodden. Sodden and smeared. Sodden, smeared, and *ruined.*

She stared at the dripping envelope. Could she extract the pages and either lay them out or clip them to the line to dry? Would the dried pages even be legible?

Hadley eased the wet copies from the envelope, cursing when

pieces of mushy paper tore off despite her caution. She gingerly lifted one corner of the top sheet and separated it from the stack bit by bit. Holding the wet sheet aloft, she walked toward the lamp.

Her idea might have worked if she hadn't stored letters written with fountain pen ink in the same envelope. Blotches of purple ink obscured most of the typed words that might otherwise be salvageable. All the other pages were sure to have the same problem.

Dammit, dammit, dammit. She tossed aside the worthless carbon copy and plonked down into a chair with her head in her hands.

"And here she is." Bizzy held the tent flap open for JoJo and Stella. "We haven't seen you all day. Is your stomach better?"

"About that . . ." Hadley let her words trail away and pinched the bridge of her nose. Confessing her white lie about the stomach issue would be the best place to start. After relating the story of her day's adventures and misfortunes, she sighed. "So Mrs. Brinkman set me one task after another all day long, which was frankly far better than I expected or deserved."

"I've been up with pilots several times." Bizzy waved a hand dismissively. "Bad luck you ran into a Japanese plane and then got caught, that's all."

"You've been up?" Stella stared at Bizzy.

"Oh, sure. Loads of times." Bizzy rolled her eyes. "The boys love to show off their piloting skills. And let's face it, fun date options are thin on the ground in New Guinea."

"Even so." Hadley kneaded the back of her neck. "I'm sorry I lied to you about being sick. That lie might be what started my streak of bad luck."

"Somewhere in that long, convoluted confession, I heard you mention Skip." JoJo opened a box of cookies and held it out to Hadley. "Your dishy pilot is upset again?"

"Skip is not *my* pilot." She took a cookie and muttered, "Definitely not now anyway."

"Like we haven't heard that before." Bizzy grabbed a cookie

and bit into it. "You say that every time you two are together."

"There's nothing between us." Stella melodramatically mimed fainting. "We're over. He hates me. I hate him."

"Then the minute you see each other again, it's off to the races." Bizzy winked at Hadley. "Every single time."

"Not this time." Hadley shook her head and pointed toward the umbrella stand. "What happened to our musette bags?"

"No, no, no." JoJo wagged her finger at Hadley. "You can't fool us by changing the subject. We'll come back to swoony Skip. But as for our bags, we figure storm winds knocked the stand over. We came back before dinner and found it on the ground, with our bags sitting in puddles of rain water."

"They'll dry," Stella said. "Well, as much as anything ever does in this jungle."

"Not necessarily," Hadley muttered. She grabbed the wet paper she had tossed aside and held it up. "These are my carbon copies."

"Uh oh." JoJo grimaced. "Well, at least your editor sends you clippings of your pieces. Were those in there too?"

Hadley shook her head. "They're in my trunk. Problem is, he didn't receive my interview with Mrs. Roosevelt."

"Oh no. Will you have to rewrite it from scratch?" Stella asked.

"Looks like it. Good thing I've got my notes." Hadley retrieved the notebook she had used for her interview from the bedside table beside her cot. Walking back to where the others sat, she opened it.

Oh, no. Her chest constricted. She halted and clutched the back of a chair for support. In her haste this morning, she had left the notebook out — and ants had chewed huge holes in each page. If she had returned for her usual mid-morning break, she would have seen what was happening and tucked the notebook back in her trunk.

Stella frowned. "What is it?"

"I *had* good notes. But the ants had other ideas." Hadley held up the notebook for the others to see.

She couldn't keep the others awake with her typewriter at this time of night, but she resolved to pull a fresh notebook from her trunk and record everything she remembered from her interview, her feature article, and today's flight before she went to sleep.

Tomorrow is another day, she mentally recited in her best imitation of Scarlett O'Hara.

CHAPTER TWELVE

Skip clutched the yoke and stared in disbelief at the spinning altimeter.

"Buckle up," he barked into the intercom. He and Mike were strapped into their seats, but the duties of other crewmen kept them on their feet.

A hellish she-witch of a storm pitched the ship up and down through the turbulence. He was unable to control the plane manually and only barely by instruments. Based on their position over the Owen Stanley range before the enormous thunderhead had sprung up in their path, he needed to gain altitude to avoid a crash.

He could avoid intense downdrafts and turbulence by taking her to a lower altitude, but with a blinding deluge pelting the ship, he couldn't be sure they wouldn't slam into a mountain. Better to climb as high and as fast as possible.

He pushed the throttles forward to pull maximum power from the engines so he could make a rapid ascent while he still had enough control to execute the action. "Sixteen?"

Mike nodded.

Taking the ship up to sixteen thousand feet would tax her engines, not to mention her fuel supply, but if the intense downdrafts sent them hurtling down a few thousand feet, they would at least have some cushion. The mission had been uneventful on the outbound leg, so fuel shouldn't be an issue. Skip plowed ahead through the raging storm with nothing but swirling black clouds in every direction, as the wind buffeted the plane up, down, and sideways. Trusting the instruments took every ounce of his control.

Finally a tiny square of blue sky up ahead grew larger, and the dark clouds lightened, thinned, and then broke apart. Turbulence gradually subsided, and Skip's shoulder muscles tingled as he allowed the tension to seep away.

Now he only had to determine their position. Leo squatted in the space between Skip and Mike, recording instrument readings.

"Doesn't make any fucking sense," Leo muttered as he rose. "Hang on. I'll recalculate."

They had crossed the Owen Stanleys, Skip was sure of that. Yet they must have gotten off course, because the landscape below held no familiar features.

Leo reappeared beside him with a map, which he held up for Skip and Mike. That wasn't good news. If he only needed them to make a simple course correction, he would have used the intercom.

"We're here." Leo jabbed his finger at a point near the coast that was well west of their route. "Halfway between this Australian airfield at Merauke." He pointed out a spot on the southern coast of Dutch New Guinea. "And our fields at Moresby."

Skip groaned.

Leo traced his finger across the water from their current location to Port Moresby. "Best course would be to overfly the Gulf of Papua, like so."

Skip flicked his gaze to the fuel gauges, and a knot of pressure tightened across his forehead. Fuel *hadn't* been an issue, until now — when they were hundreds of miles farther west than they should be. "Gulf would be, what? About two hundred miles across?"

"Correct," Leo confirmed. "Two twenty-five, to be exact."

Skip clicked off his throat mic and looked at Leo. "We don't have enough fuel."

Leo frowned. "But . . . that's the shortest distance back to base."

"I know." Skip glanced from Leo to Mike. "Way I see it, we can either ditch in the sea or find a coastal airstrip or flat delta land where we can set her down. Only airfields on the southern coast are Merauke and Moresby, correct?"

"That's right."

"And inland?" Skip knew the answer but had to ask.

Leo scowled. "Only Tsili Tsili. And that's —"

"Too far. Too dangerous." Landing in the jungle or on the side of a mountain would mean certain death.

Mike looked at Skip. "Wouldn't we be within range of Moresby radio if we headed out over the gulf?"

"Depends on where we run out of fuel." Skip gripped the throttles. "That's the downside to flying across it. An aircraft might spot us and report our location, but . . ."

But no one would be looking for them there. Mission routes rarely took crews in that direction. Sending out distress calls on Rafe's radio would only work if they were within range of Port Moresby or an Australian coast watcher outfit. Aussies had outposts inland from the coast and in the mountains, but those locations were top-secret.

If they were flying in formation or had a wingman, Skip would follow the conventional wisdom that ditching into shark-infested waters held a higher chance of survival than going down in the treacherous jungle. But with no one to report they had ditched, those odds didn't look as good.

Bringing her down on land would be preferable, but he would need Mike to be engaged or at least capable of following instructions. That he had contributed to the conversation was a positive sign, but Skip needed his copilot to actively contribute if he was to have any prayer of landing this plane on a beach without killing them all.

First things first. "Your maps don't show the Aussie outposts, right?"

"Negative," Leo said. "Can't risk the enemy being able to locate 'em."

"You have any topo maps?" Aussie coast watchers were said to operate from locations near their pre-war rubber and coconut plantations. Skip frowned. "Anything that might show cleared areas? Agricultural land?"

"Got a good one that shows all the fucking swamps between here and Moresby." Leo riffled through a stack of maps. "Like that'll help."

"Whole island's a damned swamp." Mike tapped his fingers on the instrument panel.

Skip gritted his teeth. "What else is marked on those maps? Roads, surely."

Leo snorted. "Roads?"

"Or whatever passes for a trail in this hellhole."

"There's no road — *or trail* — that runs all the way to Moresby, Skipper. Not to mention that we'd have to cross about a thousand rivers and streams," Leo said.

Skip clenched his jaw. Like he didn't know they couldn't walk hundreds of miles down the beach and ford a gazillion bodies of water?

"Not roads for *us*," he snapped, turning to look at Leo. "Roads that transport rubber and coconuts and shit to the coast. Aussie plantation owners took to the hills near their old estates when the Japanese invaded, right? We need to land near one of their plantations and find them. Connecting with a coast watcher might be our only hope for survival."

"You shoulda said. Look here," Leo pursed his lips and spread out a detailed topographic map of the Papuan coastline. "The plantations are on the coast and near rivers."

"The one north of Moresby, past the waterfall," Skip said, "is nowhere near the coast."

"Yeah, I know. Owner's still working it. I spent the night there a few weeks ago."

"What?" Skip swiveled to stare at Leo. "Why?"

"Your girl Hadley and another Red Cross Girl took a group of us up to Rouna Falls for a picnic and then over to visit the plantation. A storm blew through, and the owner offered to put us up for the night. You didn't notice I was gone?" Leo grinned.

Skip had noticed but had been too preoccupied to ask for details when Leo returned the next day. Hadley had been there? "You didn't mention Hadley."

"She asked me not to say, said you were sore at her."

Was he angry with her? He *was* pissed at that hotshot fighter pilot . . . Blanchard. Or *Blan-char*, he irritably exaggerated the French pronunciation in his head as he tightened his grip on the control column.

"She's got a new fella," he said. "Doesn't matter."

His crewmate raised his eyebrows and shook his head. "Not judging from the way she looked when she talked about you, Skipper."

"Back to the map, Leo." Skip inclined his head toward the fuel gauges.

Leo bit his lip. "Right. So that planter said most of the plantations are on the coast or near a river. So I reckon we should aim to land about here." He used two fingers to indicate a stretch of coastline.

Skip examined the map. Endless swamps, rivers, notations of *dense jungle*, and mountains. The stretch of beach near Cape Possession that Leo had pinpointed didn't contain large swathes of swampland or rivers flowing into the sea.

Trouble was, the area also seemed unlikely to have been used to grow crops. They would still need to trek in one direction or another to find a plantation, then somehow reach the Aussies who had melted into the jungle.

Skip gulped air into his constricted chest. First thing he had to do was figure out how to land this damned plane on a sandy beach without killing himself and his crew.

"Thought about how you're gonna land her?" Leo asked. "A beach is —"

"Thinkin' that through now," Skip broke in.

Leo mimed paddling a boat. "Why don't we ditch off the coast and get into our inflatable dinghy? Then we could just aim it toward shore."

"For starters, the currents might push us away from the coast." Skip shook his head. "Then there's the danger of landing too close to shore. Landing in shallow water might kill us on impact. Besides, we'll need our survival gear from the plane. Hell, we can even sleep in it for a while to stay dry and safe."

Safe not only from jungle wildlife but also from the island's human inhabitants. The villagers around Port Moresby were friendly and helpful, but this enormous island was also home to a number of distinct indigenous tribes, some of which might know nothing about the war and be less than thrilled to see them.

"Wet sand," Mike said. "Won't be the same as landing on Marston-matting, but it'll be hard-packed and smooth."

"Think the wheels will hold on the sand without causing her to flip?" Skip had assumed that wet sand would be their best bet, and it was reassuring to have his copilot reach the same conclusion. If Mike remained focused, his help would be invaluable. Skip met his eyes. "Or should we go in for a belly landing?"

"No." Mike clicked his tongue. "I'd go in wheels-down."

"I agree." Skip tapped the map and looked at Leo. "Route us and give me the heading."

"Got it." Leo stood and moved toward his seat.

Skip flipped on his throat mic and spoke into the intercom. "Crew, the storm took us off course, and as a result, we've got a fuel emergency. We're going to land on the coast. I'll alert you when to brace for impact. Acknowledge."

Charlie, whose injuries in August had only kept him out of action for two missions, spoke first. "Countin' on you to save my ass again, Skipper."

Laughing, Dewey and Rafe each acknowledged in turn, and Leo gave Skip the heading over the intercom.

When the coastline appeared on the horizon, Skip spoke again, "Crew: remove the interior covers on the escape hatch, put on your helmets, and locate your survival gear. When we come to a stop, abandon ship immediately — and take your bag if you can do it safely."

He descended and flew over the beach between rivers for several miles in each direction but saw no sign of human habitation or agricultural use. Finding a water source would be critical because the rivers that poured into the Coral Sea contained a brackish mix of fresh and saltwater. Locating one of the inland rivers marked on Leo's map would be better.

The fuel gauges hovered barely above the red line when Skip shifted his focus to identifying the most likely stretch of firm sand near the water's edge. He descended toward the beach and buzzed a potential strip. The area was awfully narrow, but the sand looked firm and ought to be long enough. His heart juddered wildly in his chest. He sucked in a deep breath and ran his fingers over the light meter secreted deep in his pocket.

"We'll put her down here," he said. "Prepare for crash landing. Acknowledge now."

One by one and without a hint of fear, his crewmates

responded. They had confidence in him, trusted he would land safely. Adrenaline heightened Skip's senses. He clenched his fingers around the yoke.

"When I yell *now*," Skip said to Mike, "cut the power switches, the fuel mixture, and the gas selection valves."

Mike nodded.

Skip glanced over his shoulder at Leo and raised his eyebrows. His navigator tightened his seatbelt and nodded. Leo was familiar enough with the controls to step in if Mike choked.

Skip took another deep breath and lined up his approach. "Wheels down."

Mike pushed the wheels control lever.

Skip descended lower and grasped the throttles, allowing his gut to dictate how much speed he needed to keep her nose up. Hovering ten or fifteen feet above the ground, he shifted his hand from the throttles to the control column and yelled, "*Now!*"

Mike flicked the power and ignition switches, then shut off the fuel mixtures and gas valves. Skip eased the throttles forward until the back wheels skimmed the sand before pulling back to glide several inches above it. Back and forth, back and forth. *Easy does it, easy does it.*

He clenched his jaw, pushed the throttles forward, and pointed her nose into the flare before allowing the back wheels to settle onto the makeshift runway. His heart lodged in his throat as he pulled back on the control column until it nearly touched his chest, adding more and more back pressure to slow the plane's roll.

Now for the real test. Skip released the nose wheel, and it hit the sand with a sharp jolt before smoothing out and rolling over the hard-packed sand.

"Thirty miles per hour," Mike called out.

Sweat slicked the sides of Skip's face. He pulled up on the control column.

Slower, slower, slower.

"Twenty-five . . . twenty."

Come on, sweet girl, slow down.

"Ten."

Nearly there, nearly there, come on.

Thud. The plane lifted off the ground, nose up, and then *ka-thunked* back down as if they had hit something. He peered out the windshield but didn't see an obstruction. The back struts absorbed the shock, and the plane continued rolling forward, although the nose wheel jigged sideways. Skip struggled to steer the plane out of the skid, but the wheel dug into the sand and the plane pitched forward, nose down, and cut a deep furrow in the sand for at least a hundred feet before coming to an abrupt stop.

Skip and Mike slammed forward, and Skip's head hit the control column. Good thing he was wearing his helmet. He lifted his head, straightened, and looked at Mike.

"You okay?"

"Yeah, I think so."

"Everybody okay?" Skip asked over the intercom. He glanced back at Leo, who had tumbled into the back of Mike's seat and now had a dazed look. Leo rubbed the back of his neck.

"I'm okay." Rafe sputtered.

"Same here," Charlie called out.

"Okay here too," said Dewey.

"Get out and away from the ship. Take your bags and guns if you can. Now!" Skip released the escape hatch above the cockpit and gestured for Mike to climb out first, handing him his survival bag and tommy gun from under his seat. Then Skip offered his hand to Leo. "Grab your maps. Can't lose those."

Leo stuffed them into his survival kit, zipped it up, and tossed it out of the hatch before clambering out himself.

Skip slung his tommy gun over his shoulder, tossed out his bag, and used Mike's seat as a lift to pull himself up. He jumped onto the ground, grabbed his bag, and hurried toward the side hatch door where the other men waited.

He then led them a few hundred feet away from the plane.

"Any injuries?" He met the eyes of each man in turn. Even a graze or small cut ought to be washed and bandaged. Infection was bad news in the jungle.

Once he was satisfied everyone was in decent shape, albeit rattled, Skip ran a hand through his hair. "We'll wait here for a few minutes, but there shouldn't be much chance of fire."

"Once it's safe to go back inside, I'll test the radio," Rafe said. "Shouldn't be a problem with the batteries."

"The radio won't help us — doesn't have enough range to communicate with our planes, even if one flies in this vicinity." Skip waved his hand at the sky.

Dewey frowned. "We should try the Gibson Girl, right?"

The emergency signals transmitter. Skip had forgotten about it. Nicknamed *Gibson Girl* for its wasp-waisted form, it might be just what they needed. Maybe they wouldn't have to traverse the jungle in search of the Aussies after all.

Port Moresby monitored a shortwave emergency station at all times, so in theory, they could send a signal using the transmitter that would allow the station to put a fix on them.

He nodded at Dewey. "That's the first thing we should do." Skip glanced back at the plane. "All right, I reckon we would've either seen or heard any fire by now. Let's go check her out and set up the transmitter."

Dewey and Rafe scrambled back into the ship first, reappearing a few minutes later carrying the bright yellow transmitter bag. Leo helped them maneuver it down the ladder, then Rafe took it and set it on a flat patch of sand. He popped open the door, unwound the antenna cable and stretched it across the beach, where he attached it to the trunk of a tall palm tree.

Dewey peered at the instructions printed on the metal plate affixed to the top of the transmitter near the hand crank. He readied the transmitter as instructed before turning the crank to switch on the interior generator to power its signals.

He turned the crank over and over, while Skip and the others crouched around him and waited for the triangular light indicator to glow red and confirm that they were successfully transmitting a signal.

Nothing.

"Let me try." Charlie elbowed Dewey out of the way and turned the crank, slowly, faster, and then at intervals.

Still nothing.

Rafe scowled and took a small screwdriver out of his tool kit. He unscrewed the transmitter's front casing and peered inside. Skip leaned closer. So many wires, tubes, gadgets, and springs. Rafe poked, prodded, tightened, and tested.

"Transmitter seems okay," he muttered. He opened another section of the interior casing, examined it, and frowned. "Umm, here's the problem."

Rafe held up the tiny generator, visibly marred by scorch marks. "Got overheated."

"Damn," Dewey said.

Leo passed the yellow bag to Rafe. "It's pretty small. Is there a spare in here?"

"Not sure." Rafe searched every compartment and pocket but failed to find one.

Dismay and worry marked the faces of Skip's men. He swore to himself. He checked his survival kit every damned day, so why hadn't either Rafe or Dewey bothered to check the transmitter? It had probably been defective since it was issued to them. He bit back the question — it would rightly be heard as an accusation. Crew unity didn't need one more conflict. Not given the pickle they were in. Besides, if anyone was to blame for their current predicament, it was him. He should have aborted rather than flying into bad weather.

No, the idea of using the transmitter had been only a temporary reprieve. He had spent the last hour or more assuming their survival depended on finding Australians — or anyone else with a functioning shortwave radio.

"I've never heard of anyone being rescued using one of these transmitters anyway, fellas," Skip said. "We'll proceed with my plan."

"What's that?" Charlie raised his eyebrows.

Skip stood and slapped his thighs to dust off the sand. "Three of us will stay with the plane, while the other three walk west. If they fail to find anything, they'll come back. Then the other three will walk east, while the first three get some rest."

"What are we looking for?" Dewey asked.

Skip met the anxious eyes of his men. "Anyone or anything that can get us out of here."

***

November 23, 1943, 3:30 p.m.

Durand Airfield (17 Mile Drome), Port Moresby, New Guinea

Hadley parked their Jeepmobile, *Papuan Papaya*, behind the ambulances lined up along the airstrip. She stepped out and circled her stiff shoulders. The seventeen-mile drive from Moresby over the rainy season's muddy roads had taxed her nerves.

Stella shaded her eyes and scanned the sky. "I'm getting my poncho. Want yours?"

"No thanks. It's too hot." The raincoats issued by the Red Cross were too warm, but even the army rain ponchos they had sweet-talked from the quartermaster in Port Moresby were too heavy to wear in the sweltering heat. Besides, the ponchos didn't have hoods, so they still had to secure a cap or scarf over their hair to keep it dry.

"All right, but you know how deluges spring up out of nowhere." Stella joined her at the back of the Jeepmobile and tightened the closure on her poncho.

Hadley stood on tiptoe, opened one of the cans of lemon cordial, and stirred it. "I'll take my chances."

She wasn't trying to impress the fellas, especially not here. She had avoided serving at Skip's field until today. Maybe he hadn't flown and wouldn't need a cold drink and a cookie.

Stella peered into the other canister. "The ice is melting fast. I hope the boys hurry."

"We'll take some while it's cold, sweetheart," one of the ground crew workers clustered around the strip called out.

Many of the men were shirtless and wore only khaki pants ripped off above the knees despite the army's constant admonitions for the men to reduce their risk of contracting malaria by wearing long-sleeved shirts and long pants.

Hadley waved them over. "Come on, then."

They always brought enough lemon cordial and cookies to serve the ground crews, who worked so hard in all weather, along with the crash crews, who waited in the ambulances.

Hadley ladled lemon cordial into paper cups and passed them to the men who had gathered around them. A dog brushed her leg, and she leaned down to pat him.

"If I give you a treat, buddy," she said to the dog, "the others will swarm over here, and before you know it, you dogs will have eaten all the cookies meant for the crews."

One of the men whistled, patted his leg, and held out a cookie, and the dog bounded over to him. Hadley smiled.

"What's the latest ETA?" Stella asked as she passed around another platter of cookies.

One of the crew chiefs ground out his cigarette and took a cup of lemon cordial from Hadley. "Should be any second now."

Another man cocked his ear toward the intelligence tent. "Sounds like the lead plane is radioing in now."

Crackling static, a call sign, and a muffled male voice rang out from the tent, followed by the shrill whine of static. Hopefully the intelligence officers could understand what he had said.

Several officers exited the tent and joined them beside the Jeepmobile. Hadley gave each of them a drink, while Stella refilled the cookie platters.

Assessing their mood was tricky. Boosting morale was part of the officers' jobs, but Hadley detected a hint of worry underlying their lighthearted conversation.

"What's the dope?" one of the crew chiefs finally asked. "We all got a ship comin' back or what?"

"One missing." A captain lit a cigarette and took a long drag on it. "Our fellas hit a beast of a storm coming back over the mountains. Could be it got separated and will turn up later."

Might turn up later. Hadley's neck seized with tension. Just as easily — maybe even more likely — it wouldn't return at all.

She and Stella would drive the Jeepmobile to each revetment after the planes landed, unable to anticipate which plane hadn't made it until they came upon an empty revetment and a distraught ground crew. And they would drive on, doing their level best to paste smiles on their faces and dispense cordials, cheer, and charm for the next crew.

"Here they come," one of the ambulance drivers shouted.

Droning bombers peeled off from the formation one by one and glided into a landing pattern. Planes with mechanical issues and/or wounded men aboard were always permitted to land first. The first bomber touched down with a jerk, its rubber wheels grinding against the Marston mat's perforated steel surface as it shot down the runway. No red flare to signal a medical emergency or a yellow flare to indicate mechanical problems.

Hadley replaced the lid on the canister and prepared to move on to the revetments.

"The first one didn't shoot any flares," she said to the men standing nearby. "So does that mean the rest are in good shape too?"

"Not necessarily," one of the intelligence officers said. "That one was probably almost out of fuel."

Sure enough, the second bomber sent up a bright red flare as it landed, and one of the ambulances sped off toward the end of the runway.

The next bomber sent up a yellow flare on its approach.

"Back up, back up!" three MPs yelled, chopping their hands to signal for folks to clear the area near the runway. Several men jumped into vehicles parked nearby and moved them away, while the MPs urged everyone on foot to move fast. "Farther back now!"

Stella stubbed her toe on a tree root, and Hadley grabbed her elbow to keep her from falling.

"Owww, damn that hurts," Stella complained as she limped away beside Hadley.

Meanwhile the injured bomber continued its cautious approach, seemingly reluctant to touch down.

"Can you tell what's wrong?" Hadley asked a crew chief.

He pointed toward the plane's underbelly. "The right wheel is jammed, so he's only got the left one and the nose strut. That's why he's slowing his approach."

The pilot kept the nose high and the front wheel off the ground as long as he could. When the nose wheel finally touched the runway, it skidded sideways, while the right side of the fuselage scraped the steel matting, sending up sparks. Swirling clouds of smoke enveloped the bomber, which careened to the right and stopped just short of a parked jeep.

The men clapped and whistled.

"Is it okay?" Stella asked doubtfully.

One of the ground crew boys grabbed a cookie from her platter. "Aw, sure. Look, the pilot's already moving her over to the perimeter."

Another bomber shot down the runway, seemingly undamaged.

"Okay, fellas, stack your empty cups in here." Hadley held out a large pail. "You can grab another cookie if you want, but we're about to move out to the revetments."

They secured the refreshments in the back of the Jeepmobile and soon bumped over the perimeter road.

Hadley wheeled the Jeepmobile to a stop near the intelligence jeep at the first revetment. When she stepped out, her boots sank into the mud, and sharp blades of kunai grass swished against her legs.

The crew stood talking to the debriefers with guns over their shoulders and flight bags at their feet. With the men talking over each other, Hadley wondered how the debriefers could hear anything useful.

Stella set out a platter of cookies while Hadley walked around the Jeepmobile and ladled cold cordial into cups on another platter.

"All right, fellas, good work up there," one of the intelligence officers said. "Go get yourselves a cold drink from those Red Cross gals."

Whooping and joking, the men swarmed toward them. As always, they were exuberant to find themselves back on the ground in one piece and ready to enjoy female company.

"You gonna wear those ugly old boots with your pretty dresses when you get home?"

"Say, where's the best place in Australia to go on leave?"

"You gals heard who won the Army-Navy game?" another fellow asked, followed by a fourth man's derisive, "You drip, that game's next week."

The men regaled them with stories containing dramatic retellings of aerial derring-do from the day's mission, then peppered them with more questions until a truck pulled up to transport them to the mess.

Hadley and Stella waved them off, collected their discarded cups, and hopped in the Jeepmobile to speed over to the next revetment.

Ten crews later, the *Papuan Papaya* chugged around a corner and headed toward the last cluster of revetments. Over a burned section of Kunai grass, they sighted what should have been their next stop — but it was empty.

No plane. No debriefing officers. No happy, chattering air crew.

"Oh, damn," Stella muttered.

Tension rippled through Hadley. She hated to barrel past the forlorn revetment, since the ground crew might not have gotten any refreshments yet. But she and Stella always left in bad spirits whenever they attempted to console a grieving ground crew, then had a difficult time shaking off the gloom for their next stop. Torn with indecision, Hadley eyed the ground crew's tent.

No. No, no, no.

Her heart jumping, Hadley slammed the Jeepmobile into park. Ignoring Stella's startled exclamations, she hopped out and jogged toward the tent, where a wallaby hopped around on a rope leash. Skip wasn't the only serviceman with a pet wallaby, but this was his base and the animal looked heartbreakingly familiar.

"Lucy?" Hadley called out halfway up the hilly slope.

The wallaby's ears didn't even twitch, and it remained absorbed with munching grass.

Hadley's erratic heart rate slowed a notch. *See, it isn't Lucy, it isn't Skip's revetment, it isn't where my heart shatters.*

The ground crew chief stepped out of the tent. "They aren't like dogs, you know. They don't come when you call 'em. How do you know Lucy?"

The wallaby *was* Lucy. Hadley's stomach twinged.

No. Skip didn't fly today. He didn't fly. He isn't missing.

He could be laid up in the hospital tent with an ear infection. Nothing serious, just any one of the many tropical ailments common in this miserable climate. That's why the ground crew had brought Lucy here, so they could watch her for him while he recuperated.

"I sailed to this theater on the *West Point* with Skip — Lieutenant Masterson — and we've seen each other a few times since then." Hadley knelt and held out her hand.

Lucy hopped closer in response.

He pursed his lips. "You're a Red Cross Girl with a southern accent, so you must be the inspiration for the name of our ship."

"What's that?" Hadley kept her eyes averted, leery of whatever truth might be written on the man's face. She pulled a blade of grass and handed it to Lucy.

"He named her *Bourbon Street Belle*, and the fellas said he named her after some Red Cross gal from New Orleans he was sweet on."

He named his plane after me?

A flush spread up her neck. Well, her namesake was missing. But was her normal pilot also missing? Hadley couldn't contemplate it, couldn't ask, couldn't look up.

Stella caught up with her and put her hand on Hadley's shoulder. "He's missing?"

"That's what they say. Wingman lost him in the storm, and no one's seen or heard from them since. I'm Nate, by the way. I'm the crew chief." He scuffed his boot through the grass.

Anchors settled at the bottom of Hadley's lungs, and her vision fogged. Nate would have said by now if Skip hadn't flown today's mission. His poor parents. They had already lost one son to the war. How would they bear losing the other?

And me. He was so disappointed in me the last time I saw him. She drew in a shaky breath. He had pegged her as impulsive, self-righteous, and stubborn. All of which were true to one degree or another. Still, she would have liked the chance to prove him wrong.

"They could still turn up, right?" Stella asked. "If they got lost in a storm, it may take them longer to return."

"We'll keep watch, but . . ." Nate trailed off.

But they would have run out of fuel by now. That's what he didn't say. They might have landed at another field. The intelligence fellas might pull up at any minute and explain that after Skip and his crew refueled, they would be on their way back to base.

"They probably landed at another base." Hadley stood.

Nate shoved his hands into his pockets and kicked at a dirt clod. "Maybe, but —"

"I know there aren't many options, but Skip is innovative. He would've thought of something," she said with ferocious certainty.

"Could be." He nodded. "A few crews have found their way back."

"He's *not* missing. Skip is too good a pilot," she said. "He has a plan, and they'll be back."

"Hope you're right, doll." Nate met her eyes. "He's a good man."

"I'll take care of Lucy," she announced, grabbing Lucy's leash. "Until Skip is back."

"Hadley —" Stella began.

Nate shook his head. "We've got her enclosure here. I'll take care of her, don't worry."

"No, he'll want to make sure he's got her when he's back." Hadley's voice wavered, and she blinked back tears. Men divvied up the belongings of those who failed to return from missions.

Nate placed his hand on Hadley's arm. "I won't give her away, I promise."

Tears stung her eyes. She clenched the rope leash. "I want her if . . ."

"We'll take good care of her. Don't worry, she'll be here waiting," Nate assured her.

She'd be waiting. Waiting for whoever comes back to claim her.

***

November 24, 1943, 8:30 a.m.

Southern coast of Papua New Guinea, between Kerema and Port Moresby

Skip pushed his hand inside his pocket and gripped his light meter to keep from scratching mosquito bites. They were all covered with hundreds of bites, but as he had instructed the others, scratching would open sores and cause them to bleed — and open wounds could turn dire in the jungle.

He had also insisted that each man take an Atabrine tablet last night and again this morning. "If you die from malaria, it won't matter if it causes sterility," Skip had said to quash the muttered complaints of his crewmates.

Sleeping last night had been miserable. After discovering the interior of the plane was far too stuffy for them to rest inside it, they had slept in shifts beneath its wings with only face nets to ward off the hordes of mosquitos and sand flies.

They weren't worried about the Japanese discovering them. Enemy troops controlled vast sections of New Guinea's northern coast, but the only ones Skip and his crew might encounter here would be in the same fix they were, stranded from a bail-out.

"Isn't it time to turn around?" Charlie asked.

Skip stopped and shaded his eyes to read the sun's position. "Well —"

"It's nine-thirty. Why in hell haven't you fixed your watch?" Dewey asked.

He ignored the question. Now wasn't the time to talk about Chet and Pearl Harbor. But he did want to allow the others ample time to walk the other direction and return back to the plane before nightfall. "Guess we can turn back here."

He tugged his collar higher on his neck. They all already had deep suntans, but none of them had spent as much time exposed to the intense tropical rays as they would for the foreseeable future.

Walking back to the crash site didn't hold the same appeal as their earlier journey had, when they had left the plane in hope of discovering anything that could extricate them from this primeval wilderness. They walked on, their steps in time with the crashing surf.

Skip planned to ask Dewey and Charlie to fish for their dinner when they got back to the plane. They had both been avid fishermen back home, so Skip had selected them to accompany him on today's first walk-out. With any luck, they would catch enough to feed all of them.

Taking stock of their cumulative rations from the plane had not allayed Skip's worries. They needed to conserve their rations. Breakfast this morning had been date bars from their packs and coconuts he and Rafe had scrounged not far from the plane.

Dewey opened his canteen and took a long swig of water.

Droplets glistened on his chin. Skip pinched his lips together, clenching and slowly releasing his fists. Did his crewmates not appreciate the peril they were in?

He cleared his throat and looked at Dewey. "Remember, we've gotta conserve every ounce of water until we find a source for something drinkable."

Dewey didn't respond but hunched his shoulders and lengthened his stride.

Water was Skip's most pressing worry. The potable amount they had on the plane wouldn't last much longer. He had hoped to find a fresh-water source on their trek, but so far they had only crossed a few brackish streams. He suspected they would need to venture into the jungle to find a lake, freshwater river, or spring. If they had to do that, they would, but even armed with a compass and Leo's maps, Skip was leery of moving into the dense forest, which teemed with danger and could prove disorienting.

Birds chattered in the trees and seagulls called over the crashing surf. Skip kept his eyes trained inland, hoping to spot something they had missed earlier. Signs of a rundown coastal plantation or a native village tucked away at the edge of the bush.

They picked their way over rocks to cross a trickling stream, then continued on for several miles before reaching the next body of water, which had no built-in path across. Charlie poked a large branch into the murky, brackish water, as they had done when they had crossed it the first time. In addition to typical swamp wildlife dangers, water this close to the sea might also be home to sharks and venomous sea snakes.

"All right, let's cross quickly. Stomp around a lot." Skip grabbed a loose vine for balance to keep from slipping in the mud slicking the bank and then stepped toward the water.

Dewey yanked on his arm and pulled him back. Charlie grabbed his other arm to keep him from toppling backward into the mud. Skip caught sight of one yellow eye and a craggy, bumpy reptilian head the same color as the muddy water as the crocodile sank below the surface. The water barely rippled with the animal's stealthy movement. *Fuck.*

"Christ, how'd you spot it?" Thankful for his friends' quick action, Skip wiped sweat from his brow.

Dewey crooked his mouth. "I grew up in south Louisiana, spent my whole life fishing in gator country."

"We oughta shoot it." Charlie put his hand on his gun.

"No." Skip shook his head. He pushed his hand into his pocket and closed his fingers around his light meter. "We can't afford to waste our ammo."

"Waste it? If that monster doesn't pose a danger, what does?" Charlie scowled.

"Not easy to shoot a gator. Skin's too tough," Dewey said. "Besides, the thing's underwater now. You can't aim worth a damn when your target is submerged."

"Well, I'm not going into that water now." Charlie jerked his head toward the turbid creek.

Skip exchanged glances with Dewey. They had to cross the creek to get back to the others. "You might not have a choice."

"We could walk upstream and see if there's a better place to cross," Dewey muttered.

Skip scowled. "Better, as in what? What are the odds the water will be any clearer or less infested with predatory prehistoric creatures?"

"We shoulda brought the lifeboat from the plane," Charlie said.

Skip held up his hand. "We all agreed the boat was too heavy and cumbersome to carry. It would have slowed us down."

"The survival manual says we can build a raft out of bamboo and shit." Charlie turned in a half-circle and surveyed the surrounding trees. "Do you see —"

"A raft?" Dewey broke in, pointing at the gurgling creek. "You can cross that sucker in ten good-sized steps."

"Assuming a crocodile doesn't eat you on step one," Charlie shot back.

"If we take time to build a raft, we'll be here all day," Dewey said. "Look, Charlie, be reasonable. We've crossed it once already."

"Yeah, but now we know that fucker's lurking in there, biding his time. I tell you, I'm not going near that water." Charlie crossed his arms.

Dewey gave Skip a *be-the-commander look*. Skip's near-miss with the crocodile made him more inclined to agree with Charlie. Yet they had to cross the creek.

He gestured toward a group of stones scattered higher up on the bank. "What if we heft some of these large rocks into the water and build a bridge?"

"Let's give it a shot," Dewey agreed.

They climbed up to the stones and then used Charlie's branch to make a smooth path down the embankment. He and Dewey carried several of the larger stones to the water's edge. The first sank to the bottom, but when Skip set a second stone on top of it, it peeked out of the muddy water. Dewey set a third one atop the second, and they were in business.

They spent over half an hour building their makeshift bridge and then several more minutes persuading Charlie to use it.

"For fuck's sake, Charlie," Dewey finally shouted from the other side. "Skipper and I stood out in the middle of the damned creek creating this bridge for the past twenty minutes. You think that croc is lying in wait for *your* sorry ass?"

Charlie wasn't wrong. That's exactly how crocodiles attacked, lurking in the water and then attacking in a flash when their prey got too close to the water's edge. But all the churning from throwing rocks into the creek had probably scared off the damned thing.

Charlie puckered his brow and gingerly stepped onto the first stack of rocks before hopping quickly over the others while stabbing the large branch into the water.

"He'll go 'round the twist if he slips and falls while he's jabbing that stick around like that," Skip muttered.

Dewey laughed.

"What are you snickering at?" Charlie demanded. "God, I need a smoke."

"Who's afraid of the big bad croc, the big bad croc, the big bad croc," Dewey sang out, mimicking the big, bad wolf song from Disney's *The Three Little Pigs*.

Skip whistled along with him.

"There's nothing funny about any of this shit." Charlie tossed his branch into a thicket of trees and stormed up the embankment toward the beach.

Dewey caught up with him and clapped him on the shoulder. "You're right, pal. Sorry." He turned and winked at Skip.

They reached the plane at noon. Irritated and alarmed by how long their morning foray had taken, Skip weighed his options. He could caution the others to walk no more than two hours along the coast before turning back. The midday heat would slow their progress and make them even thirstier than his group had gotten. Or he could send them into the jungle to look for fresh water. Water. They needed *water* before anything else. Coconut juice wouldn't work for long.

Looking for water would also prolong their options for another day. Skip hadn't yet wrestled with the plan they would need if they couldn't connect with any Australians or natives and were stranded here indefinitely.

He drank only enough water to slake his thirst and then motioned for his crewmates to gather in the shade of a cluster of coconut palms.

"Fellas, we need to make a couple of decisions. I'd hoped we'd get back an hour ago, so you three —" He gestured toward Mike, Leo, and Rafe. "Could walk east for a few hours and get back before dark. But we were delayed —"

"By a fucking murderous crocodile." Charlie tipped ashes into the sand. He had lit up a cigarette the minute they had returned.

"Thought you weren't gonna cross any rivers," Leo said.

"We crossed a creek, no more than fifteen feet wide, and we'd already crossed about five others." Skip held up his hand to forestall any more questions. "We'll tell the croc story later. Look, I'm worried about our water supply. So instead of sending you fellas east, I'm more inclined to send you inland in search of fresh water."

"Inland? You mean, *into the jungle*?" Rafe gaped at him and pointed toward the dense bramble of vine-laden trees only a few hundred yards away.

Skip nodded. "Leo's a navigator. You'll take his maps and compasses and hack your way through for no more than an hour. If you don't find anything, then turn back."

Rafe cut his eyes toward the jungle's impenetrable gloom and bit his lip. "Besides crocodiles, snakes, and giant spiders, what else lives in there?"

"They told us to watch out for cassowaries, remember?" Dewey said. "And if you see a wild pig, shoot it, and we'll eat well."

"No tigers, panthers, or bears around here," Skip assured them. "Gather your maps and a compass," he said to Leo. "You should also take your survival kits — and your weapons."

Charlie raised his eyebrows and blew out a smoke ring. "No need to worry, fellas, just man-eating crocodiles, snakes that can kill you in a minute flat, and aggressive seven-foot tall birds that can run faster than a car."

CHAPTER THIRTEEN

November 25, 1943, 10:30 a.m.

Southern coast of Papua New Guinea, between Kerema and Port Moresby

Skip frowned at the trickle of water dripping into his canteen. He would have to cut several more vines to fill it but couldn't justify using one of their precious purification tablets on anything less than a full container.

Two forays into the jungle, and they still hadn't located any fresh water. Their survival guide included instructions for tapping native rattan palm vines as a water source. The resultant liquid didn't look particularly refreshing, but it would have to do. Rhythmic undulations of the surf rolling gently onto the shore only served to irritate him. Surrounded by water, and none of it was fit to drink.

Their food supply was better. Dewey and Charlie were good

fishermen, and they had caught plenty of fish for both dinner last night and breakfast this morning. Mike had also located plenty of papayas and bananas.

Skip supposed they could survive on fish and fresh fruit, assuming they could locate water, but isolation from civilization would eventually wear them down. Day three and tempers were already fraying. Adding to the tension was his growing alarm that they truly were isolated. Skip had walked east with Rafe and Dewey yesterday morning and seen no evidence of human habitation.

Anxiety gnawed at Skip as he and Leo pored over their maps and debated their options. Attempts to draw Mike into their conversations had come with mixed results. When he was alert, he added good insights. Yet as time wore on, his focus waned.

They had already stretched the limits of exploration in both directions, not to mention having ventured into the jungle via different paths in search of water. If they wanted to go any further, they all must go, and that meant abandoning their ship and carrying everything critical to their continued survival with them. Such a trek promised to tax their stamina, not to mention their strained camaraderie.

Beyond *when* to pack and go — not *if*, because they were now convinced rescue would not come to them — they had to decide which direction would present the fastest route to extraction out of this hellscape. Skip's first instinct told him to go east toward Port Moresby, even though they were closer to Kerema. There were no air bases at Kerema, but Leo was convinced the Australian Army operated in that vicinity.

Rafe's laughter pulled Skip from his geographic musings.

"What's so funny?"

"This." Rafe sat in the shade beneath the plane's wing. He grinned and held up their jungle survival handbook. "Says here we can learn how to identify which plants and berries are edible and which are poisonous by *making field trips, talking to natives, and visiting botanical gardens and museums*."

"Who do I see about touring the botanical garden, Skipper?" Leo called out. "Can the Red Cross Girls set that up for us?"

Skip joined in their laughter, but his thoughts turned to Hadley. Did she know he was missing? He had noticed that Bizzy and JoJo were the ones who most often served them cold drinks and cookies at his base at Durand. If they had heard, they might let her know. Or perhaps they would consider it a kindness to withhold that information. Would she even care?

He hadn't handled things well at Kila Kila. He'd been both stupid and unkind when he had directed his anger at that fool Blanchard on Hadley. Skip had lost a chance to apologize to her for his defensiveness that night on the beach at Yorkeys Knob and had then compounded the problem by lashing out at her more than he had at Blanchard. If . . . no, *when* he returned to Port Moresby, he would find her and put things right. No reason they shouldn't be on friendly terms, even if she was dating Blanchard.

"Say, Skipper?" Leo's voice broke into his thoughts. "Um . . ."

"Yeah?" he answered without looking up.

"Not a botanical garden, but looks like we can do one of the other things the manual suggests." Leo's voice held both relief and trepidation.

Skip turned.

About a dozen Papuans stood clustered just inside the tree line, watching them. Three men, four women, and several children.

His heart pounded, and his mouth went dry. They had been searching for someone to help them find water, help them survive, help them return to Moresby. Yet now that their salvation had come, he froze. Not with fear exactly. He, like the other airmen based around Moresby, had visited surrounding villages and interacted with the locals who worked on the bases.

Except these tribespeople lived in isolation away from the war raging on other parts of this vast island. Some of the highlands tribes were said to be cannibals, although the army and the Australians had both assured Allied soldiers that the people who lived in the coastal areas were friendly. Many of them were also devout Christians, thanks to missionaries.

These people might not know about the war, but odds were high they had encountered westerners before. Communicating with them might be their biggest challenge. Yet somehow, he and his men must convey their dire need for drinkable water.

"Everybody up." Skip stood. "Let's go say hello."

His crewmates signaled nervousness with each step.

"Smile, dammit," Skip hissed through clenched teeth. "We don't want to scare them."

"They don't look too happy." Mike put his hand on the sheath of his knife.

"Don't pull out any weapons. They aren't armed, fellas," Skip said. "We're supposed to act friendly in this scenario, remember?"

"How do you know they aren't armed? They look pretty fierce to me," Rafe whispered.

"Uh, maybe 'cause they aren't wearing much and have nothing in their hands?" Westerners might read hostility into the array of tattoos and body piercings favored by the tribespeople, but Skip focused on their expressions and body language. "Come on, walk with me. And for God's sake, *smile*. We need their help."

Skip grinned and walked casually toward the waiting group. The Papuans stepped forward, talking among themselves, and met Skip and his men between the jungle and the sea.

One man stepped out in front of the others. A long bone pierced his nose, like some they had seen worn by local men near Port Moresby. He and the others also wore elaborate shell necklaces and headbands. Skip held out his hand, palm up, and offered the man a dime from his pocket. The man took it, held it out for the others to see, and grinned.

"Do you speak English?" Skip glanced at each of them in turn but saw no flicker of understanding.

"*Sprichst du Deutsch?*" Leo asked. He waited a beat, and when that got no response, tried again with, "*Begrijpt u Netherlands?*"

"What language is that?" Rafe asked.

"I tried German and Dutch," Leo said. "Missionaries from both countries have been here for decades."

"Use simple words they might recognize," Skip suggested. "Like the word for water."

"*Lebensmittel? Wasser?*" Leo paused. "*Voedsel?*"

Still no response.

Skip mimed drinking, then eating.

Another man stepped forward. "*Yupela laik drink. Yupela laik kaikai.*"

"Yes." Skip nodded. The man was speaking Pidgin. If he'd had much contact with either the Australian government or missionaries, he probably knew the mixture of English and his native tongue. Skip was certain that *yes* was the same in Pidgin as in English. "Yes. Drink."

"*Water belong drink.*" The man pointed toward the jungle. "*Man ee go-go-go-go.*"

"Okay." Skip inferred the jungle had a fresh water source, but how far away was it? A large section of the *Pocket Guide to New Guinea* was devoted to common Pidgin phrases. "I've got a copy of the *Pocket Guide* in my bag. One of you go get it, please."

"I'll go." Rafe backed away and hurried toward the ship.

The man pointed at the plane and mimed a plane crashing to earth. Skip then used his hand to elaborate, while waiting on Rafe to return with the book.

"Here you go, Skipper." Rafe pressed the little paperbound book into Skip's hand.

He flipped to the back, skipped the pronunciation guide, and skimmed to find the phrases for distance. Once he found the one he needed, he met the man's eyes.

"*Drink, man ee go lo-ol-o-ng way?*" He hoped his inflection was clear, even if he had botched the words.

The man once again pointed toward the jungle. "*Ee-got, drink ee go-go-go.*"

Skip skimmed more. Was there a phrase for *take me to water*?

Leo, reading over Skip's shoulder, pointed out another way to ask about the distance.

Skip nodded to Leo, then sounded out each word carefully. *"Suppose me loose-im place here along, by'n'by sun . . . uh . . . bell-o-kai-kai, ee stop now where me come up along drink?"* If I leave here at noon, when will I reach water?

The man's responding gesture indicated something less than an hour's distance away.

"Good." Skip traced his finger over another phrase. *"You come line-im me along road?"* Will you lead us to water? He fished another dime from his pocket and held it out.

The man took it, and his face split into a wide grin. His teeth were stained black and his gums were bright red from chewing betel nuts. He spoke to the others in a torrent of words in their native language. After their excited conversation, the man gestured for Skip and his men to follow them.

"Should we all go?" Dewey asked.

Skip exhaled. "Yeah, we'd better stick together. But we should secure the plane first."

He held up a finger to let the man know they needed a moment.

"Charlie, you stay here and make sure they don't leave." If curious children from the tribe backtracked to explore the plane, Skip wanted to be certain they couldn't hurt themselves or cause any damage.

Charlie nodded.

Skip and the others hurried back to the plane. Mike dropped their remaining rations out and told Charlie to divvy them up among their survival packs, while Dewey put waterproof covers over the turret guns. Then he helped Mike and Leo remove the firing pins, dismount, and store the other guns inside the bomb bay.

Rafe and Skip disconnected the battery leads so no one could turn on the ignition or the radio. They then locked the rudder, elevator, and flap controls, while Dewey collected the parachutes and stored them alongside the guns in the bomb bay.

Although it seemed unlikely the radio transmitter could fall into Japanese hands, Skip told Rafe to destroy it. They then closed all of the windows, climbed out of the plane, and shut both escape hatches.

"Take your survival packs, weapons, and canteens," Skip said.

Mike picked up his gun and nodded toward the waiting people. "You're sure?"

"Yeah." Skip shrugged his pack on and looped his harness and gun over his shoulder. "We're armed, and they're not."

"Maybe so." Mike raised an eyebrow. "But others who are armed might be waiting in the jungle to ambush us."

"Fellas," Skip said quietly. "None of these tribes have guns. And besides, we're taller and heavier than they are." They had all noticed the height discrepancy with the locals around Moresby, and similarly, none of these people were much over five feet tall. Skip waved for his men to follow him. "Let's go."

If they were near the northern coast, he might be worried that these people might betray them to the Japanese, but not here. So unless this tribe practiced cannibalism, Skip couldn't see how they could be in any danger. Following them into the jungle seemed far less treacherous than trekking through the formidable territory on their own.

All the same, they should employ caution.

"Stay alert as to where we are," Skip murmured to Leo. "And how we can get back."

Leo nodded.

The man who had spoken with Skip led the way, with the others trailing along behind him. He took a path Skip hadn't noticed before. He doubted he would have ever recognized it as being a trail. Yet apart from being a bit on the mucky side, traversing it was easier than their other explorations had been. No gloppy swamp to skirt around or pick through.

Strange, unfamiliar birds squawked, cawed, and burbled around them, and the light filtering through the trees dispelled some of the gloom. This part of the jungle was lighter than Skip had expected, but no less fetid. The pungent odor of moist decay that had emanated from the jungle around their base was stronger here.

He did his best to track the progress of the native guides while monitoring the plants brushing against them for snakes, spiders, and other creatures. Even without creepy-crawlies, the trees and vines were weaponized with prickly, serrated spikes and thorns as sharp as Kunai grass.

They walked for no more than half an hour before the low roar of rushing water signaled they were within range of the promised source of fresh drinking water. Within minutes, the locals excitedly waved them toward the bubbling inland stream that cascaded in successive white-capped spurts over rocks.

Skip uncapped his canteen, and like the others, held its mouth close to a rock to catch the streaming water. Even Charlie joined them, having apparently lost his trepidation about crocodiles.

"Hold up," Skip called out to Dewey, who had raised his canteen to his lips. "Drop a purification tablet into it before you drink."

Even though the water appeared to be clear and fresh, it likely held parasites that might sicken them.

"*You come stop place belong ka-na-ka.*" One of the other men pointed toward a trail leading away from the coast.

Skip suspected the man wanted them to go to his village, but he pulled the guidebook from his pocket to make sure. *Ka-na-ka*, he sounded out while skimming. Yes, that meant village. Skip turned to the others. "He's inviting us to their village."

"Our survival guide says we shouldn't eat in native villages," Rafe said in a low voice. "But if we don't go, we might offend them."

"Yeah, I know. Their leader might know something that could help us." Skip drank from his canteen, then refilled it and added another purification tablet.

Mike pointed to the guidebook. "Is there something in there to help us ask?"

"Hmmm." Skip ran his finger down the page. "Greetings, time, distance, food, animals, surroundings . . ."

"*Mo*?" Leo pointed to the crew as a group and repeated, "*Mo* . . . like us? Soldiers?"

"*Soldia*," one of the men said. "*Gavman soldia*."

"Soldia . . . soldier, soldia . . . soldier," Skip said, pointing at himself, then at his men.

The man grinned and pointed to the path. "*Yes, yes, soldia*."

Was the man simply agreeing that Skip and the others were soldiers? Or did he understand that Leo was asking if he and his tribespeople could take Skip and his men to *other* soldiers? Others who were not Japanese. Skip had no idea how to ask if the hypothetical soldiers were friend or foe.

"Uh . . ." He scanned the page again. "*Soldia, how mas*?"

The man conferred with the others, with even the children chiming in.

"*One pella ten two*," he finally said. "*Soldia*."

"*One pella ten two*," Charlie chanted while Skip flipped through the guidebook to get to the section about numbers. "*One pella ten two*."

"Twelve." Leo's brow puckered. "Twelve could be real. If there are a dozen soldiers somewhere near here, they'll have a way to get us out. A radio."

"*Where stop place belong ka-na-ka*?" Skip asked.

"*Not longwe*," another man said, shaking his head. "*Not longwe*."

"*Soldias*?" Leo repeated.

He nodded. "*Yes, yes, gavman soldias*."

"They say not far. Let's go to their village." Skip stood and gestured for the others to join him. "Their chief can tell us more."

"*Em, ee stop along hap.*" The man motioned for them to follow him.

They had been correct about the distance. Their small village sat in a clearing no more than a mile past the stream. Unlike the villages around Moresby where the homes were constructed on stilts over water, this one had many tiny homes that sat on wooden posts only a few feet off the ground. Their roofs were thatched with sago palm leaves in the New Guinea style, but their sides were made from bamboo, so they almost resembled log cabins.

Chickens roamed amid the homes, and several mangy dogs lounged in the shade of the trees, rousting themselves only long enough to come inspect Skip and his crewmates.

A crowd of children skipped around them, touching their uniforms and smiling shyly.

Skip nudged Dewey, who had reached into his pocket, presumably to extract something to give the children. "Don't give them anything yet. We don't know how long we might need to call on favors."

The tribesmen who had led them through the jungle motioned for Skip and the others to follow them into one of the larger buildings. They passed several big huts before stopping in front of a high one with a crude staircase leading up to the door.

The door was adorned with several intricate carvings. Sunlight and dense, humid air filtered into the building through spaces between the bamboo stalks. More carvings hung on the walls inside. This must be the village ceremonial house.

An elderly man rose to greet them. His rendition of Pidgin, if that's what it was, was hard to understand, but his accompanying gestures told them to sit on the weathered floor. The floorboards were smooth but speckled with betel juice stains.

One of the men who had guided them here passed Skip a communal pipe. He managed to take a drag from it without choking. He passed it on, then opened his guidebook and attempted to convey the gist of their predicament to the tribesmen.

He chose his words carefully and hoped the guidebook's rough translations would help him communicate properly. The men had said they knew of government soldiers. Could they take Skip and his men to them?

The tribesmen continued to smoke and talk, little of which Skip understood. They seemed to be in no hurry. Sweat beaded on his temples and dripped down his neck. He couldn't judge from the interior light how much time had passed since they arrived. The men made efforts to be circumspect, but he was aware that his crewmates were growing wary and restless.

Unless the tribesmen could lead them to other *soldias*, he needed to allow plenty of time for him and his men to walk back to the crash site before nightfall. They now knew where to find water, so they would survive — at least until their supply of purification tablets ran out.

He tried again. "*Gavman soldias?*"

"*Yes, yes,*" the men agreed. Yet they didn't seem to understand any of Skip's questions from the guidebook about time and distance.

"Hey, Skipper — " On the pretext of checking the phrase guide, Leo leaned close and whispered, "Shouldn't we politely take our leave?"

Probably. Given the language barrier and their cultural differences, God only knew how long it would take for them to extricate themselves from the village and find the path back to the plane. Assuming they could make it back without incident. They probably should give a small gift to one of the boys and ask him to lead them back.

Skip glanced at Leo. "Yeah. Help me figure out how to tell them we need to leave."

With their heads huddled over the guidebook, they didn't see a new man enter the hut. At a nudge from Mike, Skip looked up. The tribesman squatted before him and the others.

Skip inclined his head and squinted at the man's necklaces. He wore the same elaborate ones made out of shells that many of the others wore, with the addition of a wooden cross on a simple leather chain that hung prominently in front of his other jewelry. Did the cross signify something other than Christianity in New Guinea, or to this tribe?

"Is that a Christian cross?" Skip asked, his curiosity overriding his instinct toward caution and cultural sensitivity. Not wanting to point, Skip touched his chest where the cross rested against the other man's body.

The man nodded. "Yes, cross for Christian. We call it *krusefiks*. I was educated at the Catholic missionary school at Terapo."

The tension across Skip's shoulders melted away. The man's speech was closer to standard English than the rough Pidgin the others used. They had finally found common ground.

He didn't bother to translate his next words. "My name is Lieutenant Skip Masterson." He indicated his crewmates. "We are American airmen."

"My tribesmen guessed as much from the American flag on your plane." The man winked. "I am Semu."

Relieved, Skip grinned.

Semu turned and had a rapid, guttural conversation with his tribesmen in their native tongue and then faced Skip again. "You need rescue, yes?"

"Yes," Skip said. "Your tribesmen indicated that there are other soldiers near here. If they are Australian, we would like you to take us to them. They can help us get back to our base."

"Yes, they are Australians." Semu nodded. "They are upriver."

"How far away is the river?"

"*River ee . . . Walk one hour stop ka-na-ka*," Semu replied.

Hope surged through Skip. "And the Australians are near the river?"

"How you say . . . upriver. Not an hour by boat." Semu shrugged apologetically and then smiled. "I did not master time in English."

Through Semu's curious hodgepodge of English, Pidgin, and native words, Skip gleaned that Australians were about two hours away. He wanted to make sure he hadn't misunderstood.

"Do you have a boat?" Skip pictured the narrow wooden canoes he had seen the locals use on the rivers around Port Moresby. They would need several to transport everyone.

Semu shook his head. "Australians have boat."

"What do you mean?" Skip frowned. How would the Australians know to bring a boat downriver to collect them? Asking that might stretch the limits of their ability to communicate. He mimed a boat sailing downstream. "Australians will bring a boat down the river?"

"Yes, yes." Semu grinned.

Skip drew his brows together. "How will the Australians know to send a boat?"

"I send boy to tell them. They come." Semu took a drag from the communal pipe and held it out to Skip.

He took it and inhaled as little as he could before passing it back to Semu. Verb tense mattered now. Was Semu saying that he had *already* sent a boy upriver? Or that he *would* send one? And if the latter, when?

"Have you already sent a boy?"

"Yes. He is there. We walk now to river." Semu and his tribesmen stood.

Skip and his men came to their feet and waited, uncertain about the protocol for leaving the ceremonial house. They knew from their visits to the villages near their base that they should follow the lead of their hosts.

"Come with us now." Semu gestured for Skip and his crewmates to follow him outside.

Semu gathered three other tribesmen to accompany them and then waved Skip and his crewmates forward. "We take you to river where boat wait."

Skip nodded and gestured for his men to fall in line behind him. Laughing children skipped alongside them, falling back when Semu led Skip and the others into the jungle.

As they had before, the Papuans trod an easy passage through the foliage. The new route was, however, more circuitous than the one from the beach to the stream and village.

"Not sure I could find my way back to the village," Leo whispered.

Skip nodded. "Let's hope we don't need to."

He recognized the rush of water from the river before it came into view. The tribesmen led to them onto a bluff above the fast-moving brown water, where a worn, narrow footpath led down to the riverbank.

"We wait here until they come." Semu said.

They didn't have to wait long. A few minutes later, a slender village boy dashed toward them, calling out excitedly in his native language.

"He says the boat is not far. Will be here soon." Semu smiled at them.

The drone from an outboard motor soon alerted that a boat approached. Skip's pulse jumped. Surely there weren't any Japanese forces this far south.

Moments later, kicking up a sizeable wake on both sides, a PT boat cut a neat line down the middle of the muddy river. The boat motored past them for a short distance before the boat pilot turned the craft back upstream and pointed its bow toward shore.

Skip studied the boat pilot and crew. Aussies. He hadn't realized how tense his muscles had been until a wave of relaxation turned them to jelly.

"'Ow ya goin' mates?" a member of the crew called out. He and another man dropped a rowboat tethered by a rope off the side of the PT boat. Two Papuans rowed it to shore.

Skip pointed toward Charlie and Dewey, "You fellas go down to the bank and wait for the rowboat, while we thank our kind hosts."

He and the others pulled an assortment of items from their packs and passed tins of bully beef, ham, beef stew, and tomato soup to Semu and his tribesmen. They then added chocolate bars, cookies, razors, cloth rags, and bars of soap to the haul.

Skip motioned toward the boy who had gone to fetch the

Aussies. Once he drew closer, Skip removed his hunting knife from his belt and held it out to the boy. "This is for you. Thank you for your help."

The boy's eyes widened as he accepted the knife. His broad grin said far more than the Pidgin he attempted to use.

Charlie and Dewey called out to them while waving and dancing a jig on the deck of the PT boat. "Come on down, fellas!"

"Coming!" Skip laughed and waved back. "Rafe, you and Mike can go next."

He wasn't sure if Semu would agree to shake hands with him, or if he should bow or take some other action to part company. He settled on giving the man a verbal acknowledgement. "Thank you so much. We are indebted to you and your tribe."

***

November 25, 1943, 9:30 p.m.

Shangri-La Club, Ela Beach, Port Moresby, New Guinea

Hadley circled her heel in the sand. The band's rendition of *Paper Doll*, with its soulful mood, floated across the way from the open-air *Shangri-La* club.

The Thanksgiving Day dance for men based around Port Moresby had been a resounding success. They had served sliced roast turkey, cranberry sauce, sweet potato casserole, green beans, and pumpkin pie, all courtesy of their navy contacts. Army airmen had been grateful for the traditional Thanksgiving meal.

Even without stuffing or the oyster dressing favored back home in New Orleans, Hadley would ordinarily have been just as appreciative of the special feast as the airmen had been. But she had only managed to choke down a few bites.

She had tried to dance but had fallen short there too. Bizzy gave her a quick hug and shooed her out of the club. Rather than trekking back to their encampment alone in the dark, Hadley had promised to wait on the beach until the dance was over, then help the others with cleanup. Work helped to keep her mind occupied.

Waves gently splashing onto the shore failed to divert her attention from the grief that had swamped her in steady waves since she had learned Skip and his crew were missing. Despite her friends' protests, Hadley had returned to the Durand base every day. Simply checking in with Nate and his fellas hadn't been enough.

She had strode into the intelligence tent and group headquarters on a daily basis and demanded to know what efforts they were making to find Skip and his crew. To their credit, though they might have been tempted to put her off with platitudes or insisted they couldn't divulge details, the officers had explained their protocol and its limitations. Because no one had seen his plane go down or could pinpoint where Skip had gotten separated from the others, they couldn't launch a targeted search-and-rescue effort.

"What about photo reconnaissance flights?" she had asked. If they were also gaining photographic intelligence, surely they could justify non-targeted searches.

The officers had assured her that all photo reconnaissance pilots were on alert to scour the terrain below for any evidence of a downed crew. They did this as a matter of course while over friendly territory. But if they were over contested or hostile areas, they had to focus on their own safety, although intelligence would carefully scrutinize their photographs after they returned to check for any leads.

Vast swathes of this island were nothing more than clumps of dense green jungle or forested mountains from the air. Ditching into the sea might have been Skip's best hope, but scanning the sea had the same limitations as searching the island. Even with the crew's bright yellow rafts and red flares, pilots flying overhead could easily miss them in the monotonous ocean swells. Hadley hadn't needed the officers to tell her that every passing hour decreased the survival odds for him and his men.

Bizzy and the others had urged Hadley to go with them to

Sydney tomorrow on their planned leave. She had put off packing, unable to decide which option would make her least miserable. And she had to consider Lucy. Nate had promised to look after the wallaby and be certain no one else claimed her, but Hadley worried that a three-week leave in Australia would be too long for her to leave Lucy's fate to chance, despite his assurances.

She could go to Durand and collect Lucy from Nate, then meet her friends in Sydney in a few days. Yes, that would allow her to wait a while longer . . . in case she received news, good or bad. Being in Sydney, where she would hear nothing, would be torture. Yet by the end of next week, the odds of finding Skip and his crew alive would be miniscule. At that point, Hadley would take Lucy as her pet.

Voices carried down the path. Then Bizzy called her name.

Hadley looked over her shoulder and waved. The light spilling out of the *Shangri-La* ought to be bright enough for Bizzy to spot her.

Her friend hurried toward her, half-towing an officer by the arm.

Hadley squinted at the two of them. The officer was Lieutenant Lawson, one of the intelligence officers Hadley had questioned at Durand yesterday. Her skin prickled.

"Hadley! Hadley!" Bizzy squealed breathlessly. She reached out and pulled Hadley to her feet. "Lieutenant Lawson has news. *Good* news!"

"Aussies radioed us about an hour ago to tell us one of their units picked up Lieutenant Masterson and his crew earlier tonight," Lieutenant Lawson said. "We'll go get them tomorrow. Their message was brief, but it says all of the men are safe and healthy."

A wave of dizziness made Hadley sway on her feet. *Skip is safe and healthy. Safe and healthy. Safe, healthy, and returning to base.*

"Do you know where?" she blurted, before laughing and shaking her head. Her curiosity had overridden her common sense again. "Never mind, I know you can't tell me."

"You're right. I can't divulge those details. But there's nothing to prevent your boyfriend from telling you where he's been."

"Oh, he's not . . ." Hadley stammered. "We've run into one another here and there."

"Umm-hmmm," he murmured. "Well, like I said, Lieutenant Masterson can share details with you as he chooses."

"Sounds like you'll be able to ask him tomorrow." Bizzy wrapped her arm around Hadley's shoulders.

Hadley's stomach plummeted. She shook her head. "Not unless they bring him to Sydney. We leave in the morning, remember?"

"But . . ." Bizzy's eyes rounded in surprise. "Surely you'd rather stay here and see Skip, then meet us in Sydney later. You've already said you don't plan to go with us tomorrow."

"Of course, I'm going, silly." Hadley flashed Bizzy a please-play-along-with-me smile. "I should go finish packing."

She turned and smiled at Lieutenant Lawson.

"Thanks for letting us know, Lieutenant. I'm so relieved you've located Skip and his crew. I'll hear his story when I get back."

She turned and walked toward the club. Bizzy and Lawson fell in step beside her.

"Not often we get good news," Lawson said. "The Aussies operate in such remote locations, our fellas have trouble finding them. Your friend is very lucky."

They had reached the entrance to the *Shangri-La*. Hadley turned to Bizzy. "I'll go back to our tent and finish packing, then get someone to bring me back here to help with cleanup."

"No, no." Bizzy shook her head. "You don't need to come back tonight. We can manage. Be sure to find a ride to the tent though. It's too late for you to walk by yourself."

"I can give you a lift, if you like," Lieutenant Lawson offered.

Hadley nodded. "Thanks."

Surrounded by barbed wire, the encampment area for the Red Cross Girls and nurses was located a couple of miles from the *Shangri-La* beachfront club.

"Can I see you inside for a second before you go?" Bizzy

tugged on Hadley's arm.

"I'll be right back," Hadley called to Lieutenant Lawson as Bizzy steered her through the door and into an alcove near the stage where the band members stored their instrument cases.

"Hadley, what on earth?" Bizzy said. "You've been miserable and heartbroken — no, don't you dare deny it — ever since you heard Skip Masterson had gone missing, and now you're going to pack up and run off to Australia without seeing him?"

"Bizzy —" Hadley broke off. If she saw Skip, she would run into his arms. If she saw him, she wouldn't be able to hide her feelings. If she saw him, she would be emotionally entangled but good.

Hadley looked away. She had no intention of creating any more emotional ties with Skip, who would, despite his close shave with death, soon return to combat. Her heart couldn't stand any more. It was better to disappear to Australia for three weeks than chance her heart with him. Besides, the last time she had seen Skip, he had made it clear that he had lost respect for her. She would have no chance of building a relationship with him without mutual respect.

"You don't understand, Bizzy," she finally said with a shake of her head. A sheen of tears blurred her vision. "I can't see him. I can't risk what might happen next."

CHAPTER FOURTEEN

November 27, 1943

Sydney, Australia

Hadley pointed at the city map in her Red Cross brochure. "Let's go to the Botanical Gardens today and take the tram to the zoo tomorrow."

"Stretching our legs after traveling yesterday sounds good to me," Stella said.

All told, with stops along the eastern Australian coast before their commercial flight from Brisbane to Sydney, they had been in transit for fifteen hours. They had slept until late morning after stumbling into their reserved room at the Red Cross leave home for women after midnight.

JoJo smoothed her jacket. "It's a gorgeous day to be outdoors. We aren't sweltering for the first time in months, ladies."

"All the fellas are bound to be enjoying this nice spring weather too." Bizzy pulled a compact and lipstick from her purse.

Hadley, JoJo, and Stella exchanged amused looks. Bizzy was well-rested and ready to line up her usual succession of dates. She would have little trouble. The city was swarming with American servicemen.

Bizzy puckered her lips, inspected the effect, and snapped her compact shut. "Well, what are we waiting on? Let's go."

They set off and soon found the formal botanical gardens, where they strolled along the path admiring the beautiful profusion of fragrant jacaranda trees in full bloom. They slowed their pace and chatted with a number of soldiers who were also enjoying leave. To no one's surprise, Bizzy managed to arrange dates for the entire week within an hour.

"How will you ever keep up with all of them?" Stella asked. "Do you even remember their names or what they looked like?"

"Shouldn't you take notes?" JoJo asked. "Hadley probably has a notepad in her purse. She's never without one."

Bizzy made a face and rattled off names, ranks, hometowns, and days and times for her dates with each man.

"That's impressive, cher." Hadley winked. "Whether it's right or not remains to be seen. Your date tomorrow night might actually be with Joe from Tuscaloosa, rather than Joseph from Tallahassee. Who can say?"

They stopped to buy ice cream cones before ambling into the park known as *The Domain* that adjoined the botanical gardens. Hadley suggested they visit the national library, but the others prevailed on her to leave that for another day. The delightful, crisp breeze and blue skies overhead presented a far too tempting contrast with the sluggish New Guinea heat.

"The view from *Mrs. Macquerie's Chair* is supposed to be lovely. Should we walk in that direction?" JoJo traced her finger along the path marked on the brochure map.

Hadley licked the edges of her ice cream cone to catch the dribbles and savored the sweet, cool taste of chocolate. "Sounds swell. Then we'll need to go back to the hotel so Bizzy can get ready for her date."

The path winding through *The Domain* was even more crowded with servicemen than the gardens had been, and before long, Bizzy had scheduled another week of dates.

Bizzy fluffed her halo of frizzy blond curls. "Why aren't you girls accepting any invitations?"

"I'm too exhausted." JoJo stifled a yawn. "I'll go out after I've caught up on my sleep."

"And you?" Bizzy looked at Hadley.

Hadley frowned. Dates? No, she'd rather rest and sleuth out more story material during her free time. With any luck, Dupre had already received the second version of her interview with the first lady — and she had told Bizzy that avoiding Skip was crucial to her emotional well-being. Dating other men would not help. She met her friend's inquisitive gaze. "Who, me? I don't think so."

"Yes, you," Bizzy said. "If Lieutenant Dreamboat really is only a friend, you should see other men."

"Ooh, look at all those pretty kites." Hadley pointed at the sky. The path curved toward a large field where children were flying colorful kites in the spring breeze.

Bizzy wagged her finger at Hadley. "You're not being honest with yourself, or with *him*. Just admit it—you don't want to go out with other men because you're gone on him."

"Honestly, Biz, our leave is supposed to be relaxing," Stella said. "Stop fretting about us and worry about keeping track of the men you've made plans with."

"Yeah, here comes another group of fellas right now," JoJo said.

Bizzy turned to look and tittered with cascading rolls of giggles. "Yes, and look who's front and center."

Hadley tore her gaze away from the kites.

Oh God. Flutters flitted through her belly. Skip strode toward them, a smile lighting up his face.

Dammit. She wasn't surprised he was on leave. The military usually rewarded men who had undergone a harrowing experience. But with all the locations on the continent of Australia, why had he chosen to come to Sydney?

"Stop laughing." Hadley elbowed Bizzy.

Skip had only been missing for three days, but he looked leaner than he had the last time she had seen him. Lean, tan, and dishy.

"Imagine meeting you gals here," Leo called out as they approached them.

JoJo laughed. "You boys didn't want sun and surf on the gold coast beaches this trip?"

"We've had enough sand and surf for a while. Being stranded on a beach for a few days put us off the experience." Skip winked at Hadley.

Her pulse jumped. Carefully avoiding his eyes, she smiled and directed her gaze toward the group at large. "We were relieved to hear that you had been rescued."

"Bet that's some story," JoJo said with a hopeful look.

"A story we can hear later," Hadley cut in. "We shouldn't keep you from enjoying this gorgeous day. I'm sure you've got plans."

"Not really." Leo shook his head. "We don't —"

"Do you have one of these guides with a map?" Hadley asked, pulling a copy of the Red Cross brochure from her purse and holding it out.

Rafe brandished their copy. "We're all set."

"What have you seen so far?" Bizzy asked.

Dewey jerked his thumb behind them. "We just climbed to *Mrs. Macquerie's Chair.*"

"That's where we're going." Hadley tucked her hair behind her ear. "We should let you be on your —"

"We went to the botanical gardens," Stella broke in, cutting her off.

Leo started laughing, and his convulsive hoots spread like wildfire among the men.

Confusion mingled with a flash of hurt across Stella's face. She had confided to the others that it had taken more than the usual two interviews for her to persuade the Red Cross that her shyness shouldn't disqualify her from serving overseas.

"What's so funny about the botanical gardens?" Sharpness saturated Hadley's tone.

Skip's grin slipped. He coughed. "Sorry, but our jungle survival manual says we can learn to distinguish edible plants from poisonous ones by visiting local botanical gardens. There were, um . . ." His laughter bubbled up again. "A few *minor* problems with that line of advice."

Bizzy dissolved into tinkling giggles. "Sounds like something the Red Cross would put in their materials."

"And how." Stella nodded and smiled.

"I bet the gardens here don't have the same crazy plants we see in New Guinea." Leo looked at Hadley. "Remember the spiky ones Mr. Sefton showed us on his rubber plantation?"

"Yeah," Hadley said, stifling her instinctive chatty response. She was desperate to move on and escape Skip's heady presence. "Well, fellas, the gardens are lovely, so —"

"Where were you headed before you spotted us?" JoJo asked.

Rafe clapped Skip's shoulder. "Skip wants us to go to a *library*." With his inflection, the *library* might as well have been a prison.

Bizzy waved her hand at the blue sky. "It's way too pretty to be indoors, but Hadley also wants to see the library."

"No." Hadley shook her head. "Not today."

"Perfect." Bizzy's breezy tone belied her calculated agenda. "Now the rest of us won't have to come along."

"I'd love to accompany Skip to the library, but we can do that another time." Hadley tapped her fingers against her skirt. "We need to return to the hotel soon, remember?"

"Bizzy has plans for tonight," Stella put in with a shy smile. "But you don't."

"Stella's right. You should go enjoy yourself." JoJo pointed at the description in the brochure. "The library has a priceless collection of books and manuscripts."

"The afternoon is almost gone," Hadley said. "It probably closes soon."

"Not until five." Stella read the brochure over JoJo's shoulder. "You have plenty of time."

With laughter and joking calls for them to enjoy the library, Skip's crewmates departed in the company of Hadley's friends.

"Well —" She cleared her throat and trained her eyes on the brochure to keep from looking at him. "This says we should take this path —"

"Hadley, wait," he broke in. "I need to say something."

She shook her head and stared at the map.

"I'm sorry."

"There's nothing for you to —" Hadley shook her head.

He edged closer. "Yes, there is. I was a complete ass that day at Kila Kila."

"You weren't wrong. I am impulsive. Stubborn. Self-righteous. Single-minded —" Hadley said, unfurling her fingers one by one as she rattled off her flaws. "I can keep going."

"That may be true." Skip's lips twitched. "But it doesn't give me or anyone else license to treat you unfairly. I was out of line."

"Don't worry about it."

"I also messed up my chance to apologize for what happened in Cairns," he continued. "I wanted to tell you I was sorry for how I behaved that night, and then I messed that up too." He ducked his head until she met his eyes. "So I'm gonna say it now. I'm sorry. I'm sorry for —"

"There's no need for you to apologize. You don't owe me anything."

"Yeah, I do." Skip stepped closer. "Not being able to apologize would have been one of my biggest regrets if we hadn't gotten out of the jungle, Hadley. Thought about it a lot while we were lost. Promised myself if I got outta there alive, I'd find you and make things right."

Despite her assurances to Nate and her friends that Skip was fine, Hadley had been heartsick to think she might never see him again. Men downed in the jungle didn't often survive. She bit her lip. "You thought about *me* while you were lost in the jungle?"

"Yeah." Skip locked his clear green eyes with hers. "I think about you all the time."

Hadley's heart flipped and thudded in her chest. "I think about you too. All the time." The truth tumbled out before she could rein it in.

He cupped her face, his feathery light touch sending shivers snaking across her shoulders, and leaned closer. "What about Blanchard?"

"We're just pals," she whispered. Her lips parted. "That's all. I tried to tell you."

"You're sure?" He traced his finger around her mouth.

Goosebumps stole up her arms. She inhaled the cedar-moss scent of his aftershave and fixed her eyes on the faint spray of freckles dotting the bridge of his nose.

Was she sure Blanchard was only a buddy? That she was ready to cast aside her worries about becoming emotionally entangled with Skip? Or that she hovered on the edge of kissing him senseless?

In answer, she rose onto her tiptoes and kissed him, twining her fingers into his hair and wrapping her arms around his neck to tug him closer. Skip slid his arms around her waist and pulled her tightly against him, then trailed kisses along her jaw and groaned softly in her ear before reclaiming her mouth with scorching intensity. *Lordy*.

He opened his mouth over hers, and raw hunger consumed her. Blood coursed through her veins and pounded in her ears. As she had learned at Sans Souci, Skip Masterson knew how to send her. How to get her all hot and bothered.

Wolf whistles and catcalls from the crowds of passing servicemen persuaded them to disengage from canoodling in such a public space, but Skip held fast to her waist to keep her snugly against him. He smoothed her hair off her forehead and lifted his eyebrows.

"That was some kiss, Miss Scarlett."

"Um-hm." Hadley's belly tightened at the low, sultry notes in his voice. "Maybe we could try that again. Somewhere without an audience."

"Umm-hmmm, I like that idea." Skip caressed his index finger over her mouth. "But first, how about you let me be a gentleman and take you to dinner? Your friends already confirmed you're free tonight."

"You owe me a trip to the library first." Hadley inclined her head and smiled.

Skip grinned and took her hand. "Wouldn't miss it."

She laced her fingers tightly with his. God, he was a dish. She was a goner.

***

Electrical sparks pinged through Skip's gut as he approached the door to Hadley's hotel. What was it about her that had so inveigled his emotions? He hadn't stretched the truth when he had confessed how often he had thought of her in the jungle. She had gotten under his skin all right.

Uniformed servicemen waiting on their dates crowded the lobby of the Red Cross hotel for women. Skip inclined his head to check the time on another fella's watch.

Five more minutes.

He leaned against the wall, holding the bouquet of flowers he had purchased at a nearby stall against his chest so no one would crush the blooms. They smelled fantastic, an intoxicating blend of sweet and herbal scents.

Skip spotted Hadley before she saw him.

Jesus. All the breath left his body. He hadn't realized she would have civvie attire with her or that the Red Cross would allow her to wear it. Her filmy red evening dress clung to her slender figure, accented her curves, and sent his blood raging through his veins like all those New Guinea rivers.

She paused at the bottom of the stairs, bit her lip, and scanned the crowd without her normal confidence or chatty demeanor. A pink sheen tinted her fair skin.

God. Skip tightened his trembling hands around the bouquet. He was as nervous as she appeared. Old Skip had always been suave and seductive. But now?

He sucked in a deep breath and called out Hadley's name.

She turned and recognition flashed in her eyes. She smiled and cut through the sea of men, oblivious to their good-natured banter. Her dress was attracting more than her usual bevy of admirers. A surge of heat stabbed Skip's chest as she drew close.

"Thought you might like these." He thrust the bouquet toward her.

Hadley brought the arrangement to her nose and inhaled its heady scent. "They're gorgeous, thank you."

"Would have bought roses if I'd known you'd be wearing such a pretty red dress." He skimmed his fingers up her arm and stroked her silky sleeve. "You look beautiful."

"Thanks." Hadley flashed him a brilliant smile, then glanced around. "I'll see if one of the staff can find a vase for the flowers."

"Oh, right." What a numbskull he was. Of course she wouldn't want to carry flowers around all evening, and she was staying in a hotel. He should have brought her a box of candy, something she could slip into her purse.

"Ooh, those are beautiful." Bizzy appeared at Hadley's elbow with a bright smile. "And they smell tropical, don't they?"

"I thought you'd already left," Hadley said.

Bizzy eased the bouquet from Hadley's grasp. "I forgot my clutch. Shall I take these up to the room for you?"

"Oh, um . . . sure." Hadley ran her fingers over the fabric of her skirt. "Thanks Bizzy."

"I'll find a vase. Go on — skedaddle and have fun." Bizzy shooed them away.

Skip opened the front door for Hadley, then followed her down the steps onto the sidewalk. The evening remained warm and pleasant, nothing like the smothering blanket of wet heat common in New Guinea.

The neighborhood surrounding the Red Cross facility, however, was seedy and run-down. Why on earth had they housed nurses and Red Cross Girls at a hotel situated in the red-light district? Someone must have decided that having women here would be better than putting restless servicemen near the city's brothels and nightclubs. Hadley had assured Skip that they had been advised to use taxis rather than walking in the area.

Sure enough, a taxi pulled up, and three nurses disembarked from the back seat. Skip grabbed the door and leaned in. "Can you take us to the Australia?"

"Yup."

"Thanks." Skip held out his hand and helped Hadley climb in before scooting in beside her.

"The Australia?" She tilted her head and studied him.

He smiled. "Um-hmm. Got us a reservation at the Bevery restaurant. Good thing too, with you all decked out. Like I said before, you look beautiful."

"Thanks." She parted her lips. "I haven't needed this dress once in New Guinea."

Skip chuckled.

The driver pointed out various landmarks as they made their way out of the questionable environs of Hadley's hotel to a more affluent area of the city.

"Here we are," the driver said, swinging the car to a stop on Martin Place.

Skip passed him the fare, got out, and offered Hadley his hand.

"It's amazing." Hadley peered up at the immense polished granite Art Deco facade of Sydney's see-and-be-seen hotel.

"Wait until you see the inside." Skip grinned and tugged her toward the gray and white marble staircase. "It'll knock your socks off."

"You've been here before?" Hadley stroked the smooth red granite of one of the Doric columns gracing the front entry.

He grinned. "I'm staying here. Figured I was entitled to a treat."

Hadley lifted her eyebrows. "I didn't realize posh Australian hotels were letting rooms to Yanks."

"I might have greased the wheels a bit." Most of the nice hotels that hadn't been commandeered by the government or the military catered to wealthy civilians and high-ranking military officers. Snagging a room at Sydney's most upscale hotel hadn't been easy, but Skip could see little point in hoarding his combat pay. He had nothing to spend it on in New Guinea. He'd had to part with more money than he had anticipated when the hotel clerk had spotted Lucy. But staying here was worth it.

Lucy. Damn. He needed to make certain she hadn't destroyed the room while he was gone. He and the fellas had taken her out for a while this afternoon, so she should be konked out. But she sure could make mischief when left unsupervised for too long.

A doorman opened the door for them, and Skip ushered Hadley inside ahead of him. She lifted her head and looked around the elaborate foyer lined with its colonnade of black marble columns topped by a glass-paneled ceiling. An elliptical staircase led to the upper public floor, winding through walls of striking black glass decorated with silver birds and foliage.

As she stood in the sumptuous entryway in her eye-popping red evening dress with the black-and-silver-etched glass as a backdrop, she was a vision. Skip tilted his head, framing what could be a prize-winning photograph if only he had his Graflex.

She curved her lips in a beautiful smile. Pale pops of pink in her cheeks only added to her glamour. With her sultry allure, she was a dead ringer for actress Hedy Lamarr. A dream puss.

"I've wondered." She angled her head in question. "Why do

you do that?"

He frowned. "Do what?"

"I catch you doing it all the time." She fixed her eyes on his. "You lean back, tilt your head to one side, and close one eye. Makes me think of a photographer. Not a newspaper photographer who takes a jillion shots, but an artsy one. You put me in mind of them."

"Old habit." He shrugged. "I played around with photography before the war."

She stepped closer and took his hand. "Will you show me some time?"

"Show you what? I don't have a camera." Not with him right now, that much was true.

"What you see. *How* you see." A husky note took her normally throaty voice from sexy to take-me-to-bed-right-now.

He gulped and took a deep breath. The spicy notes in her perfume dominated its tangerine citrus scent. He didn't know how to confess that he hadn't picked up a camera since December 1941. Not for lack of opportunity — he'd had plenty of down time between missions. Not for lack of suitable subject material — for all its discomforts and dangers, New Guinea's untouched, pristine wilderness was both fearsome and spectacular. Not for lack of means — his Graflex still sat in its case, deep in the recesses of his trunk.

"It's been awhile," he whispered. "I —"

"I know." Hadley drew him closer. "Me too."

They weren't talking about photography anymore.

She stroked his neck with her warm fingers, then tweaked his earlobe. A shiver slid over his shoulders.

"Uh . . ." Skip cleared his throat. "If you're comfortable waiting, I need to dash up to my room and check on Lucy before we go to dinner. Be sure she hasn't ripped the draperies off the wall or something."

"How about if I come with and say hello to Lucy?"

He raked his gaze over her form-enhancing dress, and his pulse quickened. Heat radiated through his body. *No. If I take you up, all bets are off. I'll want you in my bed.*

He tore his gaze back up to Hadley's face, to the pretty golden sunburst earrings set with dark red stones visible through her dark curls, to her cheeks pinked with excitement, to her dark eyes sparking with a hint of challenge.

Her eyes said it all. She knew exactly what they might get up to in his room.

He traced his finger around one of her sunburst earrings. "Nate told me how you offered to take Lucy. To keep her safe for me."

"I'm not sure I *offered,* so much as insisted." Her throaty giggle sent waves of heat to his core. "I was more belligerent than pleasant."

"He told me that too." Skip grinned. Nate had said he'd had a hard time dissuading her from taking Lucy. Skip's chest swelled. Wasn't like she thought Nate would mistreat Lucy. She had simply wanted to safeguard his pet *for him*, and that was everything.

Scuffing his boots on the ground and not looking directly at Skip, his crew chief had imparted another interesting tidbit from his conversations with Hadley. "Boy, sure hope a woman looks at me someday the way she looked when she was talking about you."

And damn if she wasn't right here looking at him just like that. Skip's pulse raced.

She moistened her lips and locked her eyes with him. "Let's go up to your room, Skip."

"Hadley, I'm not sure that —"

"Shh." She arched up onto her toes and brought her mouth to his ear. "It's the best idea."

Tingles zinged down his spine at her breathy whisper. He knotted his fingers in her dress sash, tugged her close, and pressed his body to hers. He wanted her to feel how hard he was.

She drew in a sharp breath and grazed his neck with her fingernails. She pushed herself against him and moaned softly in his ear while suckling his earlobe.

"You're sure?" His rising desire injected a gruff note into his voice.

She trailed kisses along his jaw. "Very sure."

He slipped his hand into hers and disengaged from their embrace. "Lift's this way."

Flutters tumbled through his gut as they made their way up to his room. Last time he had taken a woman to bed had been before. Before Pearl Harbor. *Before everything changed.*

And Hadley isn't just any woman, and this isn't a casual tumble.

When they reached his door, Skip released her hand and pulled the large brass room key from his pocket. The lock clicked. He turned the knob and paused on the threshold.

Hadley met his eyes, smiled, and strode inside ahead of him.

***

A shiver ran over Hadley's skin as Skip closed the door behind her with a soft snap, extinguishing the harsh light from the hallway. Brown-out regulations had been eased during the summer, and dusky hues of twilight streamed in through the window.

Lucy moved around inside her pouch.

"Good, she's asleep." Skip touched Hadley's arm. "Hang on. I'll get the lamp."

"We don't need more light." She turned, wrapped her arms around him, and locked her mouth on his. Her resolve to avoid an emotional entanglement with him had evaporated with his admission that she had been on his mind while his life was in peril. The kicker though — the kicker had been the vulnerability in his expression, his stance, his voice when she had asked him about photography. That had undone her. Something had happened during the war to shut down that side of him, and she intended to find out what it was.

For Skip, all this might be only physical attraction and nothing deeper. And he wanted the kind of stable domesticity Hadley couldn't give him. A wartime fling, that was the extent of it. Yet Hadley was certain that for this one night, she could make Skip

Masterson forget about the war, about whatever troubles he was suppressing, about *everything*.

He crushed his lips against hers. Hadley opened her mouth, slid her tongue over his, tasting him. A hoppy note suggested he'd had a drink before picking her up. Her belly went taut with flutters of mounting excitement. He hugged her close, and the solid ridge of his erection pressed in just the right spot. She wiggled and elicited a deep guttural groan from his lips.

Skip backed her toward the bed, his breath coming hot and fast. His hands fumbled across her back, skimmed her waist and hips.

"How do I get you out of this thing?" he muttered in her ear. "I can't —"

"Buttons," she gasped. A neat row of tiny ones ran down her back. "Buttons below the vee in the back."

"Okay." His fingers found the top one. He struggled to undo it.

Hadley untwined her arms from around his neck and reached back to the bottom button, deftly pulling the fabric loop over the tiny bud with her thumb. She moved up from there until she hit the beaded band at her midriff, the point where she couldn't reach any higher.

"You'll have to get the last two. Take your time."

When he finally managed to undo the last one, Hadley wasted no time in sliding the sleeves down her arms and stepping out of the dress.

Skip held up his hand and backed up a few steps. "Hang on . . . I want to see you. *All* of you. Want to drink you in."

There it was again. He inclined his head to the side and squeezed his left eye shut. Framing a picture. Hadley shivered. Then he closed the space between them and ran his fingers over her bare skin, sending showers of gooseflesh down her arms.

"Tell me," she whispered against his throat, moving her mouth to nibble on his earlobe. "Tell me what you see."

"Beauty," Skip murmured. He unhooked her bra, lowered the cup away from her left breast, and rubbed the pad of his thumb over her nipple. "But mostly I see strength. You exude strength from every angle, Hadley Claverie."

She couldn't speak.

"Strength, principles, courage," he continued as he trailed kisses along her clavicle, his thumb still twiddling with her nipple. It hardened under his touch.

Hadley gasped with pleasure. Warmth suffused her from her hairline to her toes. She tugged off her bra and cast it aside.

Skip moved to bury his head against her chest, but before he could, she plucked off his service cap and tossed it onto the chest of drawers.

"Not so fast, Lieutenant Dreamboat," she murmured with a smile. "You're still wearing far too many clothes."

"Enough of the *Lieutenant Dreamboat* rubbish."

"Shhhh." She adroitly unbuttoned his jacket and unfastened the belt. She tossed the jacket to an armchair, unknotted his tie, and went to work on his shirt. So many buttons. When he finally shrugged it off and flung it onto the floor, adrenaline jolted straight to her core.

Oh God.

She had seen Skip shirtless before, onboard the *West Point* and at the beach in Australia, and she hadn't been immune to his attractiveness. But Lordy, with her already half-naked, and the anticipation of bedding him hanging ripe in the air around them, he bowled her over. Broad shoulders and a lean, well-defined chest that tapered into a V at his trim waist, drawing her eyes to his navel and the trail of hair that was the same tawny caramel as that on his head.

She traced her fingernail through the whorls of hair, then slid her hand inside his trousers and grasped him. Skip caught his breath. She stroked the length of him, and he moaned and dug his fingers into her lower back.

"You're driving me wild," he rumbled low and deep, the pitch of his voice setting her nerve endings on fire.

A soft laugh escaped her lips, even as his mouth closed over hers. She leaned into his smothering kiss and continued fondling him.

"Less clothes," he murmured, backing her against the bed frame. "You. Please."

"Umm-hmm." Hadley unhooked the top button of his trousers. Then the next, and the next. Then — she gasped in frustration. "Hang it, how many buttons are on these things?"

Skip laughed. "Five, but you don't have to undo them all." He pushed the pants down his legs and kicked them off.

Right. Skip had always been lean and fit, but the days he'd spent in the jungle had taken a toll on him. Hadley didn't doubt that as the plane's commanding officer, he would have taken only a small portion of rations for himself.

He gripped her waist, which was also smaller than when she set sail a year ago. In one smooth motion, he slid her silky slip down her body.

Stepping out of the garment, she feasted her eyes on the full-length view of him. He had foregone the usual olive drab undershorts. He was a dreamboat, a *dishy* dreamboat. And for tonight, he was all hers. Crackles of chemistry coursed through her and over her tingling skin, cascading deep into her core.

Skip knelt before her and gently unhooked her garters from her stockings before easing them sensuously down her legs one at a time. Then he glided his fingertips up her legs, setting off another volley of fiery tingles.

Not anxiety jitters of sexual inexperience. Hadley wasn't a virgin, but her previous sexual experiences hadn't been . . . well, they hadn't been all she had hoped. Tonight held far more promise. Skip was . . . *more*. More everything.

He slid his fingers into the waistband of her girdle, sending a fresh wave of thrilling flutters spinning through her. He took his sweet time removing her last undergarment, an act of exquisite torture that made her tremble. Yet instead of pressing her onto the bed now that she was naked, Skip kissed his way up her thighs, between them, and then . . .

"Skip, *oh my God*." She gasped, kneading her fingers restlessly through his hair.

Her continued moans urged him on. He cupped her bum and explored her with his tongue, his movements becoming more demanding, more insistent, until Hadley panted and rocked herself against his mouth. Now this? *This* was new. Her other lovers had merely taken what they needed, with no regard for her pleasure. Skip had already scored points, and they hadn't even made it to the actual bed yet.

All at once, with no warning, convulsive spasms rolled over her in waves, and she cried out his name in a high-pitched voice she barely recognized as her own. She didn't register that he had surged to his feet until he pulled her against him and tugged her onto the bed. Hadley tasted herself in his hot, intimate, devouring kisses. His hands flew everywhere at once, her breath came in ragged bursts, and they intertwined their limbs.

When he finally pressed his erection between her legs, she was ready. *So* ready. So much more ready than she had ever been before.

Skip slapped the bedside table.

"What are you doing?" Hadley murmured.

"Condom. I left the tin here." He grimaced. "I know I did, dammit."

Hadley grinned. "Optimistic, were you?"

"*All* men are optimistic, but usually without good cause." Skip said, his voice redolent of a steaming cup of chicory coffee. "Where'd it go?"

He rolled off the bed and jerked his foot off the floor in pain. "Ow, dammit!"

Hadley clapped a hand to her mouth to smother a laugh.

Skip bent to retrieve whatever he had stepped on and held up a smushed condom tin. "Lucy must have knocked it off the table — and now I've flattened it."

"Does that change their effectiveness?" Hadley giggled.

Skip sprung back onto the bed, opened the tin, and fished out a rubber. He cast her a wry grin and ran his fingers down it. "Seems no different. But if it worries you, I've got more."

"There's that optimism again." She laughed.

He made to get up, but Hadley grabbed his wrist. "Skip?"

"Yeah?"

She smiled. "Put it on. That one. Put that one on."

"Sure thing." He bobbed his head, shot her a lopsided grin, and rolled the condom on.

Hadley reached for him, and he swooped down to claim her mouth. His kisses were demanding, yet tender, as he pressed his hardness between her legs. She returned his kisses and squirmed against him. Her pulse accelerated to a blinding crescendo.

"This isn't your first time." Skip trailed warm kisses along her jawline and nipped at her earlobe. His words carried no questioning inflection, but were merely a statement of fact.

She opened her eyes and looked up at him. "No."

"Then I intend to make sure it's your best," he said, his breath hot in her ear.

He was well on his way to reaching that goal. Hadley pulled him against her and let her roaming lips and hands and restless hips signal her readiness. He eased inside her, settling his weight atop her and allowing her to relax.

Oh, God. Yes.

Though she had shied away from admitting her attraction to him, let alone their growing emotional connection, his brush with death had shaken her reserve, her caution, her vulnerability.

"Skip," she whispered.

His eyes had gone dark with need. He locked them with hers and moved with slow, steady strokes that soon lengthened and gained speed, friction, and urgency. Streams of heat flooded Hadley's senses. She scraped his back with her fingernails and trailed her mouth over the strong, defined muscles of his shoulders, carefully bypassing the knots of healing mosquito bites, and then kissed the tawny hair dusting his chiseled chest, all while moving in rhythm with his slick, pulsing strokes.

Having already had her moment — which neither of her other lovers had bothered to awaken in her — Hadley was shocked when more clenching waves of pleasure built within her. Her urge for release mounted with white-hot intensity, and she shifted to change the angle of Skip's entry.

"There, right there," she cried with a gasp, her insides clenching with anticipatory tension as she crested atop a mountain before spinning pell-mell into a sweet, drenching release that washed over her in relentless waves.

Skip's strangled moans moments later signaled that he too had sated his need.

They remained tightly entwined with Hadley's legs locked around Skip's waist, while he continued to move inside her, this time with intimacy rather than his earlier driving fervor. Her frenetic heart rate gradually slowed, and the zinging of her pulse eased.

God, I could stay here forever.

"That did not seem like a man who's out of practice." She trailed kisses down his neck. "Thought you said it had been awhile."

"Umm-hmm, it has." He nibbled her earlobe. "Before the war."

"And photography — you said that had been awhile too?" Hadley tightened her hold on him.

He held her eyes for a long pause, long enough that she wondered if she had pressed too far, asked too much. "I was taking photographs that morning," he whispered.

She winced. *That morning* could only mean one morning — December 7, 1941 — the morning of the attack on Pearl Harbor. She caressed his jawline.

"Tossed my camera inside the villa where I was staying and raced to the harbor to help." He gave a little shrug. "Since then, haven't had time for hobbies."

She suspected photography hadn't been a casual hobby for him, but the tension in his muscles prompted her to shift their conversation to something more relaxed.

"Well, Lieutenant Dreamboat," she drawled with a smile, "Your body remembers everything just fine, trust me."

"Is that right?" His hands roamed restlessly over her body. "They say practice makes perfect, so —"

He broke off as Lucy hopped onto the bed with them. Her tail smacked Skip's face, and she sniffed curiously around Hadley's face and neck.

"Nice timing, Luce." Skip gently pushed her away from them.

Hadley chuckled. "Could have been worse."

"True enough." He grinned and swiped a lock of Hadley's hair off her forehead.

Giggles rolled through her belly, building into a deep laugh. "She probably wonders what all that racket was."

"We may want to put her into the bathroom from here on out."

"There's that optimism again." Hadley's lips twitched.

"Is it? Am I just being optimistic?" Skip cupped her face with warm, gentle fingers. His voice was light and teasing and he wore that dishy, devil-may-care smile, but the look in his eyes told her he cared very much about her answer.

Hadley traced her finger over his lips. "Good thing you sprang for the swanky hotel with an en-suite bathroom."

She turned to Lucy, whose inquisitive eyes and quivering nose were still unnervingly close to hers. "Sorry cher, looks like you'll be spending quite a bit of time in the bathroom."

CHAPTER FIFTEEN

March 28, 1944

Near Nadzab, New Guinea

Skip squeezed Hadley's hand. "Close your eyes."

"Never thought I'd hear anyone advise me to close my eyes in the jungle — least of all you." She shook her head but did as he asked.

He led her through a gap in the trees. "Trust me, this isn't the real jungle."

"Whatever you say." She laughed.

The area might not technically be a jungle, but the dense vegetation still helped to conceal the sight and sound of his surprise. As the roar of rushing water grew more audible, Skip checked to make sure she still had her eyes shut. "No peeking."

He pushed aside several hanging vines with his free hand and tugged her through the opening. Her ears would have already told her they were approaching a waterfall. He couldn't keep that a surprise. But he could relish her excited expression when she saw this special place for the first time. "Okay, you can open 'em now."

She opened her eyes.

He followed her gaze. If there were ever a paradise on earth, this secluded swimming hole was it. Several mountain streams cascaded down over the rocks above to form a trio of peaceful waterfalls that splashed into a vibrant turquoise swimming hole surrounded by lush ferns, towering trees — and best of all, a group of rainbow eucalyptus trees with bark striped bright green, blue, purple, and red. The sight took his breath away.

Hadley's amusement segued into astonishment, until her mouth formed a perfect O of surprise. She tightened her grip on his hand and turned in a halting half-circle.

"Skip . . . Oh my God, it's paradise."

"It's Eden, all right," he said, still surprised that the hellscape of New Guinea also contained this amazing Shangri-La. He was tempted to pull his Graflex camera from the recesses of his trunk to capture this idyllic tropical paradise, but doing so would be a pointless exercise without color film.

He and Hadley were now both based at Nadzad, but with hundreds of men on base — a base bordering an isolated, fetid swamp on the edge of a jungle — they hadn't had an opportunity to be alone. The Red Cross tents were surrounded by barbed wire, with an armed sentry guarding the encampment. Official rules dictated that women could go on double dates, but only if each man carried his side-arm.

The surrounding swamp and jungle made the inland base miserably hot and only worsened the primitive conditions. Skip couldn't justify bouncing down a rutted dusty road for more than an hour to reach the beach near Lae, for it too would be swarming with soldiers. Coming to this isolated swimming pool with the beautiful waterfalls was the perfect solution. Skip had taken the precaution of giving his best bottle of whiskey to the man who had shown him the way and asked that he keep its location secret.

Skip squeezed Hadley's hand. "Care to go for a swim?"

"Is it safe?" A small frown creased her brow. "It's gorgeous, but —"

"It's safe," Skip said. Allied forces disregarded posted warnings about currents and sharks to swim in coastal waters but tended to heed repeated admonitions about staying out of inland rivers. They had all seen crocodiles and the venomous snakes often found in those bodies of water.

Skip grinned. "Buddy of mine told me about it. He's been here plenty of times, and I've already checked it out."

"Really?"

"Look, see how clear it is?" He tugged her closer to the pool. "You can see all the way to the bottom."

Skip had scouted the place earlier this morning with one of the local boys from the base. The boy explained in halting Pidgin that the water was too cool for crocodiles and since the pool was created from freshwater streams, it couldn't support the venomous sea snakes that thrived in the ocean and brackish coastal rivers. He didn't hesitate to jump into the water to prove his point. Skip had followed suit, quickly concluding that the small pool held no danger. It was only ten feet deep in the center, and the bottom was entirely visible.

"What about all this *around* the water?" Hadley gestured toward the thicket covering the inclined slope and the mass of boulders encircling the pool. "What lives there?"

"You're not usually this cautious, Louisiana girl." Skip winked. "Our friend Kina told me that the pool is too far from the nearest river for it to be home to crocodiles. They don't venture that far across land."

Hadley lifted her shoulders in an *okay, then* shrug and set off down the path through the tall grass toward the pool. Skip hurried after her.

She halted atop a large flat boulder near the water's edge and stepped out of her shoes, then bent to remove her socks. She turned to face him and unbuttoned her khaki shirt one button at a time, revealing the same red-and-white striped halter bathing suit she had worn on the ship.

Skip's blood heated in a rush. Since returning from Sydney, he and Hadley hadn't been able to find enough privacy for a date, let alone to make love. His body signaled his eagerness to remedy their prolonged sexual drought.

Hadley eased her shirt off one shoulder and then the other. He swallowed hard.

She locked her eyes with his, carefully folded her shirt, and set it on the rock. Her lips tugged up into a sly smile as she reached for the side buttons of her culottes.

"Coming?" She indicated the pool.

Skip raised an eyebrow. "I'd sure like to."

"Me too." Hadley's eyes told him she understood his innuendo, then offered him an invitation mixed with a measure of challenge.

Were condoms waterproof? Military training films should have covered that.

She slid her culottes down her legs in a tantalizingly sensuous manner. Once she stepped out of them, she lifted them with her toes and placed them atop her folded shirt. Mesmerized by her dexterity and the sight of her curves in a bathing suit, Skip failed to anticipate, let alone prevent, her leap off the rock into the center of the pool.

His pulse rate accelerated, steadying only seconds later after she surfaced. *Guess she conquered her trepidation about crocodiles.*

"Oh, Skip, it's wonderful. So cool and refreshing." Hadley bobbed in the water and swiped a strand of wet hair from her face. "Hurry up, slowpoke!"

"Coming." Skip shucked off his clothes and shoes and jumped in after her. He surfaced, shook out his wet hair, and gripped Hadley's shoulders. "You didn't ask how deep the water is before you jumped. Could've hurt yourself."

"The rock isn't that high up." Hadley pointed at the boulder where they had left their clothes. "And like you said, I can see all the way to the bottom."

"Okay, but I wanted to get in first and check it out." Something might have slithered into the water since he'd been here with Kina.

Hadley shook her head and stroked the side of his face. "You worry too much, Skip."

Yes, he did. Old Skip sure as hell wouldn't have been concerned about diving or crocodiles — or anything else, for that matter.

She slid out of his grasp and swam a lap around the perimeter of the pool using a smooth crawl stroke. He grinned. Hadley might act nonchalant, and she would surely tease him if she guessed what he was doing, but he couldn't relax until he had confirmed that they *weren't* sharing the space with any unwelcome wildlife. He ducked beneath the water, opened his eyes, and scanned the sides of the circular pool. Only a few small, darting silver fish swam with them. He came up for air, then dove under again, this time kicking down to make sure nothing had camouflaged amidst the rocks scattered across the bottom. Several laps around the pool later, he resurfaced and rubbed the water from his eyes.

Hadley had flipped over onto her back and was poking her toes into the spray beneath the waterfall. So peaceful and relaxed. Relaxed and off-guard.

Skip curved his lips, took a deep breath, and slipped beneath the water. He swam forward with wide strokes, flutter-kicking his legs, and positioned himself beneath her smooth white ones. He searched around on the bottom with his toes until he found a flat rock to use for leverage, then propelled himself upward. He latched on to Hadley's left leg and tugged. He came up just in time to hear her scream his name.

"A little jumpy, are you?" he teased, pulling her snugly against him.

"No," Hadley huffed. "I knew it was you. That's why I yelled at you."

"Yelled *at* me? Sounded more like you were yelling for my help." Chuckling, he ducked out of reach of her playful swat. "Easy now."

"You failed miserably, but trying to scare me wasn't very gentlemanly, you know." Pops of pink flush on her neck belied her bravado.

Skip leaned close and murmured, "You're more worried about crocs than you let on."

"No. You startled me, that's all."

"Right." He lay his palm over her heart and smiled. "Your heart's beating awfully fast for someone confident about her safety."

"I'm always safe with you." Hadley murmured, her eyes warm and soft.

His pulse roared like the water rushing over the falls. *No. No, you're not. No one's safe with me.*

Hadley licked her lips. Her moist, plump, kissable lips.

"My heart's beating fast because of *you*." She circled her arms around his neck. "Because we're here together. Together and finally, *finally* alone."

Skip's stomach muscles tautened. He would correct her misimpression of his reliability later. Right now, his body had other ideas. He closed his mouth over hers and tightened his hold on her waist. She crushed her soft, pliant lips against his with unexpected fervor. Every nerve in his body stood at attention, crackling with heat at odds with the cool water enveloping them.

Hadley wrapped her arms around his neck and suckled her lips along his jawline and around his lips. "I love how your stubble feels under my mouth, how it tastes."

"Hmm?" He rubbed his cheek, catlike, down her neck and over her chest, urged on by her sighs and groans of pleasure. He tugged the knot of her halter open, pushed down the straps, and kissed her again, his lips pressing feverishly against hers.

A strangled gasp escaped her mouth as she opened it under his and dug her fingers into his hair, the scrape of her pretty nails sending zings of chills down his spine. Skip kept one hand around her waist to hold them upright and pushed aside her halter cups with the other. He fondled each of her breasts in turn, using the pads of his thumbs to caress each nipple, thrilling at how they stiffened to pert little peaks at his touch.

She tore her mouth away from his long enough to gasp, "Oh God, Skip."

He shifted her higher and nuzzled his stubble against her breasts. His heart thundered in his ears in response to her squirms of pleasure.

Hadley traced her fingers down his back and under the waistband of his bathing trunks. This time he moaned as she slid the cool smooth tips of her nails over his ass. She cupped his butt and thrust her searing hot tongue into his mouth, devouring him.

Skip's breath came in strangled gasps. He pressed the flat of his hand against her sex and probed her folds through the material of her swimsuit, all while suckling on her earlobe.

"You're wet for me," he moaned into her ear.

Titters burbled in her belly and built into full-throated laugher. "We're both wet, honey."

"Question is, Miss Claverie," he said, tilting her back and ducking her head under the cascading waterfall to elicit more giggles. He paused with his mouth hovering over hers. "Are you wet-wet, or water-wet?"

She laughed.

"I can keep doing this," he murmured, stroking her sex again and pressing his thumb where the pressure would excite her. "Or this." He trailed his tongue around one of her nipples.

"Oh, God," she moaned.

"Or maybe this." He slid his fingers inside her bathing suit and probed her nub.

She whimpered and rocked against his hand. Her eyes, half-lidded with passion, met his. "Wet-wet, Lieutenant Dreamboat."

He rolled his eyes at her nickname for him.

With one hand wrapped around his neck, Hadley reached into his trunks and stroked the length of his erection.

"Can we do this in the water?" Skip gazed around the pool at the slippery rocks, sharp Kunai grass, shrubs, and dense trees. He had a blanket in his rucksack, but doubted they could find a decent place to spread it out.

Hadley arched her brow. "Water sex isn't in your repertoire?"

"Looks like it will be. Especially if you keep that up," Skip growled. Her feathery light strokes along his length had given way to a pulse-throbbing pace and a rhythm guaranteed to push him over the edge before long.

She leaned close enough for him to feel her warm breath. "We need to be creative."

"Creative, you say?" Skip shot her a lopsided grin, pulled her against him, and used his other arm to navigate into shallow water. When he could touch bottom, he glanced over his shoulder and assessed the possibilities. Another flat boulder sat near the one where they had left their clothing, and it might be just right for what he had in mind.

Skip lay back and pulled Hadley close, kicked his feet, and swirled his arm through the water to tug her backward toward the rock. Once he reached it, he gripped its smooth edge to keep from crashing into it.

"Getting out?" Hadley put a finger against her lower lip and surveyed their surroundings with unconcealed doubt.

He tugged his lips up on one side. "No, you are."

She sputtered with indignation, but he put his hands on either side of her waist and lifted her out of the water.

"You're all slippery, like a seal. Hope I don't drop you." He purposefully let her slip, confident he had a tight hold on her, and laughed when she squealed. Then he swiveled and set her onto the edge of the boulder.

He leaned forward, ran his hands over her slick thighs, and

rubbed at the water droplets clinging to her arms and shoulders. "You're all slippery."

"Really?"

"Yes." He nuzzled her neck and nibbled at her earlobe. "And slick."

She shivered. "How slick?"

"Slick and wet. *Water*-wet." He slid a finger inside her bathing suit bottoms. "Water-wet, and *wet-wet*. Definitely wet-wet. Sex-wet."

Hadley's low, throaty laugh sent shivers across his shoulders. She kissed her way along his jawline until she reached his lips. Then the peaceful roar of spilling water, the trill of cicadas, the squawks and chirps of birds, and the croaks of tree frogs, all faded away until only the two of them existed. Just Skip and his girl, Hadley, with her determination to experience the world fast and furious, her infectious, intrepid spirit, her fierce convictions. Hadley, whom he might be falling for. Falling hard. No, there was no *might* about it. He was a goner.

She slid her cool fingers into the waistband of his swim trunks, jolting him out of his reverie. He kissed her and murmured, "Hang on. Gotta get a rubber."

He pulled away and picked his way over the rocks toward shore.

Ow, ow, ow. In his haste, he slipped and barely managed to avoid pitching forward into the rocks. He awkwardly climbed out of the pool and scaled the boulder where they had stashed their clothes. Kneeling on the hard rock, he pulled the cardboard packet and a small tube of KY jelly from his pants pocket. He opened the packet and stared at the one remaining condom.

If he attempted to put it on in the water, he'd never find it if he dropped it, so that was a bad idea. Would it stay on in the water? The army training films hadn't covered that. He extracted the condom and removed its paper sleeve, then picked up the tube of lubricant, stood, and stripped off his swim trunks.

Standing at the edge of the pool on full display, Old Skip might have preened like a Greek god and welcomed the opportunity to showcase his masculinity. Wartime Skip couldn't summon an ounce of his former *joie de vivre* — until he turned and caught sight of Hadley's face. *Damn.* She was drinking him in. Every ounce of his self-doubt vanished.

She held his gaze and pulled her halter top off over her head. Then she finger-combed her wet dark hair and slid her swim bottoms down her legs. She pulled one foot free and left them hanging on the other so she could circle the garment in the water. With a wink, she inclined back with her palms resting behind her. Explosive warmth swelled in his chest.

Oh God.

In a rush of free-spirited impulsiveness, he jumped into the pool with the condom and tube clutched in his fist. When had he last felt this carefree, this exhilarated, this *alive*?

In Sydney. With Hadley. Not just because of the scorching sex they had enjoyed, but also because of simple pleasures. Sharing an ice cream cone in the botanical gardens, strolling hand-in-hand through the zoo, curled up next to one another while reading, his head in her lap.

He swam underwater to where Hadley lay and made a playful grab for her foot as he broke the surface. Laughter spilled from his throat as he nabbed her swimsuit bottoms, tossed them beside her discarded top, and set the tube of jelly next to it.

She giggled and allowed him to tug her forward until she teetered on the edge of the boulder. He used his toes to clear the sharp rocks and pebbles from the pool bottom, then planted his feet firmly on the sand. He pushed Hadley's legs apart and stepped between them, running his fingers sensuously over her outer thighs. His erection pressed against her folds, and the recognition of what he had in mind blossomed across her features.

Water lapped around Skip's knees, but he doubted it would pose a threat to the rubber. He rolled it on, leaned close to Hadley, and inhaled a lingering trace of her spicy citrusy perfume.

"Where were we?" he skimmed his lips over her smooth cheek.

"In a very, very, very good place," she said, a low sultry note punctuating each *very*.

The hair on the back of his neck stood on end, while fiery crackles of energy jolted throughout his body. Yet he forced himself to take his time. They had lost momentum when he had gotten out to retrieve the condom, and he wanted to be certain she was ready for him. He massaged one of her breasts while exploring every inch of her beautiful face with his lips. From her perfectly-groomed dark eyebrows, to her thin straight nose, to her rosebud mouth.

Hadley closed her fingers around him, and Skip's heart thrummed ever faster. He trailed kisses down her neck and across her breasts, suckling and teasing first one nipple, and then the other. She moaned, wiggling closer, and tightened her grip on his erection. Without breaking their kiss, he uncapped the tube of jelly and passed it to her. The intimacy of her slicking him up sent waves of heat flashing through him. Intimate and perfect, that's what it was.

He didn't deserve to keep her, to have her for always, he knew that. Hadley didn't understand how damaged and flawed he was. But for now, he could be enough. Now was now. He might not have a future to offer her anyway.

He straightened, wrapped her legs over his shoulders, and edged closer. Gripping her outer thighs, he slid inside her and moved tentatively at first, taking it slow until her face, her moans, and the arch of her body told him she was ready.

Judging from the crescendo of high-pitched cries she emitted after his shuddering release, the angle he had chosen worked really, really well for Hadley. Skip's chest swelled. He leaned forward and took her in his arms, grinning at the sheen of sweat coating her body and the ka-thumping of her heartbeat inside her chest.

"Oh, Skip." Her fingers dug into his upper arm. "Skip, Skip, Skip."

"Still feeling it?" He grinned.

She blew out a long, slow breath. "Yes. God. God, yes."

Skip laughed softly and stroked her hair away from her face. "We're going to have to figure out how to spend more time here. Lots more time."

***

Skip edged his foot beneath the waterfall, stretched back onto the rock, and soaked in the cool, misting spray. He could happily stay here all day. If only he and Hadley could ride out the war here in this oasis of tranquil beauty. He twiddled the knot of her halter top, considering if they had time for him to remove it once more before they had to head back.

"Do we have to go back?" Echoing his thoughts, Hadley trailed her finger along his forearm.

"If I didn't have to return the jeep to Colonel Tannenberg, we could stay until sunset." He rubbed his foot against hers. "We'll come back. Soon as we're both free."

"Don't count on that happening anytime soon. Not with Stella sick with another sinus infection." Hadley uncapped her canteen and took a drink. "Today only worked out because Doc released Bizzy from the hospital."

"Wasn't malaria, was it?"

"No, just jungle rot."

"*Just* jungle rot?" Skip arched his eyebrows.

She grinned. "I shouldn't be so blasé, but she only had a mild case. She went to the hospital so she could stay out of the heat and heal."

"Well, Leo had it too. Only for him, it was what the fellas call *crotch rot*." Skip grimaced.

Hadley winced. "Fortunately, Bizzy had it on her foot."

"Glad she's better." Remaining healthy was a challenge in this hostile climate. Like Hadley's fellow Red Cross Girls, he and his crewmates had been beset by a string of odd exotic ailments.

"So is Bizzy. She was going stir-crazy in the hospital. But now with Stella sick, I'll *still* have to work double shifts most days." Hadley opened Skip's rucksack and passed him a peanut butter sandwich wrapped in wax paper. "Even if JoJo and I manage to escape all the creepy jungle diseases, we're apt to collapse from exhaustion."

"Maybe we can take a break in the middle of the day." Skip set down his sandwich and twirled a strand of her hair around his finger. "Didn't take us long to get here since I was able to borrow a jeep. If I can do that again —"

"The *Kunai Club* is open from dawn to dusk," she broke in, rolling her eyes at him. "Then we're expected to sit in the muck and drizzle and watch outdoor movies with you fellas."

Skip chuckled. No two ways about it, watching movies at the base's outdoor theater was a miserable experience. Seating consisted of rough logs laid out on a hillside to maximize their view of the screen. They hardly ever received any new films, so their choices were limited, held little variety, and featured dreadful crackling audio that somehow, when it worked, comically deepened all the voices. The audience coated themselves with insecticide, donned long-sleeved clothing despite the muggy heat, and wore ponchos to protect against the inevitable downpours that soaked them multiple times during each movie.

"The Red Cross is bound to send new women soon. We're opening a new fighter strip. They'll want to operate a canteen service there." Skip bit into his sandwich.

Hadley sighed. "Yeah, well, that just means more work. We never have enough hands."

She was right. They never had enough American women to go around, especially here. In Australia, plenty of local girls came to their dances and went on dates with soldiers. Sure, that didn't please the Aussie blokes, but better a few brawls between Aussies and Yanks than the situation prevailing here. Apart from the Red Cross Girls and combat nurses, no women. No women, and thousands of horny guys.

"If they would send more women here, you could adjust your shifts so that everyone gets a few hours off each day."

"Oh, they'll send us new staff, all right," Hadley said. "And ship *us* north. They like to send experienced women in to get things up and running each time the army advances. Word is, they want more of us in Finschhafen — and soon enough, they'll move us to Hollandia."

"MacArthur's gotta win Hollandia before he can base anyone there," Skip said with a grunt. He had flown three missions there in the last ten days. Good news was that he was only two missions away from completing his tour. With Hollandia softened up now, flying two more missions shouldn't pose a problem.

Bad news was that Skip had no idea what he would do once he got his golden ticket. He didn't have a wife and kids or a house with a white picket fence and a job back home. Going home meant confronting all the ways he had fallen short. Going home meant he could no longer put off what he had resolved to do after Chet died. Going home meant giving up on his dreams and leaving Hadley behind.

If the Red Cross transferred her to Finschhafen before he finished these last missions, it might be a blessing in disguise. Because if she was still here, her presence might tempt him to extend his tour — and that would be exceptionally stupid. Going home might not hold the prospect of joy or fulfillment for him, but staying here one second longer than required would be nuts. He had no intention of volunteering for a second hellish tour of duty.

"Point is, they'll move us again and again and again." Hadley twirled her foot in the cascading water, sending a light spray over their legs. "We move and we move and we move, and I'm still no closer to the real action."

"You're stationed at the largest, most active air base in the Southwest Pacific," Skip said, frowning as he shook off the dismal picture of his stateside future. "Practically the entire Fifth Air Force is based here at Nadzab."

"I know. I'm not saying what you flyboys do isn't real action. I know too damned well it is." Hadley pinched her lips together. "But I can only write so many stories about your missions. And besides, the base was built before we got here."

"You *just* said you experienced Red Cross Girls go in and get everything up and running before you get shipped to the next place." Skip tilted his head and widened his eyes into a *what the hell* look. "You aren't making any sense."

"They don't let us in until it's safe." She kicked her feet more forcefully through the tumbling water. "Until it's *civilized.* Until it's been prettied up."

"Trust me, you should be glad they don't let you gals in while it's a cesspit. When all the mess feeds us is bully beef, dehydrated potatoes, and canned peas. When our tents sit in the mud, and we don't have any drainage ditches. There's no story there, honey." Skip rubbed the back of his neck. "Nothing anyone back home wants to read about anyway."

"I know you want me to do Ernie Pyle-type human interest stories, but I want more. All those female journalists in England will find a way to follow our troops when we invade France. You can count on it." Hadley jiggled her leg. "This isn't the front. I want to report on things as they're happening, Skip."

Well, I want to be a photographer, not an engineer. Life isn't always fair.

Skip curled his toes under the water. "They're not gonna let women storm the beaches, if that's what you're after. Not in Europe, and not here."

"I know *that.*" She jutted her chin. "But there's bound to be some middle ground. Something between accompanying the invasion forces and interviewing soldiers who serve on a secure base well back from the front."

A secure base well back from the front. Skip scowled. "Every one of the men based at Nadzab puts his life on the line. Not just on mission days either. They —"

"Wait, I'm sorry. I'm sorry. That came out wrong." Hadley grabbed his hand and interlaced their fingers. "I didn't mean to suggest that the air forces have it easy."

He squeezed her hand. He was touchy. The closer he came to finishing his tour, the more rattled he became. Well, not rattled exactly. Superstitious. Vigilant. Prudent.

He hadn't known how badly he wanted to survive until the chance to return home edged tantalizingly within his reach. Never mind that he didn't know how to wrest what he wanted from life back home. But, dammit, he wanted the chance to figure it out.

All he had to do was keep himself and his men alive through two more missions. Two more missions, and Skip would have the time and opportunity to sort out what he wanted to do with his life. What he *could* do. What he might do, if he had the chance.

Unlike many of his fellow pilots, Skip didn't want a career in aviation. Not in the military, and not even for a commercial airline. He would keep his pilot's license, but as much as he enjoyed flying, he didn't want the pressure or the instability of flying for a living. Traveling all over would bear too much resemblance to his nomadic military childhood.

Yet even though he didn't want to make aviation a career, he had been desperate to earn his wings, especially with a war brewing. When he had gotten wind that the navy brass wouldn't recommend him for flight training because of his temperament, Skip had ignored Chet's advice of letting the dust settle before flying off the handle. He had resigned his commission. Resigned his commission and pulled himself and his belongings off the U.S.S. *Arizona* less than twenty-four hours before she sank to the bottom of Pearl Harbor, taking his beloved brother with her.

Hadley wanted to find middle ground with her journalism. Maybe there was a middle ground for him as well. His plans to pursue an engineering career in Chet's place had been half-hearted at best. He had trudged through the coursework at the academy with little enthusiasm. But maybe he could find another way to use his degree. Maybe he could still fulfill Chet's trajectory without relinquishing his own talents and interests.

The strain of tamping down his natural personality had already taken a toll. Skip's month of leave with Hadley in Sydney had altered his perspective. He wouldn't have to revert to Old Skip again to relax and have a little fun. Whatever might happen with Hadley, romancing her had proven he could ease up without catastrophic consequences.

"Sometimes you've gotta picture different angles in order to look at the whole picture." He closed one eye, his range-finder view. "And in the end, you've gotta take risks to get where you want to be."

"Yeah. Yeah, you do," she whispered, toying with her beaded bracelet.

Tingles flitted through his belly. Yeah, that's what he should do. Take his time and look at the big picture without rushing into anything. Rash decisions didn't work well for him. He'd strike a better balance if he simply took his time.

Hadley continued to worry her bracelet, seemingly lost in thought.

"Hate to say it, but we probably need to head back to base." Skip squinted at the sunlight filtering through the dense foliage. "You've got the late shift, and I need to return the jeep."

"Never thought I'd say this about anyplace in New Guinea," Hadley said with a wry smile, "but I can hardly bear to leave this pool."

"We'll come back." Skip kissed the tip of her nose. "Count on it."

CHAPTER SIXTEEN

Hadley poured the last saucepan of fresh lemon cordial into the steel canister and stirred its contents. She peered into the canister and frowned. The morning had barely started, and the ice was already melting. She closed the lid and turned to Adumo.

"This can be loaded."

"Oh good," a woman said with a familiar Aussie accent. "You're about to make a run?"

Hadley turned.

"Hiya, Hadley." Lorraine Shaw stood framed in the doorway of the Kunai Club, clad in khaki coveralls. Her eyes crinkled at the corners and a cheerful grin spread across her suntanned face.

Hadley wiped her damp hands on her pants and hurried over to her. "Lorraine. How on earth did you get here?"

"Well, I didn't swim, love." Her friend laughed. "MacArthur's decided I'm bonza. Or rather, that being a woman doesn't mean I can't deliver the goods."

A sharp burn pierced Hadley's gut. She swallowed against a surge of jealousy. Lorraine had spent time in Port Moresby last fall and been allowed to accompany a crew on a mission against the Japanese stronghold of Rabaul. *Her* career was on the upswing, while Hadley's had stalled. Again.

Her rewritten interview with Eleanor Roosevelt had at last been published — in the society pages, like everything else she had written. Dupre also hadn't sent it out over the wire service so other papers could pick it up. And to her fury, he had rejected her piece about her experience with Phil on their ill-fated photo reconnaissance mission on the grounds that he couldn't publish fiction. She had exchanged several angry letters with him, but Dupre had insisted she could only have made up the story from whole cloth.

"That piece you did on the Rabaul mission was tops, Lorraine," she said.

Lorraine smiled. "I may be in MacArthur's good graces, but I'm in hot water with the Australian Army. Rasmussen is furious with me. He banished me back to Oz for months."

"I only need to box these cookies, then I'm off-duty until tonight." Hadley waved for Lorraine to follow her into the cramped kitchen. "How long will you be here?"

"Not long, I hope." Lorraine washed her hands, then helped stack cookies on an empty tray. "That's one of the reasons I was happy to find you. I need to codge a ride."

"Oh, sure. I can take you out to the other strips in one of the Jeepmobiles. Do you know which one you need?" Nadzab was twenty miles square — the largest airfield complex in the world, according to the men — and it housed six different air strips.

Lorraine gestured for Hadley to pass her another tray. "I need a ride off this base."

"Off base?" Hadley raised her eyebrows. Did Lorraine not

appreciate the base's isolation? Where on earth was she planning to go? And why?

"I've got a lead and a contact. I just need to get to Finschhafen. Well, not that far. To a place called *Mange Point*." Lorraine pulled a notebook from her pocket, thumbed it open, and stepped closer to Hadley. "See? It's northwest of Lae."

Hadley narrowed her eyes at Lorraine's scribbled notes. "You can't get there from here." She took the notebook, brought it to her face, and shook her head. "At least, not in a jeep."

"Why not?" Lorraine squinted at the map. "Are there no roads?"

"Between here and Lae, sure." Hadley left the kitchen and led her friend over to a large map of New Guinea tacked up on the club wall. She traced her finger from Nadzab to Lae. "We drove a couple of extra Jeepmobiles to the Red Cross Girls at Lae last month. It's a rough, primitive road, but jeeps can manage it."

"Well . . . " Lorraine edged closer and pointed out a section of coastline northeast of Lae. "Mange Point should be right about here."

"Okay, but these," Hadley said, touching her fingertip to each marked river between Lae and Finschhafen,"are crocodile-infested rivers with fast currents. And there's no *road*."

"You could get me to Lae though, yes?"

"Maybe." Male drivers had driven her and the other women to Lae to drop off the extra Jeepmobiles. That had probably had more to do with the ridiculous, paternalistic rules about their safety than with road conditions. She could drive Lorraine to Lae, if only to prove that going any further over land would be impossible, then enjoy a picnic on the beach before driving back.

"What journalist says *maybe* to a challenge?" Lorraine raised her eyebrows.

Hadley smiled. "Okay, fine. Yes, I can manage that."

"Manage what?" Stella walked up and peeked over Hadley's shoulder.

Hadley turned. "Oh! Hi, Stella. Do you remember my friend

Lorraine from Brisbane?"

"Yes." Stella smiled. "You're a war correspondent for one of the London papers."

"That's me." Lorraine bobbed her head. "Nice to see you again."

"Are you standing here for any particular reason?" Stella prompted, eyeing the map with curiosity. "Going somewhere?"

"Lorraine needs to get to Lae," Hadley said. "And since I'm off-duty until tonight, I'll drive her over in the *Koala Patrol*. No one should need it this afternoon."

Stella contracted her eyebrows until tiny lines appeared over the bridge of her nose. "You'll get one of the fellas to go with you, right?"

"Oh, that's not necessary. My driving is loads better." Hadley winked.

A group of airmen sauntered in, looking for coffee and a doughnuts.

"Just a second, fellas," Stella called out. She lowered her voice and leaned close to Hadley and Lorraine. "Hadley, it's not your driving that worries me, although the road is horrible. What about Japanese hiding in the jungle?"

"We're only going to Lae. It's not far." Hadley had no intention of driving any further than Lae, but having a man along meant he would get to call the shots. She gave Stella a quick hug. "Don't worry. We'll be fine."

***

Hadley slowed the *Koala Patrol* to a crawl to bypass a fallen sago palm blocking their way. Navigating over the rutted, curving road was proving to be harder than she had expected.

Tall kunai grass scraped the side of the vehicle as Hadley skirted the fallen tree. Apart from when they had passed the village of Yalu, they had seen nothing but jungle and swamp. Dense green vegetation encroached on both sides of the narrow road.

"We're definitely in the bush." Lorraine swatted at a cloud of gnats.

Hadley depressed the clutch and raised her voice so her friend could hear her over the engine. "Right. The scenery won't change until we get closer to Lae, almost to the ocean."

Sweat trickled down Hadley's neck. She wiped it away and tightened the knot in the colorful floral-patterned silk scarf tied over her hair. Her sisters had sent it to her for Christmas.

She continued forward and diverted around a variety of natural obstacles. The whine of *Koala Patrol*'s engine along the uneven dirt road kept them from chit-chatting. That was unfortunate, because Hadley remained curious as to why Lorraine wanted to traipse to a remote outpost. Her friend had volunteered no explanation for why she wanted to go to Mange Point.

Lorraine had asked if she could borrow Hadley's typewriter, so they had stopped by her tent and loaded it into the back seat before they left. Apparently during her flight from Townsville to Moresby, Lorraine and the other passengers had been forced to jettison their bags, including the one containing her typewriter. Her paper's bureau chief in Brisbane had promised that a new one would be waiting for her when she returned, but in the meantime, she needed a loaner. Lorraine was lucky she could get another one; the U.S. had rationed typewriters.

Lugging the typewriter with them seemed pointless. The road would dead-end at the airfield base, and Hadley was confident they would find no way to travel beyond Lae. Once she and the airmen convinced Lorraine of that fact, the two of them could grab some chow and then drive back. Hadley supposed that Lorraine could stay in Lae if she wanted and attempt to persuade the military to help her get to Mange Point.

Traversing this narrow road through the jungle, however, had forced Hadley to concede the folly of driving back alone. If Lorraine stayed in Lae, Hadley would have to persuade one of the men on the base to ride back with her. No way would she drive all the way back to Nadzab through the creepy jungle by herself.

She rounded a tight curve and slammed on the brake.

A large crocodile stretched halfway across the narrow road.

"Oh, lordy!" Hadley depressed the clutch as the vehicle slid to a stop. Then she shifted into neutral and clenched the wheel, her heart thudding. What if she hadn't been able to stop, and they had hit it? She was definitely not driving back to Nadzab by herself. Definitely not.

Lorraine leaned forward for a better look. "Don't worry, love. He won't charge the jeep."

"I know. We have alligators back home in Louisiana." She frowned at the enormous creature inching across the road on its belly. "They can walk on land though. Can crocodiles not use their legs out of water?"

"Yes, and they can be quite fast. This one only wants to cross to the other side of the swamp." Marshland lined both sides of the road. She leaned forward. "See, it's getting there."

"Well, it's certainly taking its sweet time." Hadley kept her eyes on the beast until it finally slid into the murky water, leaving not so much as a ripple on the surface. She shuddered.

She eased up on the clutch and accelerated, praying she wouldn't pop the clutch and send the *Koala Patrol* veering into the crocodile's swampy home. The vehicle lurched forward, and she tightened her hold on the wheel to keep them on the road.

Lorraine patted her shoulder. "That was bonza Hadley. Now we're off again!"

Hadley exhaled. They were fine and would soon reach Lae.

After bumping and jolting over the road for another few miles, the jungle vegetation grew sparser, prompting Lorraine to remark that they might be approaching the village.

"Not Lae," Hadley said. "But I know where we are. There are several old coconut plantations between here and there. No one's working them now, of course."

Japanese units had occupied Lae and the surrounding area for two years before the Allies had routed them in September. She pointed out several rows of coconut palms visible on both sides of the road. Undergrowth threatened to overtake the cultivated orchards.

"That's probably a kiln." Lorraine gestured toward a large, open-air building with a thatched roof and surrounded by scattered coconut husks.

Hadley slowed and squinted at a fork in the road. She didn't remember it from her previous trip. Which way had they gone? Coconut orchards stretched in both directions, and each road was in the same abysmal condition. She depressed the clutch, shifted into neutral, and tapped her fingers against the gear shift while she assessed her two options.

Lorraine clucked her tongue. "I'd go right. Besides, we can always circle back."

Hadley raised her eyebrows. She might be an intrepid journalist, but she still balked at following an unmarked road into the jungle — and possibly into an enemy hideout.

Beep, Beep.

Hadley shaded her eyes as another jeep approached them from the south. She threw the jeep into gear and maneuvered onto the side of the road.

The other jeep pulled alongside them, and a USAAF captain leaned out the window. "Hiya, Red Cross! Did you bring doughnuts? Our machine's out."

"Sorry, fellas. No one told us you were sinker deprived at Lae, or we could have brought some." Hadley pointed the way the men had come. "Do we take that route to Lae?"

"Yep." He gave her a swift thumbs-up and wiggled his shoulder toward the other road. "That one's so the plantations can get their goods to the Markham River. "

"Thanks!" Hadley waved, shifted gears, and took the correct fork.

Miles of coconut orchards eventually gave way to the thatched huts of the village of Lae. They waved and called out greetings to the children but didn't slow down.

Lae's single airstrip came into view before they spied the cluster of huts comprising the base's operational facilities, and beyond them, the tents where the men lived. The base housed the Red Cross Girls in a small hut amidst the operational buildings.

Hadley rolled to a stop in front of the Operations building.

"Why are we stopping here?" Lorraine asked. "Do we need petrol?"

Hadley gestured toward the Huon Gulf, lying no more than a mile off the east end of the airstrip. "That's the ocean, Lorraine. This is the end of the road. We can ask the fellas, but like I told you back at the base, we can't go any further."

"The unit I'm trying to reach is engaged in covert operations." Lorraine cleared her throat. "Cloak and dagger business. Their commander's given permission for them to talk to reporters about their training, their exploits, and themselves, for a little personal color."

Covert operations. Like the House on the Hill in Cairns.

Don't try to find it. Don't ask questions. Don't write about it.

Adrenaline jolted her nerves. Could the unit Lorraine wanted to reach be the same one she had stumbled on near Cairns? She looked at Lorraine. "Aussies?"

"I dunno." Lorraine shrugged.

Hadley wiped her sweaty palms down her thighs. "What makes you think they've been cleared to talk to you? And what about the censors?"

"No problem." Lorraine turned in her seat. "I've gotten clearance from MacArthur."

"MacArthur?" Gooseflesh rose on Hadley's arms.

"He's taken quite a shine to me." Lorraine's downturned brown eyes crinkled with her grin. "He gave me a head start, and I don't want to lose my advantage."

"Well, the fellas can probably help you get there from here."

Hadley pointed toward the Ops building. "If there are no roads and no airfield, you'll probably have to go by water."

"Thing is, duck, there are several chaps who are also after this scoop. I've gotten the jump on them, but I'm in a bit of a bind, do you see? Blokes here will dither and dather and fret about military orders, safety precautions, and all manner of rubbish."

"Lorraine —" Hadley broke off with Skip's warning about staying clear of covert operations echoing through her head. "Clearance or no clearance, covering clandestine operations is bound to be dangerous."

"If you can get me there, it'll be your scoop too." Lorraine met her eyes. "We'll write it together, and I'll share the byline with you."

Lorraine had credentials and was an established correspondent with a solid outlet for her work. Hadley wouldn't be hamstrung by Dupre's whims if she co-wrote the piece with Lorraine. She bit her lip. Driving to Lae without permission from her supervisor was one thing. As long as she returned in the company of an armed officer, she could sweet-talk her way out of trouble. But taking the *Koala Patrol* into uncharted wilderness would be a different kettle of fish. They should ask around and find an off-duty man to escort them.

"I think MacArthur's deliberately set me a challenge." Lorraine lifted her chin. "Wants to see if a woman can use her ingenuity to beat the fellas to a story."

"Maybe." Hadley's shoulders tensed. She circled them. "But women can be just as unrelenting and dogged as men, given the same opportunities."

"You're right." Lorraine tightened her jaw. "But he's probably convinced that I'll fail, which will only reinforce his preconceptions about female journalists."

Hadley drummed her fingers on the steering wheel. Driving beyond the base to investigate if there was a road past Lae couldn't hurt, could it?

Skip was right. Sometimes you had to take risks to reach your goals and make your dreams come true. If she was serious about being a journalist, she had to chase this scoop and prove that women were worthy of the job. That *she* was worthy.

Skip would never endorse a trek through the jungle in search of men engaged in clandestine activities. But he had been the one to muse about taking risks to reach one's goals.

"We can try, but I doubt we'll get very far," Hadley finally said, praying that Skip never found out what they were doing. "Let's go have a look."

"That's the spirit." Lorraine inclined her head toward the building. "We should go before they spot us and delay our venture."

True. They had been sitting here for a while without anyone going in or out of the building, but that was unusual. Hadley put the Jeepmobile in reverse, turned around, and followed the base road south toward the ocean, watching for any egress leading off to the east. About a mile from the coast, she spotted a road that was far more primitive than the one they were on. Still, it *was* a road.

"I don't reckon there's another one, do you?" Lorraine pointed toward the beach.

Hadley shook her head. "I doubt it. If there's a road to Finschhafen, this has to be it."

She turned the *Koala Patrol* onto the narrow, rock-strewn road, shifted gears, and made slow progress as they jounced and bumped over the uneven grade. She held fast to the steering wheel while Lorraine clutched the exterior handle grip on her side.

More than once, Hadley had second thoughts about proceeding. Civilization, such as it was in New Guinea, felt distant. No signs of military presence, no villages, no people.

Bodies of water, however, were quite prevalent. Fortunately, Hadley had experience fording streams and creeks in the Jeepmobile. However, she misjudged the depth of the third stream, entered the water while going too fast, and drenched them both with spray.

"Good thing it's so bloody hot!" Lorraine yelled over the roaring engine. "We'll be dry in no time."

They would dry, all right, but they would also be sticky with salt residue. This close to the coast, the stream was filled with brackish water. Hadley directed the Jeepmobile up the bank, where they continued along the so-called road.

How far have we gone? Hadley attempted to visualize the bodies of water marked on the club's wall map. The streams weren't depicted, but they should soon run into one of the larger rivers. She half-hoped they would then be forced to turn back.

The lack of human habitation jangled her nerves. No, make that the *seeming* lack of habitation. Native Papuans might be watching them, and that unnerved her even more. The tribes around the bases at Moresby and Nadzab had been friendly and helpful. She had visited several villages and attended a wonderful sing-sing near Moresby. But they had been warned that some tribes had no idea there was a war on and might have little experience interacting with Westerners.

The path took them through a series of neglected coconut groves, part of another abandoned plantation. Her unease increased as the orchards gave way to a clearing containing a cluster of Western-style buildings.

"What do you suppose these are?" Hadley asked, peering at a low building on her right.

Lorraine eyed the buildings with trepidation. "*Were*, you mean. They look abandoned."

"Hope so," Hadley muttered. If anyone was inside, they were likely to be Japanese deserters.

Her friend waved her arm. "Wait, that's a church. See the cross?"

"Oh my, this must be a mission station." Hadley pulled closer for a better look. "I hope the missionaries got out."

Several missionaries serving on Papua New Guinea's northern coast had evacuated ahead of the Japanese invasion. Most, however, met with a horrific fate. Some might still languish in Japanese POW camps, but many had been slaughtered.

They paused again after passing the church and identified what appeared to be a school and a clinic. No more than a mile past the mission, they spotted their first river. The rickety-looking suspension bridge that spanned its width gave Hadley pause.

"You think it'll support a jeep?" she asked. The muddy water, swollen from recent rains, rushed in an angry torrent below the bridge.

Lorraine pursed her lips. "Bound to, isn't it? They wouldn't have gone to the trouble of creating a bridge solely for foot traffic. And it's more than wide enough."

Hadley tapped her finger against her mouth. The Markham River near their base at Nadzab had both a suspension bridge similar to this one across it, plus a wider pontoon bridge downriver for vehicles. She looked in both directions, assessing whether or not there was a route to a safer crossing point. A trail wound up the riverbank off to her left. That might be worth a look.

"Let's head in this direction to see if there's a better option." Hadley pointed out the trail. "A pontoon bridge would be more stable."

Lorraine nodded her assent.

Hadley shifted into reverse and winced when the tires ground through the rocks and kicked up a cloud of dust.

"Sorry," she muttered through gritted teeth. Her heart pounded as she released the clutch and accelerated, then shifted gears to climb the steep bank. Her toes slipped off the clutch, and she overcorrected with her right foot on the gas pedal. The *Koala Patrol* careened forward with a sharp jerk and veered toward a large boulder.

She wrenched the steering wheel and the engine growled in protest. The tires scrabbled for purchase on the rocky incline before backsliding in a swooping plunge. Her heart plopped into her stomach. She pressed the gas, and the *Koala Patrol* roared forward once again. Before she got control of it, however, the front tire rolled up a tree trunk, and the jeep lifted off the ground, tilted sideways, and teetered on the verge of tumbling over.

Hadley's heart rose into her throat. She whipped the wheel into the lean, and the driver's side tires thudded back to earth, jolting them in their seats.

We're upright. We're okay. Breathe, breathe, breathe.

They might be back on the ground, but the impact of righting the jeep had sent them skidding toward the edge of the precipice. Hadley desperately pumped the brakes and turned the wheel into the skid to break their momentum.

Come on, come on, stop!

Dammit, they were too close to the edge, with no solid ground under the tires on the passenger side. The *Koala Patrol* slid sideways over the edge of the bank.

She screamed. All the breath left her lungs. Lorraine's cries mixed with hers.

Oh, God, Oh, God! We'll end up in the river!

Hadley frantically pumped the brakes and twisted the wheel, but neither slowed their slide. Her heart lodged in her throat. Had they left the ground? Were they falling?

Bam!

The *Koala Patrol*'s frame reverberated from a collision with the ground. Hadley's teeth jarred and her neck muscles seized. The roar of the rapids rang in her ears. Her nostrils filled with the pungent odors of mud and heavy undergrowth. She looked to her left.

Why am I so close to the ground? She turned toward Lorraine. Her friend's side of the jeep lay wedged against a large banyan tree and sat higher than Hadley.

"Are you all right?" she asked in a shaky voice.

Lorraine's eyes had gone wide with shock, but she shot Hadley a tight smile. "We aren't in the river, so I'm all right. You?"

"I-I'm okay." Pain radiated down Hadley's neck into her back. "At least, I think so."

"This stopped our slide." Lorraine pointed at the tree. "But I reckon we should get out."

Yes, we need to get out of here. Hadley struggled to clear the fog from her brain. She unfurled her fingers from the steering wheel and looked around.

Lorraine shifted in her seat, then turned to peer over her shoulder. That slight movement caused the passenger side of the jeep to wobble precariously.

Oh, my God. If it tips, it'll crush me. Hadley's heart thumped. "Don't move!"

"What the —" Lorraine froze with her hand in mid-air. All the color drained from her face. She took in the situation and whispered, "You've got to get out first, duck."

"Okay." Hadley's heart thudded in time with the roaring of the river. She swallowed past the lump in her throat. "I'll crawl out, then help you climb over the back seat."

She took her feet off the pedals and pushed her hand into the wet leaves and muck so she could crawl out over the side.

"Oh, shit. No!" Lorraine screamed and slid against Hadley as the jeep tilted.

Terror swooshed through Hadley. *Now what? Think, think, think.*

Her movements had caused the jeep to tip, so they had to keep as much weight as possible on Lorraine's side. She hitched a deep breath. "Okay, Lorraine, skootch back over toward the tree. Take it slowly, but we need to get your weight against that trunk."

"No," Lorraine whispered. "Every time I've moved, the jeep's gone wobbly."

"We can make this work. Put your right hand against the trunk for leverage. No, c'mon, over there." Hadley waited until Lorraine pressed her palm against the tree, then said with far more assurance than she felt, "Now, slide across the seat. You can do it."

"If you say so." Lorraine grimaced, but inched closer to the Banyan until her body pressed against it from shoulder to hip. She glanced back at Hadley. "Now what?"

"Now reach over and press your other hand against it too. Yes, like that." Hadley kept her voice calm and controlled. "Now, hold your weight there so I can get out."

Without Lorraine knowing, Hadley had already edged to the far side of her seat. She shifted her knees around the gear shift and leaned against the edge of Lorraine's seat.

So far so good. She exhaled, gathered her courage, and scrambled into the back seat, taking care to keep her weight on Lorraine's side. Her heart skipped a beat as she crawled across the tool box to reach the rear of the vehicle. From there, she wouldn't have to jump far to reach the ground, but what would happen when she did?

Perched over the spare tire with one hand pressed against the tree, Hadley considered her options for extricating Lorraine from the vehicle. The rear side rail had been crushed inward and now jabbed her in the ribs. The rear side panel leaned against the tree. But was it jammed against the trunk hard enough to keep the jeep from flipping when Lorraine crawled out?

"I can hop down from here," she said to Lorraine in a shaky voice. "But when I leave the jeep, it might roll. So when I hit the ground, I'll shove it against the tree as hard as I can. You need to move quickly, because I may not have enough strength to hold it there for long."

"Hadley, no!" Lorraine exclaimed. "What if it rolls toward you? It might crush you."

Hadley froze. Her friend had a point. Any number of scenarios might put the jeep on top of her. *Think, Hadley. We need to get Lorraine out, so she can jump clear after I do.*

She pressed her shoulder against the tree and winced as the rail dug into her rib cage.

"New plan," she announced. "You need to crawl over the seat and climb up here next to me. Then, you can jump off right after I do."

Lorraine frowned and paused for a few beats, "Okay, let's try."

"Turn so that your left shoulder is against the tree and keep it pressed there while you crawl over. That should keep the jeep steady."

Hang on, Koala Patrol. Please hang on.

Lorraine moved, and the jeep rocked. She went still. "Bloody hell!"

"Keep going," Hadley said firmly. "Don't stop."

"Okay." Lorraine slowly pushed herself up until her upper body cleared the seat. Moments later, she put her hands on Hadley's shoulders. "I made it!"

"Good. Now let's get off." Hadley crouched on the edge of the compartment and pointed toward a pile of leaves near the tree. "I'm going to land there. Don't waste any time jumping after I do."

"But those leaves might —"

"I know, I know. Snakes." She swallowed. New Guinea harbored dozens of species of venomous snakes, and leaf piles were among their favored hiding spots. "The alternative is jumping onto those spiny tree roots directly below us. You want to land on those?"

"Guess not," Lorraine conceded.

Hadley's knees trembled from her uncomfortable position. She took a deep breath before her legs cramped up and launched herself over the back rail, hoping all the while that she wouldn't land on a death adder or a taipan.

She landed hard on her knees, and her palms smacked into the muck. Searing pain shot through her kneecaps. Before she could get her bearings, Lorraine *ka-thumped* to the ground only a few feet away, sprawled atop the leaves. She clutched her ankle and released a string of indecipherable Australian curses.

Hadley gingerly forced herself to get up. Her knees throbbed, but she could walk. She eyed her friend. *Lorraine might not be so lucky.*

Forced to work out the fierce pain in her knees before she could speak, Hadley paced in tight circles. What should they do now? Being stranded in the jungle was bad enough. Their dilemma would be much more dire if Lorraine couldn't walk.

The pain in Hadley's knees finally eased. She walked over to Lorraine. "Is it broken?"

"I don't know." Lorraine grimaced. "Hurts like hell."

For all the good it would do for a sprained ankle, the jeep had a medical kit. Hadley decided to retrieve it. They might need it again before they got out of here.

"Don't try to stand," Hadley said. "I'll see if I can get the medical kit."

With any luck, it would contain something that would help Lorraine walk the half-mile back to the abandoned missionary station. They could shelter there.

Oh, my God. Hadley froze in mid-step and stared at the jeep. The vehicle sat in a far more precarious position than she had realized — and it was angled just up the slope from the river. If it tumbled over, it would spin into the surging water.

The kit was stored in a rear compartment on the passenger side, near where they had jumped. She couldn't reach it from the ground. Unless . . .

Hadley edged closer. One of the large exposed roots might be tall enough to boost her up so she could grab the kit. She picked her way through the mesh of thick, knotted roots that extended under the jeep. Several yards away from her destination, her boot got stuck between two roots. She twisted her foot and attempted to yank it free to no avail. A fresh wave of pain seared her knee.

Dammit. She undid her boot laces and wiggled her foot in an attempt to pull it free but tugged too hard and lost her balance. She flailed but managed to stay upright.

Stay calm, Hadley. Stay calm. She took a deep breath and inched her foot out of the boot bit by bit until it slid free.

"Argh." Hadley circled her ankle and frowned down at her boot. She couldn't walk around in the jungle barefoot, not with so many knotty roots in her path. Perhaps she could shove a branch underneath her boot and dislodge it.

"What are you doing?" Lorraine yelled.

Hadley cupped her hands over her mouth. "My boot's stuck. I'm trying to get it out."

She found a branch and poked at the boot until she finally maneuvered the branch beneath the heel. By applying pressure, she shifted the boot upward until —

"Shit!" The force of her prodding sent the boot sailing through the air. She now had no choice but to walk barefoot over the damned roots. Grimacing each time her bare foot landed on one, she had to make sure her other boot didn't get stuck and that she didn't step on a snake. Even so, she made halting progress over the gnarly root system.

"Ouch, ouch . . . Oops!" Her foot slipped. She avoided falling, but she had sent a log sliding toward the tree and the jeep. Instead of slamming into the tree, it rammed the rear driver's side tire dead-center, causing the tire to slide down the trunk until the jeep skidded sideways toward the river, picking up speed as it slid down the slope.

Oh, God, not only the medical kit — my typewriter is in there!

Hadley ran down the slope after the vehicle, heedless of her bare foot. She stumbled over rocks and roots, swatted vines out of the way, and flung herself toward the river. If she could reach the jeep, she could grab the back rail and lift herself high enough to rescue her typewriter.

"Hadley!" Lorraine screamed. "Hadley, no!"

She glanced back. Lorraine had managed to get to her feet.

Her friend waved and yelled again, "No! Don't go any closer. You'll drown!"

Chest heaving, Hadley turned back toward the river. Its fast-moving currents surged against the rocks lining the bank. Lorraine was right. Anyone standing on or near those rocks could be swamped by a wave and pulled into the current.

The *Koala Patrol* tipped engine-first into the roiling water, and white-capped waves crashed over her front seats. Then the river claimed her for its own, setting her on a wild, rollicking ride toward the Solomon Sea. With Hadley's typewriter along for the journey.

She clenched her fists and glared at the river as the torrents inundated and submerged her most beloved possession.

***

"Well, hello, ladies." Leo looked up, a jar of boot crème in one hand.

"Uh, we might not have been decent, you know," Rafe said.

Skip looked over the top of *How Green Was My Valley* to find that Bizzy and Stella had strode into the tent without warning. He cast the book aside and jumped up. "What's wrong?"

"Hadley and a friend took one of our Jeepmobiles to Lae early this morning, but they never arrived," Bizzy said. "We got worried and called to check."

"A friend? Who went with her? Why?" Skip's scalp prickled. If she had driven with a man, anything might have happened. He might have hurt her or —

"She took her friend Lorraine, a reporter she met in Brisbane," Stella said. "Said they were going to Lae, but she didn't say why."

"Lae? Like to the beach?" Leo asked.

Bizzy shook her head. "I don't think so. Her swimsuit is hanging on the clothesline."

"Maybe the Red Cross Girls at Lae called and needed her to bring something." Skip said with a frown, "and she took Lorraine along for the ride."

"No. She said Lorraine needed to go to Lae," Stella said. "We asked if their club had called, and they hadn't."

"Damn." Skip's pulse jittered. "How long ago did they leave?"

"About six hours ago." Stella twisted a ring on her finger. "I figured they had decided to stay for lunch until the afternoon wore on. Then, I got more and more worried. Mrs. Brinkman is in Moresby today, so we came to find you."

"I'm gonna go find a jeep." Skip holstered his side-arm, slung his survival pack over his shoulder, and shot out of the tent at top speed.

He hurried past the enlisted men's camp and scanned the area for Nate or another one of his fellas. At last he spotted his crew chief playing cards at a card table set up under the trees. "Nate! I'm going to Lae. If I don't make it back by dark, take care of Lucy, will you?"

"Sure thing, Skip," Nate called out.

Skip wasn't surprised when his crewmates caught up with him at the operations tent, with Bizzy and Stella not far behind. The fellas carried their guns and packs.

He pointed toward a line of jeeps parked outside the tent and yelled, "Grab one and follow me, if you're coming."

"'Course we are." Leo tossed his pack into the back of a jeep, slid into the driver's seat, and started the engine. "Let's go!"

"What's your hurry, fellas?" An unfamiliar officer leaned against another jeep.

Too wound up to reply, Skip ignored him and hopped into the one next to Leo's. Dewey threw his pack on top of Skip's and clambered into the passenger seat.

"Couple of women left here for Lae this morning and never showed up," Charlie yelled to the officer.

"Red Cross Girls?" the fella asked. "Yeah, we saw 'em this morning on our way here."

"You did?" Skip leaned out of the jeep. "Where?"

"About twenty minutes this side of Lae." The man glanced at his buddy, who nodded in agreement. "They were paused at a crossroads, but we got 'em headed in the right direction."

Skip waved his thanks. Now they wouldn't have to waste time debating whether the women had taken a wrong turn before they reached Lae.

Bizzy leaned into the passenger side to talk to Skip and Dewey. "We can't leave, but we're worried sick. Will you call us from Lae once you know something?"

"Sure." His jaw tight, Skip nodded. He flipped the ignition switch and pressed the starter button with his foot. The vehicle choked to life.

He reversed, wheeled around, and pointed the jeep toward the road. Leo and Mike followed, with Rafe and Charlie bringing up the rear. They drove full out until they reached the crossroads the officer had mentioned.

Skip slowed so he wouldn't miss any clues. The fellas had seen Hadley and her friend, but they hadn't made it to Lae. He tightened his hold on the wheel. Trouble was, if they had run out of gas or had engine trouble, someone would have spotted them because a good bit of traffic flowed between Nadzab and Lae, especially in the afternoon when off-duty soldiers often trekked to the beach. Could they have followed a trail through one of the coconut plantations?

"Check the fields on your side," he said to Dewey as he checked the groves on his left. "In case they left the main road."

No sign of movement, a jeep, or any human presence at all.

On the fringes of Lae, Skip slowed the vehicle even more. The women might have stopped here before reaching the airfield and been cajoled into staying for a meal. They might be playing games with children or listening to stories. That's what it was. They had lost track of time, that's all.

A cluster of laughing children waved and called out to them from the side of the road.

"Have you seen two women?" Skip asked, hoping he wasn't butchering the Pidgin language too much. Communication was difficult enough without his inadvertently asking the wrong question. He tried again. "White women?"

Several children waved their arms as if to say *yes*.

"Where?" Skip cut the engine and hopped out. "Take me to them."

"*No-got.*" One of the boys shook his head and mimed a jeep bumping along the road, with the driver waving good-bye.

Damn. The base sat on the other side of the village, and they hadn't stopped there. Maybe they had changed their minds and gone to the beach instead. But with her fair skin, Hadley wouldn't stay there for this long. What if they had waded into the water and —?

Skip's stomach clenched. He raked his hand through his hair, climbed back into the jeep, and called out to the others. "No point stopping at the base. Let's check the beach."

Before they reached it, Dewey spotted a trail. "Slow down. Is that a road?"

"Maybe." Skip put the jeep in neutral and peered down the narrow, dusty track. He got out for a closer look. Yes, fresh tread marks in the dirt and a few severed palm fronds indicated that a vehicle had turned here since the last rain.

Gesturing toward the tread marks, Skip waved to signal his intent to follow the trail.

"Don't you want to check the beach first?" Leo yelled.

Skip clambered out and half-jogged back to his crewmate's jeep. "No. They've been gone for hours. Someone at the base should have spotted them by now."

"Okay, but —" Leo jerked his thumb toward Rafe and Charlie's idling vehicle. "What if they go have a look at the beach and ask around while we check the trail?"

Skip pursed his lips. He had commandeered three jeeps without permission and needed to make damned sure they and his crew returned safely. Splitting up came with risks.

He jogged over to Rafe and Charlie. "Tell you what, why don't you go check the beach and talk to some of the fellas. They'd have noticed a couple of sunbathing women."

"Ok, but . . ." Rafe trailed off and knitted his eyebrows together.

Skip patted the hood. "If you find Hadley and Lorraine, leave 'em at the base and catch up with us. And if you don't . . . then wait for us at the base."

"Okay. You're in charge." Charlie tipped ashes from his ciggie into the dirt.

Yes, he was in charge and would bear the blame if any of his men got injured or were disciplined for this unsanctioned trip. His gut tightened. "See you in a bit."

He ran back to his jeep, jumped in, and bounced off the road onto the rough trail. No army engineer or work crews had done a damned thing to improve it, so why on earth would Hadley have gone this way? Was he on a wild goose chase? Maybe Leo was right, and she had fallen asleep under a coconut tree at the beach. He wanted to believe it, but his twisting gut rejected that scenario.

"Why would they have gone this way, Skipper?" Dewey yelled over the roaring engine.

Skip clenched his jaw. "Hadley and the other woman are both reporters. Something probably caught their eye."

He cursed Hadley and her damned curiosity. She could have found plenty of story material back in Nadzab. He ground his teeth and tightened his sweat-slicked hands on the wheel. The rutted pathway — which definitely wasn't a road — jolted them non-stop.

The jungle stretched for miles. Any villages nearby were well hidden. He and the others stopped several times to verify that the tread marks continued along the road.

He also strained his ears, hoping to hear the roar of a jeep approaching from the south. Rafe and Charlie would beep their horn and ride hard to catch up with Leo and Mike until they all stopped. Then the fellas would assure him that Hadley was safe at Lae, and they could abandon this Conrad-esque journey into the impenetrable wilderness.

Skip shook his head grimly as they forded another creek. What in the hell would motivate Hadley into making such a dangerous trek? Not to mention that this escapade could get her fired from the Red Cross and sent home. He slowed to a crawl and examined the rotting ruins of an abandoned coconut plantation. Nothing. No sign of human habitation or recent use.

"Reckon we'll come upon a river soon?" Dewey leaned forward. His real question was how much farther would Skip take them into this hellscape?

With a little less than half a tank of fuel left, they would have to turn back soon. A burst of tension shot through his tight jaw. *Dammit, Hadley, where are you?*

"Say, is that a village?" Dewey pointed toward a cluster of buildings off to their right.

Skip shaded his eyes. They weren't native huts. Drawing nearer, he slowed to a sputtering crawl. Hadley and Lorraine might have stopped here, although he couldn't understand why the abandoned settlement would be of interest to them. If it wasn't in such an isolated spot, Skip might have thought they were in Australia. He gazed at the large building in the center of the cluster, nudged Dewey, and pointed out the cross atop it.

"This must have been a mission before the war."

"Yeah." Dewey craned his neck. "Should we get out and look around?"

Encroaching undergrowth was already reclaiming what had once been a cultivated lawn, yet enough remained of the clearing that they should be able to spot a jeep, if one were here.

Skip frowned and swept his hand toward the mission grounds. "No. They couldn't be here without their jeep."

"Mighta parked somewhere out of sight."

"All right, let's have a quick look." Skip waved to Leo and turned toward the church.

If roads had once existed here, they were sure as hell gone now. The jeep cut a bone-shaking path through a swath of overgrown vegetation, and he grew more and more convinced that Hadley and Lorraine weren't here. The roar of their engines would have drawn the women out to investigate by now. Still, Dewey was right. They needed to check the area.

Powww-sizzzz! Powww-sizzzz!

A flash of heat seared Skip's neck. His heart clenched, and he leaned into a sharp turn to veer off their current path. After they screeched to a stop, he and Dewey jumped out and crouched behind a mass of bushes. They were soon joined by Mike and Leo.

"Enemy straggler?" Leo panted.

"Must be." Weight dropped like bombs in Skip's chest. What if the sniper had shot Hadley and Lorraine? What if they lay somewhere nearby, injured and bleeding?

What if I'm too late?

Mike swatted at a cloud of buzzing insects. "What are we

gonna do?"

"Good question." He rubbed his knuckles against his forehead. They were USAAF airmen, with no training in hand-to-hand combat or taking prisoners. He took a deep breath. "Shots came from the building beside the church, right?"

"Yeah." Leo nodded. "Seemed like."

"Could be more than one of 'em in there." Dewey peered through a gap in the bushes.

Think, think, think. Skip gritted his teeth. The sooner they captured or killed the sniper — and God forbid Dewey was right and there was more than one — the sooner he could search the grounds and buildings for Hadley and her friend.

"Fellas?" Panic suffused Leo's voice. "I dunno about the soldier, but somebody needs to take care of *this* problem first."

Skip followed his crewmate's gaze. *Fuck.*

Coiled a few feet from Leo's ankle, a death adder flicked its tongue. No doubt the reverberation of their voices was sending danger signals pulsing through its thick body. A pile of leaves had camouflaged the snake's orange and brown bands. Small wonder the creature hadn't already bitten one of them.

"Don't move." Skip swallowed past a lump in his throat. "It could strike any one of us."

"No shit," Leo hissed.

"Maybe it'll go away," Mike said.

Dewey shook his head. "They aren't active this time of day."

"It's sure as hell awake now," Leo muttered.

"Yep, and it's gonna defend its territory." Dewey drew his pistol. "Not abandon ground."

"What about your knife?" Skip asked without moving his lips.

Dewey raised his gun. "Are you kidding? You know how fast and far this fucker can strike?"

"Don't miss, buddy," Mike whispered.

"I grew up in Cajun country, shot a lotta snakes," Dewey assured him.

Sweat slicked Leo's face. "At this range?"

Dewey ignored his question and took aim. "Remember, it can still bite after it's dead, so stay clear of its head."

All the air left Skip's lungs.

Dewey's aim was true, and he hit the snake dead-on. The reptile's body twisted into a tight, defensive ball, twining and flailing in a morbid death dance, its mouth gaping open in protest until Dewey put another shot into its fearsome maw.

"Back up!" he yelled.

Like Leo and Mike, Skip lost no time in scrambling backwards to put as much distance as possible between himself and the writhing mass of coils and fangs that could still inject enough venom to kill a man in minutes. To his relief, Dewey dispatched it with two more rapid-fire shots; one to its body, and another to its head.

Skip mopped his face with his sleeve. *Shit, that was way too close.*

A flash of movement in his peripheral vision cranked up his adrenaline levels. They'd had no choice but to shoot the damned snake, but Dewey's shots had given away their location. Skip scrambled to his feet and pulled out his own pistol, and his men did the same.

Skip stepped from behind the bushes, alert and poised to fire.

Powww-sizzzz!

"No, Skip! Get down!" Hadley's shrill scream rent the muggy silence.

A cold barb stabbed his ribs. He jerked his gaze away from the enemy soldier and zeroed in on her, standing near the church. Her stance told him she intended to rush the sniper.

God, no. You'll get shot.

"Stay where you are!" he yelled in panic.

Apparently startled by their raised voices, the soldier lost focus. His hesitation was all Dewey needed. He shot the man square in the chest, and he crumpled to the ground.

Skip dashed forward, past the dead soldier, and caught Hadley in a tight embrace. He buried his face in her hair and inhaled the faint scent of her shampoo.

Violent shudders racked her body. He pulled her against him and struggled to make sense of the words tumbling out between her jerky sobs and harsh breaths. She kept mentioning a name he didn't recognize. *Cordelia? Amelia?*

"Who?" he asked. "Shhh, what's all this about?"

She said the name again, but he still didn't catch it or understand the strangled phrases. He would ask her later after she had calmed down.

As his adrenaline levels dropped, he grimly surveyed the scene over the top of Hadley's head. The fellas were checking the mission buildings. Mike soon emerged from the farthest one.

"Find any other soldiers?" Skip yelled.

Mike shook his head. "No. It's all clear, unless someone was in the church with Hadley."

"Honey, was anyone in the church with you?" Skip stroked her tangled hair.

She lifted her tear-streaked face and met his eyes. "Lorraine. Lorraine's in there. Her ankle is in bad shape, probably broken."

He caught Leo's eye and inclined his head toward the church. Leo took the hint and motioned for the others to follow him into the crumbling building.

His voice carried outside. "Hiya, Miss Lorraine. Heard you've got a bum ankle and might need assistance to get to our jeeps."

"G'day, mates." Lorraine sounded chipper.

Skip drew his brows together. "Hadley, speaking of jeeps — where's your Jeepmobile? We almost didn't stop. The place looks abandoned."

"It's — it's probably in the ocean by now." Fresh tears pooled in her eyes.

He gaped at her. "The ocean?"

"Yes." Hadley drew a shaky breath. "Last time I saw it, the river was carrying it in that direction."

"The *river*?" Learning a river was nearby didn't surprise him. Months of flying over the island had taught him just how many rivers bisected the New Guinea coastline. But how had their jeep ended up in the water? And how had they trekked from the river to here? Was that how Lorraine had injured herself? He had so many questions.

Mike and Leo emerged from the church with Lorraine balanced between them. As they passed Skip and Hadley, Lorraine patted Hadley's shoulder. "You all right, love?"

Hadley bobbed her head.

She wasn't. Skip had never seen her less composed or more on edge.

"Expect you ladies have a vehicle around here somewhere." Dewey shaded his eyes with his hand and looked around. "Should I drive it back for 'em, Skipper?"

"Their Jeepmobile seems to have met with some misfortune." Skip cleared his throat. "You can get ours started and pointed in the right direction."

"Righto, Skipper."

"Dewey?" Air expanded Skip's chest.

His crack-shot crewmate stopped and swiveled around.

"You're a damned good shot, Dewey," Skip said. "You saved our lives. *Twice*. I'll make sure Colonel Williams knows."

"Had a good teacher." A wide grin split Dewey's face. "Reckon my Pop would like to hear that."

"I'll write him too." Skip grinned. "Count on it."

He turned back to Hadley. Her color still hadn't returned to normal and sweat glistened on her temples. Mud and several jagged rips marred her uniform. He had never seen her more open, more emotional, more vulnerable. Details could wait.

He brushed his lips against hers. "You can fill me in about the jeep and everything else once we're back on base. We ought to go before it gets dark."

***

"Stop clucking." Lorraine pushed Hadley away. "I'm fine. Or I will be, once they get my ankle squared away."

"But I know you're in pain." Hadley jammed her restless hands into her pockets. "I can check to see how much longer you'll have to wait."

"No. It's only a sprain," Lorraine said. "Or at worst, a broken ankle. Most of the blokes have far more pressing issues."

"How about I make you a cup of tea, then?"

"If anyone looks like they need a cuppa — or better yet, something stronger — it's you, love." Lorraine rolled her eyes. "Why don't you go get cleaned up a bit?"

The medics had wedged a cot for Lorraine into a small room away from the main sick bays. Probably because of her gender rather than the possibility that she might contract something contagious. After all, most of the men were either nursing battle wounds or fighting tropical maladies caused by insects or the hot, humid climate. She might easily get lost in the shuffle.

"If you don't want a cup of tea, at least let me remind them that you're here."

"They haven't forgotten. Trust me." Mrs. Brinkman's soft Georgia accent was tinged with more than a dollop of disapproval.

Hadley turned to face her supervisor and arranged her expression into a mix of deference and contrition. It didn't work.

"Hadley, may I have a word?" Mrs. Brinkman beckoned her out into the hallway.

Hadley dug her fingernails into her palms. Time for her reckoning. "Of course."

"Excuse me," Lorraine said. "Mrs. Brinkman, is it?"

"Yes." The woman paused. "What can I do for you?"

"I'm so dreadfully sorry for dragging Hadley on my wild quest." Lorraine's eyes oozed remorse. "I assure you my employer will reimburse your military or the Red Cross for the jeep."

"I appreciate the sentiment, Miss . . .?

"*Mrs.* Shaw," Lorraine corrected. She didn't often use her matrimonial title, perhaps realizing it would highlight her gender more than if she allowed people to perceive her as a *career girl*. She worried incessantly about her husband, who served with the RAF in India, but downplayed her status while on the job.

"Well, Mrs. Shaw, I suspect that replacing the jeep will be much stickier than you realize. Military requisition is difficult enough, without the additional step of needing reimbursement from Australia."

"I'm a correspondent credentialed with the *London Daily Mirror*." Lorraine smiled. "I assure you the paper will expedite reimbursement to either the Red Cross or the U.S. Army, as I was on an official assignment."

"Oh, really?" Mrs. Brinkman narrowed her eyes with suspicion at Lorraine's reference to a news outlet and turned to Hadley. "We've already had several conversations about you needing to remain focused on your Red Cross work."

"Oh, Mrs. Brinkman, I'm afraid I'm entirely to blame for our diversion," Lorraine said. "I persuaded Hadley to drive me to Lae on the pretext of going to the beach."

Hadley shielded her face from Mrs. Brinkman and threw Lorraine an incredulous look. They had *not* been on a pleasure lark.

Mrs. Brinkman cleared her throat. "Be that as it may, Hadley is aware that she is required to have two armed male escorts anytime she travels that far from base."

"Yes, ma'am. I —" Hadley began.

"That is also my fault, I'm afraid," Lorraine broke in, a butter-melting smile on her face. "Unbeknownst to Hadley, I was anxious to go because I wanted a scoop. When we couldn't find any off-duty men, I persuaded her that we wouldn't run into danger since there's plenty of traffic between here and Lae. I told her we would find some blokes in Lae to accompany us back, so no one would be the wiser. So you see —"

"Leaving without a proper escort was outrageously foolish and dangerous for both of you," Mrs. Brinkman interrupted. "If you weren't healthy as a horse, Hadley, I would ship you home tomorrow."

Hadley's stomach curled into a knot. Red Cross staffing issues across the Pacific Theater had been exacerbated by the number of women who were routinely in the hospital or recuperating from various tropical illnesses. Some became so ill they had to return to the States.

"So you see, I sweet-talked Hadley into this whole shenanigan." Lorraine threw Mrs. Brinkman another pointed look. "Lae wasn't my destination, but Hadley didn't know that. "

"That still doesn't explain why on earth you two would —"

"I know," Hadley knit her hands together. "We shouldn't have left the main —"

"Hadley kept saying we should turn back, that we had gone too far." Lorraine sat up straighter. "But I urged her to continue. *I* was the one being irresponsible."

"And yet," Mrs. Brinkman lifted a brow. "the one driving —"

"Was me." Lorraine pulled a face. "We stopped to check a tire, and I volunteered to take over. I was brought up in Townsville and had driven over rough roads in the bush before. Then I told Hadley we would only go on for a short while before turning back."

No, Hadley couldn't let this stand. The *Daily Mirror* might be willing to send Lorraine a new typewriter, but they wouldn't be keen to reimburse the U.S. Army for the lost jeep. Lorraine could lose her credentials and even her job. Hadley turned to Mrs. Brinkman.

"No, it was all my fault. I —"

"Repeatedly insisted we turn back," Lorraine cut in again, her eyes sparking with new challenge.

Hadley couldn't dispute that she *had* suggested turning back at least a dozen times, but she couldn't let Lorraine lie to protect her. She shook her head. "Lorraine wasn't driving when we —"

"Drove off the main road. But *I'm* the one who had the

accident." Lorraine met Mrs. Brinkman's eyes. "The doctor should evaluate her for a concussion."

"Excuse me, Mrs. Brinkman?" An orderly leaned inside the door.

"Yes?"

"Gals at the Kunai Club gave us a jingle. A fight broke out, and they'd like you to help sort it out. We've got a jeep waiting out front if you want a ride."

"Fine, yes, lead the way." Mrs. Brinkman rubbed the back of her neck and nodded at the man. Then she turned to Hadley. "Come find me after the club closes so we can continue our discussion. Your good health may not be enough reason to allow you to stay. If you want to be a reporter so badly, perhaps you should go home and do that."

"I'll come find you." Hadley bobbed her head and pressed her lips together.

Mrs. Brinkman wagged her finger at Lorraine. "In the meantime, you two should get your story straight."

Hadley leaned around the door and waited until Mrs. Brinkman disappeared down the hall before spinning back to face Lorraine.

"No, no, no," she hissed. "You are *not* taking the fall for me."

"Oh yes, I am." Lorraine held up her hand and beckoned Hadley over to the bed. "What's my worst-case scenario? My editor will be impressed by our pluck, even though we fell short. They'll sort out the jeep with the military blokes, no worries."

"A jeep isn't on par with a typewriter, Lorraine."

"You, on the other hand," Lorraine pressed on, "stand to lose quite a lot. Look, I know you've been frustrated by your inability to report on the actual war, but —"

"I'm done reporting." Hadley shook her head.

Lorraine rolled her eyes. "She won't send you home, despite her bluster. She can't afford to lose you. And love, I know your typewriters are rationed, but I'll find you another one."

"I'm done writing," Hadley said in a trembling voice. "It's

brought me nothing but trouble, mostly for people I love. I'm done."

"You're overwrought." Lorraine found Hadley's hand and gave it a squeeze. "A nose for news isn't something you can turn on and off like a hosepipe. Writing is who you are. You'll see. This will all look better in the light of day."

No, it won't. I nearly lost Skip. He had come close to paying the same price for her and her curiosity that Fanelia's son Gabriel had. Hadley's heart constricted into a tight ball. She should have given up writing long ago.

***

Hadley stepped out of the hospital and into a puddle of muck. She crinkled her nose at its cloying stench. Dank humidity hung over the base like a wet blanket.

Twilight, so fleeting in the tropics, teetered on the knife's edge of its precipitous descent into full darkness. Frogs croaked, birds called, and insects chirped from the jungle.

"How's Lorraine?" Skip stepped out of the shadows and took Hadley's hand.

She entwined their fingers. "Her ankle is fractured. She'll stay here until she can travel."

He made a noncommittal noise and led her to a bench outside the PDX, which was set away from the central base buildings and had the added advantage of being closed for the night.

She braced herself to face another reckoning. Skip would want to know what had led her and Lorraine into making their perilous trek without an escort. Her stomach churned at the idea of recounting the details, but nothing less than total honesty could stand between her and Skip.

Silence stretched between them. Each time she opened her mouth to apologize for placing him and his men in danger, her throat closed and she strangled on the memories thrown into sharp relief. Just as Gabriel had done in the dark byways of Tremé, Skip had also put his life in jeopardy as a result of Hadley's foolish gadding about after stories.

Unlike Gabriel's story, which remained unexamined, unpaid, and untold, Hadley must recount to Skip what had transpired today. He deserved nothing less. She loved him and would never have recovered if she had lost him today. She wouldn't divulge the deeper impetus that drove her dogged quest for the truth, but she would tell him how she and Lorraine had ended up in the abandoned mission station in an isolated and dangerous slice of New Guinea jungle.

He pressed his warm, solid weight to her side and squeezed her hand in encouragement.

"I'm sorry," she finally whispered, the words which were both the beginning and the end of what she must say.

Skip jerked his chin in acknowledgment and stared down at their clasped hands. "You want to start at the beginning?"

Not the very beginning, no.

"Lorraine arrived on an early morning flight and said she needed a ride to Lae." Hadley swallowed. "She told me she wanted to go to a place near Finschhafen."

"Finschhafen? You can't get there except by sea."

"That's what I told her, but she wanted to try." Hadley swiped a lock of hair from her face. "I figured we could drive to Lae, where the men on base would confirm that there isn't a land route to her destination."

"Why didn't you take an escort?" He rubbed his thumb over her fingers. "Isn't that your usual procedure?"

She hesitated. Red Cross Girls delivered doughnuts, cookies, sandwiches, and cold drinks to all the airstrips on the sprawling base here at Nadzab and sometimes operated out of small canteen huts with thatched roofs and open-air sides. On other days, they drove Jeepmobiles out to the revetments or even to the flight line. They forded the many creeks and billabongs that crisscrossed the twenty-square-mile base and covered many miles each day.

But whenever they left the base, they never went unescorted.

Considering the dangerous wildlife, natural hazards, harsh road conditions, changeable weather, the possibility of vehicle trouble, and of course, the chance of encountering enemy soldiers like they had experienced today, it was little wonder.

Why *hadn't* she and Lorraine taken that simple precaution? They wouldn't have had any trouble finding a bored off-duty man or two who would have jumped at the chance to drive to Lae with two women. Why had Hadley been so blithe about Stella's worries that, in retrospect, hadn't even scratched the surface?

"The truth is," she said, pausing to lick her dry lips, "I'm not sure why we didn't find someone to go with us. I suppose I was worried that someone might try to stop us and figured it would be easier to beg forgiveness than ask permission. Lorraine was antsy too, afraid some man would scoop her story."

"I'm sure you could've found some low-level private who would have played along and not raised any objections." Skip twiddled with her bracelet.

Hadley sighed. How could she explain it? *He* never had to ask permission. Yes, he was subject to military orders, but what nagged at Hadley — at all the women, to one degree or another — were the chafing restrictions on the most basic facets of their existence. How could she explain that leaving with Lorraine sans escort had been nothing more than acting on instinct, with an impulse to fly free?

"I could have . . . *should* have," she corrected, "enlisted a fella to ride with us. You're right. I underestimated the danger we might run into driving there."

Skip didn't speak, but his deep inhale and the way his forearm muscles strained, signaled his escalating frustration with her.

Hadley plunged on. "I figured Lorraine could stay in Lae and work out how to get to Mange Point, while I —"

"While you did what?" he broke in, the derision in his voice drowning out his concern. "Drove back here alone?"

"Of course not." Remembering the slithering crocodile crossing the road, she suppressed a shudder. "No, believe me, I would have asked someone in Lae to come back with me."

"Bizzy said you never made it to the base at Lae, that no one had seen you."

"I-I know." Hadley bit her lip. She couldn't get around the fact that she and Lorraine had been foolhardy from that point on. Driving to Lae without a male escort had pushed the limit but pressing on into uncharted wilderness without a plan had been rash, reckless, risky. Yet they had employed their own brand of courage, rooted in their burgeoning determination to prove their worth and credibility in a man's world. Whether she intended it or not, Lorraine had framed her plan in a way designed to trigger the best and worst of Hadley's impulses. Male dominance in her chosen profession had taken its toll, no question about it.

"Guess I just figured there was no harm in seeing how far we could go before we were forced to turn back. I honestly didn't think —"

"No, you definitely didn't think." He accented each word with pops of sizzling heat.

The hairs on the back of her neck prickled. "I honestly didn't expect to find a road. I assumed we would either have to head to the beach or back to Lae within minutes."

"So when you saw the road, you just took it? Without even considering going back to the base to ask where it might lead or to get someone to go with you?"

"Yes, but —" She hadn't thought the road would take them far, yet she had indulged her desire to prove that women reporters could do the same job as men. She glanced at him and cleared her throat. "It's like you said at the swimming hole, about taking risks to get what you want out of life."

"I didn't mean risks that could cost you your life," he shot back.

She shook her head. "I wasn't trying to risk our lives. That road could have been perfectly fine. It might have led all the way to Finschhafen, where we could scoop the story Lorraine was after. That would have been a big break for both of us. It's like you said.

Sometimes you have to take risks."

"I was talking about *me*, not you!" Skip snapped, dropping her hand.

Hadley bolted to her feet. "Oh, so men are the only ones entitled to take risks?"

"That's not what I said," he spat between clenched teeth as he rose beside her. "But risks you take for your gain shouldn't put other people in danger!"

A familiar vise tightened across Hadley's chest. Her face flushed, and jumbled memories flashed through her mind. He was right. She couldn't put him or anyone else in danger. And the best way to avoid that was to keep her distance from anyone she might put in harm's way.

"Well, you won't need to worry about me putting you in danger again, Skip Masterson. Maybe the Red Cross will ship me home. Or transfer me back to Australia. But either way, it won't matter." She blinked back tears. "A relationship between us was never going to work. We've known that all along."

CHAPTER SEVENTEEN

April 16, 1944

Mission to Hollandia, Dutch New Guinea

"Fuck radio silence, you've gotta tell him." Leo thrust the map toward Skip and jabbed his finger at their position. "He's taken us miles off course already."

Skip gave his crewmate a non-committal jerk of his head. Why should he risk pissing off Major Howe? This was their last mission, dammit. Finish it in one piece, and he could go home. And since Hadley had broken things off, going home had never looked more enticing.

Space, that's what I need.

"We got a late start, and you can set your watch by the afternoon storms," Leo snapped. "If thunderheads slow us down on top of this bullshit, we'll be in a real pickle."

The weather guys had wanted to cancel today's mission but had been overruled. MacArthur intended to launch amphibious landings at Hollandia within days and wanted the Fifth Air Force to make one final push to extinguish Japanese resistance.

Storms at Nadzab had delayed their departure by two hours, adding to everyone's unease about flying through nasty weather on the return leg.

Skip glanced at the fuel gauge and ran calculations in his head. They'd be cutting it fine, but they could make it back, even with the usual storms. "I'll break in if he doesn't correct our trajectory soon."

"If he doesn't, we'll have to scrub the mission," Leo said.

Skip scowled. *No.* They needed this mission credit. *He* needed this mission credit. Getting the hell out of this damned war was more important than ever now. He no longer had any reason to prolong his stay in the South Pacific.

"Let me know when —" He shook his head. "Dammit, I know, I know. You think we've already wasted too much fuel but let me know when we've reached the tipping point."

Sensing Leo's mounting frustration, Skip kept a careful watch on the fuel supply. He had just moved his finger over the call button when Major Howe's voice crackled through the intercom with a terse route change. Now they were on course, albeit with less fuel.

"About damned time," Leo muttered.

Skip rolled his eyes. "Stop beating your gums and put on your bombardier hat for once."

No strafing today. They would bomb from medium altitude, as they had trained to do initially. The war had come full circle.

In the end, on this final mission, they may as well have been dropping sandbag bombs over the Arizona desert again for all the resistance the Japanese lobbed at them. Enemy ack-ack was light and inaccurate, and they encountered no fighters. Best Skip could discern, their mission had been unnecessary; the Hollandia airfield complex had already sustained enough damage to put it out of commission.

Now they were done. All that remained was to land safely back at their base, and they could pack their bags.

Skip banked into a sharp turn over Tanahmerah Bay before nosing along the coastline with the purple, rain-shrouded Cyclops Mountains on his right. He shut one eye and framed several shots using his mental rangefinder. He would likely never see these mountains or the Bismarck Sea ever again. This was it. No more New Guinea. No more missions.

No more war.

No more Hadley either, even though Skip planned to try again. What they had shared made it worth another try. Maybe she would hear him out this time. Why had she made this a gender issue? He didn't believe that men *or* women should have license to take personally beneficial risks that endangered others.

For God's sake, he wasn't asking her to give up being a journalist. He only wanted her to be more sensible and more cognizant of risks, especially in hot combat zones. That Japanese soldier could have raped and/or killed both Hadley and Lorraine. Not to mention the natural perils the women had faced while trekking from the river to the mission station — and she still hadn't told him how they got out of the jeep before it fell into the rushing Busu River.

He shuddered.

"Damn." Mike leaned closer to the windshield. "Look at that."

"What?" Skip gave his head a little shake and stared at the storm brewing around them. How had conditions changed so quickly? Light rain and coastal squalls they had just flown through had given way to far more threatening conditions. A colossal thunderhead loomed ahead.

He frowned at the billowing clouds swirling outside both side windows. Weather formed fast in New Guinea, but Skip had never seen a storm explode at this rate. Not even the violent storm back in November that had thrown them off course and depleted their fuel supply.

Fuel. Skip eyed the fuel gauge and bit his lip. Little room for error. His instinct was to climb and attempt to overfly the thunderhead, but that would cut into their dwindling reserves.

Major Howe's voice crackled through the intercom: "This is gonna be rough. We can't hold formation in this weather. Try to stick with your wingman best you can."

"Bob, you copy?" Skip couldn't see his wingman's ship through the thick clouds and the torrent of rain crashing against the windshield.

Bob didn't answer. Maybe the other plane's intercom or radio had been knocked out.

Skip poked *Bourbon Street Belle*'s nose along the front's leading edge. Nothing doing. That roiling maelstrom was dangerous and how.

He swiped sweat from his forehead with his sleeve, then turned to Mike. "Reckon we should take her up and look for clearer weather?"

His copilot scrunched his nose and pointed at the fuel gauge. "Dicey."

"That's what I thought." Skip pushed the yoke forward and descended lower. "Let's follow the coastline for a while, see if we can find an opening."

The menacing clouds were jet-black at the bottom, where they blended in with the jungle foliage, before segueing into varying shades of blacks and grays, threaded with swirls of silver and white, into higher altitudes. The monster thunderhead stretched for miles in all directions and churned out unprecedented turbulence. The lower he descended, the more the strong vertical currents buffeted and tossed them around, sending *Bourbon Street Belle* into stomach-dropping pitching and yawing. He clutched the control column with all his strength and descended as far as he dared. With the irregular coastline and rain pelting in sheets across the windshield, he didn't want to risk flying too low and running into a tree. Keeping her at about twenty feet in altitude and about fifty feet off the coast, that should do it.

Faint, crackly chatter on the pilot's channel suggested some fighter boys had tried to go over the front with no luck. Their reports said the front topped out at over forty thousand feet. *Bourbon Street Belle* couldn't go anywhere near that high. No point in wasting their fuel to try.

If they couldn't go over it or around it or through it, how about under it?

Skip had heard a pilot recount a daring escape made by flying *under* a weather front through a valley. Similar to what Skip had done in August, on that fateful day when Pat and his crew had died and Charlie had been injured. Yet flying fast and low over rivers in clear weather was one thing; trying it now, with no guarantee of visibility, would be risky.

"Cockpit to Navigator: Any idea if we're close to the entrance to the Ramu Valley?"

After a short pause, Leo barked a harsh laugh. "Hell no, I don't know where we are. My instruments and maps have been flying all over the place. Hang on."

Leo squatted between Skip's and Mike's seats, gripping the edge of Mike's for support. "Might have better luck looking out the damned window than with instruments."

"Why are you asking about the Ramu?" Mike asked.

Skip squinted through the windshield. "For one thing, that's our stated route."

"What's the other reason?" Leo scribbled down some numbers and shook his head.

Skip was reluctant to voice it. If they could identify the river with any certainty, he might dare it. They could theoretically fly under the front and navigate back to Nadzab by visually following the river. Downdrafts, however, posed a significant danger.

Wind danger aside, however, his plan was rife with other potential problems. Torrential rain might hinder their ability to keep the river in sight, and flying off course could send them slamming into a mountain. They would also need to be certain, absolutely certain, that they were following the correct river. If they confused the Ramu with the Sepik, they would end up far from any Allied base.

He gritted his teeth. They should head to Saidor. It was on the coast, meaning they could stay over coastal waters and keep their ship out of the storm's whirling vortex. Rain and hail already tore at it, and pockets of turbulence wrenched at the wings. Skip couldn't imagine how frightful the conditions might become if he attempted to barrel *through* the front.

"Get me a header to Saidor." Skip white-knuckled the yoke.

Leo snorted. "That assumes we've got an accurate fix on where we are."

"Our only option is to assume we do." Skip fought to keep the plane level.

Mike looked at him. "Is Saidor operational?"

"Best I can tell, they're trying to be." Their bomb group had abandoned radio silence, and he had overheard many pilots saying they were headed to Saidor.

"What about Bob? Any idea where he is?"

"Nope." Skip had lost sight of his wingman, Bob Prewett, who piloted *Pacific Prowler*, long ago. Nor did he know where any other ships in their squadron might be. Bob hadn't identified himself on the radio, and Skip couldn't distinguish individual voices in all the chatter.

Leo gave him a heading to Saidor, and Skip adjusted course. By the time they were within range of the Saidor tower, he was certain of two things: They would not receive clearance to land, but they would land anyway.

He had no other choice. Leo had been right to worry about fuel consumption. Skirting the worst of the storm had used even more, and their rear tanks were now empty. Front tanks were in little better shape. They couldn't stay airborne much longer.

"Cowpox, this is Dusky-B. Dusky-B requesting permission to land," Rafe intoned over the radio. He repeated the call several times and then said, "Radio to Cockpit: Tower isn't responding."

Skip had figured as much, based on what he had gleaned from the pilot channel. From the sound of it, pandemonium reigned both in the sky and on the ground at Saidor. It was every man for himself.

The arrows on the fuel gauge for the front tanks clicked down another notch.

He gulped, trying to suck air into his tight chest, and flicked the selector switch to the pilot channel frequency. Then he pressed the call button.

"Dusky-B here. Cowpox tower isn't responding, but I've got a fuel emergency. I'm descending now."

A bubble of protests broke out. Apparently there was some sort of unofficial queue for landing, despite the tower's lack of direction and oversight.

The fuel gauge arrows slipped further still.

Fuck, fuck, fuck. He tightened his jaw. They didn't have the reserves to circle and wait their turn. They could either ditch into the storm-tossed sea or land immediately on the Saidor strip.

"Dusky-B here," he broke in again. "I'm claiming priority landing rights. I've got less than five minutes of flying time left. Descending and lining up. Over."

Skip flipped the selector switch over to the ship's intercom. "Pilot to Crew: Prepare for immediate landing."

He tightened his grip on the yoke and ignored the selector switch. No point in hearing whatever protests the other pilots were throwing his way. He had claimed fuel priority. They needed to stay the hell out of his way.

That assumed the others could see him. He had so little visibility he couldn't tell if he was flying into someone's path in a sky congested with desperate ships. He appreciated the risks. Earlier reports of utter chaos on the ground suggested they might not find enough runway as it was.

His resolve wavered. Should he pull up, head out over the water, and ditch? What if he used up his remaining fuel only to discover he couldn't land? Sweat slicked the sides of his face. Seconds. No time to consult with Mike. He was the commander and must decide immediately whether to commit to landing, despite the risks, or head out to sea.

Skip steeled himself. "Pilot to Crew: Brace yourselves for imminent crash landing."

As bad as their landing might be, he would rather chance crashing on the runway than adding his men to the scores of pilots and crews hoping to be pulled from the drink. Lots of fellas had called out their coordinates in desperate Mayday calls as they went down into the white-capped, angry swells of the Bismarck Sea.

"One thousand feet," Mike called out.

Clouds swirled, and raindrops pelted the windshield.

Where the hell is the strip? Skip gripped the yoke. Leo had said the runway ran from the edge of the water to the base of the Finisterre mountains. Who in hell had put a landing strip between the ocean and a mountain?

Mike deployed the landing gear and opened the flaps, then called out, "Seven hundred feet." He toggled the fuel boost pump switches.

Still nothing but clouds and rain. Skip's heart leapt into his throat.

Should have taken the risk and plowed under the front into the Ramu valley. Should have ditched in the sea. Should have done something, *anything*, else. They could all die. He had put his friends' lives in danger, he was responsible. His old self wouldn't have hesitated to dodge under the front, risks be damned.

Instead, because of his caution, they were in peril. No telling where the fucking strip was, how long it might be, whether it was surrounded by natural obstacles like trees, or whether there were other desperate pilots attempting to do exactly what he was doing.

He was literally flying blind. Black squares pressed close on him, as if someone had thrown a photographer's hood over his head. He struggled to regain his peripheral vision.

"Three hundred feet," Mike called out.

Blood thundered in Skip's ears. He tightened his hold on the yoke and used his other hand to push the throttles forward.

"Two hundred feet."

He held his breath. He still couldn't see a damn thing. How was it possible for the ceiling to be so low?

"One hundred feet." A tinge of panic infused Mike's words.

Through a swirl of fog and mist, a runway popped into view, but Skip had overshot it, thanks to the low visibility. Apparently too terrified to speak, Mike jabbed his finger at the fuel gauges, warning Skip they had no fuel to circle around for another try.

He knew that. They couldn't circle around. They didn't have enough fuel, and another ship might be making its approach directly behind him. He acted on instinct, pulled back on the yoke, and pushed it to the right to ascend and turn.

As Skip banked left, Mike yelled, "Are you fucking crazy?"

"No other choice!" Skip pulled the ship into another sharp turn and lined up again. Landing from the wrong direction was exceptionally dangerous, but his only other option was to crash into the mountain or the base.

Visibility was clearer from this direction, and he had no trouble lining up his approach. He spotted several wrecked planes scattered on and around the runway. No wonder the tower had abandoned hope of directing landings at this field.

Ground crews and equipment raced pell-mell along the strip, attempting to clear wreckage. About midway down, a bulldozer chugged up to the edge of the runway. Skip willed its driver to look up, to pause, to hit his brakes. He exhaled as the vehicle halted.

Skip pulled back on the yoke to lift the nose, then brought her down onto the slick Marston-matting. He planned to slow and veer off onto a taxiway, out of oncoming traffic where another plane might materialize at any moment. But the back left tire blew on touchdown, and the plane skidded sharply left with a piercing screech and a cloud of smoke.

Skip pressed hard on the pedal and struggled to keep the plane on the runway. He leaned into the skid and fought for control. Hot waves of adrenaline shot through him. He tilted the yoke and pumped the pedal to correct the skid, trying desperately to slow the ship. *Bourbon Street Belle* stubbornly continued her precipitous slide through the muddy puddles and clipped a stationary A-20 parked on the taxiway with her left wing.

Screech, Screeeeech, Screeeeeech, Grrrrinnnddd.

Vibrations rocked the plane.

Shit! The unexpected contact sheared off *Bourbon Street Belle's* wing. Skip didn't need to look back to confirm it. The plane finally slid to a stop parallel to the runway.

"Pilot to Crew: Call out your status." Skip held his breath as one by one, all of his men reported they were fine. He drew in successive deep, gasping breaths.

They were on the ground. No one was hurt. Well, his ship was in bad shape, but his fellas were okay. They hadn't paid a terrible price for his failings. And by God, they were done. They had survived. Barely, but they had. He was *done.*

No more missions, no more strafing, no more war.

"Pilot to Crew: Follow emergency evacuation procedures."

In other words, don't fool around with normal shutdown. He wanted everyone out. He wasn't concerned about the wing shear causing a fire, but he was worried they weren't in a safe spot. Last thing they needed was for another plane to turn *Bourbon Street Belle* into a fireball.

"Oh, shit, no!" Horror permeated Dewey's voice.

Skip peered out his rain-splattered windshield, and his heart dropped into his stomach.

Boom! Kaboom!

Blasts of heat seared the ship as a P-38 fighter, either following Skip's lead, misunderstanding the tower, or having his own reason for landing from the wrong direction, skated down the runway at full-speed and crashed into a B-25 landing from the correct direction.

An enormous conflagration enveloped the entire runway. Ground crews scattered.

Skip shoved open the front hatch and yelled, "Out, now!"

Mike and Leo scrambled from the plane without hesitation.

"Everyone out?" Skip yelled, sticking his head out of the hatch.

Dewey jogged around the ship and gave him a thumbs-up sign. Relieved, Skip tossed out their kit bags, pulled himself out, and dropped to the ground.

His men had retrieved their bags and run a safe distance away, where the Saidor ground crews huddled together. Skip jogged across the runway to join them.

Oblivious of the pouring rain, the pinging hail, and the piercing wail of sirens, the men stared at him with shell-shocked expressions. Skip's hair stood on end as emergency vehicles raced down the runway, and medics dashed toward the blazing planes. Had his missed approach and split-second decision to land opposite to incoming traffic contributed to — or caused — this horrific accident? Had the fighter pilot mimicked Skip's risky flight path out of confusion, or for his own reasons? Skip's throat burned.

He stepped forward to join the emergency crews, but Leo grabbed his arm and shook his head. "You'll only be in the way. They know what they're doing."

"Do they?" Skip rasped. They were young men like him and his crew, men with little preparation for what the war had thrown their way.

He stared at his feet and skimmed his boot through a puddle of rainwater. He had put his crew, his buddies, his brothers-in-arms, in grave danger with his bad judgment. And now, he might be responsible for this tragic loss of life.

He had made it through the war all right, but no thanks to his aviation or leadership skills. No, he was a failure, just as he had always been. He would never measure up. The wrong Masterson son had died two years ago. Skip was more certain of that than ever.

CHAPTER EIGHTEEN

August 25, 1944

Clovis Army Airfield, Clovis, New Mexico

Skip tapped his pencil against the clipboard. He had already crossed off most of the names on the training roster because the men scheduled for this morning's B-29 instruction flights had come up with the usual laundry list of excuses. Most cited illnesses ranging from allergies to appendicitis, while a few claimed a superior officer had tapped them for other duty.

Cowards. Yes, the engines were finicky, but the B-29 Superfortress was a smooth ride if you knew how to handle her. She was a dream. None of the roaring-can't-hear-yourself-think noise or herky-jerky, clattering awkwardness of the B-25. No, the B-29 was elegance personified, and with a pressurized cabin that allowed the crew to fly in comfort.

The USAAF believed the B-29 could win the war in the Pacific. From the right bases, it alone in the USAAF fleet had the range to bomb Japan. It alone could fly high enough and fast enough to evade much of the enemy's defenses. But its rush through production had left it with vulnerabilities and sensitivities that had already led to several high-profile accidents, accidents that left many men unwilling to fly it.

If only the trainees would stop thinking of her as a death trap. Skip had oozed charm and his best persuasive tactics to get them to fly, and, when that had failed, he had resorted to threats. Yet no ground duties he had the authority to impose convinced the men the B-29 was safe to fly.

"Captain Masterson?"

Still unnerved by his new rank, Skip turned.

"Sir, operations wants you to round up some trainees and bring them to the runways by ten o'clock. We've got a ship en route they'll want to see," the sergeant said, hurrying away without waiting for a response.

Skip raked a hand through his hair. What a cryptic, problematic message. If the men were, as they alleged, in sick bay, how could he entice them to come watch a plane land? Especially when he had no idea why watching this particular landing would interest them.

Shortly before ten o'clock, Skip had finally managed to assemble a group of twenty men at the runways, though most of whom groused in frustrated undertones.

He ignored them, shaded his eyes, and searched the sky until he spotted the sleek outline of the incoming Superfort silhouetted in the clear blue sky. Engines purring, it made a perfect approach and landed down the center of the runway.

He caught snatches of muttered complaints from the men.

"Still a flying coffin."

"Those engines catch fire too damned often."

"Those fellas make it look easy, but hell —"

"I'm still not gettin' in that widow-maker."

Skip rolled his eyes and shook his head. When he had left New Guinea months ago, he had resolved to never fly another military plane — and yet here he was. He had been reluctant at first to train in the complex B-29, but the plane was such a beaut, he had quickly succumbed to her charms. He grew increasingly frustrated with so many men refusing to fly her. Being a flight instructor paid well and was a low-risk way to pass the duration of the war. But he couldn't instruct the trainees when they concocted every excuse imaginable to avoid him and the planes.

Ladybird rolled to a stop in front of the cluster of men. Skip squinted up at the artwork adorning the plane's fuselage just below her name. A picture of a woman, only not the scantily clad or nude one usually depicted on the noses of most military planes. This one wore clothes and goggles. *Aviator* goggles.

And exiting the plane was — Skip leaned closer — a pair of female pilots.

The women descended the hatch from the nose wheel well, each dressed in dark blue slacks paired with crisp white blouses. The wings insignia above their left pockets, even from a distance, marked them as pilots.

He cocked his head and surveyed the expressions on the men's faces. Dumbfounded appeared to be the prevailing emotion, mixed with a discernible measure of chagrin. Skip curled his lip. What a stroke of genius. Wounded male egos would spur these fellas into flying the B-29s in no time.

He turned back to the approaching women, who had been joined by their male passengers. The women were petite, especially when compared to the men. A colonel with wavy black hair and dark bushy eyebrows exuded a certain presence, not so much because of his height or his solid barrel-chested build but something more indefinable. The other man, who was rangier and leaner, was a sergeant, perhaps a flight engineer or a radio operator.

One of the women, with light hair and a peaches-and-cream complexion, cupped her hand over her mouth and called out, "Hi-deho, fellas! Beautiful day for flying, isn't it?"

"She's a real dreamboat, isn't she?" The other woman, a brunette, gestured toward *Ladybird*. "Bet you boys can't wait to fly her!"

The colonel beckoned to Skip.

Skip saluted. "Captain Skip Masterson, sir."

After returning Skip's salute, the colonel gave a curt nod. Something in his expression signaled he already knew who Skip was. "Pleased to meet you, Captain Masterson. Colonel Paul Tibbets."

The other man saluted Skip. "Sergeant Duzenbury, sir."

Skip returned Duzenbury's salute, then turned to the female pilots. "That sure was a smooth landing."

The women, Women Air Service Pilots, introduced themselves as Dora Dougherty and Didi Moorman before launching into a replay of the flight, including the adjustments they had made to the usual takeoff procedures, their voices pitched to carry over to the cluster of trainees.

Skip fought to tamp down his grin and pointed toward the ready room. "It's not much, but you can get a decent cup of coffee in there while you wait."

"They're staying," Colonel Tibbets said. "Plan is for them to take trainees up for demonstration and instructional flights."

"For the day?" Skip asked.

"No," Colonel Tibbets said. "For the foreseeable future."

Confused, Skip rubbed his chin. Was he being supplanted or demoted? Granted, three other flight instructors were also based here at Clovis, but he was the only one who had been instructed to gather trainees and congregate at the flight line.

"Major Spellman has arranged accommodations for Miss Dougherty and Miss Moorman in town." Colonel Tibbets turned to the women. "Ladies, you'll find him waiting for you in Operations. You can drop off your bags at the motel but plan to return here by noon. We'll have time to take up a few groups today."

He bobbed his head at Sergeant Duzenbury. "Why don't you

walk over with them?"

"Look forward to having you here." Skip smiled at the women.

After the women waved and walked away, he eyed Tibbets. The man clearly wanted a private word with him. If he was being replaced, the USAAF would transfer him elsewhere, and that was fine by him. Clovis certainly hadn't been his first choice.

"Been to Washington to visit your family since you returned from New Guinea?"

"No." Skip strove to keep his voice neutral, even as flush popped up across his neck and temples. He tilted his head and sized up the colonel. Had Tibbets simply made a lucky guess? "The army sent me to Grand Island to get checked out in B-29s."

"Didn't give you a thirty-day pass?" Tibbets raised one bushy eyebrow. "Isn't that customary for soldiers returning from overseas duty?"

"Timing wasn't good." Skip shrugged. He would have liked to have spent time with his sister Molly and his mother, but seeing his father was out of the question. Facing any of them was a painful prospect.

"I see." Colonel Tibbets said. "And how do you like it here in Clovis, Captain?"

"Weather's far better than it was in New Guinea, sir."

"Does your pet wallaby agree?"

"She likes it at the moment." Skip stuck his hands in his pockets. Lucy wasn't a secret on base. Major Spellman might have mentioned Skip's exotic pet. "Winter may be a different story."

"I expect so." Colonel Tibbets lifted his chin. "What I'm about to offer you won't give you better winter weather for your pet, but you might find it more . . . fulfilling."

"Sir?" Skip only wanted to pass the duration of the war with minimal effort. Contentment didn't enter into the picture.

Colonel Tibbets pulled out a pack of cigarettes and held it out, but Skip shook his head. The colonel lit up and pushed the pack and matchbox back into his pocket.

"You fit the profile of men I'm looking for, Captain Masterson. You do your job, and you do it well. They say you mastered the B-29 in no time. But more importantly, you keep your head down and your trap shut."

Skip made no reply. He couldn't see why his reserve would be of any consequence for a new flight instructor assignment.

"You keep your head down and your trap shut," Tibbets repeated, before fixing his dark eyes on Skip's. "*Now* you do, but you haven't always been this circumspect, have you, Captain?"

This too didn't seem like a lucky guess. Skip swallowed. "No sir."

"A hell raiser, by all accounts. Or a troublemaker, depending on the source." Colonel Tibbets tipped his ashes. "*That* Alton Millard Masterson wouldn't meet my needs."

The compression in Skip's chest loosened. His formal name was in his military records. Colonel Tibbets must have secured access to Skip's file, that's all. That's how he knew Skip's legal name, that's how he knew who Skip's parents were, that's how he knew about Skip's checkered past. All of that would be noted in his file.

"War changes men," Skip said. A platitude, but a believable one.

Colonel Tibbets took a long drag on his cigarette and blew out a smoke ring. "That it does. Question is, how lasting is that change, in regard to your temperament?"

Quite lasting. He barely remembered Old Skip. Hadley had glimpsed him; she had coaxed some of his former self out of hiding. But then he had lost her.

"That's all in the past," Skip said with finality.

Tibbets coughed, then cleared his throat. "Good. Good because I need pilots who can handle the B-29 — and handle it well."

Skip's eyes narrowed. This no longer sounded like a flight instruction assignment.

"Which B-29 training base are we talking about, sir?" There

weren't many. He had trained in Grand Island, Nebraska and had no desire to return there either. A handful of other training bases were scattered across the Midwest, but none were located in an appealing location.

"Wendover. In Utah."

"Utah?" Skip racked his brain. Clovis wasn't pleasant, but he imagined Utah would have harsher winter conditions. "Sir, I'm not sure —"

"In addition to B-29 pilots, I also need someone with photographic expertise, someone who knows what he's doing with Fastax cameras, someone who has both the photographic and engineering understanding of high-speed photography." Tibbets again made eye contact. "You have that knowledge, Captain Masterson — no, don't deny it."

Skip had shook his head, but more from disbelief than attempted disavowal. He did have extensive experience but had hidden those skills from the military. He hadn't sought out an assignment with a photographic reconnaissance squad, even though he would have considered it a plum assignment before Pearl Harbor. How in hell did Tibbets know about his photographic experience, let alone with such specificity?

"I *did*," Skip emphasized. "But I haven't taken so much as a snapshot in years, let alone handled such complex equipment."

"That puts you about ten steps ahead of anyone else in the military, especially anyone else who also happens to be a seasoned combat pilot with solid experience in a B-29," Tibbets said. "Don't worry about that now. We won't need those skills until later. My immediate need is to find men to train in B-29s with new and . . . *innovative* tactics."

"So you want to train me to teach these tactics to combat crews before they deploy?"

"No." Tibbets ground the butt of his cigarette under his boot. "I want to train you to use them yourself."

Oh, hell no. He wasn't signing on for another combat tour. He had done his duty and earned his cushy stateside job.

Skip shook his head. "With all due respect, sir, I'm not interested in volunteering for another tour."

"I understand," Tibbets rasped. "You've done your part."

"I flew fifty-five missions over New Guinea." He had done *more* than his part.

Tibbets shaded his eyes and scanned the isolated base's desolate, treeless landscape and drab buildings. "You've done your part — and this isn't a bad place to pass the war. The army could send you to worse places."

Skip's gut tightened. Not an overt threat, but the colonel's observation was a subtle reminder that Skip still served at the whim of the army.

Tibbets nodded. "Hear tell they're looking to send a few men to Washington to serve as USAAF liaison with the navy. Nice desk job."

That was a threat. A double-edged threat from every angle. Skip could think of nothing worse than working in direct contact with his father. And a desk job, under his father or anyone else, was the last thing he wanted.

His pulse sent jittery alarm bells zinging throughout his body. He struggled to find an appropriate response. Tibbets clearly knew who Skip's father was and how that remark would land. He eyed the colonel warily and pressed his fingers against a nerve pulsing in his neck.

"Seems inefficient for the army to train a man to fly the B-29, then ship him off to a desk job."

Tibbets snorted. "Your years in the military haven't taught you that the one thing the army excels at is inefficiency?"

"Yes, sir. But the B-29 is an expensive aircraft, making that training more valuable." Even the army wasn't so shortsighted as to transfer a skilled B-29 instructor to a desk job.

"Perhaps." Tibbets shifted his weight. "They might find your skills too valuable to waste and send you to one of the new training bases. Heard about the one in New Orleans?"

A cold spike stabbed Skip's ribs, but he fought to keep his expression neutral. Tibbets couldn't possibly know about Hadley.

"That assignment would be a treat, wouldn't it?" Tibbets toyed with his matchbox. "The Red Cross might post your girl back to her hometown."

Skip's throat was suddenly parched. He struggled to swallow. How, how, *how* could this man know about Hadley? And how did he know his words would punch Skip in the gut? Despite dangling a post in New Orleans as a reward, Tibbets clearly knew the opposite would be true.

The colonel stuffed the matchbox back into his pocket and turned. "Let me speak plainly, Captain Masterson. Perhaps you haven't heard about General Arnold's recent decree — official air forces policy says a man isn't entitled to an indefinite stateside assignment by virtue of having completed one combat tour. Your acquiescence to another tour is not required."

That *was* news. Skip had dismissed it as rumor. He pressed his lips together.

Tibbets directed a piercing stare at Skip. "I'm recruiting a group of men for specialized, highly sensitive training. I have the highest authority to commandeer exactly what and *who* I need for my work. As I'm sure you've no doubt realized, I know all about you, your skills, your background . . . *and* your vulnerabilities."

"Yes, sir."

"You should also not be surprised that I have the power to cut orders for your immediate transfer into my group or make certain you receive an assignment guaranteed to make your life miserable should you not embrace the opportunity I'm offering with sufficient enthusiasm and discretion."

"Yes, *sir*." Skip spit out the courteous term of address even as his body pulsed with anger. Discretion, fine. Enthusiasm? No fucking way. He couldn't fake delight while being railroaded into another combat tour.

"I can't divulge specifics, but I believe you'll find this assignment satisfying, Captain Masterson. I assure you that any man who has seen comrades killed or lost a loved one at the hands of the enemy," Tibbets said, pausing for Skip to meet his eyes, "will find his work with my group extremely gratifying."

Chet. Tibbets knew about Skip's family, so he knew about Chet. And Chet — and the opportunity for Skip to exact vengeance for his brother's death — was the colonel's final enticement. He swallowed past the constriction in his throat. "When do I report to Wendover, sir?"

"I'll cut your orders for two weeks. In case you want to see friends or family."

"I'll report to you when I arrive."

"There's one more thing, Captain." Tibbets turned and looked into Skip's eyes. "Every man under my command needs to understand this very clearly. Your ability to keep your mouth shut was a selling point. But if you fail to keep everything you're doing or learning under wraps, you won't like the consequences. Discretion — no, *secrecy* — is the watchword of the day with my operation. Are we clear?"

"Understood, sir."

"Good." Tibbets's mouth creased with a hint of a smile. "Bring your wallaby in with you when you report at Wendover, Captain. I've never seen one."

***

December 25, 1944
Wendover Airfield
Wendover, Utah

"Nah, I'm gonna head back to base and try to get a call through to my folks." Skip waved off invitations for a night of booze, gambling, and carousing.

He had no intention of calling his family, but the excuse would allow him to avoid the debauchery and shenanigans the men would engage in across the state line inside the casinos and brothels in Nevada.

At the suggestion of Colonel Tibbets, he and the other men of the 509th Composite Group had eaten Christmas dinner at the State Line Hotel in Wendover. All one hundred residents of this pit of a town must be working at the hotel's restaurant tonight in order to turn out so many steak dinners.

Skip stepped out into the frigid night air and paused beside the front window to tug on his gloves. The warm glow of the lights illuminated clusters of officers inside enjoying the holiday evening with their families. Colonel Tibbets' two young sons were busy arranging an entire battlefield of toy soldiers in front of the fireplace.

As Skip watched the boys play, his heart contracted with a sharp pang. He and Chet had passed many hours playing with their miniature armies, although theirs had been hand-painted tin soldiers, not the green plastic ones so popular now.

How different Christmas 1944 might have looked for him if the Japanese hadn't attacked Pearl Harbor three years ago. His brother would still be alive; they both might have children of their own. Not kids old enough to play with toy soldiers, but they might have had a start on the future Skip craved.

A future that no longer included Hadley. Of course, he wouldn't have met her if not for the war. But he had met her, and a pang that matched the sharp, bitter winds blowing on this winter night whipped through his heart. Thoughts of Hadley brought him nothing but persistent, piercing pain.

He had bought her a Christmas gift but left it in his trunk, wrapped in crisp brown paper and twine. A soft leather notebook and a new Cross pen. After he'd made the impulsive purchase at Wendover's tiny general store, he had even written her a letter. Then another. And another. He had ripped each one into bits when he couldn't find the right words.

His trunk also held something he had bought for Hadley last Christmas. He had spotted the ruby engagement ring in a jewelry store in Sydney. One afternoon while Hadley was shopping with her friends, he had gone into the store and asked to see the ring. The moment he had held it up, Skip had known it was meant for Hadley. He had bought it on the spot and spent the rest of his leave searching for the courage to pop the question.

He would find her after the war. Proposing and giving her the gorgeous ring that was so suited for her might never come to pass. She still might reject him, might have met someone else. But he had to try, had to take another shot at love and happiness.

He shook his head and cast one last look at the boys sprawled before the hearth, his heart contracting with the memories flooding through him — along with the realization that these boys, like Chet and Skip, would also know the pain and loneliness of being ripped away from their friends with each move the military ordered for their father. Would one of them also die in a war, like Chet? Would the other be left with a hole inside, gripped by gnawing guilt and grief?

Skip tore his gaze away from the window and set out for the base. Once he reached the guard station, he pulled out his ID and handed it to the MP on duty.

"Merry Christmas, sir." The man passed the card back to him.

He forced a smile. "Same to you. Did you get any dinner?"

"Yes, sir." The MP pointed toward a mess kit on the small desk inside the post.

Skip nodded. He might be miserable, but at least he had enjoyed a good meal in a warm hotel. "That's rotten luck, pal, being stuck out here on Christmas. Hope you get off duty soon."

"Thanks, sir. Enjoy the rest of your evening."

He thanked the man, then walked through the desolate, wind-swept base at a fast clip. Though his barracks were hardly warm and comfortable, they at least sheltered him from the biting cold and bone-piercing wind. No doubt Lucy was burrowed deep inside his bedding.

Skip was so focused on his destination that he nearly slammed into Chuck Sweeney, another pilot, as he approached the barracks. "Hey, sorry. Didn't see you there."

"Don't worry. It's pretty damned dark out here. Just stopped to look up at the stars . . ." Sweeney trailed off, tucking a crucifix under his jacket. He must have thought now was a perfect time for reflection and prayer with the base so empty and quiet.

"Don't let me interrupt you," Skip said.

Chuck shoved his hands into his pockets. "That's all right. Too cold to stargaze anyway."

"The colonel could hardly have picked a worse base, huh?" Skip quirked his mouth. The tiny ramshackle town situated in the middle of the Great Basin Desert was miserable, a town on the edge of nowhere. Or as Bob Hope had wryly dubbed it, *Leftover Field*.

Chuck snorted. "The colonel loves it, says it's perfect for our training."

"Training," Skip repeated. Contrary to what Tibbets had told him in Clovis, men in their group already knew how to fly B-29s. Exercises here focused on dropping pumpkin-shaped dummy bombs from high altitude into the centers of a series of concentric circles marked on the desert ground, followed immediately by a steep diving technique Skip had yet to master.

"What do you make of this work on those crazy steep turns?" Skip asked.

Chuck glanced over his shoulder in each direction before answering in a low voice. "I don't think B-29s were designed to do what he wants. It's dangerous."

Dangerous all right. Throwing the heavy bomber into a steep sixty-degree diving turn from high altitude while racing to build maximum airspeed, then hurtling down to lower altitudes at a breakneck pace, risked putting the ship into a stall. The bomber protested this mistreatment by screeching and groaning, with every rivet straining to comply with the pilot's demands. Miscalculating by only a few degrees or pulling too hard on her controls could easily shear off her wings.

"You done it?" Skip stuck his hands into his pockets.

"Hit it a couple of times." Chuck scuffed his boots in the rocky soil. "You?"

"Nah, not yet." Although his tone implied it was only a matter of time, that he was on the verge of conquering the technique of those breakaway turns, Skip wasn't even close. He had seen others do it, like the colonel and a few of his hand-picked pilots. He understood what he was supposed to do. He only needed to summon the nerve to put it into action. Skip glanced sideways at Chuck. "Why do you reckon we're learning this tactic?"

Chuck cast another look around but didn't answer.

"Seems like an escape maneuver," Skip pressed on. "Like we might need to outrun the bomb we've dropped."

"I wouldn't . . . I wouldn't repeat that, especially where the colonel's boys might hear." Chuck slipped a note of warning into his voice. "Not unless you have a hankering to see Alaska."

Skip nodded. No, he needed to keep his mouth shut. The base was crawling with FBI agents tasked with not only making sure the men complied with the colonel's strict secrecy protocols, but also with tracking their personal exploits and foibles. Tibbets kept close tabs on anything that might compromise the men under his command. He had already shipped several off to Alaska's Aleutian Islands because they had asked too many questions or stepped out of line.

Skip turned and looked each direction. He couldn't see how anyone could possibly overhear them, as they were well out of earshot of any buildings where an agent might lurk. Most were still enjoying the warmth and festivities inside the State Line Hotel or the temptations and pleasures offered across the state line in Nevada.

"Can't swing a dead cat without hitting a G-man or a scientist," Skip murmured. Even on this sprawling base, he hadn't missed the large number of civilian scientists coming and going.

Chuck shrugged but didn't reply.

Skip tried a less controversial line. "What do you make of them moving us to Cuba for a month?"

"I think it sounds a hell of a lot warmer there than this place will be in January." Chuck stomped his feet to ward off the cold, crunching frost-coated sagebrush under his boots. "Speaking of warmer, I'm gonna go brew some coffee. Want some?"

"That's okay, thanks." Despite the friendly tone, Skip sensed that Chuck was anxious to steer their conversation onto safer ground, or better yet, end it altogether. He shook his head. "I should probably go check on Lucy."

"Imagine she'll be happy to see warmer weather too." Chuck's easy grin resurfaced, now that Skip had dropped the conversation that could land them both in hot water.

Skip laughed, turned onto the road leading to his barracks, and waved to Chuck. "See you later, Sweeney."

He hurried on along the dark, winding path toward the series of flimsy wooden structures nestled at the base of the Silver Island mountains. Skip climbed the three creaky steps leading to the door of his barracks and pushed it open with his shoulder. It jammed in cold weather.

He removed his gloves, shoved them into his pockets, and hung up his coat. Then he stepped out of his boots and left them by the door. He winced at the cold seeping between the floorboards and hurried toward the lavatory.

Toiletry done and teeth chattering, he plugged in all three space heaters before threading his way between the rows of bunks. A copy of *The Razor's Edge* sat on his night table, and someone had tossed this week's mail onto his bed. He ought to respond to the ones from his crewmates in New Guinea. Leo had garnered a plum assignment on Oahu and was soaking up island life. The enlisted fellas had all been assigned to flight schools as instructors: Dewey in California, Rafe in Florida, and Charlie in Texas.

Mike sounded better. He had married Fiona, Pat's younger

sister, in July. Skip hoped she would help him continue to heal but worried about the hastiness of their wedding. Shortly after Skip had returned to the States, Mike had written that he had been discharged. The military wasn't currently discharging healthy veterans, so Skip had inferred that his copilot had been discharged for mental unfitness.

A painful lump filled his throat. He checked his cot and found Lucy, buried deep under the bedding. Skip patted the wallaby through the covers and picked up the stack of envelopes, unable to stop his heart from thumping as he scanned each return address, the handwriting, and the postmarks. As usual, his heart squeezed into a knot once he confirmed he still had no word from the person he most wanted to hear from.

He could write to Hadley and apologize again. But he had intuited that something deeper was at play with her and that no apology would reach her until he understood what that something might be. Words alone wouldn't heal their rift. Skip had replayed their last conversation many times, futilely searching for clues, but he still couldn't make sense of it.

After the war.

He would find her after the war. He wanted — no, he *needed* — to understand why she had rejected him and repeatedly refused his overtures begging her to talk it out.

With a sigh, he pulled back the blankets and sheet and slid into bed. Lucy squiggled closer to him until she nestled against his side and her tail thumped his stomach.

"Cuba will be warmer, Luce," he whispered to the wallaby. "And maybe it won't be too much longer before we go back to the Pacific."

They were training for something big, something that might end the war on Allied terms. No one had said they would deploy to the Pacific, but his gut told him that whatever their mission might be, they were more apt to take it to Japan than to Germany.

And although Sweeney hadn't wanted to talk about it, Skip was sure he was on the right track. That dive — that improbable, shattering dive with maximum speed and power — gave every appearance of a plane and its crew desperate to escape the force of whatever they had dropped from the bomb bay.

***

March 9, 1945

Harmon Airfield

Guam, Marianas Islands, Central Pacific

Hadley jerked awake when the C-47 hit the Marston-mat steel planking with a bone-rattling thunk and screeching wheels.

"Wake up." Bizzy elbowed her in the ribs. "We're here."

"Not exactly." One of the nurses seated across from them gestured toward the cockpit. "We've been talking to the pilots. We've landed in Guam to let the men off. They'll refuel, then inspect the plane before we take off again."

"Guam?" Hadley rubbed sleep from her eyes and glanced at her watch. Their flight from Biak island, where they had been posted for the last six months, had taken eight hours. She frowned. "How much further is it to Tinian?"

"It's only a short hop," the copilot said as he appeared in the aisle. He nodded at Hadley, Bizzy, and Stella. "But we'll be here awhile, so you ladies can get off, grab some chow, and stretch your legs. You'll probably find one of your Red Cross clubs here on base."

Hadley unbuckled her harness and stood. Thank goodness for the parachute seat pack. The bucket seats were cold, hard, and uncomfortable without any cushioning. She followed the others to the hatch and took the hand of a lieutenant so young he probably didn't need to shave. He helped each woman navigate the staircase to the ground one by one.

The young officer pointed toward a long, low white building

situated a short walk from the runway. "You'll find a snack bar and lavatory facilities in there, ladies."

"Thank you." Bizzy smoothed her hair and smiled at him. "It's a shame we're only here for such a short time."

Stella and Hadley exchanged exasperated looks and walked toward the terminal. Hadley would have thought Bizzy would be sleepy and stiff from the long flight, not wide awake and ready to flirt. Besides, the boy was way too young for her.

"I heard there are over twenty thousand men on Tinian," Stella said with a sly smile.

Hadley shook her head. "And Bizzy will meet them all."

"Meet all of who?" Bizzy caught up with them.

Hadley stepped through the terminal doors. "All the men stationed on Tinian. All twenty thousand of them."

"Oh, lordy, twenty thousand?" Bizzy widened her eyes. "Well, goodness. With that many fellas, we should be able to find someone for each of you too."

Hadley shot her friend a sharp look. She had told Bizzy she wasn't interested in dating, but Bizzy had been after her to at least go on daytime double dates. Hadley had finally taken on extra shifts or evaded her friend to avoid her efforts. Bizzy meant well, but Hadley had no intention of putting her heart on the line for anyone.

Once they joined the other Red Cross Girls and nurses from their flight in the queue for the lone women's bathroom, she changed the subject. "Anyone heard about where we'll be housed on Tinian?"

"I haven't." Stella's shoulders slumped. "But I doubt it'll be as nice as our beach tents on Biak. I loved that view."

"The view was tops, but I won't miss all those creepy crawlies," Bizzy said.

Hadley shivered at the memory. Green tree pythons were prevalent on Biak island, and the women had often found them climbing the tent poles or curling themselves around the bases of their cots. Large tarantulas also wandered into the tents at night, and the rats commonly found in New Guinea had been significantly larger on Biak. Not to mention the flying foxes that swooped through the encampment each night as they left to go hunting.

"Ugh, those tarantulas were the worst." One of the nurses shuddered.

Hadley silently agreed. Knowing a large spider might be climbing the tent wall or lurking on the floor kept the women pinned under their mosquito bars. Nighttime visits to the latrine dwindled to nothing on Biak.

Now, as Hadley exited the bathroom, she looked around for the others.

Stella waved her over to the snack bar. "Peanut butter or egg salad?"

"Neither." She wanted a piping hot New Orleans shrimp po-boy, dressed with spicy remoulade, crispy lettuce, and fresh, juicy tomato slices.

No wait, it was March now, wasn't it? March was crawfish season. For the briefest moment, the aroma of Fanelia's crawfish étouffée, redolent with onion, garlic, oregano, thyme, and a pop of cayenne enveloped Hadley's senses. She wasn't on an island in the middle of the Pacific, thousands of miles from the familiar rituals and rhythms of her childhood, of her entire life before the war. A sharp pang of homesickness swept through her.

She came out of her reverie with a shake of her head.

"You don't want a sandwich?" Bizzy gestured for Hadley to join them in line. "We haven't eaten in hours."

"You should eat something," Stella urged.

Hadley exhaled. "Fine. Egg salad, I guess."

"It's not bad, you know."

Hadley turned to the woman who had joined the line behind her. Her khaki coveralls bore no patches or other indicia indicating her role. Red Cross Girls wore khaki blouses and culottes, with a Red Cross patch on their right sleeve and their insignia pinned on their lapels. Nurses were also identifiable, thanks to the insignia on their lapels or jacket.

"What's not bad? The egg salad?" Hadley asked.

The woman's thin face cracked with a grin. "They've got good refrigeration, if that's what you're worried about."

"Oh, I know these gals won't serve us spoiled food." Hadley knew firsthand how army refrigerators were prone to malfunction. She moved forward in the line. "It's the monotony of our choices that's getting to me."

"Umm-hmm, limited choices." She tightened the belt on her coveralls. "But at least we get plenty of food."

"That's true. I'm Hadley Claverie." She gestured toward her friends. "And this is Bizzy Talbott and Stella Alfonsi. We're en route to our next assignment at Tinian."

"Shelley Mydans." She smiled at them. "I'm a correspondent with *Life* magazine."

Hadley gaped at her. Shelley Mydans had been caught in the fall of the Philippines and imprisoned with her photojournalist husband. Notices for a book she had published about her experiences in a Japanese prison camp had been in all the newspapers.

"Hadley's a correspondent too," Stella said. "For the *Times-Picayune* in New Orleans."

"A former reporter, not accredited," Hadley corrected.

"I don't know any *former* journalists." Shelley winked at Hadley. "It's in your blood, right? I'll bet you've got gobs of material from your service over here."

Oh, she sure did. Not just the human-interest pieces she had sent to Dupre from Australia and New Guinea, or the interview with Eleanor Roosevelt that would have gotten many more readers if Dupre hadn't chopped it to bits and printed it in the society pages. She hadn't bothered to write about the darker side of war, knowing that he would never print a column that painted anything less than a rosy picture of well-fed, well-adjusted American boys doing their duty. Not stories about the boys who failed to return from missions, the grievously wounded boys, the traumatized boys with invisible, but deep psychological wounds. Young men who were doing their duty, not dying of tropical diseases, perishing in vehicle accidents, or being killed in a takeoff crash.

"She wrote stories every night and sent them home," Bizzy piped up. "Until she lost her typewriter in an accident."

"I can still write without my typewriter." Hadley rolled her eyes. "People wrote without them for centuries."

"But you haven't," Stella said. "You've only written letters, and not many of those."

"Well," Hadley pasted on her everything-is-fine smile, the one she wore on duty. "We've been a little busy, in case you haven't noticed."

"I'll bet you have," Shelley said. "I have so much admiration for what you gals do for morale. I've only been back here for a few months, but you ladies are an inspiration."

"Shelley, egg salad?" Bizzy called from the counter. At Shelley's nod, she turned back. "Four egg salad sandwiches with a side of pickles, if you've got them. And four Cokes, please."

A wave of heat splashed over Hadley. Continuing her conversation with Shelley Mydans presented a challenge. She hadn't realized that her friends had noticed she had stopped writing. She would have to steer their conversation away from journalism. She had no intention of revealing her resolution to give it up or confessing why she had cut herself off from such a vital part of her makeup.

Stella motioned for Hadley and Shelley to follow her. "Let's nab a table while Bizzy gets our food."

Once they found one, Hadley perched on the edge of her chair, tapping her foot and mentally scrounged for a safe topic that wouldn't circle back to writing.

Before she could open her mouth, Stella leaned toward Shelley. "You said you've only been back a short while. Did you go home on leave?"

"I suppose you could call it that." Shelley's mouth curved up on one side.

Hadley pulled a few napkins from the dispenser and passed them around. "Shelley and her husband were Japanese prisoners, Stella. They were released in a prisoner exchange."

"Oh golly. You're the one who wrote the book about the prisoner of war camp?" Stella asked. "The one that's been advertised in the papers?"

"Yes." Shelley shifted so Bizzy could pull out a chair and join them. "My husband was dispatched to Europe a few months after we returned to the States. I wrote the book at my family's home in California. Catharsis or boredom, I'm not sure which."

"I thought your husband covered MacArthur's return to the Philippines." The question popped out before Hadley could bite it back.

"He did. *Time* sent him directly from the liberation of Paris back to the Pacific." Pride jostled with envy in Shelley's voice.

She's frustrated. Frustrated at being left behind, while her husband gets all the opportunities, all the prestige, all the glory.

"That photograph of MacArthur wading ashore at Leyte," Hadley told her friends. "That was her husband's photo."

"Is he still in the Philippines?" Stella asked. "While you're here?"

"Yes, he's attached to the army. So am I, for all the good it's doing me." Shelley held up her hands. "MacArthur won't permit women to cover frontline action."

"Really?" Bizzy wagged her finger at Hadley. "I thought MacArthur let your friend Lorraine report from the combat zone in New Guinea."

"He did," Hadley said. "But she's Australian. The Aussie military wasn't happy that MacArthur let her do it. He might have been playing a power game with them."

"Probably." Shelley nodded. "He enjoys reminding the Australians who's in charge."

"Egg salad sandwiches and Cokes," the snack bar worker called out.

Hadley stood and went to help Bizzy retrieve their food. She returned to the table juggling their bottles of Coke.

Stella took one. "Good news, Hadley. Shelley thinks she can get you a typewriter."

"Oh?" Hadley's hands slipped on the slick bottles, and Bizzy grabbed two of them to keep her from dropping them. Hadley forced a smile, set the remaining bottle onto the table, and slid into her chair. "Thanks, but I'm sure they need everything here for the military."

"Not really." Shelley shook her head through a bite of sandwich and waved her hand. After swallowing, she said, "They've consolidated several bomb groups here, and there's a large office at headquarters full of unused office equipment."

"Bet they'll need it later," Hadley said.

Bizzy speared a pickle and wagged it at Hadley. "Take it. No one will miss it."

"Maybe." Hadley waved her hand noncommittally. She was anxious to push their conversation in another direction, so she asked Shelley about the weather and conditions on Guam. They were delighted to learn that no snakes lived in the Marianas islands.

Shelley turned up her nose. "But there are lots of rodents. Large rats and field mice."

"But no crocodiles, snakes, or tarantulas." Bizzy smiled. "That's bound to also be true of Tinian."

"I'm afraid to ask," Hadley grimaced. "What about mosquitos?"

"They're spraying regularly, and it seems to be working." Shelley shrugged. "But we're in the dry season right now."

"Ah good. There you are."

Hadley and the others looked up as a general, flanked by several other officers, approached their table. He took his pipe out of his mouth and nodded at Shelley.

"Got a story for you," he said, "if you want to cover it."

"Of course." Excitement flared in Shelley's brown eyes. Hadley recognized the adrenaline rush of covering a scoop. Whatever the general was offering was bound to be of significance. USAAF generals didn't usually seek out correspondents without good reason.

"Be at the briefing hut at sixteen hundred," he said. His gruff voice was so soft-spoken as to be nearly inaudible, issuing his brusque phrases through clenched teeth. Hadley's jaw ached just watching him speak to Shelley. "Don't be late."

"I won't, sir. Thank you."

"Good." He raised one dark, bushy eyebrow and pointed toward the Red Cross patch on Hadley's shoulder. "Hard workers, you Red Cross Girls."

Hadley opened her mouth to murmur her thanks, but he was already halfway to the door.

"That's General Curtis LeMay, Commander of Twenty-First Bomber Command. A man of few words, but he gets results and the men look up to him." Shelley laughed. "Mind you, they'd just as soon avoid his company, but they respect him."

"LeMay . . ." His name was familiar to Hadley. She must have read some of his quoted statements in newspapers. "Has he always been here?"

"No. He's only been on Guam for a few months." Shelley sipped her Coke. "He came here from India, but he was with the Mighty Eighth in England before that."

That's where Hadley had heard his name. Vivian had written about him while she was working at an Aero-Club on his base in England. Hadley would have to write her friend that she had met LeMay. In her last letter, Vivian had reported that she was now in Germany, following the army's march toward Berlin.

Hadley repressed a bubble of envy. She wasn't writing anymore, so having access to good communication no longer mattered. She didn't need to follow stories alongside the likes of Martha Gelhorn, Margaret Bourke-White, Iris Carpenter, and the other women making names for themselves in Europe. It no longer mattered that Hadley had been sidelined in the Pacific Theater.

Yet watching Shelley root around in her pockets to confirm that she had her notepad, Hadley couldn't suppress the pang of longing that spread through her chest. Couldn't stop herself from wondering what kind of scoop would send the likes of General LeMay to find the only credentialed correspondent on base here in Guam — and a woman, at that.

CHAPTER NINETEEN

June 30, 1945

Tinian, Marianas Islands, Central Pacific

Hadley discretely slid several sandwiches wrapped in wax paper and three Hershey bars into her canvas knapsack and then looped it over her shoulder.

"Are you covering West Field this morning?" Bizzy added more lemonade powder to a galvanized jug and stirred the cold liquid.

Hadley covered the last tray of doughnuts and passed them to Stella. "Yes, I'm driving *Pacific Palms*. Stella is taking *Easy Breezy*. Where are you going?"

"Up north island to that new group." Bizzy latched the lid and turned toward a waiting sergeant. "This is the last jug."

"The super secretive group?" Hadley asked. The new B-29 group was the talk of the island. Not only had they ejected the Navy Seabees from Tinian's prime living quarters, but they had also secured their space with curiously high security — with guards stationed at every entrance, grim-faced men armed with rifles who inspected badges and searched the bags of anyone coming or going. Rumor had it they were FBI agents. G-men or not, they patrolled the perimeter fences around the clock.

Bizzy fluffed her wild curls. "I'm going in with Mr. Corbin to look over a building they may want to allocate to us."

"Really?" Hadley asked. Her friend's careful primping had to be connected to the prospect of meeting hundreds of men new to the island. "They plan to put one of our clubs inside their super-secret area?"

"Apparently so." Bizzy pulled a tube of lipstick from her pocket and applied it without aid of a compact.

"Do they realize that means they'd need to let us in to run it?"

"I dunno." Bizzy capped the tube and slid it back into her pocket. "I'll know more after we've talked with them. The place is located only a short walk from our barracks, so they shouldn't need to house us there."

The Red Cross Girls bunked with nurses in Quonset huts on the western slope of Mount Lasso, one of the two highest points on the island. For their safety rather than for military security, their compound was also heavily guarded. Mount Lasso sloped at a gentle grade on this side, but the eastern side consisted of steep cliffs and a dense network of caves and tunnels that still housed Japanese holdouts. Enemy soldiers occasionally wandered from their hideouts to give themselves up, but more often, they sneaked down at night to raid American food supplies. As a consequence, no women could go out at night without an armed escort.

The sergeant stuck his head through the door. "All loaded."

"Thanks." Hadley waved at Bizzy. "You can tell us at chow tonight if the rumors we've heard about the place are true."

Whether the new group really did eat steak and drink whiskey at every meal, had hot showers, and enjoyed both a private movie theater and a bowling alley. Whether they hadn't flown a single mission to Japan since they had arrived and only made short runs to several uninhabited islands nearby to drop oddly shaped dummy bombs. Whether they believed they had been sent to do something extraordinary, something that would end the war.

After confirming the doughnut trays and jugs of lemonade and coffee were secure, Hadley slid into the driver's seat of *Pacific Palms*. She had avoided driving in New Guinea and Biak after her accident last year, but conditions on Tinian were dramatically different.

The terrain was level, and the island sported a good network of paved roads. Savvy Seabees had noticed that Tinian's overall shape and size resembled that of Manhattan, so they had laid out the roads in a grid and named them accordingly. She would take Riverside Drive to West Field and return via Broadway.

No rugged roads, no rivers, no jungle. The Seabees had cleared enough land to accommodate two large airfields and living and workspace for thousands of men. All that remained of the original island was a wide, flat expanse of former sugar cane fields that had been given to the U.S. military.

Hadley turned onto 42nd Street and slowed to maneuver through the congested roadways south of West Field where the 58th Bombardment Wing had its facilities. She would serve the ground crews in their tents at the hardstands and then stop at the recreation facility.

Her varied duty schedule on Tinian had gone a long way toward reviving her spirit. The immense scope of military facilities on the island allowed the Red Cross directors to rotate women among the various clubs and Jeepmobile duties. Hadley had worked occasional shifts at a snack bar and led recreation activities at one of the five Tinian clubs, but she preferred the stints of Jeepmobile duty that took her from the docks at Tinian Town in the south, to North Field at the other end of the island, and everywhere in between.

Hours later, she tossed several empty five-gallon jugs into the back of the Jeepmobile and turned to Stella. "I'm stopping at Camp

Chulu, so I won't be back until late afternoon."

"Okay." Stella stepped into a spot of shade near *Easy Breezy* and dabbed a handkerchief against her face. "Are you teaching another English class?"

"No, but I told Min-ah I would spend some time with Ari this afternoon."

"How old is she?" Stella opened the spigot on a water jug and poured herself a glass.

"Ari turned one last month." Hadley passed her canteen to Stella. "She's picking up so much. I think young children absorb language faster than adults."

"Maybe so." Stella gave Hadley's canteen cup back to her. "But what good will English do her when the war's over?"

Hadley took a drink, screwed the cap shut, and shrugged. "I'm sure we'll keep occupation forces all over, for who knows how long. I expect she'll be able to keep it up. Besides, Min-ah is educated. She'll want the same for Ari."

"Won't they rejoin her family in . . . is it Korea, or Okinawa?"

Camp Chulu housed over ten thousand civilians who had surrendered to American forces last year. Roughly half were Japanese, and the others were a mix of Koreans and Okinawans. Because most of their homes had been destroyed, a small number of native Tinian islanders also lived at Camp Chulu.

Most of the internees left the camp each morning to work in the fields and gardens or provide labor around the bases. When the U.S. had first occupied Tinian, the civilians worked outside the camp under guard, but they now moved freely about the island during the day.

"Min-ah is Korean." Hadley left unsaid that Min-ah hoped to emigrate to America.

"All right, have fun." Stella slid into the driver's seat of *Easy Breezy* and started the engine. "Don't forget about the dance tonight. It starts at seven o'clock."

Hadley gave her the okay sign, waved, and climbed into the

driver's seat of her own Jeepmobile. She followed Stella for a short distance before turning on Broadway to go north toward Camp Chulu. Min-ah had finished her shift in the kitchen at the Riverside Inn club over an hour ago.

Hadley had met Min-ah in one of the English classes the Red Cross Girls taught at Camp Chulu. Impressed with Min-ah's mastery of the language, Hadley took time after each class to offer her more conversation. Through these discussions, Hadley had pieced together the story of how the bright young Korean woman had come to be on Japanese-occupied Tinian.

Although Hadley hoped their language issues painted a darker picture than what had really happened, she was reasonably certain she understood the essentials. Some two years earlier, Min-ah and her older sister Sonja accepted jobs as secretaries overseas — but instead of being taken to their supposed new home, they had been brought here to Tinian to the confines of what was euphemistically known as a *comfort station*. Though the name created an illusion of purity and peace, it was completely at odds with the reality of the enslavement of hundreds of women who served to satisfy the Japanese soldiers. Tinian wasn't the only location where duped or abducted women were brutally violated and traumatized, but it was where Min-ah ended up.

Last July, U.S. Marines had stormed the beaches on the northwest coast of the island, and the women had joined Japanese soldiers and civilian workers in a retreat to the cliffside caves along the steep bluffs in the southeast. Yet food and water supplies soon dwindled, and Tinian's prevailing breezes couldn't cut the sweltering heat inside the congested caves.

Desperate chaos broke out when the inevitable end arrived, and squadrons of tall, fit American Marines moved from cave to cave, quashing resistance from weakened soldiers and taking both military and civilian prisoners. Though the Marines treated the women and children with kindness and special care, many chose — or were forced by fervent Japanese soldiers — to jump out of the caves into the ocean below, where heavy surf crashed into jagged boulders and dense jungle vegetation. Min-ah's sister Sonja had apparently been one of them, although Hadley hadn't pressed for details. Min-ah had somehow saved Sonja's daughter, Ari.

Hadley's resolution to give up reporting and writing had wavered the moment she heard Min-ah's story If she wrote about it, she could illuminate a grievous wrong that would set public opinion aflame. Once people understood that the Japanese hadn't limited their atrocities to the battlefield or the well-publicized torture of Allied prisoners, the U.S. government would demand consequences. She had finally settled on sending details of Min-ah's plight to Lorraine instead but so far hadn't heard whether or not her friend had pursued the story.

She parked *Pacific Palms* near the tree line outside the camp's perimeter, where Ari, her face chubby with baby fat, peered at her through a gap in the barbed wire fence. The child stood back, already aware that the barbs were sharp. Hadley flexed her fingers around the steering wheel. Barbed wire might be the cheapest fencing material available, but she couldn't understand why they needed to intern innocent civilians.

"It's for their well-being," Colonel Williams had assured her when she confronted him about it.

She had glared at him. "We can't provide a mess hall, a clinic, and recreation areas without fencing them in?"

He never gave her a satisfactory answer — and that was another story she believed ought to be told. She had included the details in her last letter to Lorraine and also conveyed specifics about the rough and unsanitary state of Camp Chulu during its earliest months.

Thank goodness conditions had improved. Hadley shaded her eyes and smiled at the children playing dodge ball and blind man's bluff on the playground. Off-duty men and Red Cross Girls spent time teaching games and crafts to the children and leading English classes that were open to both children and adults. The fellas had also constructed a makeshift stage, and the internees enjoyed dancing and performing skits and plays. Most cultivated small gardens and traded fresh vegetables to the military. Amenities weren't tops, but everyone had pitched in to improve the facility. If not for the fence, Hadley wouldn't complain.

She waved at the bored guard, and he unlatched the gate and ushered her into the camp. Ari toddled toward her.

"Hello, Ari." Hadley smiled and knit her fingers into the child's small little fist. "Are you taking me to Om-ma?"

"Yes, om-ma. Om-ma. Mama. Om-ma. Mommy." Ari spoke in a burbling mixture of Korean and English, just as Min-ah had intended.

Hadley allowed the little girl to tow her along, although she had already spotted Min-ah sitting on the stoop of the shack she shared with several other women. Min-ah never let Ari out of her sight. She still wore the toddler in a sling while she worked at a Red Cross club.

Min-ah's Tinian friend Tosh waved to Hadley, held out her arms, and called to Ari in a mixture of Chamorro and English. Chamorro, from what Hadley could discern, had roots in Spanish and was a byproduct of centuries of Spanish colonial influence.

Tosh was cutting dried pandanus leaves into strips, and she deftly moved the knife out of Ari's reach. She had promised to teach Min-ah how to weave baskets, bags, and mats from the leaves of the common tropical tree. Several days ago, Hadley had helped the women strip thorns from the leaves, boil them, scrape them with a shell to smooth them, and stretch them on boards to cure in the sun. The leaves were now a pale khaki rather than their usual bright green and were ready to cut into strips for weaving.

Native Tinian islanders earned extra cash selling the hand-woven items to Americans. Hadley had already sent several items home to her mother and sisters and purchased a handbag, mat, satchel, and several baskets for herself. With all the souvenirs she had collected in Australia, New Guinea, and now Tinian, she might need to buy a second trunk for her trip home.

She took the sandwiches and candy bars out of her knapsack

and gave them to Min-ah for later, then passed the rest of the afternoon playing with Ari and watching Min-ah and Tosh cut strips of pandanus. With an eye on the sun as it dropped lower in the sky, she finally stood to leave. "If I come back tomorrow, will you show me how to weave?"

"Leaves ready now." Tosh nodded.

Hadley had cut it close. Dusk was settling over the island as she wheeled the Jeepmobile into a parking spot near the Riverside Inn club. She had already missed the ride to their barracks for women who worked the afternoon shift and would miss curfew if she waited for it to return. Given all she and the other Red Cross Girls had experienced during their wartime service, she found it ridiculous that those not on the evening shift must return to the compound before nightfall. She flagged down a passing jeep.

"Can you fellas give me a lift to Mount Lasso?" she asked. "I missed the bus."

"Sure. We're headed there to pick up our dates." The passenger got out and hopped into the back seat so she could ride shotgun.

They turned onto Columbia Avenue to find themselves in a long line of jeeps filled with men waiting to check out their dates for the evening. They might sit in traffic for half an hour.

"Thanks, but I'll hop out and walk from here," Hadley said as she scrambled out.

Inside headquarters, she cut through throngs of milling men to reach the register on the counter. She hastily scrawled her signature and scribbled down a time two minutes earlier than it actually was. The receptionist glanced at the clock and lifted her brow.

Hadley shrugged. "Lots of traffic."

She nearly collided with Bizzy at the entrance to their hut.

"Oops. Sorry." Bizzy clutched a freshly ironed blouse in both hands. "I had to wait over half an hour for the iron."

"I don't know why you bother," Hadley said. "If you're going to the movies, you're gonna get soaked, and you'll be no better off at one of the clubs in this sticky heat."

"Oh, you know — first impressions." Bizzy laughed.

Hadley rolled her eyes and followed her friend into the hut. "Where is everyone?"

"You're late. They've already left." Bizzy removed her wrinkled blouse and shoved it into the laundry bag. "Did you forget about the dance?"

"Yeah." Unsure if she could summon the energy to be charming and social tonight, she sighed, stepped out of her work shoes, and kicked them under her cot. "I'm not feeling tops. I might just stay in."

"Oh, don't be a fuddy-duddy. It's with the officers of the new group," Bizzy wheedled.

Hadley turned on another lamp and stretched out on her cot. "Oh, that's right. How was it today? Are the rumors true?"

"Hmmm. Well, lunch was delicious, and they do have a nice movie theater." Bizzy tucked her fresh blouse into her skirt.

Hadley spread her hands. "So are we staffing a club inside the super-duper secret area?"

"Not exactly." Bizzy dabbed a powder puff around her face. "Sounds like we'll take Jeepmobiles to the crews in their section of North Field."

The 509th didn't only keep their living compound secure, but they had also stationed armed security around their allocation of hardstands and facilities at North Field.

Hadley riffled through the stack of magazines on the night table between her and Stella's cots. "But not inside their living quarters?"

"I don't think so." Bizzy capped her lipstick tube. "Which is why you should get ready and come with me. Might be your only chance to see it."

"Nah, you go on. You gals can tell me about it later." Hadley held up the January issue of *Vogue*. "This sounds more fun."

"I wasn't going to say anything." Bizzy bit her lip and fiddled with her necklace. "And I could be wrong. I only saw him from afar —"

"Who?" Hadley looked up.

Her friend sighed. "Lieutenant Dreamboat. Only, he's *Captain* Dreamboat now."

"Skip? No, he can't be here." Hadley's pulse juddered. She swallowed and shook her head. "You couldn't have seen him. He went home over a year ago."

After Black Sunday's heavy losses, Hadley had checked with the officers in Skip's group to make sure he and his crew had survived. One man told her Skip had been on the list to rotate stateside. She had double-checked a month later and confirmed that he had indeed left. He had been dead set against signing up for a second tour, so she hadn't been surprised.

"Come see for yourself," Bizzy urged her.

Hadley hesitated, then repeated, "He went home."

"You never know." Bizzy grabbed a skirt from atop Hadley's trunk and held it up. "Come on. You can wear this."

Skip couldn't be here. But if he was? Nothing had changed. They'd had a war-time fling, that was all. Thrilling and fun while it lasted, but a fling all the same.

Still, it couldn't hurt to see the swanky compound. Bizzy was right about that.

Hadley stretched out her hand and took the skirt.

***

"Into the air their secret rose —"

"Where they are going, nobody knows," a deep, drama-infused voice cut in.

"But take it from one who is sure of the score, the 509th is winning the war!" Derisive laughter erupted. Showers of rocks pelted the hut's tin roof.

Skip clenched his fists.

Bart, one of the men who shared his hut, opened the door and shouted, "Fuck off!"

He wasn't the only one irritated by the song. The shouting and shower of pinging stones had startled Lucy, who jumped into Skip's lap.

"Those bastards think we asked for this?" Bill slammed his trunk shut.

Mack tugged an undershirt on over his head. "I'm sick and tired of that damned song."

They were, to a man, angered by the taunting refrain some witty fella had penned after the 509th had arrived on Tinian. Even more disturbing was their inability to prove him wrong. Much to their dismay, the men of the 509th were doing exactly what they had done at Wendover. Dropping dummy pumpkin-shaped bombs — only this time on uninhabited islands instead of the desert. They hadn't flown a single combat mission against Japan.

Other B-29 crews couldn't enter the 509th compound, but that didn't deter them from standing outside the fence and singing that infuriating song day and night.

"You coming to the dance?"

"Nah." Skip sprinkled chopped carrots onto his cot for Lucy. "Not tonight."

"Not often we get a dance, buddy." Mack stooped in front of the mirror to check his tie.

A dance required admitting women into the compound. Negotiations with the colonel had finally yielded the concession of one dance per month, as long as they didn't serve alcohol. Inebriation loosened tongues, and if anything, their security protocols had only tightened after they had arrived in the Marianas. Not that prohibiting alcohol at the dance guarded against inebriation. Mack and Bart each took a swig from a flask Bill had unearthed from his trunk.

"You'd better gargle with Listerine before you leave," Skip warned, shaking his head at the proffered flask. "The dance will be swarming with G-men. You can count on that."

The ever-present FBI agents loitered inside the compound and paced the perimeters, reportedly monitoring gossip across the entire island and staying vigilant for any leaks.

"Good point." Bill took a long drink, capped the flask, and stashed it inside his trunk.

"Sure you want to miss out on a chance to cut a rug with real American women? Lotta pretty nurses will be there." Bill ran a dab of Brylcreem through his hair and combed it back.

Nurses and *Red Cross Girls*. Skip hadn't spent much time in areas of the island beyond North Field and their compound, but he assumed Red Cross clubs existed here. Then today he had seen Bizzy — and if she was here, Hadley likely was as well. They had been together since the beginning. Their two years of overseas duty had ended in February. Well, assuming Hadley hadn't been sent home after the debacle with Lorraine last April.

He hadn't been keen to go to the dance but seeing Bizzy had cemented his resolve. Skip couldn't face Hadley. Not yet. He still needed to find out what had gone wrong between them, why she had let what should have been a simple disagreement end their relationship. But not here, not now, not with the stress of being back on active duty in the Pacific.

Skip held up *Cannery Row*. "This is my company tonight."

"A book over dancing in the arms of a pretty gal and smelling her perfume, maybe stealing a kiss?" Bart whistled. "You're nuts."

"Seriously?" Mack raised an eyebrow. "You aren't hitched, are you?"

"Nope." Skip flexed his shoulders. "Plenty of time to settle down after the war."

"Got someone in mind back home?" Bill straightened his tie.

"I do," Skip fibbed, quirking his lips and pointing toward the Betty Grable poster that hung above Bart's cot and miming her figure with his hands.

With her dark hair, perfect eyebrows, and sultry smile, Hadley was more Hedy Lamarr than Grable, but Skip's words were enough to deflect attention from his lack of a dating life.

"Gonna be a remnant party on the beach after the dance. Will you bring our stash?" Mack pointed toward the liquor bottles lining the table between his and Bart's beds.

"Okay." Skip nodded. The men usually pooled whatever remained of their monthly alcohol allotment with remnants that ranged from a few sips to half a bottle, at a beachside party at the end of each month. The women would already have been escorted back to Mount Lasso for curfew before the party, so he shouldn't run into Hadley if he went.

Several hours later, he set his book aside, stood, and stretched. Lucy was sound asleep inside her pouch. Skip wrapped each bottle in a rag and placed them into his knapsack, then stuffed a few undershirts around them to keep them from clanging together.

The orchestral rendition of *Sentimental Journey* rang through the compound as he left the hut. The dance was winding down, and he took a path well away from Tinian Tavern, the officer's club, on his way to the beach.

At the gate, the guard asked for Skip's badge, checked his sidearm, and inspected his knapsack. "Where are you going with this, Captain?"

"The beach." Skip jerked his thumb toward Chulu Beach. "Boys are having a little remnant party after the dance."

The man bobbed his head, and Skip took that as assent. He was certain the guard would intervene if he showed any sign of not heading in that direction. One of the FBI agents would probably tail him down Riverside Drive, then lurk out of sight so he could monitor the party and insure that no one wandered too far afield.

A light ocean breeze ruffled Skip's hair as he descended the wooden stairs onto the stretch of white sand. Someone had started a campfire, and the branches crackled and sputtered as the flames took hold. Faint against the shroud of tropical darkness enveloping the island, the light cast by the fire was a subtle signal of change. No more blackouts or enemy bombing raids that would send them scurrying into trenches.

Skip handed the bottles over to the fella who had set up the bar and took a seat on a log. He would have a quick drink once the others arrived and then call it a night.

He stared out at the water, squinting to make out the dark, crashing waves that were more audible than visible in the tropical night. Only the murmur of scattered conversations from men who had either skipped the dance or left early broke the peaceful silence. If not for the side-arm on his hip, he might be sitting on Waikiki Beach on Oahu, before the war. The night before the world had been upended. A night like this, with camaraderie, dreams, and peace. Chet's last night. The last time Skip had shared a beer with his brother.

Footfalls clomped down the wooden stairs the Seabees had constructed down the steep slopes to the beach. Low, rumbling chatter mixed with jokes and laughter signaled the arrival of men from the dance. Skip knitted his eyebrows together.

Was that a tinkle of feminine giggles mixed with their chatter? He stood, turned toward the staircase, and scanned the clusters of people arriving on the beach.

Dammit. Somehow the fellas had indeed brought women. He had heard that a few dollars could entice sentries to look the other way as a woman sneaked in after curfew, after one of her friends forged her name on the sign-in sheets. Yet this laughter definitely came from more than one woman enjoying a tryst. A large number of them mingled with the men walking toward Skip, and one of them was unmistakably his. *Had been* his.

He hitched a breath, and his heart performed gymnastics at the sight of her. He had nowhere to hide. With only a handful of men already on the beach, Hadley was bound to spot him. He glanced over his shoulder at the thick jungle undergrowth blanketing the bluff. That was why the Seabees had built the stairs. Still, he might

—

"Skip?" Surprise and uncertainty, mingled with hope, infused Hadley's voice. Her distinctive throaty tone filled with the spice of Southern Comfort and a smidge of honey. Oh, that voice. The one he had longed to hear for more than a year. He ignored his thrumming pulse and willed his features to portray nonchalance.

She stepped closer. One whiff of her citrusy perfume, and he was a goner.

Without consciously deciding to do it, he pulled her into a tight hug. God, having her in his arms again felt so right.

"I've missed you," he murmured into her ear. His pulse accelerated like a bomber shooting down a runway. Why had he said that? She might have moved on, might even be engaged or married, for all he knew. They had broken up more than a year ago.

Hadley tightened her arms around him, and tingles flitted down his spine. Surely if she had another fella, she would have slipped out of his embrace by now instead of leaning into him. If she had someone else, she would have jerked away at his whispered admission.

She pulled back a moment later, still clutching his arms, and looked up at him with wide eyes. "Skip, what on earth are you doing here? You went home. I checked . . ."

She had checked. Had cared enough to make sure he had survived his tour. His heart thumped double-time.

"I did." Skip inhaled and let her scent flood his senses. "Got checked out in B-29s."

She widened her eyes, a signal that she wanted to hear the rest of the story. A story he couldn't share. Not in a way that would satisfy Hadley's curiosity.

"You always said you wouldn't volunteer for another tour." To his disappointment, she released her hold on him and stepped back.

"This was Uncle Sam's doing, not mine." He cast her a wry smile. "Guess I shouldn't have proven to be so competent at flying B-29s."

"Couldn't you have requested an assignment as a flight instructor?" She crinkled her nose. "Surely they need good instructors. The boys all say the B-29s are tricky to fly."

"Did that for awhile. Then they tapped me to, um . . ." Skip let the words trail away. Mentioning his training at Wendover would lead to questions he couldn't answer. "To join this group and ship out."

"You're part of this group?" Hadley swept her hand around the now-crowded beach. "You weren't at the dance."

"No, I didn't feel much like dancing." *Didn't want to risk running into you.*

"But you're part of the 509th?" Hadley asked.

He bobbed his head, then decided to ask a few questions of his own before she could press for more details. "And you? Wasn't your overseas tour up months ago?"

"Yes. I could have requested rotation back home, but they needed experienced women to open new clubs. Some of my friends went to the Philippines. You remember JoJo, who was in New Guinea? She's there. We've heard they'll soon need us on Iwo Jima and Okinawa too."

Maybe they would transfer her. A spike of relief and dismay, mixed with intense longing, pierced Skip's gut. He pushed his internal turmoil aside and met her eyes, hoping to keep the conversation focused away from him. "How long have you been here?"

"Since March."

"You came straight here from New Guinea?"

"Sort of," Hadley said. "I left Nadzab in August, then spent six months on Biak island."

He nodded. The consequences she had faced after losing the jeep apparently hadn't involved demotion to an undesirable post. He cast around for something that would keep the conversation going, keep her close. He hadn't wanted to talk now, but he might not get another chance. They might be dropping dummy bombs again this week, but that could — no, *would* — change at any time. No guarantees he would survive the war.

He swallowed past a lump in his throat. "Hadley, can we . . . can we take a walk? Not far, just . . . somewhere where we can talk."

"Well . . . " She glanced over her shoulder, perhaps hoping Bizzy or another friend might extricate her from their conversation. "I don't know if this is the best —"

"Please?" Skip threw caution to the wind, stepped closer, and took her hand. He squeezed it and kept his eyes trained on hers. "Just a short walk."

"Um . . . okay." She took a deep breath.

He set off and led her past the makeshift bar, waving away proffered drinks and ignoring the appraising looks and whistles from other men. They knew him as a loner, a man who, while friendly enough in the mess and barracks, didn't seek out social interaction. They had also noted his lack of a dating life.

The sandy strip of Chulu beach was narrow, even at low tide. Skip clutched Hadley's hand tightly to help her navigate over the uneven stones and tangled clumps of seaweed as he steered her toward a cluster of large rocks. The campfire's flickering light and the low roll of mingled voices, punctuated by laughter, were still audible, yet he and Hadley would have a measure of privacy away from the crowd.

Skip ran his free hand across the surface of a large rock to make sure it was dry and smooth. "This seems all right."

He sat close to her, torn now that he had no excuse to hold her hand. Did he have any right to assume she would welcome his touch? Skip settled for pressing his arm against hers. Nervous jangles bounced through his heart, like colorful fish darting through Tinian's crystal-clear water. He had imagined how this conversation might go for months now, hoping it might end with reconciliation. Yet now that the moment was here, he didn't know how to start.

"Meant what I said. I've missed you." Raw emotion crackled in his voice, pitching it lower than usual, when he finally dredged up the courage to speak.

Hadley knit her hands together in her lap.

"After I shipped back home," Skip continued in a whisper, "I told myself I'd find you and figure out where things went wrong.

Even if you wouldn't take me back, even if you had someone else, I needed to understand."

"What is there to understand?" She lifted her chin. "We had an argument."

"I went over and over it in my head, Hadley, and nothing about it makes sense."

"It isn't complicated." Her soft, honeyed voice made Skip's chest contract, as though he were again searching for an opening in a mass of tropical storm clouds. "Really, it's not."

"We argued." He scuffed his boot against a clump of seaweed. "But what should've been a normal disagreement became something bigger. And it felt like — still feels like — you weren't telling me everything."

"Skip . . ." Hadley held up her hand, palm out.

He should backpedal, yet her simple invocation of his name undid him. Someone had brought a a Victrola to the party, and the opening notes of Vera Lynn's *You'll Never Know* rang out over the beach. His heart swelled. He and Hadley had danced to it in Sydney.

In a fierce rush of nostalgia and longing, Skip grabbed her hand, laced his fingers with hers, and leaned closer. "I was gonna wait until after the war," he said. "But, we're here now, and Hadley — I'm back in combat. I might not have an after, so I'm claiming now."

At the word *combat*, Hadley tightened her hold on his hand. Uncertainty clouded her expression, but a hint of tender protectiveness glittered in her eyes.

He pressed his advantage. However slight it might be, he might not get another shot.

"Look, we don't have to rehash the past, if that's too hard. But we can make a fresh start and see where it takes us." He paused, and his heart stilled as if he waited atop a precipice. "That is, if you aren't involved with someone else."

Hadley shook her head.

Skip's pulse jumped. Was that *no thanks* to beginning anew or *no, I don't have someone else?* He scrutinized her expression and waited for her to clarify it for him.

"No, I don't have another fellow," she finally said, peering down at their clasped hands. "Of course I don't. How can I? Not when I'm still in love with you."

Love? She loves me? Skip's heart skipped a beat. He gently tipped up her face and stroked his fingers along her jawline. "I've never stopped loving you either."

She parted her lips.

"So is that yes to a fresh start?" he whispered, closing in on her moist, lush lips.

She edged closer in answer, and Skip seized the moment. Kissing Hadley, his heart thumped as a tide of emotions pulsed in time with the crashing surf.

She loves me. I have another chance. A second chance. A chance I cannot squander.

CHAPTER TWENTY

July 26, 1945

Tinian, Marianas Islands, Central Pacific

Hadley paused on the top step just outside the hut's door. Her heart had been thudding since the first thunderous explosion shook the windows and blossoming clouds of thick, black smoke unfurled to the north.

Skip wasn't flying today. He had complained about it last night, grousing that he hadn't been on the roster in over a week. He might not have volunteered to come here, but as long as he was, he wanted to be useful. The other bomber groups' escalating resentment of the 509th's cushy existence did nothing to alleviate his low morale.

"Oh, no. Not another one." Stella banged against Hadley from behind. Take-off crashes occurred with alarming frequency. B-29 bombers, were heavily loaded and tricky to fly under the best of circumstances, and they often met with a violent end on or in the sea just beyond the crushed-coral runways.

This harsh reality was largely unknown to the folks back home. News reports painted a rosy picture extolling the power of the large, sleek, bullet-like bombers and their heroic crews, predicting that they alone would end the war and forestall the need for a protracted bloody land war in Japan. While living with B-29 crews for weeks on Guam before his tragic death from gunfire last spring, Ernie Pyle had written a series of pieces that touched on the gritty reality of the dangers faced by the air crews, but even he had shied away from exposing just how few USAAF deaths in this theater were linked to enemy action or how many men perished in senseless tragedies like takeoff crashes or because of bad weather or poor navigation.

Stella squeezed Hadley's shoulder and edged around to face her. Consternation in her expression asked the question she didn't want to voice.

"Skip wasn't on the roster today." Cold comfort, that. He could have swapped duty with another man, or his squadron commander may have substituted him as a replacement for a sick pilot or copilot. Hadley wouldn't relax until she saw him again.

When she had agreed to take up with him again, she had told herself this was only a continuation of the fling they had started in Australia, nothing serious, nothing lasting. Nothing had changed. When the war ended, he would still want what Hadley couldn't give. Yet her incessant worry, once held at bay while she assumed he was safely back in the States at some cushy desk job, told a different story. She was in deeper than she had intended to get.

She averted her eyes from the massing clouds of black smoke. Loved ones of eleven other men hadn't been so lucky today. Men rarely survived violent takeoff crashes.

"The others are waiting, so we'd better go." Hadley turned her back on North Field and its latest tragedy and strode toward the mess.

Breakfast held no appeal for them, so they soon headed to the Riverside club, where they would pick up a Jeepmobile for today's assignment.

Ms. Williams paired Hadley with Stella in *Sweet Sugarcane* and tasked them with serving navy sailors at Tinian's harbor.

"A large cruiser arrived in port this morning," Ms. Williams informed them. "They'll take you out to it in an LCV. They aren't docking or letting off any of the sailors."

Their drive to the harbor would take them in the opposite direction from North Field, where evidence of this morning's tragedy would hang in the air for hours. That alone made today's assignment a welcome deviation from their usual routine.

"The Jeepmobile is loaded and ready to go." Ms. Williams waved them toward the row of vehicles parked outside the club and beckoned to Bizzy and Virginia. "Let's see, right. I'm sending you two ladies to the Nurse's Roost."

Bizzy pulled a face. Hadley and Stella exchanged grins. Working at the recreation club with the nurses wouldn't put them in contact with any men. To boot, temperatures inside the hillside club, unrelieved by ocean breezes, would be sweltering by mid-day.

"I'm gonna stop in the kitchen and look for Min-ah," Hadley told Stella. "I'll meet you at the jeep in a jiffy."

The kitchen bustled with activity and was saturated with the strong scents of cooking oil and sugary doughnuts. Dozens of civilian internees worked the early morning shift and churned out thousands of doughnuts. Having cooked her fair share of sinkers in the persnickety doughnut machines, Hadley was grateful to have that duty eliminated from her routine.

Exchanging greetings and smiles as she threaded her way through the sputtering doughnut machines, percolating coffee pots, and a cooktop sizzling with bacon and pancakes, Hadley at last spotted Min-ah. Her friend was elbow-deep in another batch of dough, with Ari asleep on a pallet in the corner.

Hadley tucked several stray strands of hair beneath the edge of Min-ah's cap. "What time will you finish today?"

"Um . . . at four. Yes, four o'clock." Min-ah kneaded the dough.

Four o'clock? Hadley frowned. Even if her friend had just arrived, which she hadn't, she would be working a long shift. Of course, voicing concerns for anyone, let alone for internees, would fall on deaf ears. Wartime footing required everyone's around-the-clock efforts.

Hadley patted Min-ah's shoulder. "I'll see you after that. I have something for Ari."

"Thank you." The woman smiled.

Hadley hoped Min-ah would soon consent to leave Ari with another woman at the camp while she worked. As she got older, the toddler would likely be underfoot while Min-ah went about her duties. Hadley worried about her getting burned by the sizzling doughnut fat, the hot cooktops, or the ovens that ran around the clock. Only a few seconds of inattention would allow the child to come in contact with a hot surface.

Stella had the Jeepmobile running by the time Hadley went back outside. She glanced at the overflowing stacks of boxes in the back before climbing in. "They boxed the doughnuts?"

"Easier to transport on an LCV." Stella reversed around a stand of coconut trees.

Tinian's harbor town, the only true settlement of any size on the island before the war, now buzzed with military activity. But today held a different level of energy. The traffic backlog on the outskirts of the village was their first signal.

"I'll go see if anyone knows what the holdup is." Hadley climbed out.

She asked several men but was met with nothing but shrugs and flirtatious remarks, so she trudged back to the Jeepmobile. "No one can say for sure, but one fella said getting off on 42nd and taking it to Broadway might be faster."

The early morning air was already uncomfortably warm, especially sitting in stalled traffic. Stella tugged a handkerchief from her pocket and wiped her face.

They inched forward bit by bit until they were finally able to turn left onto 42nd Street, although it was also clogged with heavy traffic.

Stella pursed her lips. "At least Broadway will take us to the docks."

"Eventually," Hadley muttered, knotting her silk scarf under her chin to keep her hair from plastering against the sides of her face.

They stopped to chat with a few nurses who had pulled over to get a look at one of the hospitals under construction.

"Aren't they about to finish the one on Mount Lasso?" Hadley asked. The large five-hundred bed hospital was near completion and would be convenient for nurses housed there.

"Oh, they are," one of the nurses said. "But they want at least six hospitals here. For the invasion casualties."

Hadley stomach clenched. Even with the destruction the Twentieth Air Force had rained down on Japan over the last few months, the military still estimated they would need a force of a million men to invade Japan. Newspaper reports suggested that the invasion would most likely commence in the fall.

They chugged south on Broadway in *Sweet Sugarcane* for another half hour before the clear turquoise water of Tinian's harbor came into view.

Hadley's clothes clung to her sweat-dampened skin, and she had never been more tempted to plunge into the stunning cerulean water. Technically, many of the beaches were off-limits to female personnel, although plenty of women visited them on their own or with dates. Skip had taken her to Chulu Beach, the one reserved for his group, but only at dusk. He had promised to borrow a pair of snorkeling masks for a daytime swim the next time she had a free day.

She was due one free day per week, but it never seemed to materialize. The war in Europe had ended, yet the Red Cross was still stretched thin from covering operations over an ever-widening area in the Pacific. Not to mention the still-active China-Burma-India Theater, where her old Washington roommate Audrey had been sent.

Plus, they also provided services to the occupation forces in Europe. Vivian and Jack had married in early June, but she was already hard at work in Germany after their honeymoon and a short stateside leave.

Stella finally found a place to park. "Guess they'll send fellas to unload the doughnuts."

"I hope so." As the ocean breeze cooled Hadley's skin, she untied her scarf and stuffed it into her pocket. She raked her fingers through her hair. Maybe she would have time to shampoo it before tonight's dance at the 509th compound. Now that they were together again, Skip was happy to attend this month's dance.

Crowds thronged around the docks, with many MPs interspersed among the men.

Hadley shaded her eyes and peered at the large cruiser anchored out in the harbor. Nothing noteworthy struck her about the vessel.

Stella nudged her and pointed through the crowd. "Isn't that General LeMay? The officer we met on Guam?"

With dark bushy eyebrows set in his florid face, General LeMay puffed on his cigar. He was based on Guam, not here. He was also surrounded by several generals and admirals.

"Wonder what's brought the brass here this morning?" Hadley edged closer to the milling officers, hoping to overhear a tidbit that might shed some light on the hubbub.

A landing tank craft sailed in beside the cruiser. The cruiser's crane extended its boom and swung out a jib with a long line and hook attached to it. Several sailors attached a wooden crate as large as a car to the line.

"Careful, careful," the man next to her muttered. "Easy does it."

Hadley glanced at him out of the corner of her eye. A civilian. Looking around, she spotted a significant number of other civilians interspersed through the crowd.

She had already noticed swelling numbers of them on Tinian, with most connected to the 509th group. But when she had asked Skip about them, he had dodged her questions. Ever persistent, she had asked him again a few days later during the intermission of *Meet Me in St. Louis*. That time, Skip had used the spattering rain as a pretext to pull her poncho cap over her head, lean close, and beg her to drop the subject. Later that night, pressed close against him in the backseat of a jeep, with their double dates in the front, Skip had repeated his admonition in starker terms. Over the roar of the engine and the chatter of their partners, his warm whispers had urged her to stop asking questions if she wanted to remain stationed near him on Tinian.

The crane operator lowered the crate onto the deck of the waiting LCT. Seconds later, Hadley caught sight of a crane mounted on a second LCT simultaneously transferring an odd piece of cargo. She squinted at it and made out two metal canisters about the size and shape of ice cream freezers, each balanced on either end of a long pipe. Men carefully lowered it onto the empty deck of the other LCT. Two other men scrambled down a rope ladder, sat near the strange contraption, and hung on as the LCT sped toward shore.

"Excuse me, ma'am," a man in a truck called out. "I'm backing up."

She hurriedly moved out of his way. He reversed near the edge of the pier as the LCT carrying the strange canisters sliced through the water, aiming for the pier.

"Ladies, afraid you need to move on out of the way." The MP shooed them toward the next pier.

Stella turned to comply, but Hadley grabbed her friend's elbow and hung back. "Blend in with the crowd," she muttered. "I want to get a better look at this delivery."

Several MPs moved in and cleared a wide perimeter around the waiting truck. The other LCT, with its wooden crate, cruised close behind the one carrying the mysterious canisters.

The hairs on the back of Hadley's neck prickled. The men were being exceptionally careful with the aluminum canisters, all while distracting everyone with the large crate. The cargo truck waited in a cleared area, a large number of high-ranking military officials had gathered at the harbor this morning, and — most significantly — Skip's secretive bomb group, touted as having the means to end the war, had recently arrived on the island.

Once the men secured the first LCT to the pier, two men on board passed their kit bags to waiting soldiers. Under their direction, navy sailors passed the pipe with its suspended canisters from the LCT to men on the pier. Hadley had spent enough time around the docks to know how carefree the swabbies usually were while unloading freight. But these men had obviously been instructed to treat this new cargo with the utmost care.

Trepidation played across the faces of the young officers aboard the LCT until the men placed the contraption inside the truck. They then disembarked and hurried to the truck, climbing not into the cab, but into the back, as if unwilling to let the canisters out of their sight.

Meanwhile, the first group of men had lowered the enormous crate onto a large flatbed truck parked behind the one carrying the canisters, and both vehicles pulled out onto Broadway, their tires kicking up pebbles as they sped away. Jeeps filled with high-ranking officers from all of the service branches barreled along close behind.

A man behind Hadley let out a low whistle. "That's some serious shit, whatever it is."

Several MPs pulled their vehicles across Broadway to create a roadblock, a signal that the military didn't want anyone to know where the shipment was headed.

Hadley clenched her teeth in frustration. She already had an enticing story, but she would love to know more. Setting the stage for a dramatic speculative piece would be easy.

No. You aren't writing anymore, remember? Not even about this. Especially not this.

Chasing the story would come to no good end. Besides, it was pointless. If the unloading process she had witnessed was any indication, security around it would be sky-high.

She turned to Stella. "We need to find our ride out to the ship. The sailors are probably antsy for doughnuts."

***

Hadley tucked apples and oranges she had saved into her knapsack. She added several Hershey bars and a few cartons of M&Ms she had nabbed from the PX before they had sold out as treats for Ari and the other children, then slung the knapsack over her shoulder.

Unfortunately, the pack couldn't accommodate the bigger gift she had for Min-ah. The army had distributed thousands of Sky Courier radios to the troops, so many that each Quonset hut or tent had at least two. A young officer had brought several into the Riverside club yesterday on the assumption that they might be of use there. Little did he know all that the Red Cross clubs on Tinian had more than enough radios for each room.

A radio would entertain Min-ah and her friends. Not only could they listen to music, but the songs, news, and other broadcasts would reinforce their English skills. The more Min-ah and Ari spoke, the more likely they would be able to emigrate to America after the war.

Since radios were so plentiful, no one would bat an eye at Hadley carrying one out to the Jeepmobile. But getting it past the MP at the gate to Camp Chulu would be another matter. Hadley suspected he would prohibit her from taking it in, let alone leaving it there. She couldn't imagine what harm could come from it; the internees were mostly women and children and having entertainment would improve their English. But she figured the military wouldn't see it that way, so she planned to park the Jeepmobile near the line of trees closest to Min-ah's quarters and slide the radio under the barbed wire fence and into the shrubs. Once she entered the camp, she would retrieve the device and deliver it to the women.

She curled her fingers around the handle of the radio's metal case and hefted it off the table. Billed as portable, the radio and its battery was fairly heavy.

"Where are you taking that?" Bizzy asked.

Hadley settled the radio into the Jeepmobile beside the coffee canisters. She looked over her shoulder, then stepped closer to Bizzy.

"It's one of the extras that Clarkson fella brought in yesterday. Thought I'd give it to Min-ah, so she and the other women can listen to music."

"You think they'll let you give it to her?" Bizzy scratched her nose. A slight frown creased her forehead. "The guards, I mean?"

"Guess I'll find out," Hadley said breezily as she climbed into the passenger seat.

"Well, I predict you'll be hauling it back inside later." Bizzy started the engine. "The military won't want them to have anything that might aid the enemy."

Aid the enemy? Hadley shrugged. Min-ah and the mostly uneducated women with whom she lived wouldn't know how to disassemble the radio or what to do with its components, even if they did. Besides, the tubes inside it couldn't possibly transmit a signal thousands of miles away to Japan. The radio wasn't military grade.

CHAPTER TWENTY-ONE

August 4, 1945, 2:45 p.m.

Operations Briefing Room, 509th Composite Group, North Field

Tinian, Marianas Islands, Central Pacific

"Pass." The MP held out his hand

Skip handed over his pass. The MP scrutinized it, then ran his finger down a roster attached to a clipboard. He put a checkmark next to Skip's name and handed the pass to a second MP.

"ID, please," the man demanded.

Skip extracted his ID from his pocket and handed it over.

The man glanced between the ID and the pass several times before handing them back to Skip. He inclined his head to signal Skip to proceed into the briefing area.

Although the appearance of the briefing room struck him as

normal, with the usual strong odor of smoke, the murmur of conversation, and the black drapes covering the blackboards, a distinct pulsing energy crackled through the space today. Apart from the charged atmosphere, other indications told him this would be no ordinary briefing. High-ranking officers from all service branches, including the British and Australians, filled the seats near the podium.

Civilian scientists also streamed into the room alongside the air crews. Some of their faces were familiar to Skip, because they had frequently visited Wendover. He had no idea why he was here. He was the only man from his crew on the roster. Presumably he had been slotted as a replacement, but he couldn't pinpoint any of the crews without their usual pilots.

Playboy Claude Eatherly, with his usual swaggering grin in place, joked with his men. Straight arrow George Marquardt, the polar opposite of Eatherly, leaned against a wall, smoking a cigarette. Chuck Sweeney, who had been friendly to Skip, sat cloistered with his fellas. Skip also recognized three other pilots, John Wilson, Charles McKnight, and Ralph Taylor.

He sat next to Chuck Sweeney and exchanged remarks with the man's crew. Several of them were seething over the news that the cruiser *Indianapolis* had sunk, losing more than three-quarters of its crew and passengers to sharks and dehydration. The loss of the *Indianapolis* might go down as one of the U.S. Navy's most catastrophic losses of the war.

"Tinian was her last port of call before she sank." One of Sweeney's gunners shook his head and kneaded his hands together.

Skip didn't bother to correct him. The *Indianapolis* had spent a couple of days at Guam after it left Tinian. The cruiser's objective, however, had been to make a delivery to Tinian harbor. Hadley had mentioned seeing it and naturally had questions galore about its unusual cargo. He had urged her to desist from pursuing any answers.

Colonel Tibbets arrived precisely at three o'clock. Flanked by several intelligence officers, he approached the podium and motioned for quiet. Chatter petered out faster than normal. Everyone wanted to learn why they were here with this odd assemblage.

"Gentlemen, the moment has arrived," Colonel Tibbets said in a grave tone.

Skip's stomach flipped. The colonel had stood on a soapbox at Wendover field last September and spoken in tones just as solemn.

"Your mission would end the war," Tibbets had proclaimed before launching into a stern recitation of the rules for the 509th group. No questions, no speculation, no divulging details to family or anyone outside the group.

As ever, Tibbets now cut straight to the point. "This is what we've been working toward. The weapon we are about to deliver has been successfully tested in the States. We have received our orders to drop it on the enemy."

At Tibbets's nod, two intelligence officers stepped forward and removed the black cloths from the blackboards. Skip squinted at the titles of the three maps displayed on them.

Hiroshima, Kokura, Nagasaki.

"Hiroshima is the primary target." Tibbets picked up a pointer and tapped the first map, then stepped to the right. "Kokura is first alternate." He tapped the final map. "Nagasaki is the second alternate."

"Three reconnaissance planes will leave an hour before the strike force to scout weather conditions. This is a critical piece of our mission, gentlemen. The bombardier must be able to visually sight the target. Assignments are as follows: Eatherly, Wilson, and Taylor."

Disappointment, resentment even, flashed across Eatherly's face. For all his flamboyance and exploits on the ground, he was all business in the air. Despite the colonel's emphasis on the importance of accurate weather scouting, Eatherly doubtless believed he would miss out on the main action.

"McKnight and his crew," Tibbets continued, "will fly to Iwo Jima and wait there in case we need a replacement aircraft for the strike force."

Will I be part of the strike force? Skip's gut churned.

"The strike force will consist of three ships. I will command the plane loaded with the special weapon. Major Sweeney" he continued, looking at Chuck, who sat up straighter, "will command the plane carrying scientist observers and bomb measurement equipment."

Bomb measurement equipment? Skip exchanged a quick glance with Sweeney.

Colonel Tibbets aimed his pointer at George Marquardt. "And finally, Major Marquardt's ship will carry photographic equipment to record the blast."

Skip deepened his frown. He had looked around as the colonel named each crew. They all had a copilot. Why in hell was he here?

"Marquardt's ship, in addition to its crew, will also carry several photographers." The colonel scanned the crowd and locked in on Skip. "Captain Masterson, one of the civilian photographers has appendicitis. You will fly in his place."

A pumpkin-shaped bomb dropped to the bottom of Skip's lungs.

No. No, no, no.

Tibbets had mentioned the possibility when he cut orders to transfer Skip to his command. He had known then that Skip's background might prove useful.

"The bomb you are going to drop is new in the history of warfare," another voice said.

Skip pushed his anxiety aside and looked up as Captain Parsons, a tall, balding navy officer Skip had seen at both Wendover and Tinian, walked up to the podium.

"It is the most destructive weapon ever produced, with a destructive force equivalent to twenty thousand tons of TNT. We believe it will destroy everything within a three-mile area."

All the air left the room. Every fidget stilled, every breath paused. Absolute silence fell over the crowd.

Captain Parsons directed a technician to turn on the projector.

The man did so, and the film sputtered to life, jerking on and off for a few seconds until a shrill whine and fast whirring indicated the film had gotten tangled in the sprockets. The technician switched off the projector before it ripped the film.

"The film you are apparently *not* about to see," Parsons said, amid titters of nervous laughter that briefly cut the tension, "was made during the only test of this new weapon, which was performed in New Mexico last month. I'll tell you instead what the film would've shown."

Skip leaned forward.

"This weapon will knock a man flat at ten thousand yards and be heard a hundred miles away from the blast site. The light it produces is ten times more brilliant than the sun."

No one moved. Every man had his eyes fixed on Captain Parsons.

Those steep diving turns. That's what those turns were about. Skip swallowed.

"No one knows exactly what will happen when the weapon is dropped from the air. But we do expect a cloud shaped something like this," Parsons picked up a piece of chalk and drew a mushroom-shaped cloud. "A cloud that will rise more than thirty thousand feet into the air. You must avoid flying through it, gentlemen."

Parsons motioned for one of the intelligence officers to bring him a box. He fished out a pair of tinted welder's goggles and dangled them by the strap.

"You'll all be issued these." He slipped them over his eyes, indicated a knob on the nose bridge, and demonstrated turning it. "You'll need to have it on the lowest setting, so the goggles let in the least amount of light, or you'll risk being blinded by the intense light."

The men's faces paled, and they exchanged worried glances. The silence remained absolute. Skip narrowed his eyes in consternation. He had never attempted to take photographs while wearing glasses, let alone goggles fitted to let in as little light as possible. How would he operate a Fastax when he could hardly see?

The intelligence officers gave each man a pair of goggles, then Tibbets reclaimed the podium and concluded the briefing.

"Gentlemen, everything I've done, everything each one of you has done, up to this point is small potatoes compared to what we're about to embark on. I'm proud to be associated with each one of you, proud of everything we've achieved so far, proud of what we're about to do."

Tibbets shuffled the papers on the podium.

"Goes without saying that what you've learned this afternoon is top secret. You're now the hottest crews in the air force. So it should also come as no surprise that you'll be confined to the 509th compound until our operational briefing tomorrow evening. No talking about anything you've heard this afternoon, not even among yourselves."

He paused, looked around the room, and nodded in satisfaction. "Dismissed."

***

August 5, 1945, 5:30 p.m.

Tinian, Marianas Islands, Central Pacific

Hadley dried her hands and tossed the damp dishtowel into the laundry basket. She was done for the day and had nothing on her agenda for tonight, so she would have time to catch up on correspondence and relax for once.

She hadn't seen Skip in two days and doubted he would materialize tonight. Bizzy had reported that the 509th compound had been closed off since the previous afternoon when she had made a Jeepmobile run. Stella said parts of North Field had also been blocked off. Whatever mysterious mission Skip's group had might be in the offing at last. Zipping pings flitted through Hadley's stomach.

"Miss Hadley?"

She turned. Soon-ja, one of Min-ah's friends, stood in the doorway, twisting her hands.

"Hello, Soon-ja. Can I help you?" Hadley smiled. She might have said "What brings you here?" but the woman's knowledge of English wasn't strong enough for her to grasp idiomatic expressions. Besides, Soon-ja's obvious agitation told Hadley that now wasn't the time to give her additional instruction.

"Min-ah, she . . . she . . . ." Soon-ja was clearly struggling to find the English words she needed. She gave up and mimed a facial expression that was either sad or . . . ashamed?

"Soon-ja, why is Min-ah ashamed?" Hadley stepped closer. "What happened?"

"Radio goodbye. Radio Japanese. Min-ah go catch."

"What?" Hadley frowned and attempted to make sense of the woman's phrases. The radio was gone? And Min-ah had left to search for it. But what was that about the Japanese?

"The radio is missing? Gone?" Hadley waved bye-bye as she might with Ari to confirm what she thought the woman wanted to convey.

Soon-ja nodded vigorously. "Bye-bye."

"Okay. And Min-ah is looking for it?" Hadley mimed searching for something.

"Yes, yes. She . . ." Soon-ja made an undulating hand gesture that made no sense to Hadley, who shook her head.

Soon-ja wrung her hands, and Hadley pulled out the notebook and pencil she carried in her pocket out of habit. Soon-ja drew a fence and a stick figure crawling under it.

Min-ah intended to sneak out of Camp Chulu? She must believe the radio had fallen into the hands of Japanese still hiding in Tinian's cliffside caves, but where would she get that idea?

Hadley looked out the window. She didn't have time to go to Camp Chulu and get back to her quarters before evening check-in. Hadley looked from Soon-ja to the Jeepmobile keys hanging on pegs near the back door. She motioned for Soon-ja to follow her.

Babs and Ginny, who were on duty until closing, cast curious glances at Hadley and Soon-ja, but they didn't comment. Hadley surreptitiously pocketed the key to *Sweet Sugarcane* and waved at them.

Outside, she directed Soon-ja to climb into the passenger seat before starting the engine and driving north on Riverside Drive. Fortunately, Camp Chulu was only a short distance northeast of the Riverside club.

At the gate, Hadley passed her card to the MP and gestured toward Soon-ja. "She's been working for me at the Riverside club."

"You didn't need to bring her back yourself." He returned her card. "She could have come in one of the trucks."

"I kept her late. They had already left."

"Hmph," he grunted, disapproval in his voice. At least he hadn't said anything disparaging that Hadley would have found impossible not to challenge.

He waved for Soon-ja to go into the camp but held up his hand to prevent Hadley from following her. "Only internees are allowed in after dark."

"I have to pick up costumes from the stage area," Hadley said, having anticipated this. "They borrowed them earlier today, and we need them back at one of our clubs for a performance tonight." She smiled. "I'll be back in a jiffy."

"All right." He nodded tersely. "But be quick about it."

Oh, she would be quick, all right. She intended to locate Min-ah and warn her off her foolhardy scheme. If the MPs caught Min-ah outside the camp without permission, especially at night, they would imprison her without access to Ari — and once they were separated, Min-ah might even lose custody of her niece.

Hadley set off for Min-ah's hut, with Soon-ja half-jogging to keep up. Hadley jerked the door open and strode in, calling out her friend's name. Startled faces greeted her.

"No Min-ah. She go." Soon-ja tugged on Hadley's sleeve.

A babble of conversation, occasionally in English but mostly in Korean, broke out among the women. Hadley looked around and finally spotted Ari. The little girl was absorbed with a pile of wooden blocks in a corner and didn't notice that Hadley had come in. Ari was never more than an arm's-reach away from Min-ah, yet Min-ah wasn't here. The radio was also gone.

"Tell me." She held up her hand to silence the women. "The radio is gone?"

They all nodded in agreement.

"When?" Hadley ran a hand through her hair in frustration when she realized they didn't understand her question. Had they covered the concept of time in their English classes?

Min-ah's English was by far the most advanced. But one teenage boy had absorbed almost as much. Hadley racked her brain for his name. Jiho?

"Jiho? Can you get him?" She tried to mime what she wanted, and one of the women at last spoke rapidly to Soon-ja, who disappeared.

Minutes later, to Hadley's relief, Soon-ja reappeared with the right boy.

"Jiho, I gave a radio to Min-ah and these women." Hadley gestured around the room. "Someone took it, and Min-ah thinks the Japanese have it. Can you ask them if that is correct and also when the radio disappeared?"

Jiho questioned the others and turned back to Hadley. "Radio gone after sun came up —"

"Today?" she interrupted.

He nodded. "Yes, today. Min-ah talk. Japanese prisoner take it, put it under fence."

Camp Chulu had been divided into two sections. This side was Korean, while Japanese and Okinawan civilians were in the other sector. If Hadley understood Jiho correctly, Min-ah believed that a civilian from the other sector had taken the radio and planned to slip it under the fence to one of the uncaptured enemy soldiers still in hiding on Tinian.

"What good would that do?" Hadley hadn't known that the Japanese could already communicate with Rota, a nearby island still under Japanese control, when she had first given the radio to Min-ah — or that Rota relayed that information on to Japan. Skip had told her in passing that Tokyo Rose's broadcasts had reported the comings and goings on Tinian in considerable detail. The Japanese would only have that information if the enemy soldiers hiding in the caves were transmitting it to Rota.

"They use inside radio," Jiho said. "*Pieces* in radio."

"No, they already talk to Japan." Hadley shook her head. "They don't need any more radio parts. Where is Min-ah?"

"She wait. Catch Japanese come get radio."

Min-ah was waiting on the other side of the fence, hoping to intercept the civilian planning to give the radio to a Japanese soldier? Where she could be shot or captured by a jumpy American Marine as easily as by the Japanese?

***

August 5, 1945, 8:00 p.m.

Tinian, Marianas Islands, Central Pacific

Skip paced back and forth in front of his hut, with Lucy hopping along behind him.

He should go to sleep, but he wasn't the only man too worked up to rest. He had stopped by the huts of some of the other men slated to fly the mission. The colonel was playing poker with his trusted navigator Dutch van Kirk, bombardier Tom Ferebee, and a handful of others. Smoke hung thick in the air around their game table. A few fellas were writing letters. No one was sleeping.

Skip couldn't divulge any details from yesterday's briefing to his crewmates, so none of them understood his agitation. Not even reading distracted him from his worries.

The weapon the colonel had mentioned was not conventional. He had been on the right track in thinking that the insane high-speed diving turn Tibbets had made them practice over and over for nearly a year was an evasive maneuver. Clearly the planners and scientists expected a plane dropping a weapon of this magnitude to be in danger from the bomb's explosion and after-effects. Their lives would depend on their execution of that jarring diving turn at a fast enough speed to outrun the bomb.

Yet his anxiety wasn't only tied to whether or not they could escape the blast or even to being behind the lens of a camera again.

Gratifying. Tibbets had said any man who had lost a loved one by enemy hands would find his duty with the 509th to be *gratifying.* Skip slid his hand into his pocket and gripped his light meter. He would at last be able to avenge Chet's death, the deaths of his shipmates, and the deaths of thousands of other Americans who had lost their lives at Pearl Harbor. Why then did the prospect of retribution make him sick to his stomach?

From what Tibbets and Parsons had said, the new weapon would annihilate in one swoop far more people than the number that had died in the firebombing raids on Tokyo in March or the destruction of Dresden in February. Many innocent people would die, including women, children, and elderly people going about their daily lives, unaware of the peril about to fall from above. Yes, Hiroshima was an industrial city of strategic importance with many military installations, as were the secondary targets of Kokura and Nagasaki. But the new weapon — if it worked as Tibbets had described — would destroy considerably more than military targets.

The Japanese targets at Pearl Harbor had been military. Civilians had also paid a price, but not on the scale Skip imagined tomorrow's bomb would deliver.

Could he do his duty, do what the military needed from him? He wasn't the only photographer on base. Should he fake an illness to get pulled from the roster? He would need far more than a vague complaint to get out of this mission. Tibbets would demand evidence of some dire illness, especially given that Skip was already a replacement. As sick as he felt inside, he doubted he could will his body to produce enough visible effects to get him excused.

He raked a hand through his hair and continued to pace.

***

August 5, 1945, 9:00 p.m.

Tinian, Marianas Islands, Central Pacific

Hadley rocked back on her heels, grabbed a branch, and pulled herself upright. Her thigh muscles cramped. She had been crouched in one spot for too long.

She had already searched the perimeter outside the Japanese/Okinawan sector of Camp Chulu and although she had looked for the actual radio, which was probably well-hidden, she had been most watchful for any sign of Min-ah. Hadley had been torn between making her presence known in an attempt to lure Min-ah out of the shadows versus keeping a low profile to avoid drawing the attention of American security forces.

Should she stay put in this spot or keep moving? At first, she had circled the perimeter fence looking for the radio. But she had finally decided it could be anywhere, as the fence around this sector was at least a mile. The radio wasn't here, someone had already taken it, or it was obscured by foliage. She had fished around in the bushes along the fence, with nothing to show for it but an aching back.

Hadley figured that the Japanese soldiers still hiding on the island had worked out a system with sympathetic internees months ago and set up drop points for passing items outside the fence. Whether Min-ah knew where they were, Hadley couldn't guess.

Unless . . .

No, Min-ah couldn't possibly be a Japanese sympathizer. The Japanese had tricked her and Sonja and forced them into a horrific situation. Hadley shook her head. Min-ah might know or guess where to watch for the men who came to retrieve items, but Hadley refused to believe her friend was complicit in the radio's disappearance.

Finding Min-ah had to be Hadley's biggest priority. She had wasted enough time trying to find the radio. But if Min-ah were lurking somewhere nearby, waiting for an enemy soldier to take the radio, shouldn't she have already spotted Hadley?

Probably. Yet if Min-ah wanted to stop the radio from falling into enemy hands, she would be reluctant to make her presence known. She might think Hadley planned to force her to return to the camp.

How on earth did Min-ah intend to prevent a soldier from taking the radio? She had no access to weapons. Hadley knit her hands in frustration. Dammit, the radio's whereabouts weren't critical. If only she had mentioned to Min-ah that Skip had said the Japanese already had the means to send news from Tinian to Rota and from there to Japan.

Could Hadley tell Min-ah this without drawing notice from American guards? She had only seen one patrolling inside the fence, and he had made only one half-hearted pass in the last hour. Most internees had no reason to violate curfew. But if Hadley called out to Min-ah to tell her the radio wouldn't help the Japanese, even a disinterested guard would investigate.

Hadley held her watch close to her face. After nine already? *Damn.* The later it got, the more issues she would face. She could claim she had inadvertently forgotten to sign the check-in register by six o'clock, but if she also missed date-night curfew at eleven, she would definitely be in hot water.

She pinched the bridge of her nose and turned in a half-circle. She needed help. Ultimately, she was to blame; she was the one who had smuggled the radio into Camp Chulu for Min-ah. But that's not how the military would see it. Min-ah should never have left the camp. That was the tricky part. And if Hadley told anyone what was happening, the military would separate Min-ah from Ari, no matter what Hadley said. She couldn't run the risk of having Min-ah permanently separated from her niece.

Skip could help her. Yes, he would utterly disapprove, but he would help. Yet getting his help at this time of night would be impossible. If he were anywhere except inside the ultra-secure 509th group compound, Hadley could drive there and ask someone at group headquarters to look for him. But not at the 509th compound. Heavily armed guards stationed every few feet around their fence wouldn't let her in without a pass. And Bizzy had told her that they had ratcheted up their usually stiff security only yesterday.

She glanced into the darkness beyond the fence, where Min-ah had to be hiding and toyed with her bracelet. Her heart jittered at the memory of the last time she had needed to search for a friend in the darkness. A friend who, like Min-ah, had a mistaken impression Hadley could have corrected.

She had to do better by Min-ah than she had with Gabriel. She had to set aside her guilt and summon the courage to find her friend and avert disaster.

***

August 6, 1945, 12:00 a.m.
Combat Crew Lounge, 509th Composite Group,
Tinian, Marianas Islands, Central Pacific

Skip followed the other airmen into the Combat Crew Lounge for the second time that evening. They had already had their standard operations briefing and received their flight route, altitudes, and expected weather, along with the locations of air rescue units, surface ships, and submarines along their briefed route.

Even without the crews from the weather scouting planes, who were eating a pre-takeoff breakfast and would proceed to the flight line within the hour, the briefing room was far more crowded than normal. Far more crowded, yet far quieter and more somber. Perhaps Skip wasn't the only one tussling with moral reservations about the new weapon, whatever it might be.

This final briefing was for the crews of the strike plane, which Tibbets had dubbed *Enola Gay*, named for his mother, and the two observation planes that would accompany it to the target. From here, they would go to the mess for a pre-mission meal and then head to the flight line.

Skip's stomach churned.

"Sweeney will position his ship roughly three hundred feet behind the strike ship," Tibbets said. "At the point of release of the weapon, his crew will release the bomb measurement equipment, then Major Sweeney will breakaway to the left, while the strike ship breaks right."

Tibbets nodded at Marquardt. "You will position your ship several miles south of the release point so the photographers can do their job."

The room remained uncharacteristically silent. No one moved.

"Tonight is the night we've been waiting for, gentlemen. Our long months of training are about to be put to the test. We will soon know if we have been successful or if we have failed. With our efforts tonight, it is possible history will be made."

History. Skip gulped.

"Remember, you must wear goggles when we approach the aiming point. You must prove you have them with you before you board your ships." Tibbets swept the room with his piercing gaze. "Obey your orders. Do your jobs. Don't cut any corners, men."

He beckoned to the group's chaplain, William Downey. After indicating that everyone might bow their heads, Downey read a prayer he had composed specifically for this mission:

Almighty Father, Who wilt hear the prayer of them that love

Thee, we pray Thee to be with those who brave the heights of Thy Heaven and who carry the battle to our enemies. Guard and protect them, we pray Thee, as they fly their appointed rounds. May they, as well as we, know Thy strength and power, and armed with Thy might may they bring this war to a rapid end. We pray Thee that the end of the war may come soon, and that once more we may know peace on earth. May the men who fly this night be kept safe in Thy care, and may they be returned safely to us. We shall go forward trusting in Thee, knowing that we are in Thy care now and forever. In the name of Jesus Christ. Amen.

Skip and the others rose in silence and filed out of the room.

CHAPTER TWENTY-TWO

August 6, 1945, 12:15 a.m.

Tinian, Marianas Islands, Central Pacific

Hadley's ears pricked. The leaves rustled. Having spent the last few hours lurking in the darkness near the perimeter fence, she had become hyper-attuned to the night's normal noises. She was in just as much danger from a skittish guard or Japanese hold-out as Min-ah. She stood stock still and examined the immediate area. Probably just another rat.

She shifted and prepared to resume her circuit of the fence, when more rustling echoed through the night. She went still.

If only the sound had come from Min-ah passing close enough for Hadley to grab her and whisper about the missing radio being of no consequence, then lead her to the Jeepmobile.

She squinted into the silent grounds inside Camp Chulu and

caught a flash of movement. Was someone going to the latrine, or had a rodent scurried along a roofline? Or had a night breeze caused a forgotten item of clothing to sway on the clothesline?

Hadley couldn't decide and trained her gaze on the ground near the fence. Something glinted in the meager light. The metal casing of the entertainment radios the army distributed was dull and drab, but the band displays were bright white.

She stepped forward to investigate but halted when a man crept out of the darkness and slinked stealthily toward the fence. He hadn't seen her. She sucked in a shaky breath.

God, he materialized out of nowhere. The hairs on the back of Hadley's neck tingled, and adrenaline gushed through every muscle, every nerve. If Min-ah was lying in wait, she would soon show herself to either intervene or follow him.

Hadley didn't know which would be worse, and not only for Min-ah. If a confrontation broke out, the noise would alert the guards. But if the man grabbed the radio and ran, Min-ah would follow him — and Hadley must summon her courage and do the same, as she should have years ago, to avert a tragedy.

Assuming she *could* follow them. The man would probably disappear even more quickly than he had emerged from the shadows. He had to have been lurking nearby, waiting for someone to stash the radio, so he had probably also seen Hadley.

A cold shiver snaked down her spine. If he had seen her and taken no action, did he not consider her a threat? Or was he not armed?

He stooped and pulled a white canvas laundry bag out of the brush, slung it over his shoulder, and turned to slip back into the foliage. Yet before he could disappear, Min-ah dashed forward and attempted to wrest the bag from him.

A gleam of a blade flashed in the moonlight.

No! Hadley ran forward and barreled into the man, knocking him down and splitting the bag open. K-ration cans of Spam and green beans, jars of peanut butter, and a half-wrapped loaf of bread spilled out. The soldier scrabbled up onto his hands and knees.

"Food?" Min-ah yelled. "Where is radio?"

"Never mind." Hadley grabbed Min-ah's hand. "Quick, come with me!"

The soldier turned and ran, but she knew he would come back for his food. And once he realized he had been jumped by two unarmed women, he might prove to be more dangerous.

"Radio!" Min-ah wrenched free and dove into the bushes. "It must be here."

"No, Min-ah, the radio doesn't matter." Hadley tugged on the woman's arm. "I'll explain in the jeep. We need to go before he comes back. Let him have the food. He's hungry."

"If he takes radio —"

"It doesn't matter," Hadley repeated. "They already have a radio. I'll explain more later. Please, let's go before he comes back."

When Min-ah nodded, Hadley linked arms with her and set off at a fast clip, skirting the perimeter, careful to stay out of sight of any guards.

As they hurried along, Hadley whispered that the Tinian holdouts already had a transmitter that allowed them to communicate with Rota, and thus Japan.

"They don't need anything else," she assured Min-ah. "An entertainment radio will not improve their ability to communicate with Japan."

Min-ah's English might not be strong enough for her to grasp the finer points of Hadley's explanation, but she seemed to accept that locating the radio wasn't critical.

Hadley was thankful she had moved the Jeepmobile to make the guards think she had left Camp Chulu. The jeep would provide a safe place for her to explain everything to Min-ah.

She gestured for Min-ah to climb into the passenger seat. Then Hadley slid in the driver's side and clutched the steering wheel with shaking hands.

"Safe now." Min-ah laid a soft hand onto her shoulder.

Hot tears rolled down Hadley's face. Her shoulders shook. She had saved Min-ah but could no longer contain her regrets from the past that tonight's intrigue had forced her to face.

"I had to find you. I-I couldn't let anyone else die because of my mistakes." She choked up and paused until she regained her composure and finally allowed herself to voice the one story she had never been able to tell, the story she had held inside for far too long. "Gabriel was the son of my nanny, Fanelia. He was her only child."

Fanelia didn't bring her son with her to the Claverie home each day, but Hadley had met Gabriel when he came uptown after school to wait for his mother. They became friends and often sat outside and talked to pass the time, always careful to remain visible so no one could claim their friendship was improper.

Gabriel raised her awareness of the racial injustices and stark inequities so prevalent in New Orleans and ignited the spark that set Hadley down the path of becoming an investigative reporter.

Soon after his sixteenth birthday, Gabriel left school, got a job, and quit stopping by as often. Hadley hadn't seen him in months before the muggy June evening she found him waiting for Fanelia and told him she planned to sneak out of the house. Not to meet a boyfriend, or even to go to a backatown dance club with friends. No, she intended to go to a secret meeting of a group interested in racial egalitarianism that was organizing a local CIO union. The meeting itself wouldn't be a problem, but its location would put Hadley in one of the city's more crime-ridden neighborhoods.

Gabriel urged Hadley to abandon the idea because venturing into that area after dark was too dangerous, especially for a young white girl. He failed to dissuade her, and she stubbornly rejected his offer to accompany her.

"So I climbed out my bedroom window and walked to the nearest trolley stop," she told Min-ah. "Later, I changed to the line going into Tremé, even though the conductor questioned me."

Min-ah bobbed her head as if she understood.

"Once I arrived . . ." Hadley glanced at her friend, then let her words trail away and knit her trembling hands together. "I-I realized what Gabriel had tried to tell me. I was too young, too inexperienced, too easy a mark."

"Didn't take me long to realize I was in over my head. Much as I hated to admit I had made a mistake or retreat from a story, I was too uncomfortable to stay. So I went home, never once remembering that Gabriel had said he was going to the meeting too, whether I wanted him there or not."

Min-ah patted Hadley's shoulder. She might not understand every word pouring out of her friend's mouth, but she innately understood Hadley needed comfort and kindness.

"Someone killed Gabriel that night, only a few blocks from where they held the meeting." Hadley drew in a quivering breath. "And the police never found the murderer."

Min-ah pressed her hand over her mouth.

"I-I knew he wanted to watch out for me." Tears slid down Hadley's cheeks. "I should have looked for him and confessed I was too scared to stay. He would have walked me to the trolley stop. But I was only thinking about myself."

"Maybe he not there." Min-ah drew her brows together.

Hadley swallowed. "What do you mean, *not there*?"

"Not at meeting." Min-ah stared at her. "You say he killed at different place."

Hadley rubbed her temples. She had always assumed that Gabriel had followed her to the meeting and somehow lost her on the street, even though Fanelia had said that Gabriel had simply been in the wrong place at the wrong time. He had played the trumpet and desperately wanted to join a jazz ensemble performing in one of the many New Orleans nightclubs.

Wracked with guilt, Hadley had never confessed that she and Gabriel had argued that night and that she believed he had been murdered because of her. She had spent the last decade certain she could have saved his life if she had looked for him rather than jumping back onto the trolley without a second thought.

Min-ah's simple question prompted Hadley to consider Fanelia's scenario. All this time, Hadley assumed he was killed trying to locate her. But now she was able to make connections guilt had blocked all this time. Gabriel's mother hadn't been surprised that he'd been in Tremé, home to some of the best jazz clubs in the city. And now that Hadley recalled her conversation with him, he *had* given her the impression that he planned to be in that area of the city anyhow. *De rien,* he had said.

The constrictive pressure around Hadley's chest eased, and she drew in a deep breath. Gabriel's death might have been inevitable, yet she still should have thought about him, should have let him know she was going home. Nothing could remove the sting of that failing. But she had been only sixteen and had just glimpsed a more dangerous world where her skin color and social standing did nothing to insure her safety. Gabriel would have wanted her to put herself first.

"I am sorry about friend," Min-ah said. "The boy."

"Thank you," Hadley whispered, shooting Min-ah a grateful smile. She would always carry guilt about Gabriel's death, but saving Min-ah and confessing the story from her past had eased her burden. She might now be able to forgive her teenage self, the frightened young girl who had made the safe choice, if not the perfect one.

She blew out a long, shaky breath, wiped her eyes, and drummed her fingers on the steering wheel. Then with a heartfelt sight, she lifted her watch to her face.

Nearly one-thirty.

She turned to Min-ah. "We're out too late."

Min-ah nodded.

Hadley swallowed. By five-thirty, a truck would transport many of the internees to work at the clubs and mess halls. Min-ah might be able to slip in with them, but would the other women in her hut report her absence when they awoke? Did the guard check people off a roster as they boarded the trucks?

Getting Min-ah back inside before dawn would be much more

prudent. She was small enough to crawl beneath the fence, so Hadley got out of the jeep and motioned for Min-ah to accompany her back the way they'd come. They both remained alert for any movement.

Before she slid under the wire, Min-ah hugged Hadley.

"Careful," she whispered, pointing toward the road.

Hadley nodded and waited while Min-ah cleared the fence, dashed across the yard, and disappeared inside her hut. She waited an extra beat to make sure no one caught her friend, then scurried back to the Jeepmobile and started the engine.

She cringed at its loud growl, hoping the noise was carrying less in the still night than it sounded in her ears. She clutched the wheel with trembling hands, reversed, and headed north toward Mount Lasso and her bed. Lost in thought, she drove at least a half mile beyond the turn-off. Once she realized it, she stopped but decided that making a U-turn on the narrow road in the dark wasn't a good idea, so she continued on toward the roundabout at North Field. At this time of night, she might even get to see B-29s leaving on a mission.

Dammit! In the dark, she missed the correct road off the roundabout and found herself still headed north. The MPs at North Field's guard station would be sure to direct her onto the right road — and might even order some unfortunate fella to drive her back.

She slowed as she approached the entrance off Lenox. The field hummed with unusual activity. Must be a maximum effort mission.

Hadley inched forward as the guard waved through jeep after jeep in front of her.

"Press?" the guard asked when she pulled up.

Hadley nodded reflexively. *No wait, I'm not press, I —*

He gestured for her to pull forward, and she snaked around the field behind the line of jeeps. How had the guard failed to notice that she was a woman on her own? She had planned to tell him a flimsy fib about staying late at a club and then getting lost. Well, she certainly wasn't lost, but she had no business being here. What would warrant all this hoo-haw?

Mobile generators hummed, and floodlights mounted on klieg stands bathed Runway Able and the lone bomber parked there in dazzling light, like a star-studded, red-carpet Hollywood premiere. As she pulled closer, a scrum of reporters and photographers came into view. She tensed and put her foot on the brake.

Whatever was going on was sure to capture the interest of the Japanese hiding out in the cliffside caves atop Mount Lasso. The man she and Min-ah had encountered had obviously been distracted from this spectacle, but there were dozens, perhaps hundreds more, who might be transmitting critical information to Rota at this very moment. For a group that was normally so secretive, the 509th was being anything but circumspect tonight.

"They'd better get the show on the road," she muttered, her heart thudding erratically.

Is Skip here? Is he flying this special — and probably dangerous — mission?

***

August 6, 1945, 8:00 a.m.

Near Hiroshima, Japan

Skip compulsively checked the settings again, even though he had already made more than a dozen minor adjustments during the six-plus hours since they had taken off from Runway Charlie at North Field. He swiped his damp palms on his thighs.

Many of Marquardt's crewmen had fallen asleep and lay curled at both ends of the thirty-foot tunnel that ran over the unpressurized bomb bay that connected the front sections of the B-29 with the rear. Marquardt himself had turned on the autopilot, left his copilot to monitor the instruments, and napped for a few hours until they rendezvoused with *Enola Gay* and *Great Artiste* over Iwo Jima.

Brilliant sunlight streamed through the plexiglass sections of the nose where Skip sat, in what was normally the bombardier's station. The Norden bombsight had been removed and replaced with a high-tech version of the equipment used in photo reconnaissance planes.

Behind Marquardt and Anderson in the cockpit, Bernard Waldman, a scientist and photographic engineer, had dragged his hand-held equipment into the cramped space already occupied by the navigator, flight engineer, and radio operator. Waldman would operate a hand-held Fastax 16 mm camera, designed to capture ten thousand frames per second. The device required a hundred feet of film per second, so he had over six hundred feet of spooled film with him to record the blast — plus another hand-held Fastax for still photographs.

The typical photo reconnaissance setup included a trimetrogon, with one camera pointing downward and two others positioned at oblique angles to capture each side of the flight path. But today, because they had to avoid the mushroom cloud, they had modified the usual configuration by mounting Fairchild K series cameras in Skip's space to allow him to capture stills of the blast once Marquardt made a ninety-degree turn to face the cloud.

He also had a hand-held Fastax 16 mm, similar to Waldman's. Once Skip turned on the mounted cameras, he would aim the Fastax out the plexiglass and shoot.

With his nerves on edge, he nudged his kit bag hidden underneath the bombardier seat. At the last moment, impelled by emotions he hadn't examined, Skip had pulled his own Graflex out of his trunk and stashed it inside his gear bag. It wasn't authorized, but he had seen others hiding cameras in their bags — and at least *he* was an official photographer.

He put on his goggles and checked the viewfinders in both the mounted cameras and the handheld, then fiddled with the light setting knob on the goggles. Even using the highest setting rather than the lowest as ordered, he couldn't see much. But hell, if the blast blinded him, he damned sure would never take pictures again.

His stomach swooshed in rhythm with the willowy bouncing action in the nose seat. Skip had always flown in the cockpit. The view here was spectacular, yet the feeling of exposed vulnerability in the ship's nose came as much from the teeter-totter effect of its seat as from his Plexiglass nest. He felt as if he were perched on the edge of a swaying branch.

His headset crackled with Marquardt's voice. "Gentlemen, the strike ship is approaching the aiming point. When you hear the tone, put on your goggles and leave them there until I tell you it's safe to remove them."

Like a shark undulating through crystal-clear water, *Enola Gay*'s silver fuselage whipped through the clear blue sky ahead of them, illuminated by bright sunshine.

Even from this altitude and distance, the city of Hiroshima sparkled before them in the early morning sunlight. No cloud cover, perfect visibility. It could be a perfect hit.

On another bright sunny morning not unlike this one, unleashed bombs had rained down and scored one knockout punch after another, leaving physical ruin and mental scars on the psyche of a nation in their wake. Countless lives had been lost, upended, and forever altered since that fateful December morning.

Skip clenched his hands. They had to do this. They had to, he reminded himself. Ending the war was critical to *both* sides to avoid the expected heavy casualties if the Allies were forced to invade Japan's home islands.

But couldn't they have demonstrated this bomb over a sparsely populated island instead of dropping it onto a large industrial city? Or better yet, couldn't they have shown the Japanese the film of the test done in New Mexico, the one that Parsons had attempted to show their crews two days ago?

A high-pitched tone pealed through Skip's headset. He jumped, and jitters rolled through his belly like a plane riding over pockets of turbulence.

He began counting the sixty seconds inside his head. At the end of that sixty seconds, *Enola Gay's* pneumatically controlled bomb bay doors would open, and a ball of concentrated hellfire would tumble from the bomber, aimed directly at the Aioi Bridge over the Ota River. Forty-five seconds later, the bomb would explode roughly eighteen hundred feet above the ground.

Skip unzipped his bag and took out his Graflex. The camera's solid weight triggered warring impulses within him. Resolve to avenge his brother, his lost comrades, and his country vied with a toxic mix of guilt, grief, and determination to live in place of his brother.

He slid his hand into his pocket and closed his fingers around the light meter. Chet had given it to Skip to encourage him to follow his own path. Skip's brother wouldn't want Skip to live in *place* of him. No. Chet would want Skip to live for himself.

He hung the Graflex around his neck and turned it on. Then, racked by indecision, he put on the goggles but left them atop his head. If the explosion blinded him, many of his options would disappear. Yet his job here and now depended on his being able to open the shutters on the various cameras, then focus, frame, and take the necessary shots.

Shots the world needed.

The tone in his headset abruptly ended. He had between twenty and forty-five seconds to either pull the goggles on or take his chances. He swallowed, hard.

Like a silver bullet racing through the air, *Enola Gay* executed her steep, hair-raising breakaway right turn, and moments later, Sweeney's *Great Artiste* dove left in her own gravity-defying turn. G-forces would have pinned every man to his seat in both bombers, and Tibbets and Sweeney would be putting as much muscle as possible into controlling their respective dives while gaining maximum power and airspeed.

Marquardt turned their ship ninety degrees to give Waldman and Skip the best vantage point for capturing the historic moment.

Can I do it? Skip had been surprised by how fast the steps, considerations, and functions of high-tech photographic equipment came back to him. Not that he had taken any photographs yet, but he had prepped the equipment and made sure he understood all the mechanisms. He was confident he could operate the equipment and take the photographs from a technical standpoint. Whether he could confront the emotions intertwined with photography was another matter.

The last time he had taken photos had been on that clear, sunny morning on Oahu, when he, like the unsuspecting citizens of Hiroshima, had no idea what an unseen enemy had already set in motion above him.

Already set in motion. The bomb was already in play. Nothing Skip did or didn't do would change that. Tension in his chest loosened. But recording the blast for posterity might dissuade others from ever unleashing such power again.

"Ten . . . Nine . . Eight . . .Seven. . .," Marquardt intoned.

Skip looked into the camera's rangefinder and pressed his hand to his forehead below the goggles. Before he could decide to pull them over his eyes, an intense white light exploded before him, vibrating, spinning, and jarring the atmosphere before flaring through his body and enveloping the plane. An ethereal glow coated the cameras and instruments.

Dimly aware that he had not been blinded, instinct took over, and he flipped on the mounted cameras. He then grabbed the handhelds and shot picture after picture, alternating between the Fastax and his Graflex.

Bright orange-red light lit the cloud cover beneath the ship, followed immediately by an angry fiery-red ball racing upward in a great circular mass of dark air. The towering explosion then morphed into the mushroom shape Parsons had drawn on the chalkboard.

Skip focused on it, but saw to his horror, even from this distance, that the landscape, which only moments earlier had been the city of Hiroshima, was now a boiling black cauldron of bubbling tar dotted with hundreds, maybe thousands, of orange-red conflagrations.

The angry cloud hadn't merely risen; it had also grown wider and expanded in volume. The fearsome spectacle now towered miles above them in altitude and gave every impression that it might engulf them, an impression reinforced by a violent shockwave that rattled through the ship like a firestorm of ack-ack shells, causing it to wrench up and down.

Marquardt, perhaps not expecting such a violent and physical reaction from the blast given they were positioned miles from impact, hurled the plane into a steep breakaway turn. The resultant G-forces threw Skip against his seat, preventing him from lifting his hands to hold the camera. The mounted one was still running, but in this wild turn, it would no longer be focused on the cloud or what was left of the city.

Once the ship leveled off, Skip overheard Marquardt speaking, presumably to Tibbets.

Then he said into the intercom, "All right, fellas, the colonel says the scientists think we ought to be in the clear now, and he reckons I should tell you boys what he just told his crew." Marquardt cleared his throat. "It seems we've just dropped the first atomic bomb in history."

Skip let out a long, low whistle. He *had* been on the right track, even if he hadn't made the full scientific connection.

"The colonel says we'll circle the cloud for a while, now that we don't expect it to send anything more at us." Marquardt turned the ship broadside to face the burning city.

Skip lifted his camera again and despite the untold horror reflecting back through the lens, being behind a camera again wasn't the source of stress and anxiety he had anticipated. He was revulsed by the suffering and tragic deaths of the people caught up in the maelstrom of the apocalyptic cloud, yet he had a strong desire to record the cataclysm for posterity, in the hopes his photographs might deter others from ever again using such ruinous force.

The purplish-black cloud seethed, burbled, and heaved as

though animated by human emotions as it weaved ever upwards into the stratosphere. Vibrant colors, including every shade of the rainbow, threaded through the roiling mass. Even color film wouldn't do justice to the full spectrum splashed across the sky in such vivid, brilliant hues.

Marquardt followed the other two planes as they orbited the city and the cloud several times before turning southeast into their heading back to Tinian. Finally forced to tear his gaze away from the devastating spectacle they had unleashed, Skip shut off the cameras.

More than once over during the next hour, he considered turning off his headset to eliminate the stream of chatter Marquardt seemed disinclined to squelch. Crew members speculated about whether Japan would have surrendered before they landed and wondered about various aspects of atomic energy and radiation, including whether they might all now be sterile.

Skip only wanted to be alone with his thoughts. Thoughts from the past, thoughts about what they had done that day, and thoughts about the future.

A future that now shined bright because he was now certain he *had* a future.

The Japanese might not surrender before they returned to Tinian, but if not today, they soon would. He hoped they would do it before America felt compelled to drop another atomic bomb — assuming they had another. Connecting everything he had observed over the past year at Wendover and Tinian, he was certain the bomb they had dropped had been expensive and wasn't the sort of weapon homefront industrial workers could churn out on an assembly line.

Confident for the first time in years, Skip turned over possibilities in his head. Not only what he might do for a living once he demobilized, but where he and Hadley might live, how she might pursue her ambitions, what their children, should they have any, might look like — assuming he could convince Hadley that their relationship was much more than just a wartime fling. He was certain what they had was lasting and real.

As soon as they landed and debriefed, Skip would find her, do his best to convince her he was worth the risk, and describe the frames of their future he had composed today.

***

August 6, 1945, 3:00 p.m.

North Field, Tinian Island, Marianas, Central Pacific

Hadley wormed her way closer to the runways through the crowds that had gathered to welcome the bombers home.

"There they are!" someone shouted.

Another man yelled, "Look! Here they come!"

Two other bombers circled in the sky above, hanging back, but all eyes were on the one in the landing pattern, the one lined up to land on Runway Able.

When its wheels touched down and it shot down the runway, a roar went up from the growing throng. The whole island now knew that Tibbets and his Glory Boys had indeed delivered, had in all probability brought an end to the war with today's historic mission.

An atomic bomb, that was the word.

Skip had to be here somewhere. Hadley had managed to learn from a friendly fellow in operations that Captain Masterson had indeed been rostered on this mission. The weather scouting planes had returned two hours ago, and he hadn't been among their crews. Nor had he been on the ship that had waited on Iwo Jima, ready to act as a replacement.

Enola Gay taxied to a hardstand near where Hadley stood and she, like the others, converged on it for a better view of the men as they disembarked. Colonel Tibbets descended the ladder first, smoking a pipe, with the others following close behind.

The crowd clapped and cheered.

The colonel barely made it twenty steps past the propellers

before General Spaatz marched up to him. An officer yelled for the crowd to back up and give them some space. Tibbets hastily transferred his pipe into his left hand.

General Spaatz pinned the Distinguished Service Cross onto the breast of Tibbets's rumpled flight coveralls, then stepped back a few paces, and exchanged salutes with the colonel. Photographers snapped picture after picture of the short ceremony.

Once the MPs holding the crowd back signaled that everyone was free to move again, *Enola Gay*'s crew was mobbed by well-wishers and shouted questions. Blinking in the bright afternoon sun, the men looked more tired than triumphant.

Hadley had no doubt that they would revive after debriefing and would hurry to join the parties already in full swing across the island. Parties with unlimited food and booze, exhibition sports games, pie-eating contests, shows, and jitterbug contests that had been advertised via hastily-assembled flyers pasted up all over the place.

General Spaatz and Colonel Tibbets stood off to one side of *Enola Gay*, deep in conversation. Hadley pursed her lips and stared at the gathering reporters with pads and pencils in hand, clearly waiting for an opportunity to interview the hero of the day.

Skip. I need to find Skip. Hadley sighed and turned away from the growing scrum of reporters vying for Tibbets' attention.

The crowd had hardly noticed when the two remaining bombers touched down, one on Runway Baker, and the other on Runway Charlie. They each taxied to a hardstand and were swarmed by their normal ground crews. No brass, no cheering crowds, no photographers.

Hadley cut through the excited throngs ringing *Enola Gay* and crossed Runway Able. Normally crossing a busy runway was forbidden, impossible, and dangerous, but today activity at North Field was at a standstill apart from this mission. Hadley shaded her eyes, lengthened her stride, and scanned the area for Skip's familiar figure. *Where is he?*

Passing *Great Artiste*, Hadley counted eleven men apart from the ground crew, who were identifiable because most of them were clad only in cut-off shorts. Skip was not among them.

That left the last plane, unnamed and forgotten in the melee. As Hadley strode toward its hardstand, she scrutinized the men clustered around it before deciding the crew hadn't disembarked.

Ah, there they came. Several men, enlisted fellows, descended from the rear of the plane. Next came a couple of officers, who climbed down the ladder from the front hatch.

Her heart fluttered as she waited, hoping Skip would soon climb out. He had flown countless missions, and apart from the time he had gone missing, she hadn't even known he was going up, let alone been nervous about it. Today, there were no racing ambulances or other signs of alarm among the crews of these planes. It stood to reason he was fine. Physically fine, at least. Whatever mental anguish he may have experienced today was another matter altogether.

She saw his camera before she saw him. How she knew it was his, she couldn't say. He was still wearing it attached to a neck strap.

All the breath left Hadley's body in a whoosh, and ripples of dizziness surged through her. Without intending to move, she dashed toward him, wanting only to fall into his arms, revel in his solid warmth, and delight in the fact that he was safely on the ground.

His face lit up with a surprised grin, and he pushed the camera aside before wrapping his arms around her and pulling her close. "How are you able to be here?"

"Half of the island is here." Hadley pulled back and pointed toward Runway Able, where the enormous crowds still milled around. "See?"

"Ah, a welcome party." His shoulder muscles stiffened. Hadley kept her eyes intent on his and traced her finger along his jawline.

"Are you all right?" She swept her hand toward the cheering cluster of men crowding around *Enola Gay* "With all that?"

"I understand the jubilation. But they didn't see what we saw."

He shook his head. "They don't have to live with those images burned into their memory. All they know is we've won the war."

"This is it, then? The end?"

"Oh, yeah." Skip nodded grimly, locked his hands around her waist, and tugged her close. "Maybe not today, but soon. The Japanese will have no choice but to surrender."

"I'm glad," Hadley whispered. "But . . . at what cost?"

The cost not only to the Japanese, but also to the American psyche — and to their moral standing on the world stage. The cost to their quest for global stability and peace.

If the rumors Hadley had heard rippling through the crowd today were true, thousands of people had perished in an instant in Hiroshima. Using such a horrific weapon, no matter how many lives it saved on both sides, blurred the line ever more between the Allies and the Axis powers. Hadley sent up a prayer for the victims of the atomic weapon, a prayer for those who had already perished during this long war, and a prayer for President Truman, who had been forced to weigh using the bomb against the costs of mounting a conventional invasion of Japan.

"It's a whole new world now, isn't it?" she murmured. "The bomb changes everything."

"Yeah. Yeah, the bomb . . . it'll shift everything." Skip raked a hand through his hair. "Hadley —"

The bomb. The bomb had been delivered by Skip's group. He was under Tibbets' command.

"Say, Skip?" Hadley stared up at him. "Can you introduce me to Colonel Tibbets? He hasn't started talking to anyone yet and if we hurry —"

"Yeah, yeah, I'll introduce you, but hang on. I've gotta say this before I lose my nerve." Skip took a deep breath, then said in a rush. "Hadley, I know you've wanted this — us — to be just a wartime fling. But today, I realized that I want you forever."

"I —" All thoughts of Tibbets and interviews slipped away, and a series of flips cascaded through her stomach. Hadley opened her mouth, but nothing came out.

He kept going. "I know we may have to move a lot with your job and that's fine by me. We can go anywhere you want. New York, Washington, London. Or home — home is good. *Your* home. If you want to go to New Orleans, that's okay too. Wherever you are is where I want to be."

She gaped at him. He was willing to move for her? And he understood she wanted to be more than a homemaker and a mother? All along, she had assumed he wanted what she couldn't give. A ribbon of warmth spooled from her heart. Was this a proposal?

"Skip —"

"We haven't talked about kids, but I'm okay with whatever you want to do," he babbled. A pink flush tinged his cheeks. "I'd like some, but I know your career might make that difficult. Look, I'll be happy no matter where we live or what we —"

"Skip?" Hadley broke in, cupping his chin and pressing a finger to his lips.

The anxiety etched on his face was mirrored in his voice. "Yeah?"

"Yes."

"Yes?" He moistened his lips and swallowed, hard.

"I assume there's a question in there somewhere." Hadley tilted her head, smiled, and mock-widened her eyes. "Maybe a formal one you wanted to ask?"

"I hadn't intended on asking you now, or *here*." Skip smiled and gestured toward the plane, the hardstand, the watching circle of men. "But if I'm gonna do it, by golly I'll do it right."

Hadley held her breath as he fumbled in his pocket and extracted a small box. A shiver of delight skittered down her spine. *He has a ring? When did he buy a ring?*

Skip dropped to one knee while the grinning air and ground crews edged closer, whistling and hooting their encouragement. He opened the box and held it up so Hadley could see the platinum ring with the cherry-red ruby set among a circle of brilliant-cut diamonds.

"Hadley Claverie, will you do me the honor of becoming my bride?" Skip's eyes, soft and expectant, met hers, and her heart flipped into her stomach.

"Yes. Yes, of course I will," she said, her voice ringing out with confidence. She had never been surer of anything in her life. Not ever. She laughed, wiped away the unexpected moistness in her eyes, and held out her trembling left hand.

Skip slid the ring onto her finger, paused to admire it, and then pulled her up and closed his mouth over hers while half-lifting her off her feet and twirling her around.

What a momentous day. A day of contrasts that changed not only the world, but also their future.

EPILOGUE

December 14, 1945

The Moana Hotel, Waikiki Beach, Honolulu, Oahu, Hawaii

Hadley pulled aside the window sheers and peered down at the beach below. Plenty of people were still sunbathing, swimming, and surfing. She smiled. She supposed there was no harm in having a few extra bystanders as unofficial guests at her wedding to Skip this evening.

Hadley had been surprised when Skip had wanted to marry her in Hawaii, taken aback that he would want to spend any time more than necessary here where his brother had died, where he had experienced such deep emotional trauma.

"This brings everything full circle," he had said, draping his arm around her shoulder as they looked out at the ocean from the summit at Diamond Head. "Starting our new life together here feels right. Unless you'd prefer to marry at home, with your family."

A warm ocean breeze ruffled her hair, and she shook her head. No, she didn't need or want the big production her mother would expect. Apart from anything else, booking the church in New Orleans and making plans would take months. She had written to tell her parents that she and Skip would marry here and then have a reception back home in January before they moved to Washington.

Hadley had secured a position as a reporter with the *Washington Post* thanks to her interviews with General Spaatz and Colonel Tibbets, plus the other pieces she had written after the bombing of Hiroshima, and then three days later, Nagasaki. Tibbets had been so impressed with her, he had given her access to speak with crews from both missions and had also put in a good word for her with commanders of the conventional B-29 groups on Tinian, giving her a chance to add more depth to her features.

"You celebrated our engagement for about thirty seconds before begging me to introduce you to Colonel Tibbets," Skip had said with a laugh as he teased her about those interviews. Even so, she could tell he was proud of her.

He could rib her for the rest of their lives as far as she was concerned because her dogged focus had paid off. She would have to prove her worth at the *Post* and work twice as hard as any man, but her career was off to a wonderful start.

Still bursting with pride over her success, Skip had reached out to everyone he knew in Washington in search of a job for himself. That his aspirations were still vague only complicated a job search hindered by mail delays.

His anxiety had increased as time wore on without any leads. Until only days shy of their departure for Hawaii, he received an offer from a Bethesda-based research company from an unlikely source: His father.

After hearing that his son had put out the word that he would soon move to Washington with his new bride, Admiral Masterson had spoken with friends in the defense industry and given Skip a contact at the Naval Ordnance Laboratory, a newly-established company engaged in research and development of military weapon systems. Hadley worried that Skip might refuse to pursue the lead given its source, but he couldn't turn down the chance to work as a photographic engineer — a job that would allow him to combine his passion for photography with his engineering degree and technical expertise. He would start work after demobilizing next month. Hadley had her fingers crossed that his father's gesture would lead to their reconciliation.

First, however, Hadley and Skip would marry.

After they had arrived in Hawaii two weeks ago, they had visited several local churches as well as post chapels on the island's military installations in search of a venue. Religious faith wasn't of paramount importance to either of them, and Skip had pointed out that since they didn't have many people to invite, most of the churches would look empty.

Bizzy and Stella had arrived two days ago, and Skip had made contact with Leo, his former navigator, who was also stationed on Oahu. Their crewmate Dewey had been able to get leave and transport from his base in southern California, so he was here now too.

Hadley's only regret was that she and Skip had been unable to help Min-ah and Ari leave Tinian. All available transport was reserved for the rapidly demobilizing American forces returning home and the troops moving into occupation zones. In theory, Min-ah and Ari might eventually be allowed to come to Hawaii, even though American immigration laws would prevent them from entering the United States. Hadley had promised she would continue her efforts to arrange transportation for them to Hawaii as soon as the flow of returning troops eased.

With Hadley and Skip's wedding being so small, she had finally mused about possibly having the ceremony outdoors. Skip had embraced the idea and arranged for Captain Downey, the chaplain from the 509th, to perform the ceremony. They settled on marrying beneath the Moana Hotel's famous banyan tree on the edge of Waikiki beach, then celebrating their marriage with a wedding dinner on the hotel's oceanfront veranda. Thankfully, the barbed wire that had marred the beach's beauty for the past few years had been removed.

The hotel's only stipulation was that the wedding not take place on a Saturday, when they hosted a large audience in the courtyard for the live broadcast of the long-running *Hawaii Calls* radio program. The broadcast had continued through the war years, and the courtyard had become a favorite weekly gathering place for the men and women in uniform stationed here.

Hadley was fine with choosing another day, but picking a date in December had presented many challenges. She wanted a date that wasn't too close to Pearl Harbor Day, so Skip could always mark the anniversary of Chet's death and honor his brother's sacrifice. She also didn't want a date too close to Christmas, even after learning that a Christmas wedding in Hawaii would bear little resemblance to one back home. Here, she could wear a light, filmy dress and carry exotic tropical blooms.

Someone rapped on the door of Hadley's hotel room. She turned away from the window.

Bizzy opened the door and stuck her head in. "You haven't started getting ready yet?"

"No, but come in." Hadley waved her and Stella in. "It shouldn't take long."

She had already visited a salon this morning to have her hair and nails done. Her dress hung in front of the armoire, and she had laid out her accessories on the bureau.

Bizzy and Stella wore lovely marquisette dresses they had found at the shop where Hadley had bought hers. In a nod to the season, Bizzy had chosen a ravishing floor-length red gown with cap sleeves, with ruching at the waist that separated the pleated V-neck bodice and the pleated sheath skirt. Stella had picked a modest design in vibrant forest green. Matching green illusion net set off the elaborate bows and detailing around her shoulders, and the basque waistline marked the top of the pleated A-line skirt. They each wore matching gloves.

Stella lifted Hadley's garter from the bureau and stroked the bit of blue ribbon she had added last night. "Here's your something blue. Your dress is new. What about —"

"The Bible my mother sent is both old and borrowed." Hadley pointed toward the worn white leather Bible adorned with a corsage of pikake flowers and white cattleya orchids. Her mother's note had said that she borrowed it from Hadley's Great Aunt Marie.

Hadley moved away from the window, slipped out of her skirt and blouse, and slid the garter up her leg. Bizzy took Hadley's wedding dress off the hanger and held it open so she could step into it. Stella and Bizzy then helped her pull up the form-fitting satin sheath with its filmy overlay of point d'espirit lace and adjusted the delicate illusion cap sleeves of the same point d'espirit lace that draped across her shoulders like a cape.

"My mother will have a fit when she sees this deep V-neckline." Hadley smiled at her reflection in the mirror.

Bizzy grinned and nodded at Hadley's cleavage. "Well, I know who's going to love it, and that's your groom."

"You're right about that." A flood of warmth zipped from Hadley's heart to her belly. Oh yes, Skip would definitely appreciate her plunging V-neckline.

Stella stood on tiptoes to fasten Hadley's pearl necklace. "There you go."

"Thanks." Hadley stepped into her shoes and smiled. "What else?"

"The part that will truly transform you into a bride." Bizzy held up the beaded and appliquéd Juliet cap adorned with a sheer fingertip veil. "This is so beautiful."

Hadley closed her eyes as her friends worked together to secure the cap.

"There," Stella whispered. "Have a look."

She opened her eyes and caught her breath at the sight of her reflection. Bizzy was right. The veil transformed her from a woman wearing a beautiful lacy white gown into a bride. She ran her finger along the edge of it. Her fluttering stomach felt as diaphanous as the lace.

Stella put the Bible and corsage into her hands, and Bizzy touched up Hadley's lipstick.

"Ready?" Stella asked.

A knock on the door startled Hadley. She raised her eyebrows. Perhaps one of the staff had come to tidy the suite. She and Skip planned to spend their wedding night here, while Leo and Dewey kept Lucy. After sharing a wedding breakfast with their guests tomorrow morning, she and Skip would depart for their honeymoon at the Kona Inn on the big island, while Leo looked after Lucy until they returned to pick her up after Christmas.

Bizzy cracked the door open and peeked out before opening it to admit a man wielding a camera. He nodded to Hadley.

"Hello, ma'am." He held up the device. "My name is George Lee, and I'm the photographer your groom engaged to photograph your wedding. He asked me to take a few photos of you here in the suite before you come downstairs, if that's all right."

"Oh! Of course." Hadley gestured for Bizzy to close the door. Her family would appreciate having a bridal portrait. Skip was sweet to think of it.

Mr. Lee took several photos of Hadley standing before the mirror, then some with Bizzy and Stella adjusting her veil and sleeves. After that, he had Hadley step out onto the balcony. Bizzy and Stella had done a good job pinning on her Juliet cap, because although the veil blew in the light breeze, the cap stayed in place.

"Those photographs of you on the balcony with the ocean as a backdrop will be tops," Stella assured her as they stepped into the elevator.

They walked through the lobby and the lounge, smiling and laughing as other hotel guests extended their congratulations.

Hadley paused at the door that opened onto the banyan patio and inhaled deeply, breathing in the heady floral scents of plumeria, orange blossoms, and orchids. A small Hawaiian orchestral ensemble set up under the banyan tree lifted their instruments and played Pachelbel's *Canon in D*, a signal for Stella and Bizzy to walk through the courtyard to the wedding arch.

The arch, festooned with panels of white chiffon interspersed with arrangements of fragrant plumeria, orange blossoms, pikake, and cattleya orchids, had been set where the courtyard transitioned to the beach. Hotel staff had moved the tables off the courtyard and set up rows of white chairs for their guests.

Dewey and Leo stood up for Skip, all in uniform. Skip had teased Hadley that he might wear white linen trousers paired with a print Aloha shirt instead, but she was relieved he had chosen the uniform over island attire. The sight of a man in uniform — *her* man in uniform, especially — always sent her heart spinning and her blood racing. She would always be glad to have him in his USAAF dress uniform in their formal wedding portrait.

The hotel manager had suggested they hire a local to help them choose some local wedding customs for their ceremony. Attired in exactly what Skip had said he might wear, the man stepped forward and lifted a conch shell to his mouth. Holding the shell steady, he blew two rich, resonant notes, first to one side, then the other. Next he faced the crashing surf before turning to Hadley and blowing a long, haunting call meant to bring forth the elemental powers of earth, sea, air, and fire as witnesses to their marriage rites.

Hadley had rejected Skip's suggestion that she ask one of his fellow officers to escort her to the altar and decided to walk alone — a decision reflective of their journey to each other.

After Chaplain Downey made his opening remarks and then read from the Bible, the local officiant handed Hadley a maile leaf lei and gave Skip a white crown flower lei. Skip ducked his head so

Hadley could drape his lei around his neck, and he did the same for her.

Downey smiled. They had given him traditional words to say after they exchanged leis, and so he said: "Now Skip and Hadley have bestowed upon one another these leis, as part of their vows and as a symbol of their Aloha, their love and admiration for one another."

Hadley wanted to melt on the spot. She and Skip had loved those beautiful words right away. Downey took her hand and placed it in Skip's.

"Hold the hand of your very best friend, the hand that will support your worthy goals without end, the hand that will encourage you in times of sorrow, the hand that will rejoice with you today and every tomorrow."

The red-orange sun inched lower in the sky as he spoke, while the waves broke on the shore, their soothing rhythm filling Hadley's soul with the peace and joy of the moment.

After they exchanged vows and rings, Downey pronounced them man and wife, and the man with the conch shell blew another long note to signal the end of the ceremony.

Several people strolling along the beach joined the wedding guests in applauding and cheering when Downey presented Hadley and Skip as Captain and Mrs. Skip Masterson.

George photographed the wedding party before snapping a few pictures of Hadley and Skip together. Once they were done, Skip waved the others toward a table on the veranda.

"I'd like a quiet moment with my bride on the beach before we join you, if you don't mind." He grinned and grabbed Hadley's hand.

They left their shoes beside the arch and walked hand-in-hand toward the cresting surf, with the panorama of the glorious sunset arrayed around them. Hadley hoped George would capture this moment on film, with them holding hands and facing away from the camera, while silhouetted against the infinite expanse of sea and sky.

Skip halted, cupped Hadley's face, and stroked the pad of his thumb along her jawline. "Quite a road we've taken, isn't it?"

"I don't know anyone I'd rather have by my side than you, Skip." Hadley's heart swelled and tingles surged through her from head to her toe. "You're my *everything*."

Marrying him was the perfect capstone to all she had experienced during her momentous years overseas. She was now more certain than ever, not only of her steadfast love for her new husband, but also that when she looked back on her life, however long or short it might be, these years would be the ones that had wrought the biggest changes and left the most lasting mark.

She and Skip lingered at the water's edge with warm waves lapping ever closer to their bare feet, exchanging tender words of love and giddy hopes for the future, until the sun dipped below the horizon and their friends' bubbling laughter and the orchestra's sultry rendition of *It's Been a Long, Long Time* lured them up the beach to celebrate their vows.

STAY IN TOUCH!

Follow the link below to sign up for my newsletter. Through my newsletter, you'll receive deleted scenes and sneak-peak previews of upcoming novels. My newsletter will arrive in your inbox no more than once per month (or probably bi-monthly).

Sign up at:

www.elerigrace.com/contact.html

AUTHOR'S HISTORICAL NOTE

Placing my Red Cross Girl heroines and the soldiers they served into the Pacific Theater for this novel presented a number of challenges from the standpoint of sensitivity. After the attack on Pearl Harbor, many Americans, both civilian and military, including those stationed overseas and those on the homefront, used an unending supply of derogatory terms to denigrate the Japanese and Asians in general. Australians and Americans had similar insensitive names for the native inhabitants of what is now known as Papua New Guinea. And of course, the use of atomic weapons continues to spark debate and controversy. I have done my best to honor the perceptions and emotions of the time period while steering clear of the common epithets that my characters might have used. Both Skip and Hadley recognize the moral and ethical issues relating to dropping the atomic bombs on Japan, even though, in keeping with the near-universal perceptions of the time, they celebrate the end of the war and the lives they believe were ultimately saved by avoiding an invasion of Japan's home islands.

The *Crossing the Line* ceremony is a time-honored naval ritual dating back centuries to the British navy in the eighteenth century. Those who have not crossed the equator are actually called by a name that has now become a racial epithet in Britain, so I chose to substitute the term *tadpole*. Even President Franklin Roosevelt was initiated as a shellback in November 1936, while aboard the U.S.S. *Indianapolis* (the same ship that later transported several components of the *Little Boy* bomb dropped on Hiroshima before it tragically sank days after delivering the bomb components to Tinian). Although President Roosevelt was not subjected to the full gamut of the ceremonial rituals, he didn't get off entirely. In a letter to his wife,

President Roosevelt described the two-day ceremony as being *great fun*.

The first *Armed Services Editions*, small paperbacks issued to American servicemen, were actually first distributed in September 1943, after Hadley took Skip to the Ludoma library.

Z Experimental Station (ZES) or Fairview House in Mooroobool, a present-day suburb of Cairns, served as a covert training facility for operatives of Special Operations Executive - Australia ("SOE Australia"). Known to the locals as the *House on the Hill*, Fairview House earlier served as a wireless relay station to transmit messages from SOE Australia to Dutch operatives behind Japanese lines in New Guinea. When the house became a training facility in July 1942, the isolated town of Cairns had already been partially evacuated due to the threat of a Japanese invasion. Commando operatives received instruction in weapons, tactics, signals, codes, ciphers, first-aid, survival skills, demolition/explosives, and the use of collapsible canoes known as *folbots*. *Folbots* were tested in the rivers near Cairns and then used in several successful commando raids in the Pacific Theater. Commandos who carried out Operation Jaywick, a raid on Japanese shipping in Singapore, launched from the Cairns area in August 1943.

By mid-1943, the invasion threat had dissipated, and Cairns became increasingly congested with a large number of Allied forces. As a result, Special Operations SOA ("SOA") needed a more secluded site for training commandos and subsequently moved their operations from ZES to Fraser Island in October 1943. I combined Hadley's encounter with one of the SOA commandos who would soon move to Fraser Island Commando School with Eleanor Roosevelt's overnight visit at Yorkeys Knob on September 11, 1943. I had no trouble imagining how a nosy female journalist might have also helped prompt the relocation of this special operative training site to a remote island.

Eleanor Roosevelt did indeed tour the South Pacific in August -

September 1943. She traveled under the auspices of the ARC, wearing their uniforms and often visiting, dining, and staying in ARC facilities. Marcia (Ward) Behr's memoir, *Coffee and Sympathy*, relates many details about Mrs. Roosevelt's overnight stay at the ARC rest home for officers at Yorkeys Knob outside Cairns. The uniforms the first lady wore, the dinner menu, and the last-minute upgrades the military made to the facility are all courtesy of Behr's memoir.

Photo reconnaissance pilots in the Fifth Air Force in the Southwest Pacific most commonly flew P-38 Lightning fighters that had been modified to carry vertical and oblique cameras. In this capacity, they were known as the F-4 or F-5. Without the usual armament installed in a P-38, the F-4/F-5 planes were lighter and nimbler when evading enemy fighters and anti-aircraft fire. The pilot operated the nose-based cameras via controls in the cockpit. The only weapons they carried were the ones Phil Blanchard demonstrated to Hadley, a standard issue side-arm and a Tommy rifle. P-38s were single-seat airplanes, so I had Phil's usual F-4 out for repairs and put him and Hadley in a two-seat L-4 Grasshopper.

The last large-scale Japanese offensive against Port Moresby were the daylight raids of Operation I-Go in April 1943, but the Japanese continued to send small groups of bombers and fighters, or sometimes a single bomber, over Port Moresby in nighttime nuisance raids for the remainder of the year. Japanese forces never penetrated the Owen Stanley mountain range, so USAAF personnel had no reason to reconnoiter southern New Guinea. But Phil's mission made for a dramatic scene, and one Red Cross Girl, Kay Peddle, did take what was promised to be a quick reconnaissance trip in a small plane over Morotai island (then part of the Dutch East Indies), only to find herself unexpectedly in a combat scenario similar to what Hadley experienced.

I am indebted to Garrett Middlebrook's combat memoir, *Air Combat at 20 Feet*, for demonstrating with such great detail how a pilot might have approached crash landing a B-25 bomber on a sandy beach. Like Skip and his men, Middlebrook's crew were rescued from their isolated crash site by friendly local tribespeople who helped them connect with Australian coast watchers. Skip and his crew, however, endured several more days of uncertainty, worries about water, and danger before Semu's fellow tribesmen arrived to help them find a way back to Port Moresby.

The swimming hole enjoyed by Hadley and Skip is based on Butaweng Falls, actually located near Finschhafen in Morobe Province, Papua New Guinea, but I decided they deserved a paradise secreted in the jungle closer to their miserable base at Nadzab.

The first overseas dispatches publicizing the exploits of the Alamo Scouts, covert special forces operating in the Southwest Pacific, were published in October 1944 by AP correspondent Murlin Spencer. For plot purposes, I had Lorraine persuade Hadley to help her locate their training site at Mange Point, just off the northwest coast of Dutch New Guinea, in April 1944.

Lorraine Shaw is based on Australian journalist Lorraine (Streeter) Stumm. Lorraine worked as a reporter for the *London Daily Mirror* in the mid-1930s and married RAF pilot Harley Stumm in Brisbane in July 1939. Her husband was ordered to Singapore, and Lorraine joined him there. She gave birth to their daughter Sheridan in June 1941. With Japanese forces converging on Singapore in February 1942, Lorraine and her infant daughter escaped home to Australia.

She secured war correspondent credentials in August 1942 and represented the *London Daily Mirror* at General MacArthur's Brisbane headquarters as the sole female correspondent based at MacArthur's headquarters. MacArthur agreed to send her to New Guinea at some point in 1943, and although the Australian government objected to her field assignment, they were powerless to countermand MacArthur's wishes. By spring 1944, Lorraine was anxious to reunite with her husband at his post in India. General MacArthur allegedly imparted information regarding a secret operation in Burma as a parting gift for one of his favorite journalists. Lorraine, however, was unable to make use of the information because her husband died in an airbase accident in May 1944, only weeks after her arrival. I tweaked the historical record of her life to set up a scenario to allow Hadley and Lorraine to act on a tip from General MacArthur and attempt to scoop an elite special forces unit operating in New Guinea, but in March 1944, the real Lorraine Stumm had already relocated to India. While I included a spouse for my version of Lorraine, I omitted her daughter, whom I can only surmise spent considerable time with other family in Australia while Stumm was away on assignment in New Guinea.

Then-Lieutenant Colonel Paul Tibbets trained Dora Dougherty and Dorothea "Didi" Moorman to fly the B-29 Superfortress bomber. Many pilots and crews were afraid to fly the airplane due to its frequent engine fires and takeoff crashes. Tibbets believed the sight of two petite women flying the large, complex bomber would activate male egos and insure the men would thereafter agree to train in the aircraft the USAAF believed could win the war.

Dougherty and Moorman flew *Ladybird* from Birmingham, Alabama to Clovis Army Airfield on June 29, 1944 and provided demonstration and instructional flights to male crews for several weeks. Dougherty's reminiscences published in the WASP newsletter in March 1996 include a clipping from a Clovis Army Airfield maintenance bulletin dated 29 June 1944. In it, she states that she and Didi flew only a *few* flights before word came from on high that WASPs were no longer permitted to fly the B-29. Other sources placed the women in Clovis during the month of August. I found it less plausible for Skip to have departed New Guinea, checked out in the B-29 himself, and been stationed as a B-29 flight instructor inside of two months, so I went with the later time references.

The other tweak I made to the historical timeline relates to when the army briefed Paul Tibbets on the Manhattan Project and ordered him to assemble the 509th Composite Group. The actual date was September 1, 1944, and he selected Wendover, Utah as the group's base a few weeks later. It's also unlikely, though still plausible, that Tibbets would have focused on insuring the 509th included men with technical, scientific, and/or photographic expertise. Dora Dougherty was a test pilot with the 509th Composite Group at Wendover for a time, but when the army disbanded the WASPs in December 1944, they discharged her. I also made a small tweak to Tibbets' family: Paul Tibbets brought his wife Lucie and their two sons to Wendover, but the boys were too young to have been playing with toy soldiers in December 1944.

As Skip reminds Hadley, popular American journalist Ernie Pyle made a name for himself by publishing roving human interest columns during the Great Depression. He was credentialed as a war correspondent with the Scripps-Howard newspaper syndicate in 1942 and spent significant time with army forces in North Africa and Italy and the D-Day landings (hence, he's apt to make a personal appearance in a later book). After the liberation of Paris in August 1944, Pyle returned home to New Mexico to recuperate for a few months. He set out again to cover the Pacific Theater in January 1945. On April 17, 1945, he went ashore with the invasion forces on the island of Ie Shima (now Iejima) and was killed by gunfire the next day.

On the night of March 9-10, 1945, General Curtis LeMay assembled a force of over three hundred B-29 bombers that had been stripped of most of their guns and ordered them to fly at exceptionally low altitudes and release incendiary bombs on Tokyo. Over more than two hours, Twentieth Air Force bombers dropped over 1,500 tons of bombs, unleashing fires that gusting surface winds whipped into a blazing inferno. Dubbed *Night of the Black Snow* by the Japanese, this firebombing mission was the deadliest air raid of the war, killing as many as 100,000 civilians and destroying sixteen square miles of Tokyo. This was the mission General LeMay might have invited correspondent Shelley Mydans to cover when Hadley stopped in Guam en route to Tinian. I found no stories with Mydans' byline covering Operation Meetinghouse, but she was posted at Guam at the time and was actively covering the Twentieth Air Force.

According to George Hick's *The Comfort Women* (N.Y. 1994), the sixty comfort women stationed on Tinian were all Japanese and perished during or in the aftermath of the American assault on Tinian, mostly by suicide. But on the whole, most of the comfort women were Koreans abducted or lured from their homes with deceitful promises. A significant population of Korean civilians lived on Tinian in the summer of 1944, and later that year sent $667 to President Roosevelt with a note indicating they were pleased to offer a meager financial contribution to the Allied cause. Like Japanese and Okinawan civilians, the Koreans were interned at Camp Chulu (sometimes referred to as *Camp Churo* in the historical records) in north central Tinian. The internees were permitted to leave the camp to work in the agricultural fields or in menial capacities around the military bases during the day and were paid for their services.

The women stationed on Tinian, Red Cross Girls and nurses alike, were required to be escorted by armed men at all times, day or night. Hadley's jaunts around the island in a Jeepmobile without another Clubmobiler and an escort stray from the historical record.

Secondary accounts of the atomic missions dispute what was said and by whom in the briefing on August 4th (a full 30 hours before the first planes took off for Hiroshima). Tibbets's own memoir makes no mention of that briefing, and he seems to have taken memories of his own remarks to the crews late on the night of August 5th from notes transcribed by William Lawrence, a journalist assigned to Project Alberta to give official account of the mission and its results to the general public. Other sources attribute the substance of these remarks to the August 4th briefing (which began at 3:00 p.m.), noting that the early evening briefing on August 5th was a more typical operational mission briefing, conveying the route, altitude, headers, weather conditions, and location of air rescue crews. The final briefing at midnight on August 5th concluded with a special prayer composed by the 509th's chaplain, William Downey, that was reprinted in *Yank* (September 7, 1945 issue).

The photographic results from the atomic mission to Hiroshima on August 6, 1945 were an unmitigated disaster. The military tasked Bernard Waldman, an American physicist, with operating a high-speed movie camera loaded with six seconds of film on Plane No. 91 (later named *Necessary Evil*), the photographic plane flown by pilot George Marquardt. According to some accounts, Waldman started filming too early and missed the actual explosion because he ran out of film. Other accounts claim that Waldman, in excitement or anxiety, forgot to open the camera shutter, thus recording none of the explosion. He did take still photographs with a hand-held high-speed camera, but the photo lab on Tinian stripped the emulsion, destroying whatever photos he had captured. The photos taken by the Fastax Skip operated were similarly ruined in the lab on Tinian. As for the ones he took with his personal Graflex, readers may later learn what Skip discovered from the pictures he took on the morning of Pearl Harbor and on that similar sunny morning over Hiroshima.

Two crew members on Plane No. 1 disobeyed orders and brought their own cameras on the mission. A short segment of grainy, color footage from one of them didn't surface until two weeks later, possibly because the airman didn't want to admit he had violated orders. Russell Gackenbach, navigator on Plane No. 91, kept the photographs he had taken in his personal possession for decades, inspiring me to put the Graflex and personal photographs into Skip's hands. I found it baffling that Plane No. 91 was dubbed the *photography plane*, yet officially carried only one photographer. Since, in my mind, they could have used more than one photographer given the problems, I decided I could write Skip into this scenario without too much disruption to history.

Bob Caron, the near-sighted tail gunner on *Enola Gay*, snapped the famous lasting shots of the mushroom cloud over Hiroshima with a hand-held Fairchild K-20 camera given to him at the last moment by the 509th's photographer, Jerome Ossip. Caron was not a professional photographer, yet he managed to take the historical shots while also simultaneously relating a vivid, detailed description of the cloud and its aftermath into a wire recorder from his unique position facing Hiroshima head-on in the tail section of *Enola Gay*. When the only known available photos from Plane No. 91 were destroyed in the processing lab, Ossip turned to Caron's shots, eventually choosing several to release as the official documented photographs.

Another unauthorized photograph of the Hiroshima blast was taken, perhaps within the first ten seconds of the explosion, although the U.S. Air Force has never officially confirmed the incident. The photograph was taken from a photo reconnaissance plane that hadn't received the official USAAF directive to avoid flying within fifty miles of Hiroshima that morning and got mixed in with photos taken later in the day on authorized forays into the airspace above Hiroshima.

At a reunion of the 3rd Photo Reconnaissance Squadron in 1995, John McGlohon recognized the photo he had taken that morning and recalled telling the photographic lab technicians on Guam that he and his crew, who were unaware the airspace was restricted and had followed their charted route for routine photographic reconnaissance mapping, had flown over Hiroshima seconds after *Little Boy* exploded. McGlohon didn't realize he had witnessed an atomic explosion, but he wanted the bomber to receive credit for the precise hit on its target, so he turned on his camera and captured the first photograph of the Hiroshima mushroom cloud.

As far as I know, none of the crew members of Plane No. 91 proposed to a woman on the hardstand that warm August afternoon. But for all we know, it may have happened, for none of the secondary sources I consulted make mention of what happened with either Sweeney or Marquardt's planes after the mission, apart from noting that they both slowed their airspeed to allow Tibbets to land *Enola Gay* first.

Skip did not take part in the mission to drop the *Fat Man* plutonium bomb on Nagasaki on August 9, 1945. The 509th Composite Group flew combat missions against Japan on August 8 and August 14, 1945, using conventional weapons, and other B-29 bomber crews from the Twentieth Air Force flew daily conventional bombing missions until Japan at last surrendered on August 15, 1945.

Readers may be relieved to know that the men who flew the atomic missions were not rendered sterile, although the crews did debate the topic once they understood the nature of their mission.

Exclusions against Asian immigrants in a 1924 immigration law thwarted Min-ah's dreams for a time. As a result of Hadley's persistent intervention with authorities, however, she and Ari immigrated to Hawaii in 1946, then moved to the mainland in 1952 after U.S. immigration restrictions eased. Hadley and Skip kept in touch with them through the years. George Hick's *The Comfort Women* (N.Y. 1994) is an excellent resource for readers who want to learn more about the experiences of these women.

Finally, the 509th Composite Group departed Tinian aboard the transport ship U.S.S. *Deuel* on October 17, 1945, and docked in Oakland, California on November 5, 1945. The group then moved to assignment in Roswell, New Mexico. For my purposes, I assumed that based on Skip's prior combat service in the Fifth Air Force and his connections, he was able to arrange an extended 30-day leave in Hawaii before resigning his commission and demobilizing when he and Hadley returned to the States in early January 1946. Hadley had more than met her two-year commitment to the ARC. To avoid logistical and/or transportation issues, Hadley probably would have requested leave time in Hawaii and waited to submit her formal resignation until she was back on the mainland.

I hope you enjoyed reading my continued tribute to the indomitable spirit, courage, and sacrifices of the Red Cross Girls and the men and women who served in our nation's military forces during World War II in *Carry a Crusading Spirit*.

CLUBMOBILE GIRLS NOVEL #3: COMING SOON

To keep up with publication news and teasers for the Clubmobile
Girls series, please visit my website and subscribe to my occasional
newsletter.

http://www.elerigrace.com/contact.html

ACKNOWLEDGMENTS

As with my first novel, countless individuals deserve recognition for their role in helping me bring Hadley and Skip's story to life. My editor and writing coach, Laura Mitchell, again deserves top billing for her advice, encouragement, and enthusiasm for the story.

My dear friend, early morning Starbucks writing partner, and first-look beta reader, author Caroline Leech, provided very helpful insights and suggestions that improved my portrayal of Hadley and Skip's journey. I'm forever grateful for her unflagging support and encouragement.

I extend my deepest appreciation to Melanie Noto for her excellent editorial guidance and to Jo-Anna Walker for the gorgeous interior design and formatting.

Rafael Andres of CoverKitchen Book Designers has again created an evocative custom illustration that captures the heart and soul of my novel.

Historian Donald Miller continues to be a ready resource when I hit a brick wall with historical research. Peter Dunn, founder and curator of the *Australia at War* website (www.ozatwar.com), provided many helpful responses to queries relating to Australia during WWII. Phil Crowther and David Wilson, historians of the 6th Bomb Group Association, provided invaluable assistance with locating photographs and other resources that allowed me to bring wartime Tinian to life in vivid detail.

As I noted in the Author's Historical Note, this particular novel presented a number of challenges from the standpoint of cultural sensitivity, and I am very grateful to Judy Sagara, Naomi Green, and Eiko McGregor for their feedback and suggestions.

Thank you also to those who beta-read the manuscript and provided comments and suggestions, including my good friends Carmen Pratt and Melinda Feeney.

Despite the best efforts of all these sets of eyes and the input of innumerable historical experts, there could easily be historical errors that do not fall into the category of artistic license, and I apologize for those mistakes.

I am so very grateful to the many readers who extended their compliments about my first novel, *Courage to be Counted*, and wrote reviews and/or notes to me. You inspired me to pour my heart and soul into this latest book in the Clubmobile Girls series.

To the veterans who served our country with pride and valor, we are all forever in your debt. Conditions throughout the Pacific Theater were overall fairly miserable, despite the best efforts of the military, our ANZAC and British allies, the American Red Cross, and USO entertainers. I now have far greater appreciation for the challenges peculiar to the Pacific Theater of operations and extend my heartfelt thanks to all who served under those conditions, singling out the B-25 crews of the 345th Bomb Group and the extraordinary men who flew B-29s under Colonel Paul Tibbets in the 509th Composite Group on Tinian.

As I read the memoirs and other accounts left by the former Red Cross Girls who served with such distinction during World War II, I am in awe of the indomitable and courageous spirit of these inspiring women. I am profoundly grateful for their service and hope my stories convey their character and sacrifices with the requisite respect.

Last but not least, I remain forever grateful for my children, Elizabeth and Harry. Elizabeth's spirit and strong convictions always inform my heroines, and Hadley's tenacity, persistence, and crusading spirit in search of social and economic justice are traits my daughter has in spades. The battle scenes, and in particular the details

relating to the mechanics and physics of flight under extreme
weather conditions, are greatly strengthened by the contributions of
my resident aviation expert, Harry. Thank you, Harry, for putting up
with my never-ending hypotheticals in search of more dramatic aerial
combat scenes. Elizabeth and Harry, all my love.